To seal their bond, the

Painfully introverte

heavy stammer, Lord George Albert Westin rarely ventures any farther than the club or his beloved gardens. When he hears rumors of an exotic new orchid sighted at a local hobbyist's house, though, he girds himself with opiates and determination to attend a house party, hoping to sneak a peek. He finds the orchid, yes…but he finds something else even more rare and exquisite: Michael Vallant. Professional sodomite.

Michael climbed out of an adolescent hell as a courtesan's bastard to become successful and independent-minded, seeing men on his own terms, protected by a powerful friend. He is master of his own world—until Wes. Not only because, for once, the sex is for pleasure and not for profit. They are joined by tendrils of a shameful, unspoken history. The closer his shy, poppy-addicted lover lures him to the light of love, the harder his past works to drag him back into the dark.

There's only one way out of this tangle. Help Wes face the fears that cripple him—right after Michael finds the courage to reveal the devastating truth that binds them.

Heidi Cullinan, POB 425, Ames, Iowa 50010

Print ISBN: 978-1-945116-31-5

Edited by Sasha Knight
Cover by Kanaxa
Proofing by Lillie's Literary Services
Formatting by BB eBooks

First publication 2012 by Samhain Publishing

www.heidicullinan.com

A Private Gentleman

HEIDI CULLINAN

Dedication

For Anne

ACKNOWLEDGMENTS

Thanks to Cate for research help, and Kate, Dan, and Jason for beta reading, Jules for all manner of brainstorming and mental support poles, Marie for putting up with my bitching and whining, Dan and Anna for uncomplainingly foraging for food and clean underwear pretty much all the time, and the Minions, Signy and Asrion, for platinum-level service in research, moral support, entertainment, and beyond.

Thank you as always to my patrons for your love and support, especially through this past year. I absolutely could not have come through this journey of re-release without you. Thank you especially to Rosie, Marie, and Sarah Plunkett for your exceptional support.

Chapter One

London, February 1844

STANDING IN THE receiving line outside Russell Gordon's Kensington ballroom, Lord George Albert Westin smiled and inclined his head at the other guests, trying not to let his panic show. Given the amount of laudanum he'd drizzled into his tea in anticipation of this outing, he shouldn't have any panic left to display. But were it not for the telltale sense of floating, of a world carried on clouds and fuzzy around the edges, he would have wondered if he'd remembered to add the opiate at all. The problem, he acknowledged grimly, was not that he'd forgotten. It was that once again he'd acclimated to the dose and would require more to achieve the desired effect.

"Quite a crush," a lady said beside him.

Wes blinked. To his surprise, it appeared it was he to whom she spoke. Everyone else was busy removing wraps and handing over canes and hats to footmen, and she was staring directly at him. He scrutinized her face, not recognizing her but thinking perhaps he had only forgotten her, but she seemed too singular to do so. She had a flat American accent, an elegant but eclectic dress, and flaming scarlet hair.

She chuckled. "No, you don't know me, so you can stop trying to recall where we have met. My name is Penelope Brannigan. But you may call me Penny." She arched an eyebrow. "Go ahead and be appalled at my lack of manners. I'm accustomed to it, and I don't mind."

Wes was indeed appalled. First she spoke to him as if they were longtime friends, then she introduced *herself*, and to seal the outlandishness told him to call her Penny. Unwilling to cut a woman direct, unable to form complete sentences and not knowing what he would say even if he could, Wes simply stared at her.

As the foyer quieted, he realized he wasn't the only one staring, though people were watching him, not his companion. It had taken the small crowd lingering at the door a few moments to identify him, but they knew him now. Fans and drinks shielded the gossiping tongues, but the eyes followed him as his identity spread like wildfire.

"Daventry, that's who he is! He's the Marquess of Daventry's son!"

"*Daventry's* son? Do you mean to tell me that's the Earl of Vaughn?"

"No. That's the *other* one. Lord George Albert. The stammerer."

The woman regarded Wes with new interest—and a strange empathy.

Wes left. He told himself he was only moving forward in line, that Mrs. Gordon was looking at him expectantly, wanting to perform her hostess duties, but the plain truth was that he'd cut Penelope Brannigan. He'd had to. His hands shook, the panic of so much attention threatening to drag him down. It was all he could do to keep walking as the whispers around him continued.

"Second son. I've heard stories about him. Wrong in the head, isn't he?"

"Didn't even make it through Eton. Had to be tutored at home."

"Horrible stammer."

"Very private."

"Fixated on plants. He's in some society about them."

"Never goes out. No idea why he's here now."

"Brain damage."

Wes drew a deep breath and urged the drug to temper his fragile nerves as the old black fears rolled around him. *No one will commit you to Bedlam tonight, no matter what they think of you. No matter how frightened they are of a potential madman in their midst, they're more afraid of your father.*

Mrs. Gordon pasted on her brightest smile as she held out her hand to him. "My dear Lord George. Such a pleasant surprise to see you here today."

Wes wished he could have swooped in with a smart smile and a breezy retort. *Alas, madam. The Royal Botanical Society received your invitation, but it is with great regret I report that only I was able to attend. But I am delighted to be here with a peer of science. A lady who, according to my sources, is one of the most learned botanists in all of Britain.*

Instead he said, "It-t is g-good t-to s-s-see you, Mrs. G-G-Gordon."

Mrs. Gordon's countenance transformed into pity. "How kind of you to grace our humble gathering—we are honored, my lord. Quite honored." She looked abruptly eager. "How does the Regent's Park garden fare? I have heard such wonderful things about it."

Quite well, quite well. We finally have the piping sorted, and the tropical house is finding its feet. You should see the bromeliads. Nothing finer. Would you care to stop by sometime and see them yourself? I'd be happy to give you a personal tour.

"G-G-Good," Wes said.

"Wonderful." Mrs. Gordon fixed her smile a little firmer.

Wes stood there stupidly. This was his moment, he knew. This was where he should make some small talk about her notable skill with plants, of how he longed to see her conservatory, which reportedly rivaled any in London. This was where he said, *I hear you have acquired a strange new orchid, delivered in full bloom, with an unusual shape and oddly colored lip. Could you be persuaded to allow me to see it?*

This was the reason he had drugged himself nearly

insensible and braved traffic and the crowd, the reason he'd sifted through the usual pile of discarded cards to find Mrs. Gordon's invitation. But while the drug could carry him here, it seemed it could not grant him charm, could not even loosen his tongue, and in the end Mrs. Gordon made him a curtsey and urged him to enjoy himself.

Wes moved away from the receiving line and into the room, hugging the wall as much as he could as he looked for a safe place to stand. He ended up near an ornate vase filled with flowers and greenery beside a window, an empty space which, by the time he reached it, was noticeably larger because the guests were giving him a wide berth.

He tried to tell himself it was because he was so far above the social station of everyone here, but he doubted that was the truth.

A servant offered a glass of punch to Wes, who accepted it with a nod. He didn't drink, however, only continued to watch the others in the room. They watched him back. He could not hear their conversations now, but he could imagine them.

What is he, thirty? Thirty-one? Does he have his own money?

Thirty-seven. And yes, his mother's father left him five thousand a year. He's hardly touched it, with his father covering his apartments and his dues at the club, and practically everything else. A girl could be very happy with Lord George. If she could overlook his...problem. One would have to pray, of course, that the damage would not pass on to the children.

Wes curled his lip as he raised his punch cup and pretended to sip. Even within the Royal Botanical Society, where he monthly produced papers for others to read in lecture, where no one could claim better knowledge of plants and their care than he—even there he knew they whispered of him. He was a member of all the right clubs, yes, but he got in not because of his merit but because no one dared upset his father. They all talked of the crazy lording, he knew.

What was wrong with his lordship's mind? Yes, his papers were brilliant. But why could he not read them aloud himself? Why could he not, most of the time, even be present when they were read, and at best could only stand in the back of the room? Why did he never go out? Why did he always look like a rabbit about to bolt to its den?

Why couldn't he speak even a single sentence without stammering through every consonant like some simpleton dragged out of a village gutter?

Lowering the punch cup, Wes stared down into the fruit-scented depths. This, his stammer and the public's reaction to it, was why Wes never went out. This was why it had taken a dangerous amount of Doctor Jacob's wicked little pills mixed in with his usual laudanum to bear him to the carriage and to this party. It depressed him beyond measure that even despite this he had broken into a sweat and stammered almost beyond comprehension at the door and had failed so utterly with his hostess.

This was why he should have stayed home tonight as well.

"Whatever fish it is you're trying to catch here tonight, glaring less will almost certainly help."

Wes blinked and turned toward the voice. Good Lord. "Penny" stood beside him again. Her eyes were fixed out at the crush of people. They seemed to amuse her.

"It's not a bad ball, for the Gordons. Though I think Griselda is trying too hard. That is the way of it here in England, though, as far as I can tell. The middle class crushes itself in its desperate attempts to become part of the upper class." She sighed. "I wish they'd stop long enough to realize most of the gentry is miserable too, perhaps more so because they have no one to ape, only their wealth and status to maintain." She paused and glanced at Wes with a wry smile. "This is where you tell me I am mad, or too forward, or say, 'Why, I never!'"

By God, Wes nearly laughed. "Y-You are."

Her eyebrow lifted. "Mad? Forward?"

"B-B-Both." But he was still smiling, which made her return the gesture before she turned her gaze back to the crowd.

"I'm proud to claim both. Though what I need just now is a bleeding heart, and one with money at that, as I'm running out of the latter and wearing down my former. That's why I've come here, you see. I need a patron. Someone with money who wants to do good things with it. My uncle was high enough in stature that a connection to him can get me in almost anywhere but the *haut ton*, but his money dried up long ago. So I'm here to find some for my 'little project', as most people call it. I've found I do better at the parties of the Mrs. Gordons than the Lady Somesuches. More people hoping their charity will elevate them." She glanced at him again. "That, my lord, is why *I* am here. May I press my forwardness enough to ask why it is *you* are?"

Wes rubbed his thumb against the side of his punch cup as he considered his response. Uncouth as she was, he found himself charmed by Miss Brannigan—she *must* be Miss, not Mrs.—and wanted to answer her. She had heard who he was and had sought him out on purpose. He wasn't certain this had ever happened before.

"To s-s-see a f-f-flower." He flushed, embarrassed by his stammer, but the opium made everything soft, and he pushed on. "R-R-Rare orch-ch-chid. M-M-Mrs. G-G-Gordon h-has one."

She stayed silent, and he dared another glance, worried she was appalled at his speech, but it turned out she appeared only to be considering something carefully. At last she favored him with a wicked smile. "Judging by the fact that you stand here looking frustrated and Mrs. Gordon seems to have no interest in giving you a tour, might I assume you plan to find this rare flower on your own?"

Wes hesitated before nodding.

Miss Brannigan smiled at him. "I wish you success. If you need a distraction at a doorway, let me know and I will do my best." She inclined her head at the crush. "Would you care, my lord, to return the favor, and tell me in which pool of guests I might best find *my* fish?"

Warmed by her lack of convention and her easy acceptance of his impediment, Wes decided to indulge her. He turned to give the crowd a proper study.

It truly was a gauche attendance. Merchants and bankers, West Indies plantation owners returned—a few Army and Royal Navy gentlemen, though of course none of any quality. But Mrs. Gordon had scored a coup, for a few men of fashion had deigned to attend. They were the lower sort, but they were here. It would lend credence to the Gordons's social aspirations. "I saw the most charming statue at the Gordons's party last week. Yes, darling, the Gordons." And the fops would jockey carefully, riding the line between demeaning themselves by the association and elevating slightly the reputation of someone who didn't deserve the elevation at all.

In short, London society as usual.

Wes knew none of the attendees personally, though he could guess a few by reputation. He didn't circulate in society, no, but when one did most of one's dining at clubs, the most amazing tidbits could be overheard. The short man in the striped trousers had to be Benjamin Bennett, of the Devonshire Bennetts. Yes, it would make sense that he would be here, balanced on the edge of decency, as the rumors were that he'd been left practically at the altar. Given what Wes had heard of Bennett's gaming debts, the bride-to-be had made a narrow escape. And there was the broad-shouldered gentleman with a bright blue waistcoat and an Osbaldiston knot: that had to be Fredrick Grainville. He'd married Lord Gatley's daughter and, according to rumor, left her to languish in Scotland while he chased actresses and dancers. But his father had left him a fortune from his time in India, and his brother was an admiral in the Royal Navy, fighting away in China. Plus, he was a notorious charmer. Certainly half the women in the room were swooning over him.

Indeed, Wes could scarcely blame them.

He wasn't finding anyone for Miss Brannigan, he realized.

Wes was scanning faces in a crowd he thought might be her likeliest bet when he saw the man. He was as much a darling of the crowd as Grainville, but Wes didn't know a single thing about him. He might have dismissed him, except the man was *very* charming and exceptionally pretty. Dressed in a long cream coat with tails, he looked like he belonged at a masquerade ball, or perhaps the court of George III. He drifted through the guests with such ease and grace he was almost dancing. His dark blond hair was long, unfashionably so, but on him it was so winsome as to reset the fashion itself. Blond tendrils curled artfully against his forehead and cheek, and even his hair, pulled back in a queue, had been set to the iron so that it caressed the lip of his gold-embroidered collar whenever he turned his head. He wore a cravat even more old-fashioned than Wes's own, tied loosely to offer a tantalizing view of a long smooth white neck.

The man moved in and out of conversations with the same grace he employed to drift across the ballroom floor. He was a practiced flirt, making his dancing and conversation partners blush while never managing to encourage anyone too much. He flirted, too, Wes noticed, with the men. Older men, especially those well-married and firmly off the mart. Though in truth any man who had set himself aside but smelled of money was approached with wide smiles and shining dark eyes. Laughter too—soft, beguiling laughter that was almost feminine. In fact, everything about the man was a tantalizing mix of male and female. The boldness of a male, the obsequiousness of a female. The frame of a man but the softness of a woman. And pretty. Handsome and pretty at once.

In short, he was the very sort of man Wes preferred.

"No one, my lord?" Miss Brannigan prompted, sounding wistful.

Wes startled and hastily jerked his gaze away from the blond man. He made one last sweep of the room before nodding as casually as he could at a sad-looking gentleman in a worn brown topcoat near the punch table. "Elton," he managed, after coaxing his open mouth around the "El" for three seconds of preparation. "Welsh b-b-businessman. L-Looks sh-shabby, but h-he's h-heavy p-pockets. M-M-Misses his w-w-wife. T-Talks c-c-constantly of the n-n-need for f-f-founding h-h-hospitals for w-w-women."

Miss Brannigan looked pleased. "Thank you very much, my lord. I am quite in your debt."

Wes inclined his head in her direction. "H-H-Happy to ob-b-blige."

The expression on her face went briefly enigmatic, and then she lifted her reticule and fished inside it. "I suspect you won't like my mentioning it, but I cannot help but notice you possess a rather pronounced stutter, and I would feel remiss if I did not offer this." She handed him a card. "It bears my name and address, and should you ever wish to look me up, I would be more than happy to share with you the techniques I know to overcome the affliction."

Wes did not take the card. "I h-h-have s-s-seen d-d-doctors—"

"Oh, I promise you," Miss Brannigan remarked dryly, "I'm as removed from a doctor as one can be. But as the former owner of a prominent stutter myself, I believe I might be able to help." When Wes's mouth fell open in shock, she laughed. "Yes, I know, it's difficult to believe. But from ages five to eight I said not a single word, and from eight to thirteen every one of them was better butchered than anything you could serve up." Still smiling, she tucked the card into Wes's pocket. "Ignore it for now, of course, because I know I am horribly shocking, but please don't toss the card straightaway. You might change your mind later, and in any event, I won't be moving from that address." She made a pretty curtsey and nodded at him. "And now, if you will excuse me, I believe I will take my forward self over to Mr. Elton, the lonely businessman. Good day, my lord. May your quest be profitable."

Wes watched her go, touching his hand to the pocket where she had tucked her card. *She* had been a stammerer? As he watched her go, fiery hair and straight spine and forest-green velvet dress with no hoops of any kind swinging freely as she moved—well, he acknowledged, were he a different man, he'd be in love.

Or, he supposed, if *she* were a man.

The thought made Wes's eyes slide back to the pretty young gentleman. He didn't look Wes's way, but Wes wished he would. Even just a glance. A glance and a small, secretive smile.

Flirt with me too.

He thought of the way Miss Brannigan had approached him, and for a moment he let himself indulge in the fantasy of meeting the pretty blond fop. He imagined himself striding across the room, catching the blond man's attention with a wry quip and holding it with a seductive smile. He pretended his tongue was light and cunning as air, and he imagined how the man's flirtations would falter under the assault of his own. As the man blushed, Wes would lean close and ask if he would like to step outside. Though it was cool and had begun to rain, they would go. They would find a dark corner where the young man's desire would no longer be able to be held back, and he would confess, trembling, how much he wanted Wes.

Smiling, Wes would run a finger down his cheek. "It's all right. Let me take care of you, my lovely. Let me take you back to my rooms. We can sample wine together, and then…"

God help him, and *then.*

But this, of course, was only a fantasy. The one time the pretty young man glanced Wes's way, his gaze passed through him as if he were invisible. A pause just long enough to register—and reject.

Wes made himself turn away, forcing his mind back to his true reason for attending the ball.

The room had become full as he stood against the wall. The way to the door was thick with people, and even thinking of pressing through them made him sweat. Even the indomitable Miss Brannigan had been swallowed up.

He began to feel dizzy. Though he'd been warmed by the heat of the room since his arrival, perspiration now ran down the back of his neck in a steady stream. Pressing himself to the wall, Wes fought his uneasy stomach, regretting the punch he'd sipped. He would be sick. He would be sick, and then he would pass out, and once his father found out what a disgrace he'd made of himself, and where, and *why*, he'd give Wes that long, sober look that made it quite clear that never in the history of the world had a son been more disappointing than he.

Just one more pill.

Wes shut his eyes, trying to push the thought away. He couldn't take another pill. He'd taken too many already. But the panic was too great, and the thought kept coming back. It was true, he'd taken this many once before. He'd passed out that time, but with as much tolerance as he had now, surely he'd be fine?

At this point it was practically an emergency. Because he wasn't Penelope Brannigan. He was Lord George Albert Westin, stammerer and all-around disappointment. He needed this much opiate just to haul himself to a plant.

The white pill slipped between his lips and slid into his stomach with a large gulp of punch.

Ten minutes later he made his way through the press of people toward the door, mindful of the crowd but uncaring of any of it. Uncaring, in fact, of anything at all. A few people glanced worriedly at him, but he didn't mind. What did they know? They were all liquid color anyway, nothing but stalks of feathers with eyes, swaying in the breeze. He didn't need Miss Brannigan's brass or her tricks. He had his little pills. He would be fine.

His thoughts were blurry, however, and he had to

wrench them back to his purpose. Orchid. He wanted to see Mrs. Gordon's orchid. "There's something odd about it," his source had told him. "Something strange. She paid dear for it, that much is known." A new, blooming orchid. It would be lovely, far more lovely than any of the women in this ballroom.

Perhaps even more beautiful than the man who had shunned him to flirt with a fat, balding man whose tongue never failed him, not even in his cups.

The additional opium had shaken out the dark corners in Wes's mind, and his disobedient tongue sat soft and tingling in his mouth. *I would like to show you my tongue, pretty young man. I would like to thrust it between the cheeks of your round little bottom and into the heat of your hot passage.*

Wes let the image possess him for a moment, arresting him on his path to the door. He glanced back into the room, catching sight of the man, and he waited. His breath caught when the blond head turned his way—then continued turning, as if Wes weren't even there.

Shunned not once but *twice*.

Wes let the opium swallow his disappointment as he squared his shoulders and continued to the hall, taking himself deeper into the house. The flower. He'd come for the flower, and once he found it, once he saw it, he would forget all about the indomitable Miss Brannigan and the delightfully delectable blond-haired man.

He hoped.

AS THE CRUSH of bodies in the northwest corner pushed Sir Joshua closer and the drunken baronet pressed an eager erection into his backside, Michael Vallant repressed a shudder. This was all Rodger's fault.

And damn if the bastard wasn't leaving the room, abandoning him to the grubby hands of the baronet. Without his spectacles, the world was as always a thick blur of color and movement, but Michael watched the tall, familiar tailoring and dark hair disappearing into the crush, and his panic rose. Rodger was playing an odd game, weaving unsteadily—playing the drunk? But why?—and heading for the door to the main hallway. What the devil was he about? Punishing Michael for being a fool and not staying home as he'd been ordered? Rodger was a vindictive bastard, but never like this.

Not with Michael.

Sir Joshua's hand gripped Michael's backside firmly as he thrust into Michael's hip again. "I'm going to take you upstairs, boy," he slurred, "and fuck your backside raw. And you'll love it, you whore."

"Be quiet." Michael glanced around in a panic to make certain no one overheard him. "You'll get us both arrested, you drunken sot. And I'm not going anywhere with you."

He winced as Sir Joshua's grip on his backside

tightened. "You'll go, nancy-boy. You'll go, and you'll beg for my cock. I have your fucking coin, and I'm going to buy every hole you have."

Michael didn't answer this, unwilling to antagonize the fool into shouting. Instead he held still, swallowing his revulsion and biding his time as the baronet continued to molest him. When the crush that had allowed Sir Joshua to press him into the darkened corner parted enough that he dared an escape, Michael pushed away.

He darted and wove between clusters of party guests, across the dance floor and down the hall toward the drawing room where other gentlemen were playing cards. He scanned for Rodger but saw only unfamiliar blurs. However, he did see a familiar raven-haired beauty in royal blue coming out of one of the retiring rooms.

"Darling!" he breathed, rushing toward her. He grabbed her arm, drew her back inside and shut the door.

"Michael Vallant!" she scolded him, her carefully cultivated voice slipping back into a rough Cockney. "You can't come in here, luv! This here's for ladies!"

"Then you shouldn't be in here either." After verifying they were alone, Michael let his forehead fall against the center of her chest. "God help me, Clary, but Sir Joshua is groping me in the bloody ballroom."

Clarissa stroked his hair. "Is he out of money?"

"It's control he's lost. He's off my list, and he's angry about it. Had I known he'd be here, I wouldn't have come."

"We shouldn't have come at all." Clarissa lifted Michael's head with both hands. "We should have listened to Rodger and stayed at Dove Street. He's likely to tan us both when he finds out."

Michael pursed his lips and pulled away, tugging at his coat. "He's already here."

Clarissa's eyes grew wide. "He isn't!" She frowned toward the ballroom. "He can't be here. I didn't see him."

"I did. Just now."

"Huh." Clarissa shoved her sleeves up higher on her arms and leaned back against the wall. "What did he say when he found you? And where is he now? Off dealing with Sir Joshua?"

"I don't know." Michael's jaw was tight with irritation. "Either he didn't see me, or he left me with Sir Joshua as a punishment."

Clarissa's eyes narrowed. "That ain't like Rodger at all. Mikey, you're blind as a bat. Are you sure it was him you saw? How the devil'd you see Rodger from that far away?"

"It was Rodger, I swear to you. I know the cut of his coat and the spread of his shoulders and the way he moves. He was playing fumbling gentry, from the look of him."

"Hmm." Clarissa folded her arms over her chest, but she looked thoughtful, not angry. "Well, perhaps he's on an assignment of his own. In any event, we must find him." She paused a moment, and when she spoke again, her voice was soft. "I heard Daventry's lad is out there too."

Michael hated the way even the name made him shiver, both now and when he'd heard the whispers on the dance floor. Which was ridiculous. He tried to brush it off with a laugh. "It's the second son, not Vaughn, according to the gossips. Harmless. A poor stammering simpleton." Yet even with the dismissal, the idea of encountering any of Daventry's spawn made Michael's blood run cold.

"I got a peep at him. Heard him too. Good Lord, but he can barely talk, he stammers so badly." She shook her head. "I don't know I could do a man like that. What if he went sixes and sevens on me when he was givin' me the tickle?"

Michael didn't want to talk about Daventry or his son. Though his fear shifted focus as another thought occurred to him. "Do you suppose Rodger would do anything to him?"

"Oh no." Clarissa paused. "Well—likely no. Depends on whether or not Rog was drinking." She bit her lip. "We'd best find him in case and kiss his arse, though I do long to give him a good chivey for not rescuing you."

Oh, Michael intended to do more than scold Rodger for this farce. But Clarissa was right. "I suppose we must find him and move on to the next."

Now Clarissa looked doubtful. "You want *more* of

this? I thought to go home and poke into the Dove Street ball. Might as well make a few pennies in the booth. Rodger was right on more counts than one. I haven't found a thing here. Everyone's too desperate for other things to care for a tup."

Michael waved his hand in irritation. "This is the only party we'll come into cold. The others will be better." He grinned and put his hands under her breasts to plump them playfully. "Edgar Almton is said to be at the party I plan to take us to next. Isn't he one of your favorites?"

Clarissa's eyes lit up before narrowing along with her dangerous smile. "Him and his deep pockets and great big cock—yes, he's my very favorite."

Michael sighed. "So I've heard, both about the pockets and the cock. Oh, if only he wanted to play with a pretty boy instead of a pretty girl."

Clarissa laughed throatily. "Go on, you greedy thing. You've got cocks enough, all of them worshipping your pretty bum. Let a girl have some leavings."

Michael kissed her cheek and took her arm. "Come. Let's find Rodger, call a carriage, and leave this dreary old place."

They stepped into the hall—and into the path of a red-faced, bleary-eyed Sir Joshua.

"There you are, lad," the baronet roared, his eyes full of lust as he reached for Michael.

Clarissa shoved him away. "Go on. Dodge him and meet me 'round back. I'll go find Rodger. *Go.*"

Michael gave her a brief look of gratitude as she threw herself into Sir Joshua's arms, and then he did run, right down the hall, which was filling with people as Clarissa, back in her lady form, began to squeal and protest loudly at her assault. Michael moved through the bleary figures, unsure of where he was going, hoping to God he didn't end up down a dead end.

As he rounded the corner, though, he saw a familiar figure heading up the stairs. "Rodger, you devil," he whispered, and hurried up the stairs after him.

FINDING THE ORCHID was more difficult than Wes anticipated.

He had spent the better part of a half hour hunting for it, a search which would have been easier without so much opium. Getting into Mrs. Gordon's conservatory would have been simple as shy, stuttering Lord George, but with the opium his words slurred, his feet faltered, and he kept wanting to giggle, making him appear either drunk or alarmingly unstable. He decided to sit on a stool in the hallway and flush some of the drug out with more punch, but even this act was apparently not done with enough innocence, for none other than the hostess herself was brought to him by a worried-looking footman.

"Are you well, my lord?" she asked carefully.

Heavens, no. I'm high as a kite. Wes smiled, trying not to let it appear too dopey. "Just taking a small r-rest,

Mrs. G-G-Gordon. Though I was h-hoping I might take a p-p-peek at your cons-servatory."

She looked at him with surprise at such a lengthy speech and with barely a stutter. Wes wanted to snort. *Surprised to see I'm not quite as stupid as you thought? Ha!*

Oh, but he loved opium sometimes. He bit his cheeks to keep back the giggle that threatened.

Her smile was still hesitant, though more confused than worried. "But of course." She gestured down the hall. "Just through there."

"Would you c-care to escort me yourself?" His heart pounded as he spoke the words, but the opium carried him onward, and he winked. "F-For the Society."

Ah, there—there it was, bright hope and eagerness lighting her entire face. *Hurrah for opium!* "For the Society. Yes, my lord. But of course." Blushing and beaming, she stood back as he rose, offering her arm carefully, as if to an invalid. Unfortunately, Wes was obliged to take it, overcome by the drug as he was.

She chatted absently as they stepped out the back door, over the flagstones and up to the glass door of the greenhouse, but Wes ignored her, too busy taking foggy inventory of the conservatory itself. Oh, yes, it was a beauty, and he envied every pane of glass and piece of piping. It was one of the larger stovehouses he had seen, twenty by thirty feet, likely thirteen feet high at the apex, and though it couldn't be but a few years old, it had the smell of a seasoned garden shed. Moss, mold, dirt, peat, all of it heated by stoves and damped by a series of copper pipes set to mist at regular intervals—oh, yes. This was a proper conservatory.

And her plants! Most were tropical, though she had a few fruit trees as well. She had several ferns draped from above, the usual maidenhair and sword, but there were a few he'd thought only the Society had access to: Marsilea and Pyrrosia, and another which he thought might be the Asplenium he'd been struggling with. She had more varieties of begonia than Wes had thought a private collector could have, several cyclamen, a bromeliad—and of course, an entire shelf of orchids, two of them in bloom. Cattleya, laelia—even a paphiopedilum. But not the orchid he had come to find.

"My husband's ships travel regularly to Brazil," Mrs. Gordon confessed, smiling as she reached out to stroke the petals of an angel's trumpet. "He sends along a botanist and has him treat the specimens with great care."

So that was her secret. Wes wondered how he might bribe his own botanist without losing the prizes.

"It is a l-l-lovely col-l-lection," he said.

She sighed. "I have trouble with the orchids. They so rarely survive the voyage, even with great care." She pointed to the flowers in their glass jars, clinging to their rocks and moss. "These I've had for six months, which is a record for me. But you see how the blooms begin to fade?"

Wes reached up to stroke the glass and shook his

head. "Shouldn't be k-kept here. T-T-Too unst-stable."

She frowned at him. "What do you mean, not here? Not in the conservatory? But—" He could see the light dawn in her eye. "But *yes*. The humidity is excellent, but the temperature is too variable, isn't it? Even with my servants stoking the fires regularly through the night. Of course. And that's why when I keep them in the—"

She stopped abruptly and glanced at Wes.

It was a painful moment. There was indeed a precious new orchid, or a precious something—a flower so beloved it wasn't kept where a clumsy guest could harm it or a servant accidentally might mangle it. Kept close to be watched, nursed in a private room inside the house, a room where, most likely, the temperature was more even and controlled.

There was an orchid, and she wasn't going to tell him about it.

Oh, she would have, he knew. That was why she paused. Here was his chance to clear his throat and hint that, should she show him this flower, he could perhaps give her a bit of a leg up into the Royal Botanical Society. Like so many others present, his favorable report could buy whatever he wanted from the Gordons. It was this she waited for.

It was this, Wes acknowledged with thick regret, he could not give, not even with the cleanest tongue. Oh, he was a member of the Society. But his word would get her nowhere.

Mrs. Gordon smiled, the flat, polite smile that made

it clear she would be showing him none of her prizes. "Please take your time in the conservatory, my lord. Examine whatever you like. It's a pleasure to have a member of the Royal Botanical Society present, and I do hope you will share with me any other advice you might have for my plants' improvement. Now if you'll excuse me, I must get back to my other guests."

With a curtsey, she was gone.

For a few minutes, Wes poked about the leaves, hating his stammer, hating Mrs. Gordon, hating life in general. Then he drew a deep breath of loamy air, squared his shoulders and left the greenhouse to explore.

With a much more manageable bit of opium coursing through him, he was able to move about quite easily, peering into rooms and closets. He'd meant to look farther on the ground floor, but there was a sudden hubbub in the hallway toward the ballroom, and so he escaped up the stairs.

And it was good he did, for in the very first room he came upon the orchid, whereupon he let himself inside and shut the door behind him.

It was not an area, he was sure, Mrs. Gordon intended guests to be. It was just off a bedroom which appeared only partly remodeled, with a door joining the two rooms directly. Likely at one point this had been a servant's room. Now, from the look of what was scattered throughout, this was the lady of the house's working retreat. The table was piled high with the detritus of a true botanist: clippers, bags of stones, jugs of soil and moss, pots, jars and containers of every type and size.

There in the center of it all, he saw it: the orchid. It was indeed everything he had heard it described to be. The flower was kept inside a tall glass jar. Its lid was in place but kept from a perfect seal by a small twig, which Wes took care to place on the table where he could find it again as he opened the jar to full air.

Most sailors and sea captains simply stowed the orchids they found wherever they could manage, and as a result many of them were so mangled by the time they arrived in the London docks that it took great care to nurture them back to glory. Not this orchid. Especially given how far it had travelled, it was pristine—which made it all the more tragic that it was also clearly dying. That was the trouble with taking orchids in full flower, why he told his procurers to take only plants not in bloom. At the slightest sign of stress, the flower was wont to put all its effort into seed, sacrificing itself for the sake of the next generation. A noble flower indeed. But even in its *danse macabre*, this one was breathtaking.

Wes didn't know how to classify it. It appeared to be a cattleya, but...no, not quite. The color was wrong, as was the shape. He'd seen plenty of two-toned orchids, but never one colored only on the lip. And such a vivid, dark purple—even faded, it was striking. The leaves were straplike, but the pseudobulbs weren't nearly as pronounced as others he'd seen.

Wes stood, pressing his hands together and lifting them before his lips. He was shaking, though not from fear or opium but excitement. This was *new.* This was a *new* orchid. Unnamed. Unknown.

And dying. No care would save this one now. But Wes had seen it. The hell and humiliation of the night had been worth it.

Pulling his notebook out of his pocket, he blinked a few times to try and clear his head enough to work. A great deal of the drug had left him, yes, but he was still somewhat groggy. His notes would be rough, alas, though it could accurately be argued that without the opium, he'd have no notes at all. He wondered if he dared linger a little longer to allow the narcotic to wear off entirely—ah, no, couldn't let himself be discovered by a servant who would come in vain to nurse the doomed favorite of the mistress of the house.

Still, he thought, shuffling to the window, a bit of cold air would do him good, and it wouldn't matter to the dying plant. He threw open the casement and leaned on the sill, staring out at the sea of houses below. The windows had been opened in the ballroom, letting the din spill out into the night. From here it was a noise that almost soothed, and he shut his eyes and took deep draughts of cool night air, willing it to sharpen his opium-muddled mind. The wind rippled his hair. The mist dampened his face.

A warm, firm hand took bold and possessive hold of his backside.

"No more hiding. I've found you, darling," a soft, sensuous voice said from behind him. "And thank goodness, for I am in the most desperate need of a rescuer."

Chapter Two

WES STARTLED, BUT the hand behind him slid coyly over the curve of his cheek, fingers tucking meaningfully into the crease of his buttocks.

His assailant spoke again. "You were right. This party isn't worth doing. But leaving me to that randy baronet is too cruel by half. You've made your joke. Now help me dispatch Sir Joshua, love." He stroked Wes's thigh. After a pause, he added, "I shall give you an entire night for free."

Wes fumbled at the sill, bracing against the wood to keep from falling out the window. Even if he could speak, for once, he'd have no idea what to say.

"Please, darling? Help me?" The hand around Wes's waist crept forward to the front of his thigh. "I will be so very, very grateful."

Wes might have been frozen in confusion, but his erection was not so encumbered, and it swelled to full mast, making a mighty sail of the front of his trousers. He wanted to see who this was, but fear—and lust—

kept him still. This was most certainly a mistake, and when the man learned this, the exchange would be over.

His assailant's fingers brushed sensually against the ridge of Wes's cock. The man laughed, sounding surprised. "Ooh, *Rodger.* I was jesting, of course, but—I take it this is a yes? And such a very *big*, delicious yes."

Wes let out a sharp, short, "Huh!" and turned around.

It was the pretty flirt from the ballroom, ignoring Wes no longer.

The long blond curls were even more enticing at close range, playing delectably around his elegant face, all cheekbones and sensuous lips and bright hazel eyes. The sodomite—no question of that now—smiled seductively, his expression promising carnal delight as his hands played over Wes's hips.

The man stopped, leaned forward in a squint and went very pale.

"Sweet heaven." He drew back in alarm. "You aren't Rodger."

No, Wes wasn't, and he was suddenly very sorry. But he had to put the man at ease. "N-N-No, b-b-but you n-n-needn't w-w-w—"

"You're him." If it were possible, the blond man seemed *more* terrified now. He stumbled backward, looking as if he might faint. "You're—you're *his*—Daventry. You're Daventry's son."

Wes searched for words, but none came to his aid.

It didn't help that the pretty man was no longer full of charm and wiles. He was clearly terrified.

"F-forgive me." The man's hand went to his throat, tugging weakly at the exquisite cravat. "I didn't know—I thought—P-Please. Please, don't—don't—" His hands were held out before him, warding Wes away, but he was still backing up, and on the last "don't" he ran into the wall. He did cry out then, and he flattened himself against the barrier.

"Please."

Confused and more than a little concerned, Wes took a careful step toward the blond man.

"G-g-g-g—" he began, stopped, sighed, and drew breath to try again.

The sound of a door opening roughly down the hall stayed him, though, and made the man against the wall cringe.

"Vallant?" an angry voice called out. "Vallant, you sod, come out at once."

The blond man crumbled into himself, sinking slowly down the wall.

"Vallant, when I find you, I'm going to spank that pretty white bottom until you scream."

Wes looked to the door between the sitting room and the unfinished bedchamber, then glanced at the door to the hall. Not even bothering to speak, he stepped forward, closed his hand over the blond man's elbow and pulled him into the adjoining bedchamber just as the door to the sitting room crashed open with a mighty thump.

"Vallant!"

Wes took the trembling man into the shadows with him, tugging a sheet away from a chair it was protecting. With a deft toss he draped it between the chair and end table and secured both ends before drawing the man with him in the narrow space beneath the makeshift tent. The sodomite tried to recoil from Wes, but the door into the bedroom opened, and when the shout came again, the blond man stilled.

"Vallant!"

Wes stared into the dim, blue-tinged depth beneath the sheet. His companion had stopped shaking, but he appeared distinctly unwell, and it made Wes ache. Vallant, if that was indeed the man's name, seemed vacant now, numb with his terror, torn between fear of the intruder and of Wes himself. He supposed the man feared exposure, that Wes would have him arrested for being a sodomite.

He longed to explain this was in no way the case.

Though he supposed he could simply fear Wes, stammering madman. The thought made Wes's heart heavy and sad.

The intruder's voice drew him out of his self-pity. "Vallant, you bugger, bring your lily white arse out here where I can see it, or so help me, I'll drag you back to my house and do it in front of my staff. And then do you *with* my staff." He chuckled darkly, sounding proud of his joke. He also sounded very, very drunk.

Footsteps echoed around the room before stopping not far from Wes and Vallant's hiding place. Wes heard the sound of liquid sloshing, as if in a flask.

Vallant shut his eyes.

The newcomer's words began to slur. "Nasty little sod. Don't play coy with me. You know you want this cock." Another grunt. "Yes. You want it, you filthy whore. Had a taste of it, and now you want it again. Come on." A pause gave way to a sharp slap of hands. "Come on!"

Vallant jumped at the sound. Without thinking, Wes reached out to gentle him with a hand on his knee. Vallant's eyes flashed to him, full of terror, and the sight made Wes ache. He tried to smile his most reassuring smile. He kept his hand on Vallant's knee, stroking his companion with his thumb. It wasn't exactly an erotic gesture, but neither was it innocent.

Vallant eyed him with guarded suspicion.

Wes extended his free hand, palm up. Then he lifted his other from Vallant's knee, and with a wry smile, inclined his head in a small bow.

Vallant continued to watch him.

"Vall*ant*!" Sir Joshua barked. The shout echoed against the empty walls. The baronet mumbled beneath his breath as the sound of footsteps came closer. Both Vallant and Wes tensed when the sheet rippled and the chair creaked. But Sir Joshua didn't find them, only grunted and farted as he settled back in the chair anchoring their sheet, breathing heavily.

"Fucking cocktease," he grumbled. Another grunt, another fart, and then a belch as well.

Wes and Vallant held very still. They also tried not to breathe.

Sir Joshua did not rise. After the passage of a few more minutes, he began to snore.

Wes and Vallant were trapped. They sat beneath the sheet, inches apart and staring at one another. Vallant no longer looked terrified, but he didn't look settled, either. The strangest thing, however, was that Wes got the distinct feeling it wasn't Sir Joshua who upset Vallant the most. It was Wes. And the longer they sat there, silent and staring, the more desperately Wes wanted to know what about him inspired such a reaction.

Careful not to make a sound, he reached into his vest pocket and pulled out his notebook and pencil.

Balancing the paper against his leg, he wrote, *I will not expose you.* He started to pass it over before pulling it back to add, *Not to Sir J nor to any other. You have no need to fear.*

He handed the notepad over and watched carefully for Vallant's reaction.

Vallant's first move was to lift the paper very close to his face, though after studying it, he glanced up at Wes, his look still wary. Which meant he hadn't feared exposure.

Which meant he feared the *other.*

Grimacing, Wes motioned for the paper.

I am not a madman. Only a stammerer. It is my tongue, not my mind, which is my affliction. His lips tightened as he added, *Certainly I am preferable to he whose wind gags us and uneven snores prevent us from escaping.*

He handed the pad over brusquely and waited.

Once more the pad went all the way up to Vallant's nose. This time, however, when he read Wes's note, he blushed.

"I don't—" he began in a whisper, but as soon as he spoke Sir Joshua snorted and stirred. Wes laid a finger to his lips and passed over the pencil. Vallant took it and wrote hurriedly.

I don't think you're mad. Thank you for helping me. Certainly you had no cause to.

It was kind of Vallant to say this, of course, but it helped Wes not at all. He wrote again.

Then why do you fear me?

He was ready for Vallant to object, to insist he didn't, but to his surprise, Vallant seemed abashed. He hesitated over the pad.

You are Daventry's son.

Wes glanced at him, but Vallant wasn't meeting his gaze. Wes wondered why the devil that was. Because of his father, apparently, but that explained nothing that would help him now. Fear of the office, perhaps?

He tried for levity.

An accident of birth. I'm afraid I'm nothing like my father, and he would be the first to tell you so. Emphatically. After some thought he added, *I shan't tell him anything either, if that gives you any comfort.*

The pencil stub ended up in the corner of Vallant's mouth, where he nibbled absently at it before writing his reply.

You are oddly tolerant of my nature.

Ah.

A return confession felt redundant after his reaction in the anteroom, but it seemed Vallant would demand it of him. Wes wrestled with phrasing, wanting to be clear to Vallant while being coded enough for another to fail to accurately decipher it should they find their notes. In the end he decided there was nothing for it, and he would need to burn these pages the moment he returned to his apartments.

I share it.

To his surprise, Vallant only gave a grim smile. His reply was swift.

I meant that I am a whore. Somehow I doubt you claim that nature as well?

Was it terrible that Wes felt aroused by the conversation? Likely. He tried to absorb himself in composing a reply, which took some doing, both the absorption and the reply itself. What did one say to that? *No, don't mind at all, old chap? What are your rates, perhaps I can give you some business?*

Aloud, he would have no hope of continuing the conversation. Indeed, he would never have made it this far. But here, trapped as they were… Perhaps it was all the pent-up frustration of the evening, perhaps it was the opium, or perhaps it was simply Vallant himself, but Wes suspected very much he was flirting.

If all are as delightful as you, I should hope to encounter many more of your peers. If I am mistaken, however, I shall happily embrace you as an exception.

Vallant's surprise at this reply was quickly masked, but Wes took pleasure in the suspicion that it flattered rather than alarmed him. When the notepad returned to him, Vallant presented it with a slight smile playing at his lips.

I apologize for my familiarity earlier. I honestly did mistake you for my friend.

Wes's reply was as swift as he could write it.

Pray, think nothing of it. I live in hope you make the mistake often in the future. And I envy your friend.

This time Vallant's mirth was more difficult for him to repress, though by his reply he clearly meant to keep trying. *Whores are meant to be bought with money, my lord, not flattery.*

Another quick reply, one Wes gave almost without thinking.

Perhaps it is not the whore I am trying to buy.

This, though, upset Vallant, who went still and wary at once. His reply was also swift, his hand shaking slightly.

You have only seen the whore, I promise you. And him, sir, you must purchase with shillings.

Wes cast up his eyebrow. He had no idea why Vallant thought he would swallow such a lie.

Perhaps it wasn't Wes he was lying to.

He should let it go, he knew. What he meant to pursue with such a man he had no notion. Sir Joshua was well asleep now, and they could easily make their escape. Yet he could not stop himself from writing again.

I have seen only a whore in the same way you have seen only a stammerer.

Vallant stared at the paper a long time. This time he didn't chew the pencil, but he did nibble his lip. He glanced up at Wes, searching for something in his face. Then he returned to the paper.

What is it you want, my lord?

It was a fair question. Wes wished he knew its answer. From Vallant, he had no idea. Certainly he wouldn't confess the answers that rose in his mind: it had been some time since his last congress, which had been rough and hurried. Also he was lonely, and Vallant was achingly pretty. But because he was enjoying pretending he was witty and clever, and seeing such reflected in another's eyes, he pretended to misunderstand.

An orchid no man has yet discovered and the power of speech enough to describe it to my peers.

Vallant only gave him a withering—but reluctantly amused—glance and handed the notepad back. "From me, my lord," he whispered.

Oh, devil take it. Wes wrote again.

Well, if I am wishing for the moon, I should long for a kiss, but rest assured I don't expect one.

His nerves fluttered this time as he handed it back. He'd hoped Vallant would laugh, but he didn't. Neither did he recoil, however.

As your reward?

Wes shook his head, not meeting Vallant's gaze. He felt foolish now for his confession. Yes, what was he playing at with Vallant? Did he imagine he would charm the man? Did he think this would bring the man to his bed? Vallant had made it plain that money would. Still, even as he chided himself, part of him yearned for one more exchange, one more flirtation. Because no, he didn't even want a kiss, much as he wouldn't refuse one. He only wanted to extend this strange, beautiful moment—handwritten exchanges with a male whore beneath a bedsheet while his assailant snored beside them—as long as he possibly could.

Which, he decided, was a destination he had reached.

Motioning with his head, he slipped quietly out from beneath the sheet. Vallant glanced worriedly toward Sir Joshua, but the baronet slept on. Wes extended his hand and helped Vallant rise, and together they moved in silence across the room to the door. It creaked when opened, and Sir Joshua stirred enough to murmur incoherently and release more wind, but that was all. They passed safely into the adjoining room, and Wes closed the door without a sound.

Pocketing the notepad and pencil, Wes turned to

Vallant with a smile he hoped appeared wry and not full of the ridiculous sad longing he felt. But his half smile slid away as he took in the strange look on Vallant's face. He waited, but Vallant only continued looking at him carefully. At last, Wes could take it no longer.

"W-w-what—?" he began, though he stopped as Vallant lifted a hand and pressed two warm fingers against his lips.

"Hush," he whispered. His eyes fell to his fingers at Wes's lips, and when they rose again, they were enticingly soft and open. Now it was he who offered a half smile, though his was laced with quiet uncertainty. "No more stammerer nor whore—not just yet."

Wes shook his head. "I c-c-can't s-s-s-stop it."

"I can," Vallant replied, the words tickling Wes's ear and leaving gooseflesh on his skin. Vallant leaned forward and pressed his lips to the place where his fingers had been.

In his surprise, Wes did not close his eyes, which was why he saw that neither did Vallant. The other man's eyes were slits, but they were open and watching. Their gazes held and locked as their lips met, remaining so even as Vallant drew back to end the kiss.

Wes let out a breath in a shuddering rush and lifted his own hand to Vallant's face. Brushing his knuckles against Vallant's cheek, Wes stared down at his companion in surprise. Vallant leaned into Wes's touch. His fingers pressed against Wes's chest, five pinpoints of gentle pressure.

They stared at each other a little longer.

Then, somehow, it all went a bit mad.

Wes never knew who moved first. All he could remember later was that one moment they had been staring at each other, and the next their mouths were locked as they stumbled to the small sofa near the window. Vallant straddled him and ground a rock-hard erection against his own aching cock, murmuring eager, breathless approval as Wes fought to undo both their trousers at once.

"Hurry," Vallant pleaded, sounding deliciously desperate. He dug his fingers into Wes's shoulders. "*Hurry.*"

Wes freed their cocks at last, and Vallant began to thrust and moan softly, but Wes stayed him. "W-We n-need a h-h-handkerchief."

Vallant lifted passion-bleary eyes and scanned around them before pointing to the table. "There. A cloth beside that flower in a jar."

"C-Careful," Wes admonished as Vallant leaned over to reach for it. "The orchid."

"It's beautiful," Vallant said.

"It's d-dying," Wes replied.

Vallant grinned wickedly at Wes. "But we aren't, my lord."

"Wes," Wes gasped as Vallant took them both in hand. "C-call me W-Wes."

Vallant paused in his stroke and frowned. "It makes

us sound like school chums. No, thank you." He tilted his head to the side. "Why Wes?"

Odd. No one had ever asked him that before. He even had to think to remember why himself. His father hadn't come into his title when he'd first been at school, so he was simply George Albert Westin. And yes, school chums, if they could be called such, had called him Wes. Or rather, W-W-Wes to mock his stammer. By the time he came home, he was Lord George—but George was his father. And his brother. At home his father had called him George or George Albert, and his brother called him Brat. In his own mind, he was Wes and had been since his mother had died.

He could hardly sputter all that out, and he wasn't reaching for his paper when he had Vallant's cock pressed so tightly against his own. Given the way Vallant had reacted to his father, his Christian name wouldn't do. Best go with the other one then.

"Albert," he rasped as his head fell back.

The name made Vallant stop, and so Wes opened his eyes and lifted his head. Vallant was regarding him curiously.

"M-My m-m-middle name," Wes explained. *My mother called me Albert.*

"Albert," Vallant said, as if trying it out. He smiled. "Yes, Albert will do quite nicely." He bent and nipped at Wes's chin. "Fuck me, Albert. Fuck hard against me, and I will make love to your mouth."

It was foolish, surely, to behave so wantonly there with Sir Joshua only a room away, with no doors locked and anyone able to walk in. Reckless, chasing such fleeting, selfish pleasure that would bring exquisite suffering for them both, should they be caught. Yet as Vallant eased them together, as his hand closed over their shafts, as hips began to buck and thrust and lust pounded in Wes's veins, Wes thought of nothing, nothing at all but how delicious he felt. When Vallant's tongue slipped into his mouth, the Queen of England herself could have walked in and he would have barely been able to spare her a nod.

He came first, groaning into Vallant's mouth as the whore twisted their cocks into a sweet, tight angle, as Wes fucked hard and fast into the towel. Vallant came shortly after. They hovered there, shaking and out of breath, sated and smiling against each other's mouths.

A loud bleat and snort from the other room stirred them. When Sir Joshua began to murmur and mumble to himself, sounding dangerously conscious, Vallant slid off Wes's lap and hurriedly did himself up. Reluctantly, Wes did so as well.

Before Vallant left, he turned and pressed one last kiss on Wes's cheek, so soft and sweet that it melted what remained of Wes's insides.

"Thank you." Vallant smiled.

And then he slipped into the hall. Wes did not follow, waiting as long as he could, letting Vallant move far away before he went out as well, heading toward what he hoped was the front hall stairs.

He was sliding into his coat when he realized he had not finished his sketch of the orchid. He paused, momentarily considering going back upstairs to do so, but then he caught sight of Vallant with a dark-haired woman on his arm. Wes remembered that all the pages of his notepad were full, all the room for sketches taken up by his foreplay.

Wes smiled all the way back to Mayfair and tossed the conversation with Vallant into his fire with great reluctance.

Chapter Three

IT WAS SHOCKING how very much Lord George Albert Westin looked like his father.

All the rest of the night, Michael's mind kept coming back to Lord George's resemblance to his sire. He thought of it quite a bit as he rode with Clary across town to a masquerade party where he had absolutely no luck finding a client. It flitted through his mind as he wove his way through the crowd at the Kilpatrick ball, trying not to let anyone see how he had to squint to identify people more than fifteen feet away. He even thought of it as he sucked down Mr. Kilpatrick's thick rope of semen in a dark corner of his study. And back at Dove Street, after enduring Rodger's angry lecture, he finally sank into his bed in the attic at dawn, still thinking of Lord George and Daventry.

So very alike in looks. So absolutely different in manner in every single way. Michael disliked thinking of him as Lord George, for Daventry too was a George. Only such an arrogant man could name not just his first born but his *second* son after himself.

Albert, he'd said. Call him Albert. Well, that was how Michael would think of him. It was perhaps a bit intimate for a marquess's son, but then, they'd been rather intimate, hadn't they?

Whatever he called him, he couldn't deny the physical resemblance, so he tried to focus on where they differed. The easiest was that Daventry had an older man's paunch where Albert was tantalizingly fit, and Daventry had graying, curling hair, where Albert's dark locks were straight and only slightly mussed even after a good fucking. Daventry had more sense of fashion, though. Albert didn't dress poorly, but he did dress more conservatively than most of his peers. He dressed like Rodger when he was in his gentleman's getup, which was what had thrown Michael in the first place. No, Albert and his father dressed nothing alike.

But they had the same eyes. It was so strange to look into the same pair of eyes he had hated more than any other and…not hate.

Eyes and mouth. Same shape of the lips. Even the same sideways curve when they smiled. The smiles were the worst. Michael lay awake a long time, haunted by that smile. Daventry was a cold, cunning bastard, and his smile was a portal to hell. Albert's eyes were pools of quietness, a little sadness too, and they invited, not lured. His smile was like the sun in England. Rare, dim, but in its full glory, a cause for celebration.

Good Lord, he was becoming a poet over Albert.

God knew he would never wax rhapsodic for Daventry.

Daventry's son. I have fucked Daventry's fucking son.

Daventry's son, the shy botanist. Who had hidden Michael from Sir Joshua, flirted with pencil and paper, and who loved orchids.

Michael smiled to himself at the memory.

He picked up a book to try and distract himself, but his mind would not follow the words. Eventually he simply gave up and lay down, pulling the blanket over his head. It made him think of being under the sheet tent with Albert, and there beneath his linen where no one else would know that he did it, he shut his eyes and relived the moment, that first kiss, the intake of breath…

The sofa…

Michael fell asleep. And he dreamed. He dreamed of kissing Albert, of lying naked for him, of offering up his body. He dreamed of fucking him face-to-face, of Albert sliding in deep, and Michael cried out his name.

"Albert. Oh, Albert."

But when his lover lifted his head, it was Daventry who leered down at Michael as he thrust inside him.

"That's right, my darling whore. My sweet little cunt. Moan for me, lovely. Show me how much you love my cock."

Michael stiffened, pulled back, and screamed.

He woke in a pool of his own sweat, throat hoarse from shouting, Rodger shaking him violently. When

Michael calmed down enough to sag against him, Rodger swore.

"Fucking hell, love." Rodger bussed a kiss against Michael's forehead and fumbled at his belt before pressing a flask into his hand. "I thought you was murdered."

Michael tipped the whiskey back with a shaking hand. "Dream." He wiped his mouth, forced bile down and added, "Daventry."

Rodger's swearing would have taken the paint off the walls, had they been painted. "Fucking ruddy fucking bloody fucking bastard! What in fucking hell did you fucking dream about him for?"

Michael winced, then shivered and pressed tighter against Rodger.

That's it, my cunt. Moan for me. Just like before.

He didn't realize he'd started whimpering until Rodger nudged him again. "The dream is over, love. No more, you hear me? Daventry's not here. He doesn't have you. He'll never have you again." Rodger stroked Michael's hair. "What brought this on, ducks? Did you run into the bastard somewhere?"

Michael shook his head, then prepared for his confession. "No. But I saw his son."

"Vaughn? He's a pretentious ass. I hope you planted him a good one right in the center of his fucking face."

"No. The other one. The second son, Lord George Albert." He shut his eyes tight. "I fucked him."

"*What?*" Rodger roared.

Michael put the flask Rodger had given him up to Rodger's own mouth to stop further swearing. "Drink. And listen."

As Rodger slowly drained the flask, Michael told the story of running from Sir Joshua, of mistaking Albert for Rodger, and all that came after. All of it.

"I'll be damned," Rodger said when he was done. "But what did you think I was at the Gordons's party for?"

"Well, I thought you'd followed me, and I was glad for it, because you were right: I got into trouble. But it wasn't you, obviously. I swear, Rodger, you and he have the same tailor. And you're the same height and build. Hair color too."

Though Albert's hair was much softer.

"You truly are blind as a bat, you poor sod." Rodger climbed onto the bed, leaned back against the pillow and put his feet on the mattress. "So this is Daventry's second son. I think I've heard of him. Shy fellow, I thought. Heavy stammer. Didn't know he was a mandrake. Or is he like his dear da and just likes the power?"

"No. He's a full-on sod. He knows his way around a cock, and he gives as much pleasure as he takes."

Rodger lifted his eyebrows. "You sound half besotted, love."

"I'm *not* besotted. I'm just telling you how he's different than his father. And he is. Completely." Michael tucked himself into the crook of Rodger's arm and rested his head on his shoulder. "He does stammer. Horribly. He clearly had to fight for every word. And I heard whispers of how he went into pieces just moving through the crush."

"Why on earth was he there, then?"

"I've no notion. Something about an orchid, I think, but that doesn't make any sense." Michael stroked Rodger's shirt. "He fucked with abandon, as did I. Just a heavy rub, but my God, I was shattered. I wasn't even acting. I was completely lost. I can't remember the last time I let go as I did with him."

"And now you dreamed of Daventry."

Michael stared across the room at his bookshelf. "Yes."

"You shouldn't have fucked his boy. Stirred everything back up in your damn head."

"It was a very good fuck. But you're right, it wasn't worth this." He dug his fingers into Rodger's chest. "It doesn't matter. It was just a stupid nightmare. It will fade soon enough."

Rodger grunted. "Do you want me to nap up here a bit?"

Michael glanced up at him. "Would you mind?"

"Fuck yes. It's cold as a witch's tit in your attic."

"But it doesn't smell like sweat or sex, and no one moans unless I stub my toe." Michael shrugged. "I'm sure I'll be fine."

Rodger sighed and nudged Michael with his hip.

"Roll fucking over."

Michael slept without dreaming, face to the wall and Rodger's strong, hairy arm around him.

But that afternoon as he ran some errands, he discovered the dream hadn't faded at all.

Twice he thought he saw Daventry on the street. Outside his favorite coffee shop he saw a tall man stepping out of a black carriage, and when Michael lingered to see if he were handsome, his heart nearly stopped as he found it was the marquess staring back at him, dark and hungry. When he stumbled backward into the shop window, banging his head on the glass, he opened his eyes once more and rubbed his stinging head. He saw that it wasn't the marquess at all. It was a gent, all right, but just some old toff. He didn't even look like Daventry.

This was with his spectacles *on*.

It happened again outside the dressmaker's. One of the girls wanted a new frock to try and catch herself a rich coal merchant, and Michael was leaning against the wall by the window when he saw Daventry again. This time the marquess stood by a lamppost, leaning on a walking stick and grinning like the lecher he was, staring right at Michael. He cried out and knocked over a mannequin, had half the girls in the shop rushing over to see what was wrong—and of course when he stood, Daventry wasn't anywhere.

"You need to get your spectacles changed," Rodger said when Michael told him over dinner what had happened.

"There's nothing wrong with my glasses," Michael snapped. "Just my stupid head. He wasn't there either time. I only thought I saw him." He drew his knees up to his chest and sank deeper into the ratty sofa in the back of Rodger's office. "You're right. I should never have fucked Albert."

Rodger frowned. "Albert? You're calling him Albert?"

"It's complicated."

Rodger grimaced. "Fuck someone else, love. I'll find you one of your favorites and nudge them to come round. Who would you like?"

Michael shrugged. "Billy Church?"

"Church!" Rodger laughed. "That old horse? What do you want him for?"

"He's gentle and comfortable." Michael grabbed an afghan off the back of the couch and tugged it over his legs. "He calls me his precious angel, right before he buggers me silly. Yes, he's one of my favorites."

"As you like it," Rodger said, and left to see to Billy Church's nudging.

Billy was thin and slight and had a cock as thick and long as a thimble even when erect. There wasn't any way to mistake him for the Marquess of Daventry, not even dead drunk. When he stumbled hesitantly into the room, smiling his shy smile and mangling his hat in his hands, Michael smiled back and prepared to lose himself with a comfortable old shoe. And yet once

Michael's eyes closed, once he began moaning and gasping to egg Billy on, his mind was full of shadows, and the next thing he knew he was cold and shaking and Billy was pleading in his high, whining voice for Michael to please start breathing again.

Rodger had given Billy a full refund and one of the new boys for free, and then he'd come back to Michael looking very grave.

"I'm fine," Michael insisted. "You're right. I shouldn't have gone with Billy. Find me someone rough and ready."

Rough and ready that night was a wealthy shipping man, Edgar Trowle, who liked to sing sea shanties while he fucked Michael against the wall. So at seven that evening, Michael was in that very position, gripping a well-placed bar above his head as Mr. Trowle belted out his best baritone and prepared to drive his clipper in to port.

He turned into Daventry before Michael's very eyes, and Michael began to scream.

Worst of all was that at first Trowle thought it was part of the game, and Rodger ended up coming in and nearly decking the man before Michael could recover enough to explain that no, it wasn't the very wealthy customer, it was him. Which had only made things worse, and Rodger ended up having to promise Trowle the rest of the month gratis just to keep the peace.

Once that was settled, he came storming back to Michael.

"This has got to stop, ducks," he said, his voice full of both anger and deep concern. "And if you tell me you're fine once more, I'll pin you to that mattress until you tell me the truth of what's bothering you."

Michael drew his dressing gown tighter to his body and curled against the headboard, staring sightlessly at a lewd painting on the far wall. Trowle had been gone for twenty minutes, but Michael was still shaking. "I don't know what's happening. I honestly feel fine, and then all of a sudden it shifts. It doesn't make any *sense*."

"Lord George didn't do *anything* unusual to you? Outside of rub his prick against yours, which I believe you agreed to?"

Michael nodded. And shivered. So cold, so very, very cold. "I must be tired."

Rodger sighed. "Take the rest of the night off. Go read your books and get some sleep."

Michael did. He didn't dream, either, and he woke in the morning feeling very refreshed. He came downstairs whistling, and by midafternoon he decided he was ready to work. He gave a few hand jobs in the lobby and sucked some cocks in the private rooms. He even let a fat candle merchant undress him and fondle him in front of his nervous-looking friend in one of the parlors. Relieved, Michael went upstairs with a comfortable old dock worker, stripped naked, put his arse in the air, and got ready for a delicious ride.

And it happened again.

There you go, boy. That's the way. Spread yourself for me.

Show me how much you want me to claim you.

This time when Michael started shouting, his partner stopped, concerned he had hurt Michael, and Michael was able to lie and say that no, he'd hurt himself. They rubbed cocks instead, and he did reach his zenith, gloriously pinned beneath the sweaty weight of a man. But he still felt cold even an hour later, and he didn't try to take a trick into a private room.

He told Rodger about it, though, because he had to. Rodger wasn't pleased.

"This is bad, ducks."

Michael shoved a shaking hand into his hair and averted his eyes. "I can sell some books to make up for my losses, if you want. I'm sure it will pass soon enough."

That only made Rodger angry. "I'm not talking about money, you dumb sod. I'm talking about *you.* This is bad for *you.*" Rodger sank beside him on the sofa with a heavy sigh. "Why did you have to go and fuck his lad? God above, but I wish you hadn't."

"I didn't think it would matter. It shouldn't have mattered." Michael wrapped himself in the afghan and stared at the floor. "I don't understand. I'm not upset about it, about what Daventry did to me. I haven't been for years. I get tense if someone mentions him, and I think it would be bad if I encountered him, but it isn't as if we run in the same circles. And his son is nothing like him. Albert is *kind.* Even funny. I enjoyed myself with him. But I'm not even thinking of him. Or

Daventry. Not until—" He bit his lip and said nothing more.

Rodger rubbed his chin for a long moment. "Let me have a go."

Michael drew back and looked at him in horror.

Rodger punched him lightly in the shoulder. "Don't give me that look. I've had that arse more than any man in London."

"Yes, but not for years," Michael protested. "We joke about it all the time, but we never actually do it."

"If you panic with me," Rodger dogged, "then you know something is truly buggered in your head. Pardon the pun. If you can let me do you…" Rodger gave him a cheeky wink, "…well, then you know you can at least keep up your rent."

Michael grimaced, but it was mostly for show. He never minded being fucked by Rodger. "Fine," he agreed. "But you'll not do me for free."

Rodger snorted. "I'll pay your going rate if there's come dripping out your arse, how about that?"

Michael made a rude gesture, stripped out of his clothes, and turned over.

Ten minutes later he was shaking, wrapped in every blanket the servants could find and huddled in a ball at the end of the couch near the stove as Rodger stormed down the hall, swearing so badly one of the men at the door had to ask him to please stop scaring off the customers. Once he was able to stand, Michael dressed, crawled up the stairs to his room, drank warm milk, and fell asleep.

In the middle of the night he was screaming again, the nightmare returned in full force. It came the next night as well.

And the night after that.

The night after that too.

Even when Rodger sat beside him all night, or all day, or whenever Michael tried to sleep deep enough to rest, the nightmare came back, over and over and over.

"This is insane," Michael complained through chattering teeth during the second straight week. Cold, so *cold*. He wrapped himself in blankets, but they could not warm him. He felt hollowed out from the inside.

Rodger was grim. "You should be getting better, not worse. No one's touched your arse in ten days."

Didn't Michael know it. "Perhaps I'm ill."

"Only in your head." When Michael recoiled, Rodger gentled. "Calm yourself. No one's sending you to Bedlam."

Michael sagged against the wall. "I was *rid* of this." He drew his knees closer to his body. "Until Albert."

Rodger was silent a moment. "Maybe that's what you need. Maybe you need to see him again. Hey," he said when Michael glared at him. "Don't look at me like that. It might work. Nothing else is, anyway."

Michael doubted that very much. But talking about Albert made the man linger in his mind. It made him think of his face, guarded, but so soft, so…pretty, really. He had a simple look about him, a shyness

Michael knew well, but no desperation. Just quietness. And now that he knew underneath that veneer lurked a tiger…

Rodger's hand came down on his, and he turned to him, frowning. "What were you thinking of just then? You went all relaxed and quiet. You looked almost yourself again." He glanced down, then boldly reached over and cupped Michael's groin.

"Rodger!" Michael snapped his legs together and glared. He was half-hard.

Rodger only pointed an accusing finger at him. "What were you thinking of?" he demanded.

Michael felt his cheeks pinken. "Albert. But I even got hard for you—"

"I'm going to bring him here, and you're going to fuck him," Rodger declared. "Or rather, he will fuck you." He frowned. "Unless that might make you worse. God above, I don't think I could handle you being worse." He looked into Michael's face, stripping him bare. "Do you want him, love?"

Michael turned away before Rodger could see anything. "And how will you fetch him if I do? Knock on Daventry's door and ask if you could borrow his son? You have a whore down in your bawdy house you need him to fuck for you?"

"Don't get smart. I'll send the boys out to watch for him. I doubt he lives with the marquess, at his age. Don't know quite where he'd be, but sounds like we should be looking in gardens to start." He nudged

Michael with his elbow. "But is that what you want, Michael? Do you want to see Lord George again?"

Michael stared down at the bed, the hollow cold inside him making him shake. He tried to stammer a lie, but he was too tired. "Yes."

Rodger smacked Michael's rump through the blanket. "Get yourself greased for your shy stammerer then, love. I'll have him for you by the end of the week."

And so Michael lived in a constant state of terror, half-afraid that Rodger would produce Albert, half-afraid he wouldn't be able to. Every night he dreamed, and as every day passed, the dreams got worse, and the cold he felt after them grew colder and colder, until he never thought he'd be able to get warm again.

NO PEER OR gentleman in all of England was more venerated, more wise, more admired and more emulated than Wes's father, the Marquess of Daventry.

All his estates were in perfect order. He kept up the entailed houses, and he had a few others as well. He was active in politics and a vocal and respected participant in the House of Lords. He'd provided the title with two sons, and the first had married well—third daughter of a duke, bringing in a tidy sum to boot. She'd produced two sons and a daughter already, with another child on the way.

Daventry had mourned his wife properly when she died and now kept to the life of a genteel bachelor.

There had been a few relationships, Wes suspected, but as with all things Daventry, they were discreet.

One bright March morning, Wes received a summons to visit him.

Daventry House sat in St. George's Square, boasting a lovely view of the park. Daventry himself was here, doing his duty through the Season to government and society. In fact, as Wes was ushered into his study, his father was in quiet consult with his secretary, trying to decide which balls and dinners he should attend for the next week in between attending Parliament sessions and meetings with the other leaders of his party. But when Daventry saw his second son in the doorway, he put the secretary's list down and sat back in his chair, giving Wes his full attention.

"George Albert. How prompt you are. Well done." Brown eyes danced beneath pepper-gray hair as Daventry motioned to a chair across from his desk. "Do sit. We're nearly finished here, and I shall be with you directly."

Wes sat as bid, glancing about the room as his father continued to debate in quiet tones with his secretary.

The study had been redone again. That was Daventry, never one to step out of pace. He had given way to the necktie as well. Wes touched his own cravat. He wondered if it was a particularly sad social sin to be more out of fashion than one's own father.

Daventry dismissed his secretary and turned to

Wes. Wes sat forward in his seat, trying to look alert.

"As I mentioned in my note," his father began, "I have need of your aid. You remember the Presleys." When Wes only blinked at him, Daventry's mouth flattened in dismay. "Arthur Presley. Of Devonshire. I believe you knew his son at school, before you left? Garreth?"

Before you left. The words rang in the air between them, as disheartening as the memory of Garreth Presley himself. "Y-y-yes, F-Father."

Daventry shifted some papers on his desk. "As I said, I'd like you to attend the ball with me. It seems Presley has taken a liking to plants and wants to know how to begin a collection. He's coming over for a little dinner I'm having. The usual people will be in attendance: your brother, senior members of our party in Parliament, and their wives. I told Presley you'd be there and that he could quiz you all he liked about plants."

Wes looked up in alarm. His father's "little dinners" were nothing of the kind. The last one had consisted of fifty people. "I d-d-d-don't th-th-th-th—"

"I have need of Presley's influence on a few matters, and this would go a long way to assuring his compliance." He leaned forward on his desk and looked Wes levelly in the eye. "I would consider this a great favor, George Albert. I should think you would be eager to seize this chance to be of use." He smiled a sad smile before turning back to his books. "But of course I will let you think on it." He ran his finger down a line of figures. "So. Are you off to your Regent's Park garden today? How does your work there progress?"

"G-G-Good." Wes longed to explain how he'd solved the problem with the piping in the south part of the main greenhouse and saved the society several hundred pounds in averted catastrophe, not to mention the cost of replacement for overheated plantings, but he knew better than to try to get such a complicated sentence out. Certainly his father wouldn't wait for it. "Y-Y-You should st-st-stop b-b-by and s-s-see."

"Oh, I shall leave the plants to you, boy." Daventry shuffled through the papers on his desk. "I should like to have nothing better to do with my time than see your trees and flowers. Not a minute of the day goes by without another trouble thrown at me, and here your brother has brought more for me to bear." He rose, signaling the end of their interview. "I shall look forward to next week. My secretary will send the details to your apartments."

Wes nodded, though his smile was forced, and made his way out of the room as the secretary returned.

The house was quiet, and he wondered absently what else his father had upgraded. He indulged himself in a tour.

The library was much the same, but there were several other prominent changes. The dining room had been papered, and the painting at the foot of the stairs had changed. He climbed up to the first floor, curious to see how extensive the remodeling was. His old bedroom, long since turned into a guestroom, was blue instead of the rich yellow it had been last he'd checked up on it. There was gas lighting down the entire hall as well as within the bedrooms, which made Wes smile wistfully. How he wished he would have had such a luxury when he had been a child. No need to find a bright window to read or squint at the light from a candle.

"You there!"

Leaning on the doorframe, Wes paused, uncertain, but when no one else answered and angry footsteps became louder, he stood up and leaned the other way to glance into the hall. A pinch-faced elderly man stalked toward him, looking very cross. Wes pushed aside his anxiety and forced himself to straighten. This was Daventry House, after all. He stood tall, lifted his chin and stared down at the stranger.

He said nothing at all, either, a trick which had served him well in the past and did not fail him now. The man approaching him slowed, faltered, then stopped entirely. Wes might have an idiot's stammer, but he could still give a haughty glare with the best of the Westins.

"Pardon, sir," the man said, bowing. "He's stolen my glasses again, and I mistook you for a footman from a distance. I am Martin Gibbous, his lordship's tutor. Is there any chance you've seen Lord Alten?"

The man's jaw set in a hard, angry line. "He's gone missing again."

Wes frowned. Edwin was here? But term surely had restarted by now. Why on earth wasn't his nephew back in school? "Wh-Wh-Why is h-h-he—"

He cut himself off as a towheaded figure darted out of a linen closet, ran across the end of the hall and disappeared into a small sitting room.

Understanding seemed to dawn on the tutor's face and with it a great deal of condescension. "Ah. You are Lord George. I have heard Lord Daventry speak of you." His tone took on the careful speech one used around the very young, the very old, and the very simple. "Have you seen your nephew about today, my lord?"

Wes looked Mr. Gibbous in the eye. "No."

Gibbous sighed and ran a bony hand through his remaining wisps of hair. "Likely as not he's gone into the cellars again. I should lock him down there for an evening. That would cure him." He gave Wes one more simpleton's smile and did all but pat him on the arm. "Very good, my lord. Thank you so much for your help."

Wes smiled back and remained standing in the doorway until the tutor was all the way down the stairs and in the main hallway, calling out to a maid and demanding to know if she had seen Lord Alten pass by. When all was silent, Wes pulled off his shoes, stayed close to the wall and proceeded almost as silently as he had when it had been he himself ducking from tutors. Outside the sitting room at the end of the hall, he waited, patiently, until at last he heard the sound of something heavy being shoved across the floor, at which point he smiled. A four-and-a-half-foot tall, gangly blond boy appeared in the doorway, ready to dash across the hall.

The boy froze, then tensed, ready to bolt. But then he got a better look at Wes's face and relaxed, his face breaking into a bright, wide smile.

"Oh, Uncle George," Edwin cried. "I'm ever so glad to see *you*."

"I WAS THROWN out again."

Edwin swung his legs back and forth after this confession, the heels of his boots clipping the wall behind the wooden shelf he perched on. Wes had smuggled him through the stovehouse and into the gardener's shed behind it, the gardener's silence bought with a pair of shillings and the sly touch of Wes's fingers at his wrist. The latter would cause him an awkward conversation later, he knew, for he had no intention of tupping the man a second time, but all he cared about just now was getting to the bottom of Edwin's situation.

Wes sat on a bench opposite Edwin. "T-tell me what h-happened."

Edwin's feet swung a few times. "My schoolwork."

Wes frowned. Edwin was a brilliant young man. Something else was going on, surely. He waited patiently for the rest.

It took some time in coming. Edwin continued to swing his feet, though when he lifted his head, he looked at Wes with all the sobriety of an adult. The boy was eleven, that odd age where he was both boy and man, flitting between the two without a moment's warning.

"They tease me. Everyone does. And this boy across the hall does horrible things to me. Once h-he made me eat soap. In front of everyone. It made me sick, so horribly sick. They salt my food too, and put mud in my sheets, then say that I—" He blushed furiously and averted his eyes.

The sound of the rain beat around them, pelting the windows. It was warm inside, and it smelled comfortingly of plants and damp. But the cold bite of memory washed over Wes.

"Sn-snow," he said at last. "Th-they liked to put sn-snow into my p-pants. I h-had to stand there unt-til it m-melted."

Edwin's eyes filled with unshed tears. "I didn't want to go back after holiday. I thought if I were a bad student they would kick me out. And they did. But Father says I'm a disgrace. Says I've"—he swallowed hard, looking guilty—"betrayed the family and the name." His tears spilled over. "But I can't go back, Uncle George. I can't." He wiped his eyes on his sleeve. "I told Father I wanted to have tutors at home like you did. He got very angry. He says he's going to let Grandfather punish me."

There wasn't a lot of terror in Edwin's voice, and Wes had to hide a wry smile. Punishment from Daventry? Guilty lectures, yes. Possibly some boxing lessons. But punishment? No. Wes felt a tug of envy. How he would have longed for such personal attention from his father.

"If y-you like," he said, "I c-can ask if you can h-help us at the g-gardens. G-Give you g-grueling work as w-well as an educ-cation."

It warmed him to see the way his nephew beamed. "Oh! Would you really? That would be so wonderful. I would do any work you asked. As grueling as you like."

Wes was fairly certain he could astound Edwin with new levels of disgust when he saw the manure sheds, but he also knew Edwin would wade through worse rather than go back to his torment at school. Which he would eventually need to return to, unfortunately. There would be no quiet arrangement of tutors for Edwin Westin, Baron of Alten, heir to the Earl of Vaughn and one day the Marquess of Daventry.

But Wes could give him a few shining moments while the boy was still in town.

He rose and held out his hand. "C-come. If you w-want to h-help me, you must first h-have your l-lessons. Let us s-see where your t-tutor has g-gone."

IT WAS MIDAFTERNOON when Wes finally returned to his lodgings—technically he lived only a few blocks away from Daventry House, but once he'd helped settle matters with Edwin, he went to the club for a luncheon and a stiff drink. After dealing with his elder brother for an hour, he'd thought it was the least he was owed.

"I can't coddle him," Vaughn had snapped when Wes suggested Edwin be allowed to spend some time with him at the Regent's Park garden. "It's all well and good for you to hide out with your plants, but you can't encourage that in Edwin. He's the heir. He has responsibilities, and he must learn how to manage them. Everyone has trouble in school. Everyone faces bullies. It's part of growing up."

Wes had wanted to argue with his brother, but when he'd tried to pull out his notebook to present his own position, Vaughn had only rolled his eyes.

"Do you see? This is what I'm speaking of. You would have me coddle the boy until he is like you, unable to participate in a simple conversation without a paper crutch. He must be made to be strong. I won't have him turn out like you, fit for nothing but playing with dirt in the park."

His brother had turned on his heel and stalked out of the library before Wes could recover from the blow enough to mentally prepare a retort, let alone find means to deliver it.

The insult had carried the devil's barb in it, Wes acknowledged as he leaned back in his seat on the hack ride home. His brother's verbal slap robbed him of his usual solace—"playing with dirt" as Vaughn had put it. No Regent's Park garden for him, not that afternoon. He would have nothing but cigars and whiskey and the din of men's conversation drifting into the club library. The prospect of dinner with more of the same had turned his stomach, and so he'd headed for home, content to ring up a sandwich for supper or send the potboy out for a loaf later if he grew hungry.

Though the thought of sliding into a warm bath with a large pot of poppy tea had a great deal of appeal. A bit of opium would make all the day's misery drift away. No, he shouldn't use it as such, but surely today warranted a bit of bending the rules.

It wasn't as if he were required to be of *use* to anyone tonight.

By the time the driver let him off, Wes's mood was so black he found himself wishing he had opium to smoke and could lose himself properly. He was halfway to the door and nearly resolved to fetch his purse and a warmer coat and head right back in to the City again to seek out a decent den, when he looked up to see Rawlins, the building's butler, hurrying down the walk to meet him.

Wes stopped short and blinked in confusion, but before he could form a question, Rawlins closed the remaining distance between them and made a bow.

"Forgive me for troubling you, my lord." He held out a slip of unsealed cream paper. "But a gentleman brought this by three hours ago and was most insistent I get this note to you as soon as I saw you."

Before I even stepped in the front door? Something was odd here, that was certain. Frowning, Wes took the paper from the butler.

> *Require a moment of your time to discuss a mutual acquaintance. Will stop by at four this afternoon. Sending pleasant regards from Mr. V.—R.*

Wes stood on the steps, staring at the paper, confused. Mutual acquaintance? V? Who was V?

Slowly, terribly, the words and what they meant permeated his brain.

Mutual acquaintance.

Mr. V. Which could only be Vallant. Michael Vallant.

Someone knew.

Wes crumpled the paper into his fist. "Th-th-th-th—" He shut his eyes, forced himself to calm, and tried again, but he was so rattled it was work enough to keep himself speaking. "Th-Th-Th-Thank you."

"I'm very sorry, sir," Rawlins said, sounding almost as agitated as Wes was. "It is not my wish to deliver what is clearly bad news to you so abruptly, but the gentleman was most insistent."

Wes couldn't reply. He ran a hand over his face as he pushed past the butler into the house, fighting against the torrent of potential ruinations this unknown R could bring to him and to his family. His father.

Heaven help him, he would put a pistol to his head before he would let his father hear of this—

He didn't realize he'd become so anxious that he'd passed out until he was lying on the floor, Rawlins bent over him with smelling salts.

"My lord! My lord!" Rawlins's face was gray. "Oh, I am so sorry—I should never have let the man bully me into giving you that note. I will call the authorities straightaway—"

"No!" The word came out in a sharp, desperate bark, the stammer not even able to rouse itself in time, Wes's panic was so acute, though it quickly regained its ground. His plea of "Do not call anyone" stalled at the back of his teeth, reduced to desperate spits of Ds and Ns.

"Very well, my lord," Rawlins interrupted him, clearly trying to soothe his distraught master. "I shall not call. But I shall stand ready, should you need me."

Wes wanted to balk at that as well, but practicality won out in the end. After ten minutes of sputtered assurances to Rawlins, he dismissed the man and continued to his apartments, where he took some pills and poured himself a large tumbler of brandy.

Ten minutes after that, after growing impatient for Doctor Jacob's opiates to take effect, he brewed himself some poppy tea.

When the knock on his door came at four, he had drugged and drank himself into a strange sort of calm. There was little he could do now but meet this R and hope his demands were reasonable. Upon reflection, he suspected Rawlins had been blackmailed as well, which would explain his nervousness and breaking form to meet him on the walk. Whoever this was would not be easy to dispatch. But Wes resolved not to panic. He would face this calmly and rationally.

And very, very drugged.

Wes opened his door ready to face down Rawlins escorting a greasy, shifty-eyed miscreant, or perhaps a leering, gap-toothed thug. Which was why when he found instead a polished, well-tailored man of fashion standing beside the butler, he was taken aback to the point that instead of returning the man's polite nod he glanced around the empty hall, still looking for a scoundrel.

"Lord George," the stranger said smoothly, as if Wes weren't gaping at him slack-jawed. "Such a pleasure to meet you, and so kind of you to agree to interrupt your affairs to see me. I begin our acquaintance already in your debt." The man bowed low. "I am Rodger Barrows."

Chapter Four

KNOWING HE WOULDN'T be able to utter much beyond consonants, Wes dismissed Rawlins with a stiff nod and motioned for Barrows to take one of the chairs in his sitting room. Barrows sat and waited patiently, Wes knew, to be spoken to so he could begin.

It was with some pleasure that Wes *didn't* speak. He studied his visitor instead.

Rodger. That was who Vallant had mistaken him for at the Gordons's, wasn't it? Surely he must be the same man. They were of the same height, Wes and his guest, and roughly the same build, though Barrows was a bit beefier across the shoulders than Wes. His clothes truly were exquisite. Like Barrows, Wes favored darker tones and clean lines, though he saw Barrows adopted the more modish necktie and pin rather than the cravat Wes wore. There was also a hint of flamboyance to Barrows's dress in his tie, the detail on his lapels and embroidering on his collar, ostentation that Wes himself eschewed.

Barrows, likely realizing he would wait until Doomsday to be invited to speak, cleared his throat and began, though he didn't seem put-off by the silence at all. In point of fact, he was easy, breezy and smiling.

"Perhaps it is best if I get right to the point, my lord. I understand you recently met my good friend Mr. Vallant. You did him no small service at Mrs. Gordon's party. Relieved him of the attention of a particularly rude guest."

Wes nodded once and waited for the rest. *I understand afterward he thanked you in a rather singular fashion.*

But Barrows only nodded, the gesture almost a bow. "I must thank you. By rights I should have been there to rescue him myself. I am grateful from the bottom of my heart that you were there to do what I could not."

There was an odd sharpness to Barrows's tone, and Wes's already churning insides rolled over themselves. Dear God, was Barrows Vallant's lover? That sealed it then, didn't it? Possibly the only thing worse than being blackmailed by an opportunist wanting to expose his sodomy was a jealous *sodomite* wanting to expose his sodomy. Vengeful lovers could rarely be bought off.

Barrows had paused again, giving Wes an opportunity to speak. He didn't take it.

"Ah." Barrows's smile slipped just slightly before he continued. "Well. As I have said, I am grateful to you. We both are, in fact." His smile righted itself. "Which brings me to my errand today. I hope I may humbly appeal to more of your good nature and implore you to do my friend yet one more service."

Wes laced his fingers together and leaned back, not bothering to hide his grimace. *Lend us the figure of, say, five hundred pounds. To send me and my good friend packing from London—at least until we need another five hundred pounds.*

Barrows barely paused this time, adapting to Wes's unwillingness to participate in his conversation. "I ask you, my lord, to pay a visit to Mr. Vallant. At your convenience, of course, but I implore you to come sooner rather than later. Tonight in fact would be most welcome. It is a matter of utmost importance."

Wes frowned, waiting for the rest, but now it was Barrows who kept his silence, and after a full minute, Wes was compelled to rouse his words. He said a small prayer that just once he could control the stammer, but as usual, his prayer went unanswered. "I d-d-do not underst-t-t—" He stopped, closed his eyes and visualized the word. "Understand."

"A visit, Lord George. To Mr. Vallant, at his residence." Barrows paused, though this time Wes could tell it was for effect. "His business residence."

Wes's eyes went wide, and even if words had come easy to him, he doubted he could have spoken them, not at that moment.

Barrows continued breezily, as if he had not just asked a marquess's son to visit a brothel. "It would be a particular kindness to me if you would do so. So much, in fact, that I should be happy to give you a much reduced rate."

Wes had to bend forward and press his fingers against his lips to strangle his exhalation—a laugh? A gasp? Whatever it was, it tasted of madness and terror in his mouth. *Friend.* No. Barrows was not Vallant's friend. He was his *procurer.*

Come fuck my whore, please, and I'll give you half off.

Even before the shock receded, memories were rising inside of Wes: memories of blond hair in his hands, of a sweet mouth on his, of long slender hands clutching him as a hot cock slid against his own. Of wicked laughter, a bright smile, and dancing eyes.

Mr. Barrows, tell me where he is, protect my anonymity, and I would pay you double.

Wes had a feeling that blackmail still lurked in this somewhere—likely if he refused. What he didn't know yet was why Barrows had sought him out.

"H-how do you c-care for p-plain sp-p—" Wes gritted his teeth. *Damn* the stammer. "Sp-speech," he finished at last.

Barrows's composed face broke into a wry grin. "Plain speech? You mean we stop dancing around like ninnies and say what we actually mean? Fine by me, guv."

Wes blinked. And then, whether it was pent-up shock or simply insanity settling in at last, he laughed.

"Careful," Barrows said, though he smiled as he settled back in his seat. "Now, I know you have trouble with words, and I already know you peg me for a blackmailer. Which"—he flashed Wes a dark grin—"I might yet be, though I'd rather have you as a customer. So I suggest you sit back, my fine lord, and listen as I do my best to explain."

Wes leaned into the corner of the sofa. "V-very w-well."

Barrows grinned.

"So, I've checked into you a bit, Lord George Albert Westin. As someone who looks into people regular, I don't mind telling you that you were something of a challenge. You're a very private gentleman. At first I thought, no, a man can't be that reclusive without having something to hide." He chuckled. "You do, of course. But I fell out of my desk laughing when I saw it was *plants* you was smuggling. Oh, don't look at me like that," he said, when Wes glared at him. "I don't care about that. It was me I was laughing at, really. Thought for sure it'd be guns or little girls."

Wes sputtered. Barrows waved his indignation away.

"After everything I've seen, I've learned not to be surprised." He shook his head. "Anyway. Like I said, you're private. And you're clever. And excepting your little moment with Michael, you are the most discreet buggerer I've yet met." He smiled sadly. "Unfortunately I've two servants who will swear they saw the two of you together. You and Michael, that is."

In his seat, Wes went very still. So it would be

blackmail after all. What he had feared all afternoon now had come true. Odd, how after his earlier terror, he felt oddly calm. Perhaps it was shock.

Or opium.

He straightened and gathered his words. "H-how m-much do you w-want?"

Barrows pursed his lips and tilted his head back and forth, considering. "Well, regular at Dove Street is fifty pounds for an evening. That's in a posh room, mind you. For weeklies we drop it back a bit, thinking of the long term and all, and I wouldn't mind setting that up, especially if this goes like I hope. He's right worth fifty as you well know. And should this become a regular event—which is my goal, if this works at all—you'll pay the regular rate, period. Perhaps a bit more, seeing as you're such a fine gent with pockets deep enough to bribe shipmen." He sighed. "But just now, since it's me asking you, and since even I don't know how this will go down—" He winced, then nodded in resignation. "Ten. Ten pounds, up front. And no money back, you got me?"

Wes was getting dizzy from all the earthquakes in this conversation. "You only w-w-want t-t-ten p-p-pounds to k-k-keep qu-qu-quiet?" Then he remembered the part about a "regular event". Ah, now it made sense. "A m-m-month?" Even so, that was a bargain. Goodness, but Barrows was a reasonable blackmailer.

"Well, you can come weekly, you know. And at that

rate you know you can afford to." He stopped. "Wait. Keep quiet?" He laughed. "Guv, this ain't hush money. I want you for a *customer*."

"C-C-Customer?" Wes repeated.

"You didn't figure it yet? I'm the madam, or the mister, or whatever you like. I run a house on Dove Street. Right posh we are at that. We serves all kinds, no questions. I inspect anybody who wants a private room, but once you're cleared, you're in. And before you start worrying about discretion, we keep the right palms greased, if you know what I mean."

"I kn-new who you w-w-were," Wes said, trying to take his time, but he was desperate for understanding now. "B-but wh-why—?"

"Why did I scare the piss out of you and your uptight butler? So you'd give me the time of day. I didn't feel like waiting around for you to ignore the trash on your doorstep. Same reason I put on the duds and the talk." He winked at Wes and slipped back into his formal speech. "I daresay I did quite well, don't you think? And I imagine Michael is correct. Your tailor is Garret on Bond Street?" He grinned as Wes nodded, and he went back to his colloquial speech. "Yeah. I knew an actress awhile. She taught me how to blend in. Right handy for a man in my profession. But you want to know why I bludgeoned into your life to get you to come fuck my friend for half-price, yes?"

Wes nodded. Yes, he couldn't wait to hear the answer to this one.

Barrows snorted. "Well, you ain't gonna hear. So you can sit and wonder. But the offer stands. For ten quid, you come—tonight would be lovely—and you shag Michael Vallant good and proper. In return, I will keep your visit a secret and any such visits in the future. And if you don't agree to my offer, I will spend as much effort as I did in getting your attention in letting any and everyone you don't want to know you fucked a sodomite that you did. That speech plain enough, my lord?"

Wes was hanging on to the edge of the sofa now in a vain attempt to keep the world from spinning crazily around him, but the problem wasn't with the world, just with Rodger Barrows's presence in it. Wes was intrigued, even half hoping Vallant had wanted him badly enough to extend this invitation. Add to this, of course, that Wes desperately *did* want to see Vallant again—especially for sex. The fact that Barrows was giving him virtually no choice was almost a blessing. Odd, but a blessing all the same.

But did Vallant want him?

Wes sat up and braced his elbows on his knees. What *did* Vallant want?

Had he asked for this?

"Well?" Barrows prompted. "What's it to be?"

Wes didn't move for a long second, letting the last of his doubts be strangled. When they were gone, he stared straight ahead and nodded.

"Wonderful!" Barrows exclaimed. "How about we

get started?"

Wes sat straight up. "N-now?"

"Now, my lord. We'll hire a closed hack, and I'll whisk you away. We'll set you up with a nice hot bath and brush up your clothes for you as you soak. Dinner too, if you like. And when you're ready, you can hand over your ten-pound note, head upstairs, and fuck Michael good and proper."

Wes sank back into the sofa again, too stunned to sit upright any longer. Why not now, indeed?

Barrows rose. "Would you like to ring for the cab, or should I?"

MICHAEL WAS WRAPPED in a blanket and huddled in his bed with a book when Rodger appeared in his doorway.

"Oi, Princess," he called out, startling Michael. "Put down your book. You have a customer."

Michael sat up, blinking even though he had his spectacles on. "What? *Now?*" He glanced out the window, but no, the sun was still up. His guess was it was just around six.

"He's in the bath and having tea. Yours is waiting downstairs. When you're done, head to the blue room."

Michael pushed his glasses higher up on his nose. His limbs felt heavy, and his head threatened to spin off his shoulders. "A private room? But—Rodger, I still can't—"

"You've an hour at best, love. Make yourself pretty."

Rodger started back down the stairs. Michael threw off his blanket and followed.

"Rodger! Are you insane? Or is this your sick idea of a joke?"

Rodger kept walking. "Not a joke."

Michael grabbed Rodger's shoulder and made him turn around. "Stop it. Whatever you're up to, stop it. Tell me what's going on."

"I did." Rodger's face was a mask. "You have a customer in the blue room in an hour."

"Do I get a name? A list of his preferences? A hint?"

Rodger's eyes danced with devilry. "Flowers. I think he likes flowers."

Michael's knees threatened to give way. "You didn't."

"I did." Rodger swatted Michael's backside. "One hour. Look pretty."

Rodger left. When Michael could move, he headed to the first floor to what they had all come to think of as the ready room.

He went through his ablutions in a daze. Several of the girls were there, likely sent by Rodger, and they dressed him, and he let them, moving like a doll, his mind rolling helplessly in fog.

Albert. Albert was here.

"Paint?" Clary asked as she cinched his silk banyan

and Marie applied the iron to his hair.

Michael tried to shake his head, then shouted as his ear was singed. “No.” He rubbed at the tender flesh. “No paint. And no more curls. I’ll finish myself.”

“Rodger said we was to help you,” Clary insisted.

“I say I can help myself,” Michael snapped, and he shooed them out.

They left, and he locked the door. After taking a moment to steady himself and still the last of his panic, Michael took a deep breath, exhaled and got to work.

He brushed his hair, removing the exaggerated curl and making sure his hair was as smooth and soft as possible, inviting touch. He applied no paint, but he did dust his cheeks with powder and darkened his brows just enough to highlight the contrast. He lingered over the oils, torn between floral scents and rosewood, which he favored. He went with rosewood in the end, telling himself it was still a plant, in a way.

When he was prepared, he put his spectacles back on, stood in front of the long mirror and regarded himself.

Sometimes he wished he knew what he looked like without the spectacles. Heaven knew he looked like an accountant with them, even naked. Then he looked like the *devil’s* accountant, which wasn’t alluring. Just strange.

His glasses were thick, ridiculously thick, because without them he was practically blind. He could make out things just in front of him, and technically he could read without aid, but only if he held the book four inches from his face. To go back and forth from his glasses to without often made his head hurt so badly it sent him to the icehouse, which was why, normally, he simply let the world beyond the tips of his fingers remain fuzzy and vague, navigating by broad shapes and an intricate study of hue and color. But in the past month he'd become accustomed to wearing his spectacles more often than not. To go without them for any length of time would promise quite a headache later. Obviously he would remove them before Albert arrived, but he would keep them on until he heard his footfalls in the hall.

Thinking of Albert made his butterflies begin again, so he drew his mind back to studying himself.

Outside of the glasses, it wasn't bad, he decided. He inspected the banyan the girls had given him. It had gold stitching and floral embroidery on the shoulder, and it looked quite good on him. It was one of the girls' gowns, technically, but he was fairly sure Albert would like it. His hair was limper than he'd like, but if he plumped it with powder, it wouldn't feel the way he wanted it to.

He remembered how often Albert had threaded his fingers into it.

Undoing the tie to the gown, Michael let it fall open slightly, revealing more of his chest. He pulled the fabric back farther—a dusky nipple appeared, and the plane of his abdomen. Soft, but firm. Very good. He tested revealing part of his pelvis as well, but he cinched it back up immediately. No. That would be too much. Albert was the sort who would want just a bit of a tease but plenty of promise.

Albert. I am about to make love to Albert again.

The girls had laid out a small tea for him, but Michael couldn't stomach it. He spent his remaining twenty minutes trying not to touch his hair and make it more oily.

When it was time, he went to the blue room. He lit candles and warmed the oil he'd chosen before trying out several arrangements of pillows on the bed. He rearranged the chairs and sofa too, then moved them back to their original places again.

He paced the floor for some time, and his hand ended up in his hair quite often despite his best efforts.

He was so distracted that when he heard the footsteps in the hall, he wasn't even on the bed yet, and he had to throw himself onto the pillows, arranging himself hastily, only to realize as the door opened that he still wore his spectacles.

Leave them on and get a proper look at him, the devil's accountant whispered. Michael ignored him, whipped off the glasses and leaned forward to stow them beneath the bed, rising up just in time to see the blurry shape of his lordship as he came into the room and shut the door.

The sight of Albert made Michael's heart beat faster. Deprived of his glasses, Michael strained to take the man in: the great height of him, the contrast of his coat and cravat, the color and shape of his hair still damp at the edges from his bath. His short boots peeked out beneath crisp trousers. From this far away, Michael could not see his face, but even with the lord's proper posture, his body movements belied his nervousness.

Belatedly, Michael realized he was not posed evocatively on the pile of pillows he'd spent fifteen minutes arranging, choosing instead to greet his lover dangled over the edge of the bed, banyan rucked up oddly around him and one foot lifted into the air for balance.

Damn.

He rolled to his side and tugged at the edge of the banyan as best he could as he carefully assumed a casually seductive pose. Fortune favored him at last, for his left nipple exposed itself all on its own, as well as a generous portion of his abdomen. Though he still couldn't see Albert's face, he saw his patron's body posture quicken.

Michael smiled.

"My lord. We meet again."

Across the room, Lord George Albert cleared his throat. Michael heard the careful intake of breath that meant he was getting ready to speak. "G-g-good day, Mr. V-Vallant."

Michael's pulse hammered so hard he felt it in the base of his throat. "Call me Michael."

Another breath. A pause. "C-c-call m-me Alb-b-b-b—" Albert gave up and sighed.

He was very nervous, if that much preparation still led to that much of a stammer. Michael longed to put him more at ease. Of course, it would be nice if someone would return the favor.

"Albert." He let his fingers slide into his hair and reached out his other hand to beckon to Albert. "Come here and sit on the bed." *I want to see you.*

But Albert seated himself in one of the chairs by the fire—well outside of Michael's sight range. Michael swore at himself silently. If he hadn't worn his glasses so much lately, he could have seen at least a little. Now he couldn't even read Albert's face. While reading the faces and body movements of people was usually a handy skill for maneuvering them into the place you wanted them, with Albert it was essential for simple communication. So here they were, blind and mute together.

The depths of potential disaster expanded endlessly around them.

"Wh-why am I h-here?" Albert said at last.

Michael combed his tone for clues. Caution, nerves still, and a great deal of reserve. He tried to relax him with humor. "I thought that was obvious."

The pause was lengthy. It took Albert three breaths before he was able to speak, and his first two attempts were nothing but sputters of consonants.

Michael gave in and softened. "Relax, darling. Relax. Deep breaths. There's no reason to be nervous."

Albert barked out a rueful laugh.

Michael echoed his smile. "Very well, perhaps there is a little reason." He stroked the sheet, mimicking the touch he would have given Albert, could he have reached him. "Take your time."

Albert's sigh made Michael shiver. Two more breaths, and then: "D-did you ask f-for m-me?"

Michael couldn't help a frown. "Ask?" He watched Albert's shape tense and spoke quickly. "Darling, no—don't, please. I'm sorry, it's my fault I don't understand. Did I ask what for you?"

Albert held very still. Michael could read nothing, damn it all to hell.

"D-did y-you ask him t-t-to br-bring m-me h-here?"

"Bring you?" Michael's eyes widened, and his mouth fell open. "Do you mean—Rodger *brought* you here? Against your will?"

The pause nearly killed Michael. "N-not p-p-p"—a sigh—"p-precisely."

How could Rodger not precisely bring him? Either he did, or he didn't. Michael started to ask this, then stopped. "Oh—he did bring you, but not precisely against your will?"

A soft laugh. Very soft. "Y-yes."

"But partially."

While Albert paused, Michael shifted nervously in his chair. "H-he p-p-promised t-to b-blackmail m-me if I d-did not."

Michael clamped a hand over his mouth in horror

and sat up. "He didn't."

"He d-did."

Michael felt ill. "I'm so sorry. Please—if you want to leave, I promise I'll make him—"

With what was clearly great effort, Albert overrode him, his voice coming out in a sharp breath. "I s-s-said only p-p-p—" This time his sigh was so frustrated it was almost a growl. "Only p-partially."

I'll kill him. I swear, this time I really will kill Rodger. Michael ran his hands down his face. "I *am* sorry. I had no idea. I never would have asked for this. Not like this."

The shape of Albert leaned forward. "But d-did you ask? F-for m-me?"

Heat rose in Michael, the sensation suspiciously like a blush, which was almost as horrifying as the thought of Rodger blackmailing Albert into having sex with him. He tried to give a coy smile, but he wasn't sure it worked. "Does it matter, darling?"

"Yes."

The short, clear word, delivered with no pause, cut straight into Michael. He felt dizzy, confused, and afraid. And aroused. Between the distance, the stammer and the revelation of Rodger's meddling, he hadn't been able to read the question at all. Was Albert simply curious? Was he amused? Was he besotted? Was he suspicious? Was he planning on reveling in the thought that a whore had asked for him particularly?

And while he was wondering, why did Michael care about any of this?

Because even with the stammer, he could hear Daventry in Albert's voice. Because more and more every day the dark clouds of the past closed in on him. Because somehow one night of sex with Albert had managed to take away everything he'd built in sixteen years, and now that Albert was in the blue room with him, he wasn't sure that trying to fuck him again would do anything but make matters worse.

Michael could bear no more torture. "Come to the edge of the bed," he demanded.

He watched Albert's shape like a hawk, watched him hesitate, watched him rise slowly, watched him smooth his clothing. He watched the blurred figure move closer.

When Albert stepped into Michael's field of vision, it was as if he stepped through a magic portal, morphing from shaped blob into man, into the man Michael remembered, only he was here now, not a memory but real. Dark hair, neatly combed, conservative clothes. Tall, wide frame. Same jaw as his father. Long, almost pretty nose.

Lips, parted and wet, revealing a hint of teeth.

Hands, strong and smooth, resting on his hips, fingers curved inward.

Soft, beautiful brown eyes trying so hard not to let Michael get the better of him, hoping so hard this would not be a disaster.

Michael stifled a sigh of relief.

Albert's chin came up. "D-did you ask for m-me?"

Proud. So proud. So tender and gentle, yes, but proud, and so very strong.

Sitting in the center of the bed, Michael kept his eyes on Albert as he replied, "Yes."

A blush crept over Michael at the confession, but he decided it was worth it when Albert smiled and reached up for the tie to his cravat.

Chapter Five

WES WORKED THE complicated knot of his cravat slowly, not wanting Vallant to see how clumsy his fingers were. He wanted his hesitant speech to be the only awkward thing about him just now.

Vallant was beautiful. His pale skin shone in the light of the candles strewn around the room. The room itself was nothing but sensual opulence—silks and brocade, gilded surfaces and rich carpets. A scent of something soft and exotic wafted around him—rosewood, he was almost sure of it. But Vallant was without question the most enticing part of the scene. He wore blue silk and nothing else, the garment parting to reveal a hint of skin. Wes's focus lingered on that exposed nipple, making him want to suckle it. Vallant's golden hair gleamed as it framed his face, inviting touch. His eyes were dark pools that promised a host of erotic delights. His mouth was as sensuous as Wes remembered.

The last knot of the cravat came undone, turning

the material into a long, cream-colored length of fabric draped around Wes's neck. He pulled it free, and as the material slid away, Vallant came forward on his hands and knees, prowling like a cat.

Wes reached for the fastenings of his coat. Vallant continued on, as the dark sleeves of Wes's jacket fell away before they sailed over to the chair to join the cravat. Vallant was almost to Wes now, but he didn't increase his speed, apparently content to watch the waistcoat peel away.

He asked for me.

Vallant was inches before Wes now, still crouched, but he rose as Wes undid the buttons of his shirt. He slid up the length of Wes without touching him, his breath teasing Wes's skin—a whisper along his thigh, a hot, deliberate exhale against the growing outline of his cock. He smiled as he passed Wes's midsection, lifting his gaze to Wes's own. He took gentle hold of Wes's hips, slipping fingers to the top of his waistband. By now Wes had his shirt undone, and he reached to the edges of the panels, pulling them wide, exposing his skin.

Vallant closed his eyes, leaned forward and opened his mouth over Wes's stomach.

He kissed, he laved, he nipped his way up and down Wes's abdomen, his fingers tugging at the waistband of Wes's trousers. With his stomach quavering at the gentle sensual assault, Wes let his shirt fall, and with no way to reach his trousers and nothing else to do with his hands, he slid them into the silky blond hair. Vallant sighed, then resumed his kissing as Wes massaged Vallant's scalp.

"Mmm, Albert," Vallant murmured against the top of Wes's pelvis as he took hold of Wes and made him hiss a breath. "Such a nice, firm cock. So big and fat." His hands slipped down the length of it, and his eyes tipped upward as he drew back, running his tongue from base to tip before smiling and speaking again. "I want to feel it in the back of my throat."

Wes groaned, tightening his grip on Vallant's hair. He met Vallant's gaze as long as he could, watching the pretty mouth close over him until the heated sheath of his sucking became too much. He shut his eyes and gave over to sensation.

Very quickly, though, he had to hold back, because Vallant's exquisite skill risked his coming within the first minute of the experience. It was lovely, yes, to have someone take the time to tease the tip of his penis, to apply pressure at the base, to have such a wicked tongue and rigid seal of lips pleasuring him—but since he was accustomed to the need to be fast, to not be found out, it took some focus to keep his body from rushing to release.

Vallant kept driving him toward the edge, gripping his hips, taking his cock deep, holding it there and humming around the shaft, making soft, mewing noises so submissive and carnal that they woke dark things in Wes. He wanted to hold Vallant by the hair and pump roughly into his throat. Now. But he didn't let himself.

Vallant came off his cock with a soft pop to nuzzle Wes's stomach as his hand kept up a regular rhythm on Wes's cock.

"Darling," he said, breathless, never ceasing his kissing. "Darling, shh. Let go now, and I'll build you back up again later. I promise." His tongue traced an erotic path across Wes's pelvis before he continued. "Let me taste you, love. Let me drink you down. Let me drain you before I fill you up again. I will, I promise. Trust me, darling. Trust me."

And so Wes did. When Vallant swallowed him down this time, he gave over, letting Vallant's expert tongue and mouth bring him back to the edge. He fucked that sweet mouth three times, then erupted into him. He clutched that blond head as he fought for breath, as the orgasm made him dizzy and weak.

Vallant's hands slid around him, drawing Wes down beside him onto the bed and giving him a kiss flavored with his own semen.

For several minutes they languished there, simply kissing, Vallant leading. But it was odd, because while he instigated everything, it was more that he issued invitations for Wes to do things to him. Vallant began the kiss, yes, but to lure Wes into his mouth as he made soft, desperate gasps. He pulled on Wes's shoulders, letting Wes push him down into the mattress. He tilted his head up, encouraging Wes to explore his neck.

Take me, he said without words. *I am for your pleasure.*

Enjoy me. Try this. Try that. Try all you like.

It was a heady elixir to Wes, and he accepted each one of Vallant's overtures. When Vallant arched his back, pressing their chests together and sending his banyan over his shoulder, Wes pushed it away on both sides and rubbed the soft fur of his chest against Vallant's smooth skin. Their nipples brushed, and Vallant moaned and arched again. Wes shuddered, grinding harder. A surge of power filled him, fueled by Vallant's plaintive, helpless whimpers, and the erotic sound drove Wes into a state of lust he hadn't known he had in him. With a grunt, he ground his still half-hard cock against the apex of Vallant's legs, shoving them wider with his knees as he drove him deeper into the bed.

Without warning, Vallant went from soft and moaning to stiff and shouting, his hands shoving at Wes's shoulders.

Wes pulled back at once, ardor not just doused but drowned as Vallant rolled away from him and curled into himself, tugging the blue silk tightly closed.

"Oh God." Vallant turned his face into the mattress. His countenance was pale, and his whole body shook.

Wes sat back carefully on his knees as Vallant drew tighter and tighter into himself. Wes tried to comprehend what had happened and what he should do. Had he hurt him? Had he been too rough? Even as guilt rose, it tangled with more confusion. Wouldn't Vallant have behaved differently, if that were so? For pulled hair, he would have winced. For too much pressure, he'd have directed Wes to lift up. No, there was no way to match what he'd been doing with Vallant's response. This was something else. Something… God help him, but Wes had no idea. Likely it would be best if he left.

"Damn Rodger and his ideas," Vallant whispered. "Damn me for listening to him." His hands ran up his face, covering his eyes. "God help me, I don't want to go to Bedlam."

Wes, halfway off the bed with one foot on the floor, paused. Bedlam? He glanced back at Vallant with new concern. Good Lord! Why—?

He thought back to his conversation with Rodger, with his easy familiarity with blackmail and nonchalance over the thought of human trafficking. Was that what this was? Was Vallant under some sort of duress? Had Wes unwittingly become a part of it?

Concern kept him pinned to the bed, overriding the urge of courtesy which required him to leave and allow Vallant some peace. Though a thousand questions clogged his throat, his tongue remained as recalcitrant as ever. In his own distress, he'd manage no coherence of any kind. He hovered for several seconds, searching for some other way to communicate, but in the end he could only reach over and gently, oh so gently, rest a hand on Vallant's arm.

"H-hush," he managed, the sound more caress than word. "Shh. Shh. It's all r-right."

Vallant flinched at the touch, but only for a moment, and he calmed almost immediately. On instinct, Wes left his hand there, testing for further reaction. When none came, he let his thumb brush gently across the blue silk.

Pulling one hand away from his face, Vallant closed that fist over the top of his robe, clutching at it as he spoke. "Forgive me." He swallowed hard before forcing a weak smile. "Please. There is no need for you to stay and witness my ridiculousness."

Had there been any sharpness in his tone, even a hint of coolness, Wes would have stammered something benign and done as he was told. But heaven help him, he felt as if a child had just called out to him, another boy at school trying to put on a brave face after a beating, willing his friends to leave him alone so he could weep.

The thought hit Wes like a slap. He looked down at the beautiful, confident man rendered so weak and helpless, and he ached.

"D-did s-someone h-h-hurt you?"

Vallant's sudden, careful stillness told Wes all he needed to know. *I will kill him*, he thought. His mind began to catalog the many, intricate plant-based poisons he knew, several of which were rendered tasteless in a simple cup of tea.

A soft, almost sad laugh cut off his mental indexing, and he glanced back down at Vallant, who was rubbing his forehead as if he were trying to grind something out of it. His eyes were still closed.

"It's like some mad dream. All these years, nothing, and now—with *you*, of all people." He rubbed harder. "I am living an opera."

Wes, with no notion at all how to respond to this, kept up a gentle stroking against Vallant's arm and waited for him to speak again.

"Long ago, yes. Very long ago, someone hurt me." Vallant laughed mirthlessly. "Heaven help me, but I'm so unhinged I want to tell you the whole sordid tale."

Wes remained quiet, his thumb moving back and forth against the silk in a regular rhythm. Vallant stayed silent as well, but he opened his eyes, fixing a dull gaze across the room. Eventually he spoke.

"My mother was a courtesan. When I lived with her as a child, I never truly understood what it meant. I knew men came and went, that for years it would be the same man, and when we changed houses it would be another. This was all. I understood we were risqué, somehow, for people whispered when we walked by, but Mama held her head high, so I did too." His grip on his gown relaxed slightly. "I went to school. Not an excellent school, but not a terrible one, either. I did well enough. I had the usual dreams of being a lawyer or a scholar, sometimes even an ambassador. But then I turned twelve, and I came home for the end of term."

His eyes went hard, his jaw set tight, but when he spoke, it was the little boy again, even through the cold delivery. "Mama was not there, just a man." He stopped for several seconds, his countenance growing harder and harder, his throat working with difficulty several times before he said, with perfect coolness and ease, “My mother had sold me to him.”

Now it was Wes’s turn to jolt, a soft gasp of horror escaping.

Vallant smiled a wry smile and glanced at Wes. “Do you know, Rodger still uses the story sometimes to weed out customers? Without revealing it was me, of course. Anyone who isn’t horrified is shown the door and never allowed back again. Isn’t it interesting that neither of us thought to tell it to you before tonight?” He regarded Wes. “It’s your eyes, I think. They promise something kind. Heaven help the world should you ever turn dark. You would send Satan himself scrambling.”

Wes’s hand had stilled on Vallant’s arm. Vallant reached over, touched Wes’s fingers lightly, and moved them back and forth a few times against his own skin. When Wes renewed his rhythmic caress, Vallant pulled his hand away and began to speak again, gazing into nothingness once more.

“He bought me for the entire break between terms. He stayed in the house with me except for a few times when he had to leave, and then I was shackled to the bed until his return. All the usual servants were gone and new brought in, but let me assure you, it was a special kind of hell to endure that in my own home, in my own mother’s bloody bedroom. He had me every way he liked until a few days before term was due to start again, and then he left. The night he did so is something of a blur in my memory.

"I remember him leaving. I remember my mother appearing at the bottom of the stairs from wherever she had hid herself, wiping at her eyes constantly, speaking with false cheerfulness, trying to pretend it hadn't happened. She spoke of how excited she was for me to go back to school, how the headmaster had reported me such a model student, how grand things were ahead of me, surely. She produced a treasure trove of gifts, every book and trinket I had ever asked for but never received. She produced a grand new trousseau for the next term. She promised a holiday soon, to wherever I wanted to go. I kept silent through it all, shocked at first, and then hurt, and then furious, and the longer I said nothing, the more extravagant her promises became. At last she broke down and wept hysterically.

"She rationalized it several different ways. She was out of money. She was too old, and no one wanted her. She had panicked. She was weak. She was terribly sorry, and she knew it was wrong, but couldn't I see there was no other way to keep up the lives we had become so fond of living? Didn't I want to go to university? Didn't I want grand things? What, had I thought such would come for free? Wasn't it time I provided for us, for a change? She wheedled, promising I could have it all, any and everything—so long as, every now and again, I spent some time with the man. And of course unspoken but understood was the truth that after this man, there would be another. And another. And another."

Wes hissed out a breath, and his hand tangled in the blue silk. His stomach turned and he saw nothing but red. He didn't realize how tightly he gripped Vallant until he felt fingers brush his own. He relaxed his grip, but to his surprise, Vallant did not release him. In fact, he captured Wes's hand, drew it to his lips as he turned his head, and kissed his knuckles before returning Wes's hand back to his sleeve.

"Well," Vallant said, as if this were some light gossip he repeated, "I left that night. In the true form of the fool I was, I tied my most precious belongings into a bedsheet, slung them over my back and darted out into the night." His laugh rumbled through his body, and he shook his head. "Good God, but by rights I should have learned the many horrible ways men on the streets could be worse than—" He stopped, bit his lip and sighed. "Suffice it to say, I was fortunate beyond anything I deserved. The first person I ran into—literally—was Rodger, who at the time was but sixteen, though he already ran an impressive ring of prostitutes. Mistaking me for a lordling, he proposed to ransom me to my family, only to withdraw in shock as I went into hysterics, threatening to tear out his eyeballs if he so much as dared to *think* of sending me home again. My tale came out shortly thereafter, and my life as it is fell in to place. Rodger took me under his wing, and then he took me into his bed. With my permission, mind you. Though we both tired of that quickly enough." He stopped and blushed. "I don't know why I just told you that."

His hand reached up to stroke his own hair, and his gaze across the room turned strangely pensive. "I enjoyed sex even then. Despite what she may have intended, my mother did not sell anyone my virginity, nor the concept of sex with my own gender. And as I watched Rodger's girls and boys work their corners, as I saw their power and even their pleasure, I thought of what my mother had said, of all she had promised, if I would only sleep with the man. And I thought, well, why not? Now that I had been relieved of my fantasies, there was really nothing else for me to do but whore.

"But with Rodger it would be on my own terms. There seemed a sort of justice to it—she had ruined me, but I could remake myself, even thumbing my nose at it all by taking what they had made me and doing them one better. So I did, and I did it well. I was pretty then, acutely so, and so I was popular. And I wasn't stupid. The Dove Street house was my plan, built on the ashes of my mother's schemes. Sex on our terms, for our rates. And for many years now, that has been the whole of it. I have enjoyed many fine things and as much pleasure as I care to reach for, protected and monitored by Rodger."

His eyes closed on a sigh. "Except now, for no reason I can explain, pleasure has turned to panic. I dream dark, terrible dreams, and while I can kneel before a man in a crowded room and suckle his root like a calf at a teat, while I can take his cock in my hand and draw his pleasure out of him with a skill I have taken years to hone, if you put me in a room alone with a man and let him cover me with his body, if he tries to enter me, or even sometimes if he simply moves the wrong way or the smell is right, I am so filled with panic I nearly cast up my accounts on the spot. Let me assure you this is the very devil to explain to a client who has already put his coin in Rodger's greasy hand." He rubbed his forehead. "And that is the tale, my lord. I am a whore who can no longer fuck, and I don't know why. I've had no one in well over a month." His lips pressed together. "Since you, dear Albert. No one since you."

The sordid, impossible story kept swirling inside of Wes's head—operatic indeed—but at this, Wes deflated slightly. *This is why he asked for me.* Immediately, he felt ridiculous. What had he expected? That the beautiful whore had fallen in love with him? That this was some idiot fairytale?

My mother sold me.

Wes shut his eyes and pinched the bridge of his nose, willing the disgusting thought to roll back into the depths of his consciousness, but it would not go. He thought of the hopeless case he'd been at twelve, at how he'd barely been able to leave the house, let alone speak. He could not imagine what he would have done if his father had sold him—his mother had been dead by then, so she could not have. The thought of her doing so wasn't even something he could put his mind around. Not his father either. He couldn't imagine anyone doing it. It was beyond disgusting.

I have long ago learned not to be surprised. That was what Rodger had said. Wes began to understand why.

Vallant took Wes's hand again and kissed his fingers gently. "You are a darling man to listen to all that prattle. I don't even know if that explains it properly, but hopefully this allays your concern enough to allow you to leave. I had thought—" He grimaced. "Oh, it's ridiculous, obviously. But I'd thought perhaps, with you, it would be all right. That it would cure me or something. Which now seems nothing but mad. I am sorry to have troubled you, to have exposed you to Rodger, to have involved you in this at all. Please consider yourself absolved. Whatever Rodger held over you, I promise to make him release it. I know you have no reason to believe my word, but I swear to you, you have nothing to fear from me, now or ever."

Wes stared at him in disbelief. Go? *Go?* Vallant thought he would leave, just like that? Frowning, he opened his mouth to speak.

"D-d-d-da—T-t-t-t-t-t-t—"

Growling in impotent rage, Wes swung his legs off the bed, doing up his trousers with trembling hands. He hated himself, hated his stammer, hated his tongue, his mind, his stupid timid nature, stupid, stupid, stupid—

My mother sold me.

You learn not to be surprised.

Wes stormed over to his discarded waistcoat, not even aware of what he was reaching for until the notebook was in his hand. He dug into the pocket again until he found the stub of pencil and exhaled a victorious huff. As he returned to the bed, he could see Vallant eyeing him warily, but he ignored this, sat on the opposite end and braced the pad on his knee.

You think after all that, I will leave? What sort of monster do you take me for? You think I could be that callous? No better than the piece of filth who used you, nor the soulless fiend who sold you?

He ripped off the page and handed it over, but he began a second note even before Vallant had taken the first from his hand.

Is this bastard still alive? I assume not, that Rodger had him strangled? He had to pause, forcing his grip on the pencil to lighten before he went on. *I want his name, if he isn't already dispatched. I'm not without resources or influence. And I'm very difficult to prosecute.*

He stopped writing then, but his blood was pounding in his ears, and without meaning to he crumbled the bottom half of his notepad. He had never felt such rage in all his life.

"No." Vallant's reply was short, sharp, and brooked no argument. He handed the notes back to Wes. "No, you will not have the name. Don't ask again, either. Ever."

Wes wanted to press the issue, but he knew a brick wall when he saw one. And notes could only be so persuasive. He turned over the first piece of paper and wrote again.

I want to help you.

Vallant took the paper with visual trepidation, but he laughed once he saw the words. "Well, you can't, darling. You saw where we landed."

Wes scowled. *I didn't mean help you that way. Please. You must let me give you aid. I think now you meant Bedlam as a joke, at least a dark one, but this cannot be healthy regardless. You thought something in me might help you, enough to send for me. Now that I actually know what I'm meant to do, let me at least attempt it.*

Wes watched Vallant's face as he read, but it gave him no clue. When Vallant spoke, he glanced at Wes without turning his head or lowering the note. "Aid me how? What is it you think you could do?"

Wes had no idea. He didn't write this though, pausing with his pencil over the paper as he frantically tried to think. He began a few lines only to cross them out. After three such tries, he balled up that paper, tossed it over his shoulder into the fireplace and started one afresh.

I want to keep seeing you. I don't care if we have intercourse or not. We can talk. Or write notes. Or paint bloody watercolors. I hardly care, to tell the truth. I know only that I can't simply walk out of here and whistle my way back to my apartments as if you were just some whore I fucked and nothing else.

He hesitated over that last, but in the end he passed it over before he could second-guess himself. He waited as Vallant read, watching his face to see if he laughed. But Vallant didn't, only cast him an unreadable glance when he finished.

"This argument again. Darling—I *am* some whore you fucked and nothing else." He lowered the note to his lap. His tone turned gentle, soothing. "I'm flattered, truly, but it doesn't matter. I've already impeded the ledgers as it is—I've been out of service for over a month." He grimaced. "I think I just need Rodger to hold me down a few times. Desensitize me. Or perhaps I should drink. Something to—Oh, heavens. You're scribbling again."

Wes's stomach had turned over at "need Rodger to hold me down a few times", and he'd shut his ears to the rest as he fumbled for his notepad. By the time Vallant had realized Wes was writing, he'd finished, and he handed the note to him. Vallant read it, frowned at Wes, and read it again.

"Eight hundred pounds? What is that supposed to mean?"

Wes took a few breaths. "I'll g-give it to y-you."

He enjoyed watching Vallant's eyes widen. "*You* are the one heading to Bedlam. Why would you do such a thing?"

Deciding not to risk speaking, Wes wrote quickly.

For the pleasure of your company for one month. Your company and nothing more, unless you wish it.

Vallant stared at the paper for several seconds. Then he drew it slowly to his chest. He said nothing, only looked at Wes.

Wes raised an eyebrow at him.

Vallant's laugh, bursting out of him soft and quiet, was a balm to Wes's soul. As was Vallant's self-conscious hand through his silken hair. "I can't accept it, my lord. You flatter me beyond anything I've ever known, but—"

"Al-Albert," Wes interrupted. He took a breath as Vallant paused, surprised. "Y-you c-can ac-c-cept. S-s-ay y-yes."

Vallant studied him a moment. "If I were to accept this—which I'm not saying I am—I would insist on some better compensation on your part. Given that I might never be able to give you more than witty rejoinders to your notes, I want to give something to you. I just have to think of what."

He bit his lip in an unconscious gesture, and Wes found it endearing beyond words. He warmed in a way that felt like arousal and yet wasn't at all—an internal arousal, if there were such a thing. *You don't have to give me anything. You have no idea what a gift simply being with you every day will be.*

Before he could find the way to stammer some of this, however, Vallant was shaking his head and speaking again. "But what shall we *do* if we aren't fucking? Go to the opera?" He paused and looked almost wistful. "Going to the opera and actually watching, not sucking someone off in the back of a darkened booth. That would be something."

Wes had been recoiling inwardly at the thought of the crush at the door, but at the mention of a booth, of being alone with Vallant, his panic quieted. Perhaps the opera would not be so bad.

"But what else? Dancing?"

Wes shook his head vigorously. "I d-d-do not d-d-dance."

"Hmm. That leaves out the Dove Street balls. I can't imagine your dislike of crowds would make an exception for a gaming hell, and in any event, I don't like them either." Vallant paused, then looked at Wes helplessly. "I've no notion what we would do to occupy our time, if we aren't having sex. What do *you* do all day?"

Wes smiled a wry smile. "P-Plants."

He almost laughed at how crestfallen Vallant looked. "*All* day?"

Still smiling, Wes went back to his notepad. He scratched a quick reply and handed it over. He watched Vallant's face as he read, pleased when a bit of interest lit and his eyes lifted to Wes, appearing impressed.

"You work at the Regent's Park gardens?" He turned suspicious. "*Work*, my lord?"

Wes rolled his eyes and took the notepad back again.

"Royal Botanical Society?" Vallant read when he was finished. "Ah. You study or manage or some such,

I presume. That makes more sense." He lowered the notebook. "Well, I suppose if you wish to pay eight hundred pounds to show me plants all day, I can hardly object. At least it will be warm."

Wes could just picture pretty Vallant sitting on a wooden bench in the stovehouse. It was a lovely image, but yes, the man would be horribly bored. "W-We can g-go to m-my c-c-club, if you l-like." Vallant leveled a look at him, and then Wes couldn't help it. He had to laugh. "Or n-not."

"What on earth would we do at a club?" Vallant demanded. "I don't know how to play billiards."

Wes shrugged. "Eat. W-Watch p-p-people. L-Listen." He tipped a sideways smile. "Or t-t-talk."

All at once, Vallant's eyes sparkled. "That's it! That's how I'll repay you. I shall help you with your stammer."

Wes sighed and went back to the notepad. This reply wasn't worth trying out loud.

I appreciate the thought, but there is no point. I have seen every specialist here and on the continent. He thought about mentioning the opium but decided against it. *At best, when I am very relaxed, I don't do too badly, but my stammer is part of me. You might as well try to remove my nose.*

Vallant read the note. He looked as if he wanted to challenge Wes's declaration, but he stopped and nodded. "Very well." He studied Wes's face before leaning forward, tracing a long finger down his cheek. "I will still want to fuck you, you know. And I might try, despite my inconvenient problem." His finger slipped down to Wes's neck and his chest, heading toward his left nipple.

Wes caught his hand, though he didn't pull it away. "I h-have n-no objection t-to th-that."

They regarded one another, desire filling the space between them. Wes held still, letting Vallant make the decision.

Vallant drew back. "Best not to push the matter to-day, I suppose."

Wes's hand fell to his lap. "Wh-When shall I c-come for y-you tom-m-morrow?"

Vallant was all breezy business again. "It is your shilling, my lord. You tell me when I am to be ready, and I shall be."

Wes reached out and touched the underside of Val-lant's chin. "Albert. I d-do n-not d-do this as a l-lord."

"First you want to escape your stammer, and now your title as well. Is that the attraction, Albert? Am I your escape?" Vallant met his gaze, but he appeared vulnerable and uneasy. "Why *are* you doing this?"

Wes paused, his fingers lingering on Vallant's jaw. "Because I r-r-remember how it f-feels."

Vallant went still. "How what feels?"

Wes's fingers stroked Vallant's cheek. "W-Worrying about B-B-Bedlam."

Vallant softened in comprehension. "Oh. For the stammer. But that's ridiculous. You aren't mad. Not in the slightest. Any fool can see it."

Wes shook his head. "Y-You are n-not m-mad either."

Vallant looked haunted. "How can you know?" he whispered.

Wes smiled. "Any f-fool can see it."

Vallant's hands rose toward Wes's face, though they stopped at his shoulders, suddenly uncertain. Gone was the whore. Vallant already seemed young, but now he looked much younger. So soft. So sweet.

So beautiful.

So vulnerable. Remember that.

Wes leaned forward, closing the distance between their mouths, but only to apply the briefest, gentlest of kisses to Vallant's parted lips. He faltered when Vallant's breath exhaled against his cheek, and he indulged in one last brush of flesh in acknowledgment, and then he drew back, collected himself and rose.

"El-leven." He fastened his trousers. "I w-will c-come by at el-leven." Reclaiming his cravat and coat, he paused and turned back to Vallant. "W-Will that do?"

Blinking, Vallant nodded. "Y-Yes. That will be fi-ne."

Wes nodded back. "Until t-tomorrow," he said, and left the room.

In the hall he paused, leaning against the wall and shutting his eyes. Fear and excitement swelled within him over what he had done, over what he had promised.

Eight hundred pounds. *If Father finds out, I won't*

know what to tell him I used it for.

One month. What shall I do with him for an entire month, indeed?

Dear God in heaven, but I hope we do make love again.

Don't hurt him, don't hurt him…

Don't let him hurt you.

The voices swam within Wes's head for a full half minute. Standing, he drew a deep breath and shoved them firmly down as he left, ready to find Barrows and submit his promissory note, his father's potential questions be damned.

"SO LET ME get this straight." Rodger poured a liberal amount of brandy into the two tumblers on his desk before reaching for his pipe and packet of tobacco, methodically packing the leaf as he spoke. "You couldn't let him fuck you. You told him the reason why—mostly, leaving out the fact that your rapist was his own dear da. He offered you eight hundred pounds to give him 'the pleasure of your company' for one month. He gave no stipulations for this. Not whether or not you're having sex, how often you're meeting, *where* you're meeting, or whether or not anyone else gets to lay hand or cock on you. You accept this and tell him to stop by on the morrow, would you, love? To which he says, 'Sure, ducks.' Except with an incredible stammer. Then he fastens his trousers, writes me up a note for a princely sum with a bloody seal and all on it, doffs his hat and takes off. That it, love, or did I miss something?"

Michael took one of the tumblers and cradled the glass to his chest, drawing the banyan closer to him as he stared down into the amber liquid. "That's essentially the tale, yes."

Rodger lit the end of his pipe, puffed a few times and pulled it from his mouth, shaking his head. "Bloody hell."

Michael grimaced into the glass, then downed a significant portion of it. "I made us some money, at least."

"But you still can't fuck?"

Reluctantly, Michael shook his head. Rodger swore and put his pipe back between his lips. A sudden agitation seized Michael.

"I think it might work eventually." He tangled his finger in a loose thread at the edge of the banyan. After tightening the string into a neat curl, he let it go and threaded it onto his finger. "Part of the problem, I think, is that for some reason I seem to want to lose myself in him, and that's not good business. But…well, he's so…" Michael stopped and stared at his lap, smiling faintly. "It's hard to explain. Gentle, but not gentle." He stayed quiet another moment, still lost in memory. When he realized what he was doing, he cleared his throat and placed his hands in his lap. "In any event, I think we're heading in the right direction. At least he's paying."

Rodger watched Michael as he smoked his pipe. He puffed thoughtfully for a long minute, during which time Michael drained the entirety of his brandy. His throat burned, and his head was starting to spin. Unfortunately, he didn't feel any less agitated after this glass than after any of the others he'd had. He reached for the brandy bottle to give himself another dose.

He paused, though, hand resting on the neck of the bottle when he caught Rodger looking at him oddly. "What?"

Rodger puffed once more before pulling out the pipe. "Michael, are you in love with Lord George?"

Michael toppled the brandy bottle and nearly fell out of his chair. "What? No, I'm not in love with him. Sweet Christ! I've met him twice."

Rodger righted the bottle. "Sometimes that's all it takes. Sometimes just a look can do it."

"Please." Michael curled his lip in derision. "I'm not a romantic fool. I don't even *believe* in love."

Rodger snorted a laugh. "Yeah, and them's the worst kind that falls in it. Walking around in it like a lost chicken without a clue."

"I am not a lost chicken." Michael poured himself more brandy and threw it back. His eyes burned, and his voice was rough with the sting of alcohol as he slammed the glass back onto Rodger's desk. "I am *not* in love with Albert. Stop being an idiot. And give me your damned pipe."

Rodger passed the pipe over to Michael, who

sucked on it with a vengeance. And gagged.

Rodger laughed out loud. "You're a fine mess, you are. I think you do love him. I think you took one look at p-p-precious Lord George in his greenhouse, saw his soft smile, and you fell in love."

"Ridiculous." Michael coughed. Good Lord, how did Rodger smoke the thing?

"And it upsets you because of Daventry, but it already doesn't matter. You want your Albert and only him. And that's why you can't fuck. Because he's on your mind. Inside you, mucking about. You want to let go to him, to surrender your heart, but you can't, much as you want to. Because of what happened to you. Because of who he is."

Michael glared at Rodger. "What happened with Daventry is done. It's the past. I don't care about it, and I haven't for some time. Do I like the man? No. But I don't cry into my pillow over my poor lot in life. I don't peer around corners to be sure he's not lurking there. It's over. It's been over for a long, long time."

"That's just it, love. It ain't over. Or rather, you called it over too fast." Rodger held up a hand as Michael started to sputter indignantly. "Look. I was there the night you ran off from home. I fed you your beer and looked into your wide little boy eyes."

"I wasn't a little boy," Michael shot back.

"He was there in your eyes. If you'd been the Michael I know now, I'd have just robbed you and gone on. I don't care that you was twelve. It was a wee lad I met in that alley. It was a wee lad I heard in your voice as you told your tale. It was a sad, hurt little boy that sniffled quietly in his nest of blankets on my bed while I lay by the fire. Oh, you had him snuffed out by morning, I'll grant you that. You was hard lines and indifference by breakfast, and you never looked back. I kept waiting for you to crack, but you never did. I was impressed. Always have been." Rodger aimed the mouthpiece of the pipe at Michael. "That boy is still inside you, though, no matter what you think. He's been sleeping all this time, maybe. Or maybe he lives in all them damn books you read. But he's not gone. And I think, my lovely, he's waking now. Because after all this time, he's finally seen something worth waking for."

Rodger's speech was the most ridiculous thing Michael had ever heard, but it chilled him to the bone. "I'm not in love with him. I couldn't be. I can't be." His hands tightened against his gown. "I *won't* be."

Shrugging, Rodger puffed on his pipe. "Think what you like. Just be advised that thinking you aren't in love won't change the fact that you are, if I'm right."

Michael rose, glaring at Rodger. "I'm going to bed," he declared. Cinching his robe, he turned to go, but at the last second he grabbed the bottle of brandy and took it with him.

"Sweet dreams, love," Rodger called. His voice sounded sad and possibly even a little resigned. Michael hugged the bottle against his body and slipped out into the hall.

He could hear the chatter and coo of the whores working the front room. It was whispers and giggles there, but in what Rodger had deemed the chambers down the hall came the sound of music and bawdy laughter and plenty of groans. In semiprivate alcoves around a small ballroom, men and women, men and men, and occasionally women and women joined in no more than fifteen minutes of ecstasy, unless they paid the footmen under the table to go a bit longer. Couples and groups danced in the center tonight, though sometimes special-event performances were held there instead.

As Michael climbed the three flights of stairs that led to his attic room, he passed the progression of suites the more wealthy patrons favored—where he had always worked before, and where he had met Albert just a few hours ago. Here the moans and cries were more muted, thanks to heavy padding and thick walls, but only so much could be done about a bed, and a steady rhythm of creaking springs and thumping headboards drifted out. The next floor offered the occasional swish of a whip or slap of a backside. These were the more aggressive rooms, and Michael would step nowhere near them, no matter how much fun Rodger promised they were. He'd had enough shackles and bonds to last him the rest of his life, thank you.

He walked through the last floor, full of small, crowded rooms where the whores slept during the day and the day servants slept now. At the end of this hall, he pushed open a narrow door and climbed the creaking stairs to his room.

The other half of the attic was storage and smuggling caches for some of Rodger's sideline exploits, but this nook was all Michael's. It was quite spacious, considering, and grand, hosting its own stove. His wardrobe and mirror occupied one corner with a small vanity in the space near that, and beside his bed beneath the window was a wooden crate he used as a nightstand. Everything else was books.

Shelves of books, piles of books. Rare books, worthless books, books in languages Michael knew and books in ones he didn't. Some of them were purchased, some of them were stolen, and still others he honestly wasn't sure how he'd come by them. He had penny dreadfuls and erotic notebooks and preachers' sermons. He had reprints of plays both old and new and other people's discarded journals. He had books he loved and books he despised.

After lighting a lamp, washing his face, and climbing into a nightshirt, he selected one at random. This one was in German, a language he'd never quite been able to wrap his mind around enough to read. Nevertheless, he curled up with it in his bed all the same, tucking his coverlet around his body, pushing his glasses higher up on his nose and angling himself toward the light so he could see. His eyes passed over the unreadable words, digesting sentences he could not understand. Rodger called it a "damned odd thing to do." Michael found it relaxing.

When he'd scanned his eyes over two full pages of text, he let the book fall against his chest and stared across the room.

He wasn't in love with Albert. It annoyed him that Rodger had carried on so much about it.

He wondered what in heaven's name they were going to do at eleven tomorrow.

He wondered why Albert had offered so much money for him.

He wondered why he had accepted.

He wondered what Albert expected for such a payment, despite what he'd said about only wanting Michael's company.

He wondered if he should send a note telling him not to come the next day, or ever again, and if he should insist Rodger give the money back.

He wondered what in heaven's name he should wear.

With a heavy sigh and a grimace, Michael picked up the book again, found the place where he'd left off and resumed reading, letting the comforting shape and rhythm of unknown words shut out all the thoughts rattling crazily around his head.

Chapter Six

AT TEN THIRTY the next morning, Wes stood in the shadow of the alley between a slopshop and a tavern, trying to ignore the din from the pub as he stared across the street, telling himself that under absolutely no circumstances should he cross and go into the opium den.

There was no sign on the door of the establishment, for this was the sort of place one needed to know of in advance to enter. Wes wouldn't have known the coffeehouse was anything but a coffeehouse, either, except that the last time he'd met Legs, the seaman had made mention of the business's other allure. Back then Wes would never have considered going into a den of any kind, let alone one in such a bad neighborhood as this.

This time, matters were different.

The docks were close enough that he could hear the whistles and calls of the sailors loading and unloading their ships. This part of London was never fully safe, not even at this time of morning, but it was at its quietest now, its residents largely passed out or too hungover to move. But even this relative calm was too much for Wes today. He was nervous about meeting Vallant at eleven, and now he was nervous additionally about being *late* to meet him. Legs was late, and Legs was never late, not without sending word. At the appointed time, Wes had departed from a hired cab, went up the stairs to the small apartment above the tavern and knocked four times on the door. Legs had not answered.

Legs was always there when he said he would be. Which was why Wes had lingered, but he'd lingered too long. His nerves were a wreck, he'd used all the pills he'd brought with him, and now he would never have time enough to get back to Mayfair and then over to Dove Street, not by eleven.

And there was the opium den, like an answer to his prayers.

He had never been in a den. He knew of a nicer one not far from his club, but dens of all kinds were about opium for pleasure. His pills were medicine. It seemed important not to blur the line. At least it had until now, when he was so overwrought he couldn't bring himself to hail a hack.

A sip or two of poppy tea would put everything to rights.

But would a den even have drops for tea? He'd never smoked opium, though he'd thought about it—

never seriously, but he'd do anything to calm his nerves. He couldn't face Vallant like this. He should have brought more pills.

He should cross the street, go into the den, and be done with it.

Wes studied the other buildings, reminding himself in what company the opium den was kept. On the one side was a brothel, and not the well-bred sort on Dove Street. This was one where half the girls were just that, girls, young enough that Wes had difficulty meeting their gazes. On the other side was another brothel, though this one was rumored to be a molly house. Occasionally Wes would see young boys at the windows, looking soul-stricken. In every one of their eyes he saw Michael.

His gaze drifted back to the alley, to the opium den.

Just one little bit. The filth and the likely debauchery inside would be motivation enough to contain himself. It would be a good lesson to him to see what true addiction was.

Yes. Yes, it was practically *good* that he go over. Just a quick visit. He needn't even finish his tea, or his pipe, or however they delivered it.

Shoving his trembling hands into the pocket of his coat, Wes stepped forward onto the sidewalk, heading for the street.

"I expected better of you, my lord."

Wes stopped short and turned around. It was Penelope Brannigan, his wallflower companion from the

Gordons's ball.

She stepped forward out of the shadow of a door, the toes of her plain, worn brown boots peeking out from an equally ragged hem. Gone was the velvet finery of the ball, but she spoke to him with the audacity of a duchess. "I thought you were convincing yourself you didn't need it. And you don't. A cup of plain black tea or some soothing mint will do you much better."

Wes looked the woman up and down. At the ball he had been too distracted by his mission and his nervousness, but here now he saw that she was ghastly tall and built broadly. She wore what had to be a man's jacket over an ample bosom, and her dress was the most faded thing he'd ever seen. It was brown in the way all fabrics were when they aged—brown-gray, or brown-blue, but mostly brown. She wore several petticoats beneath it as well, hinting that she lingered often in the cold.

A crash from the tavern startled him, and he glanced back toward the window nervously. The shouts inside were starting to sound like a brawl.

Brannigan nodded behind her at the narrow, unpainted door. "I would very much like you to come sit in my parlor, sir, and allow me to give you a restorative cup of tea and a moment to strengthen your resolve. At the very least I owe you that for setting me up with my favorite new benefactor."

Take *tea* with him. He grimaced and turned back to

the street, willing a hackney to be passing by.

There were none.

Miss Brannigan stood directly beside him now. "I do not wish to see you sucked into that den, Lord George." She put a hand on his arm.

Wes drew back sharply, glaring at her. "M-madam! D-d-d-do n-n-n—"

The brawl inside the tavern broke through the door and became a scuffle on the sidewalk. Shaking, Wes stumbled backward. The street was suddenly full of people shouting. He found it hard to breathe. People, people everywhere, and sound. And Miss Brannigan haranguing him, and—

His vision went black, and he felt his breakfast rising like a sea inside his throat—

Strong hands led him to the mouth of the alley, where he cast up his accounts, then brought up the ghost of them a few times more just for good measure. A fragrant but serviceable handkerchief wiped away the slime from his mouth before a soft voice led him back to the sidewalk, then to the narrow, unpainted door—and into a scene of blissful calm and tranquility.

The sofa was sagging and threadbare, but a warm quilt lay across it, as well as a pillow. The fragrant scent of rose-hip tea filled the room, as well as a hint of lavender. No gaslight hissed comfortingly in the walls, but the fragrant oil of a lamp bathed the room in a soft glow. Thick if faded curtains kept out the noise of the street as best as could be done, and the soft *click, click* of knitting needles from a gray-haired lady at the window soothed the jagged edges of Wes's soul.

He found himself immediately upon a sofa. "Hush," she said. "Rest now."

Wes tried, but his gaze kept darting around the room, trying to take it all in. There were three other people present, one napping on a chaise, one in the corner with the curtain pulled back, staring blankly out into the chaos of the street. The one in the window was a female, but the one in the chaise was indeterminable in gender and covered with another quilt. The third was a young man staring at a chessboard on the floor in front of the small stove, which kept the room cozily warm and a teakettle's water heated.

Miss Brannigan poured Wes a cup of tea and handed it to him, then picked up the quilt and draped it around his shoulders. "There, my lord. Sip that slowly. It isn't hot, but your stomach likely isn't up for much just yet. When you're feeling up to it, I'll fetch you some stew. And dumplings." She reached down to speak softly to the boy, who nodded without looking up. Once Miss Brannigan stood and turned away, he moved a pawn on the left side of the board before returning to quiet study.

Wes tried to stammer an objection, to explain to her he was not a street child to be coddled, but she pushed the cup to his lips, overriding his objection. He kept sipping dutifully until she took the cup away, smiling at him in approval.

"There you are. Well done." She was studying him carefully now. "I'd wondered if you were an addict when we met at the Gordons's, but of course I couldn't mention it there. Your eyes, though. You were using that night, weren't you?" She didn't wait for an answer, only lifted the tea to his lips. Wes drank. "Is the stutter why you seek the opium? At least, why you sought it originally?"

Wes lifted an eyebrow. Then he nodded.

She flattened her lips and sighed. "And likely a doctor told you to do it. How I'd like to smack them all upside the face and give them what for. Well, take heart, sir, that there's a much better remedy and by means far less destructive than opiates." She paused, seeming to wait for something, and when Wes kept quiet, she leaned forward and spoke in a stage whisper. "This is the part, sir, where you ask me to beg your pardon and demand to know where I get off, etcetera."

Wes couldn't stop a smile, and in truth, he almost laughed.

She smiled back and reached for his hands, clasping them between her own.

"I can help you. I know you don't believe me, that you think I'm just some mad American woman you should run from, but I swear, I can help you. I can see you are a kind, good man, and the world is far too short of them as it is. Please, do not throw your life away to opium. You are not yet lost to it—do not give it any more of you than it has already taken. I don't care that you're a lord. You're human, you're flesh, and that's all it takes for it to claim you and turn you into nothing more than a wraith. Don't let it, Lord George. Don't let it."

Wes stared back at her, oddly moved and completely unable to respond.

He was saved by a distant shout and thud. Miss Brannigan let go of him and rose, hastily murmuring an apology as she opened a door in the far wall and headed up a flight of stairs, leaving Wes alone.

He waited a few minutes, digesting it all as he sipped his tea. He watched the woman staring at the street and listened to the one beneath the quilt softly snore. He kept an eye on the boy at the chessboard. He'd found that if he looked too long at him directly, the boy would turn away, huddling tight into himself. Once he relaxed, however, he made three more moves, playing both sides of the board. He played the pieces correctly, as best as Wes could tell, but he used no strategy, and Wes couldn't tell which side he was trying to urge to win, if any.

Don't let it claim you.

You are a kind, good man.

Let me help you.

Wes's hand shook around the cup.

He wasn't an addict. He knew that. And yet he was so moved by her speech. Why? Why did he yearn for whatever it was her eyes and her gentle touch promised? Were he normal, he would have thought he was in love with her. But he knew better than that. What was it, though? What else could it be? Was it just that he, like all men, wanted salvation?

But he was *not* an addict.

When five minutes passed and Miss Brannigan still had not returned, Wes put the teacup down, pulled his notepad out of his pocket and began to write. He wrote to her, on and on and on, filling four pages front and back. The boy at the stove had stopped playing and watched him, but Wes didn't look back, only kept writing until footsteps came upon the stairs and the door burst open.

"I'm so sorry," she said, her face flushed. Her dress was dirty too, stained with footprints and—good heavens—splatters of what had to be blood. This seemed not to bother her, however, and she sat across from him in a ragged chair. "Now. Where were we?"

Wes smiled politely and handed her the stacks of paper.

Frowning, she began to read, but she spoke occasionally, usually without looking up. "Yes, I know physicians are wise creatures, but they don't always know all the tricks. And"—she paused for more reading—"ah. Good, I see you already know about slowing down. And visualization. *Good.* But I wonder if they've told you about singing—Oh!" She smiled widely and glanced up at him. "Bravo! You've accepted that it can't be cured, not completely. *Very* well done. It might however, disappear entirely one day with those you are very comfortable with." Her shoulders slumped. "Social anxiety as well. Ah. I see why you turn to opium." Another pause as she read, but then she gave him a look that by rights should have come over the top of a pair of glasses from a displeased tutor. "It doesn't matter that a physician prescribed the opium to you. Outside short-term use for pain, it's little more than a way to check out from the world, ultimately permanently, if not from the drug then from the debauchery that tends to come with it."

She lowered the papers to her lap and angled herself in her chair to point over her shoulder toward the door. "That den is full of dead lives, my lord. Very few of them took their first dip into opium on a lark. Pain, agony, desperation, desolation—every person flying into diamond-studded clouds in that place began as someone with a true life. Now they live for that drug. Mothers, sisters, friends, husbands, wives, lovers—now they are addicts only, every one. It's my mission to see no more of them. Today, sir, it's my mission not to see you become one of them. You may think me silly or ridiculous or managing or whatever you like, so long as you think it on this side of the street or riding away from this place." She rose, tossed his notes into the stove and came back to stand beside him. "Now. May I interest you in some stew?"

Bewildered, Wes could do nothing more than nod. She bustled off happily toward the kitchen, and for a moment he simply sat there, stunned by the intensity of

Miss Penelope Brannigan. Who the devil *was* she? How did she know such things? Was she brilliant, or was she mad?

Was she *right*?

Then Wes saw the clock on the mantle, startled at the time, and stood.

He pulled out his wallet, emptied it of all but what he would need for a cab, and withdrew his pad of paper.

My name is Lord George Albert Westin. But please call me Wes.

He removed the slip of paper and placed the note on the table, glancing once more around the room, but only the boy paid him any mind, and once he caught Wes looking at him, he turned away.

Wes turned away as well, moving silently across the room and out the door, where fortune favored him at last with a cab coming up the street toward him, empty. Hailing it, he climbed inside, stammered the Dove Street address to the driver, then settled back, wrenching his mind off the odd encounter with Miss Brannigan and onto his impending engagement with Michael Vallant.

ALBERT WAS LATE.

Michael sat in the front room of the Dove Street house, feet tucked up beside him on the sofa, trying to look bored instead of anxious as the day servants cleaned around him.

It was a difficult task, waiting. To begin, Michael had nothing to do. He hadn't brought anything to read, never dreaming he would need to pass so much time. He'd also never been in the sitting room at this hour of the day, drapes pulled wide as every pillow was cleaned, every stain scrubbed, every carpet aired. Michael hadn't realized the room looked so dismal and tawdry until now. To make matters worse, Rodger was hosting one of his balls that night, which meant more people than usual were passing through on their way to prepare the ballroom. Which meant they all saw Michael sitting there, waiting.

And waiting.

The only consolation he had was that Rodger had gone off on business, too distracted to do much more than ask Michael five times if he was all right, if he wanted a bodyguard, if he was sure he wanted to do this. Michael had said, "Yes, no, yes," though he suspected he and Albert would be shadowed by one of Rodger's men regardless.

Assuming Albert ever arrived.

"More tea, sir?" a maid asked him, appearing beside the sofa. She hovered uncertainly, as if she wasn't even sure she should ask. There was generally no one to tend to during the day.

"I'm fine, thank you," Michael replied, smiling thinly. Though as soon as he spoke the words, his stomach gurgled unhappily, and he wondered whether or not he should ask for a sandwich. Generally he ate a meager breakfast as he rose and a small meal at about this time, and he had barely choked down toast and tea this morning. Perhaps it would be best to eat, in case food was not on Albert's agenda. He turned around to call the girl back—and then the door to the sitting room opened, and there he was.

Tall, dark, flushed, and harried-looking—there stood Lord George Albert Westin in the doorway. He made a small, awkward bow as he approached Michael, and he trembled slightly as he handed Michael a note.

Michael accepted it somewhat awkwardly, though he supposed he would need to get used to such things with Albert. He began to read, but as Albert stood there, still looking a walking wreck, Michael stopped and motioned to the space beside him.

"Please, sit. You look as if you ran here from Covent Garden." He paused, then added, "You didn't, did you?"

Shaking his head as he sat, Albert waved impatiently at the small pieces of paper he had shoved into Michael's hand.

Michael sighed. "Very well. I'll read. But please relax, or I won't be able to digest a single word."

Nodding, Albert sat back, endeavoring to look like a gentleman relaxing. Smiling despite himself, Michael read Albert's note, which was written in a dashed, unsteady hand.

Please accept my sincere apologies for my late arrival. A meeting this morning detained me, and in lingering longer than I should have I encountered further difficulties which required me to return to Mayfair to fetch something before arriving here. In hindsight, I should have sent a messenger to explain myself. My conduct was most rude, and I hope you shall be able to forgive me. It shall be my most strident goal to keep such an event from ever happening again. Your humble servant, Albert.

Michael put down the paper and turned to Albert, startling to see how pale and distraught he appeared. Without thinking, his hand went to Albert's leg, resting on his knee. "Albert! For heaven's sake—you were simply late. Oh, yes, I was cross, but now you're here, and—" He stopped and shook his head, smiling wryly. "Well, you take all the fun out of being upset about your tardiness. Please. You have purchased my time. If you chose to use it to make me wait, that is your prerogative."

Albert grimaced, then let out a breath and concentrated for several seconds before attempting to speak. "N-N-Nervous."

Michael managed to keep a straight face as he raised his eyebrows. "Are you? Goodness, darling. I couldn't even tell."

Albert relaxed, just a little, and smiled. He reached over and placed a hand on Michael's: large, warm and comfortable. Then he rose, only somewhat unsteadily, and held out his hand to Michael as he glanced toward the front of the house in a gesture which said, clearly, "Shall we go?"

Michael nodded, accepted his hand and rose.

Albert had a cab waiting for them, a sleek, closed carriage which was nice enough that he suspected it was the man's own. Gratefully, the carriage bore no crest of the marquess. Michael wasn't sure he could have entered the vehicle, knowing it belonged to Daventry. But no, it was simply plain black with a lush blue velvet interior. It smelled of earth and Albert.

Michael settled back in his seat. "Well? Where do we go today?"

Albert rested his hands on his knees and gave a shrug and a smile. "Wh-Where would you l-l-like?"

Back to this. Michael raised an eyebrow. "My lord. I understand you are new to these sorts of liaisons, but this has nothing to do with what *I* want. The question is, where do *you* wish to go?"

Albert looked helpless. He stammered a few consonants, clutched his hands against his thighs, then shut his eyes.

Michael waited for a full minute to see if Albert would recover, but it became clear he had shut himself down. Michael sighed. Then he stood, lifted the trap and spoke to the driver.

"Drive six blocks north, please, and stop at the intersection of Dove and Oxford." Closing the trap, he remained standing and smiled wryly at Albert. "I hope you brought coin, for I'm going to make you buy me a loaf and some cheese. I'm simply—" He stopped as he realized Albert was shaking. "My lord? My lord. Albert—Albert—darling—" He sat beside him and took the shaking hands into his own.

Albert still had his eyes closed, but his face was red, and his nostrils flared as his lip curled in disgust. Michael paused, uncertain. As Albert fumbled with his pad and scratched out another note, Michael realized it was *self*-disgust.

Didn't take enough medicine, he wrote in an unsteady hand.

Michael looked up at his face in alarm. "You are ill? But why didn't you say?"

The noise Albert made through his nose was more expressive than a Frenchman's sigh. He scratched at his paper again.

Not ill. Only—

He stopped writing, crumpled the paper and tossed it angrily across the coach.

Michael sat still a moment, unsure of exactly what to do. He had the sense that this first outing with his patron was about to fall into permanent pieces. What was odd was that he felt so strongly about this not happening. Why did he care? This was Daventry's son.

Daventry's son who could not be more unlike his father. Daventry's son, who is as broken as I am.

Michael didn't know if Rodger was right or not. He

didn't know if he'd fallen in love with Albert, or if he was simply losing his grip on reason and sense. He also didn't know what to say, how to calm him.

And so he calmed him the only way he knew to calm a man.

Smiling the smile he had smiled for so many gentlemen, a smile part seduction, part gentling, part distraction, he placed his hand on Albert's thigh. "Be still, my lord," he whispered, and as his hand slid higher, he bent and placed his lips on his patron's own.

However, there the whore's game ended and something else began. His lips brushed Albert's once, twice, lingering before drawing on the soft flesh, meaning to steal his tongue inside and brush Albert's teeth. He meant it to be a practiced move, calculated and controlled. When he should have drawn back, he found himself hesitating. Instead of executing his carefully thought-out kiss, he found himself leaning forward and pressing his forehead to Albert's own.

He could not say how they ended up how they did, with himself on Albert's lap, knees straddled on either side of him, their chests pressed together as he took Albert's face in his hands and kissed him deeply. There was no art to it, no careful seduction, only a sudden flare of need that had little to do with sex and so much more to do with…something. Michael didn't know what it was, but Albert had it and he needed it, needed it desperately.

"Albert," he whispered against his lips, and when

Albert's arms closed around him, drawing him closer as he kissed back, Michael shuddered and let go.

"Albert," he whispered again, his voice straining with need. His hands trembled on Albert's ears, and he tipped his head back as lips trailed down his throat. *Albert.*

When the coach stopped, Michael startled as if waking from a dream. Disorientation quickly morphed into awkwardness, and as he realized what he was doing, how he had thrown himself not artfully at Albert but as some lovesick schoolgirl, he felt his cheeks burn, and he tried to withdraw.

Albert stopped him, gently but firmly, keeping him trapped with one arm on his waist. With his other hand he shifted the curtain away from the window and peered out into the street. He glanced at Michael with a curious frown. "B-Bakery?"

Michael's flush deepened. "Well, I'm quite hungry."

Albert's grin did devilish things to Michael's insides. "Ah." Keeping Michael captive on his lap, he fumbled on the seat for his pad and pencil. "What-What w-would you l-l-like?"

It took Michael a moment to realize Albert was asking what he wanted to eat. "Oh. Ah—a couple of meat pies would do quite nicely." He cleared his throat. "Please."

Albert brushed a kiss against Michael's lips and adjusted Michael on his lap in order to first scribble onto the pad. Rising enough to knock on the trap door, he shoved the paper through, which presumably had instructions for the driver to go into the bakery and get them food. When he returned his full attention to Michael, he seemed remarkably calm.

"No longer nervous, my lord?" he tried to quip, but the words came out breathless and uncertain. No, Albert wasn't nervous. Michael was.

Albert smiled softly, almost wryly as he stroked Michael's face. "Y-Your kiss-kisses are g-good med-medicine." Michael averted his eyes, and Albert's hand fell away. He didn't look nervous, but he did look resigned. "D-Does m-my con-con-con-condition d-d-disgust you?"

Michael frowned. Condition? Oh—the stammer. He touched Albert's chest reassuringly, but butterflies flew up in his stomach and made his hand tremble. "To be blunt, my lord, I'm too busy worrying about my own condition to bother with yours." When Albert raised a questioning eyebrow at him, Michael gave in and confessed the whole. "I don't understand my reaction to you. It upsets me. I'm accustomed to being in control. And—"

And I find I don't want to be in control when I'm with you.

He froze. The words had stopped behind his lips, but he'd heard them in his head, and they terrified him. Despite his cutting them off, somehow it seemed Albert had heard them too.

The knock on the door made them both jump, but Albert recovered quickly, gently displacing Michael onto the seat before leaning forward to open the door and take the wrapped package the servant offered. He stammered instructions as well, too quietly for Michael to hear. Then he sat back on the seat, opened the package and handed a meat pie wordlessly to Michael.

"Th-Thank you," Michael replied, but he didn't eat it, not at first.

Albert smiled, watching patiently until Michael took a bite. Then he smiled again and kept smiling as the coach pulled back onto the street, and eventually Michael gave in, relaxed, and simply ate as they rode on.

Chapter Seven

THEY DID NOTHING more that first day than drive around London.

While Michael ate, occasionally foisting some of the food on Albert, they circled aimlessly, but eventually the carriage stopped. When Michael pushed back the curtain, he saw they were in Hyde Park. It was a cold, dreary day, not quite raining as much as it was spitting in fits and starts, and so the park was not as full as it might have been. Still, a fair number of coaches circled the paths, and a few brave souls rode.

Michael, who had been to the park, had never done so in a carriage—not, that was, sitting on the seat. A gentleman he'd seen regularly a few years before had been fond of riding across the green, waving to his friends while Michael serviced him below. It made him feel a bit grand to sit in a fancy carriage with the curtain pulled back, watching London's finest promenade. He couldn't see much, just blurry blobs of color, and he longed to don his spectacles and see them better. In a moment of self-consciousness, he glanced across at Albert and found his patron watching out the opposite window, looking away from the carriages. Looking up, in fact. Quite intently.

Michael did the same, but he saw nothing but a sky full of gray clouds. Trying to be surreptitious, he leaned over and attempted to repeat the gesture through Albert's window, but it was more of the same. Frowning, he looked again, and when he realized what had captured the attention of his host, he laughed.

"Trees. That's what you're looking at, aren't you? I'm ogling the *ton*, and you're inspecting the trees."

Albert's quiet smile did dangerous things to Michael's insides. "M-Moss," he said, and pointed at a tall tree they were heading past. "On the b-b-bark."

Michael leaned forward and squinted, but of course he could only see the dark skeleton of the tree. "Ah. Is it good moss, or bad moss?"

He could hear the smile in Albert's voice. "Just m-moss." His arm extended before Michael's face, pointing to the south. "Th-That yew is d-dying. Every y-year it h-hollows out more. A sh-shame. P-Pruning would have s-saved it."

Michael had a suspicion he wouldn't have been able to tell anything about the yew even with his spectacles on, but he nodded and pretended he understood. "What else do you see when you look out your window, Albert?"

That was all they did that first day. The whole first

week, in fact, was nothing but Albert taking Michael on rides around London, through every park and borough, never looking at buildings or other carriages but always at trees and plants. In a gesture that touched Michael, Albert always brought along a fresh meat pie for Michael as well.

Michael of course never put on his glasses, but he thought he was beginning to identify a few things by their shape and hue.

Though they toured every day, spending hours and hours together, not once more after that first day did they even skirt close to anything remotely like sex. At best their hands would touch, but since he had climbed onto Albert's lap, Michael hadn't received so much as a kiss. He couldn't decide if this was good or bad. It was nice, in a way, to simply be with the man, and yes, it flattered him that Albert wanted to share his passion for plants with him. Indeed, he found himself interested despite himself. Michael noticed plants more when he was out on his own. After a week with Albert, he realized life was everywhere, even in the dingiest parts of London.

Still, he wouldn't have minded a little more personal "life". He had stopped dreaming of Daventry—he was too busy now dreaming of all the carnal things he wanted to do with Daventry's son, but in real life he received nothing at all, and it was driving him mad. He didn't know if this was some game or if Albert had truly lost interest in him sexually. Every brush of hands, every glance, became a tease, a torment. Every day Michael told himself he would kiss Albert again, that he would end this strange standoff, but every day he waited for Albert to make the first move, or at least to give him a sign. Michael began to wonder if he would need to be a plant to get more attention, and found himself constantly reaching for anything green in his wardrobe. It was sad, to be honest. But he couldn't stop.

On the sixth day of their meeting, Albert took Michael to the Regent's Park gardens.

Michael could tell even before they arrived that this tour was different. There was an eagerness about Albert that outstripped his usual mood. He pointed out trees and shrubs as he always did, but he kept glancing forward, as if he could not wait to arrive.

It was with some irony that Albert had chosen to show him something special, because today Michael was tired and had a headache. Rodger had made him a present of the newest installment from Dickens, presenting it at night when the only place available to read with gaslight was in Rodger's office. As he'd read, Michael could hear the sounds of other people's pleasure. Normally he would have ignored it, but it only made him think of how he received none, and so he'd gone to bed to read by candlelight. Which had strained his eyes. He should be wearing his glasses, and he had been wearing them, right up until Albert had come into the parlor to fetch him. Without them his vision this afternoon was beyond horrible.

Well, he would pretend he could share in Albert's delight, as always.

They came to a large, half-finished glass structure, and they were the only carriage pulling up to the door. Every other vehicle was a wagon clearly designed for service, mostly builders' carts. Also interesting was that while the scene outside was pure chaos, it didn't seem to upset Albert in the slightest. In fact, he was beaming as he lightly touched Michael's elbow and motioned him on to the door. Once there, a workman doffed his cap and bowed as he held the door open for them.

"Good afternoon, Lord George."

Michael glanced at Albert, saw the eagerness blooming brighter and brighter, saw his eyes light up, saw all the nervousness slip away, and even without being told, Michael knew. This place, however much it might belong to the crown, was Albert's. These were *his* gardens.

"The R-Royal So-So-So-Society overs-s-sees these gardens," Albert explained as he led Michael past builders and toward another door leading into a greenhouse. "It sh-should be open to the p-p-public s-soon." He glanced at Michael, eyes dancing. "I th-thought you mi-mi-mi-might like an early t-t-t-tour."

Michael smiled back. "Of course. Thank you."

Albert briefly clasped Michael's hand. Then he nodded toward the door, let go and led the way. Michael followed.

The small door was clumsily made, clearly there for temporary purposes only during construction, but it opened into a huge conservatory made entirely of glass and filled, Michael surmised from the loam-and-floral scent that assailed his senses, with plants and flowers. The air was hot and moist, a stark contrast to the cold out of doors. The room was filled with sound as well, a sonorous symphony of hisses and clicks and whirrs, of drips and drops of water and chatters of metal as pipes shifted and banged against glass and pots.

And color—Michael was blind to detail, but everywhere around him was color, in bright patches and in quick slashes that swayed in the breeze they'd made by opening and closing the door. Reds and oranges that glowed against more shades of green than Michael had known existed.

Among them moved the tall, well-shaped dark figure that was Albert, whose face, when it came into the partial focus that was the best Michael could do today, looked at him with wicked delight.

"B-Beautiful, isn't it?" Albert's voice was hungry and delightfully rough.

Michael wrapped his arms around himself, blinking against the light and his headache. "Do you work here as well? I mean," he amended quickly, "do you work with the plants?"

"Y-Yes. I h-help with acqu-qu-qu—" Albert sighed, then shook his head.

"Acquisitions?" Michael offered helpfully. He tried

to ignore the way his heart beat faster when Albert smiled at him and nodded.

"I h-h-elp with scheduling m-m-m-maintenance too." His attention had begun to wander back to the greenhouse, and as he led them deeper into the building, he paused to adjust levers or knobs and sometimes stopped for several minutes to record notes in leather journals kept near the plants. When they came to another door to a smaller section of the greenhouse, he grinned devilishly at Michael as he withdrew a key from his pocket.

"We k-keep the orchids here," he said, his stammer almost invisible in his excitement. As they stepped forward, he took Michael's hand, his grip strong and sure.

Given the build-up, Michael was disappointed. The room was actually quite sparse, housing only a few plants on three shelves off to one side, and between the distance and the glass which covered them—glass misty with condensation—Michael couldn't understand what the fuss was about. He tried to cover up his reaction. "Rare, are they? Prized flowers?"

Even without his spectacles, Michael could read the censure in Albert's countenance. "In f-fact, orchids g-grow on every c-continent in the w-world. B-But without soil." He crossed to one of the glass jars, stroking it reverently. "And w-we think they m-may be c-crossbred l-like n-no other fl-flower." He turned back to Michael, his own disappointment clear in his tone.

"Y-You d-don't find them b-beautiful?"

Michael opened his mouth, ready to lie, to wax rhapsodic on the beauty of the fuzzy pink and white blobs in front of him. He had done well enough all week, feigning that he could see the wonders Albert described. But as he stared at the orchids, the words stuck in his throat. He tried to lean forward, tried to get close enough to actually see. Any other day it would have worked, but today the blooms faded in and out of focus, overlapping one another, aggravating his headache.

He was tired of it, tired of lying, tired of being surrounded by Albert's joys and not being able to share. Which was why, his judgment repressed by a pounding head and a foul mood, he confessed the truth.

"I can't see them," he said.

He could see, just, Albert's frown. "Wh-Wh-What do you m-m-m-mean?"

"I mean that I can't see them." He gestured vaguely at the jars. "I'm horribly nearsighted on the best of days, and today I have a headache that keeps me even from pretending. I should very much like to see your flowers, my lord, but I can't. I don't like to advertise it, but I see so poorly I am practically blind. I can barely see where you are, let alone your flowers."

He averted his eyes. He felt empty and very foolish and more exposed than if he'd stood there naked with half the *ton* looking on.

A brush at his elbow made him startle, but the tender touch that followed gentled him again.

"Y-Y-You need sp-sp-sp-spectacles," Albert said, his voice further gentling.

Michael felt himself blush. "I have spectacles." Without thinking, he touched his vest pocket where they lay hidden. "But I look ridiculous in them."

Albert laughed, and the sound combined with the soft massage of his thumb against his arm made Michael's knees go weak. "P-P-Put them on, M-M-Michael."

Michael tried to pull away from Albert's touch but ended up leaning into him slightly instead. "No. I don't want to look ridiculous, not today." *Not with you.*

Albert stepped closer. Michael shut his eyes as he inhaled the sweet, familiar scent of Albert and shaving soap.

"Please."

Michael started to tell him no but said instead, "Kiss me."

Neither of them moved. Both Albert and Michael looked at each other in complete surprise, though at least in Michael's case, there was a bit of terror as well. The words hung between them, impossible to take back. What was wrong with him? Why had he said that? That wasn't what he meant.

Except he had. He wanted a kiss. He wanted a kiss desperately, and if he put on his spectacles, certainly Albert would never think of kissing him again.

Kiss me. Kiss me.

"Kiss me." He meant to speak the words this time, but they still startled him, terrified him. He tried to look alluring, tried to play coy lover, but he felt for all the world as he had that first time at school he'd looked at one of the older boys and longed for just this sort of thing. His hands were sweaty, and he couldn't make himself move, could only grip the edge of the shelf behind him and wait, barely breathing, to see what happened next.

What happened was that Albert placed his hands on top of Michael's and bent toward his lips.

Michael shut his eyes and leaned in to meet him.

Soft. Albert's lips were so soft, and the breath of his gentle exhale so hot and full of his spice. Such a sweet, almost innocent kiss, much more innocent than either of them deserved, and it made Michael ache and his head spin. When Albert's hands traveled up his arms to his neck, Michael tipped his head to the side and tried to deepen the kiss, opening his mouth, but Albert only nipped gently, at first his top lip, then his bottom. Michael whimpered, and he felt Albert smile, brushing their lips again briefly before his tongue stole out and tickled his skin, and then his teeth. Michael's knees gave out, and Albert held him in place by pressing their pelvises together as his hands slid from Michael's neck onto his waistcoat...and into his pocket, where they found his glasses, plucked them out and whisked them away. When Michael cried out and tried to reclaim them, Albert stepped back out of his reach.

Still dizzy, Michael righted himself and aimed an angry finger at Albert. "That was a devil's trick," he whispered.

Albert only smiled wryly and held out the spectacles, dangling them from his fingers. "Wh-Wh-Why will you n-not wear them? You p-p-prefer not to see?"

Michael's cock was pounding as hard as his pulse now, and as he knew neither would get release, he lost his temper. "My lord, I make my living by my looks. How many whores have you met with glasses thicker than most windowpanes?"

He doubted he'd have been able to read Albert's face even if he could see it. It made him angry, and he would have stormed out, but he couldn't leave his glasses. He'd fallen asleep before he'd finished the Dickens.

"Wh-Wh-Why d-did you ask m-m-me to k-k-kiss you?" Albert asked at last.

"Because you haven't kissed me all week," Michael shot back.

Albert's reply was measured, careful. "You w-w-wanted me to?"

"Yes." Michael folded his arms over his chest. "I did."

Albert took a step forward, his blurry form coming into partial focus. "H-How m-many c-clients h-have y-you m-met with s-s-s-such a c-c-clumsy st-st-st-stammer?"

Heat raced up Michael's cheeks. "You're different,"

he whispered.

"S-S-So are you," Albert whispered back.

Don't fall in love with him. Rodger's words rose up in faint echo, a last warning.

Too late, Michael admitted, frozen in place as Albert lifted Michael's glasses and arranged them carefully on his face.

Repulsed as he was by the idea of anyone, let alone Albert, seeing him in his spectacles, Michael couldn't help himself as he stared ahead, watching Albert come fully, sharply into focus. After a world of softness, it was always strange to see the edges and angles his glasses brought him, but to behold Albert with such vivid clarity captured him and held him in place. He could see the line of his nose. The detail of his eyebrows. The circles of his irises. The tiny cut above his lip.

His lips. Coming closer once again.

This time when they kissed it went deep instantly, and Albert ground his own hard cock against Michael's. When Albert broke away, Michael cried out in despair, but Albert only reached over and locked the door before taking Michael back into his arms, resuming the kiss with enthusiasm.

When Albert turned him to the wall and pressed him against it, Michael trembled briefly. Albert slowed and nuzzled his jaw.

"W-We can st-stop," he whispered.

"I don't want to stop." Michael's hands were shaking. He wanted to sob. "Why am I like this? I don't understand. And why are you so kind about it?"

Albert laughed into his neck. "I d-don't m-mind."

Michael's answering laugh was hollow. "You don't mind throwing a small fortune at me so you could drive me around London and show me trees? That I can't see properly?"

Albert lifted his head and looked at Michael. With his glasses on, he could see the subtle play in his eyes much more clearly, could watch the walls go down as he prepared to confess something too. "I w-would l-like t-to t-take y-you s-somewhere b-b-better. B-But I am a p-p-poor escort." He ran his index finger sadly down Michael's cheek. "Wh-Where w-would you h-have m-me take you? If I w-w-were n-n-normal? Wh-What do you l-l-long to s-s-see?" When Michael said nothing, he began to suggest sights. "V-Vauxhall? Opera?"

"Bookstores." Michael's cheeks flamed hot, but he pressed on before he lost his courage. "Bookstores and literary salons."

Albert had an odd look about him now, something like hope and hard thought all at once. "B-Bookstores I c-c-could d-d-do. S-S-Salons m-m-might be h-harder. I sh-shall ask at the c-c-club."

"Club? Oh—your gentlemen's club." He wondered if he dare ask to see one of those as well, or if he would simply seem like an eager child. He tried for nonchalance and polite interest. "Which is yours? White's, I suppose?"

Albert recoiled. "N-No. I p-p-prefer the Ath-th-then-naeum."

Michael's nonchalance melted away in abrupt, blatant envy. "You belong to *the Athenaeum*?" Michael almost wept. Every literary and scientific genius belonged to the Athenaeum.

Dickens belonged there.

Albert nodded, watching him carefully. "W-Would y-you l-l-like to g-g-go?"

Michael could not help himself. "Yes," he confessed breathlessly.

Smiling, Albert brushed another kiss against his lips. "C-Come s-see m-my orchids."

Michael did. With Albert beside him, touching his arm, Michael took in the flowers, properly this time. They were beautiful, he admitted. Not quite worthy of the rapture in Albert's voice, but they were lovely all the same. Delicate and strong at once, which suited them in a way Michael couldn't quite put his finger on. The stems were thin and long, the leaves fat and pulpy, and the petals were intricately marked, with lines and veins shot with color. The shape of the flowers varied, one looking like a star, another looking like a slipper.

Albert lifted the glass off each in turn, leading Michael's fingers out to touch the plant as he explained haltingly the name and origin of each one. He explained how the plants came from all over the world, that there was quite a race to find them and a vibrant black market for their purchase. The longer he talked about his flowers, the less pronounced his stammer became. The flowers, clearly, were the man's passion. Michael found himself intrigued more than anything by the infectious excitement in his lover's tone.

"I had no idea such things even existed," Michael said as Albert put the glass back over the last flower. "But yes, you're quite right. They're absolutely lovely. Thank you for showing them to me." He turned to Albert, smiling.

Albert smiled back.

They left shortly after that, Albert giving him another tour of the main body of the greenhouse, this time with Michael able to see. He took a moment to speak to a few of the workers and another gentleman who appeared to be a caretaker, and then, with Michael still wearing his glasses, they headed back to Dove Street.

"I w-w-will n-not c-come tom-m-morrow," Albert said as they came up to the curb. "I m-m-must take d-dinner with my f-f-family." He forced a smile. "P-P-Perhaps the day after w-we can v-visit b-bookstores and m-my club."

"Thank you," Michael replied, not knowing what else to say.

They kissed again before he exited—a brief, lingering brush of lips. Once Michael stepped out, the carriage rolled away.

Michael watched him go. Pocketing his spectacles,

he hunched into his coat and hurried inside, stumbling twice on the paving stones as he adjusted to life without clear sight once again.

WHEN WES RETURNED home that evening, Legs was waiting for him in the alley. He had his translator with him.

A thrill rushed through Wes as he hurried forward to meet the sailor, a high almost as good as opium. He'd feared Legs had met with an accident, and the very idea of trying to find a new agent for his botanical ventures had begun to make him more than a little ill. But now Legs was here and looking well.

A sailor on a merchant ship since he was thirteen, Legs had run afoul of a particularly sadistic captain and had his tongue cut out for insolence almost as soon as he began. He was first mate now on a ship that ran primarily to the West Indies and down to Brazil on occasion. He'd been due to sail to the latter on his last voyage, and he'd promised to try and secure Wes a new orchid upon his return. Though he'd been in port three days and had sent word for Wes to meet him, he hadn't showed at their appointment nor sent any follow-up correspondence. Wes was beyond glad to see him now. The fact that he was not clutching a glass jar or a plant wrapped in burlap, however, was not a good sign.

Legs inclined his head and removed his hat as he approached Wes. Wes returned the incline and touched his own brim. The rather raggedly dressed and dark-skinned woman beside him made a brusque and businesslike curtsey before returning her full attention to Legs.

Conversation began.

Wes nodded at the door to his building, then gestured to it and lifted his eyebrows at Legs.

Care to go inside?

Legs wrinkled his brow and cast a dubious glance at himself and at his escort before nodding pointedly at Wes's finery.

You sure you want us riffraff in your nice place?

It was true, they usually met at Legs's rooms. Irregular as it was to take Legs into his apartments, Wes was too eager to follow him back to the docks or to schedule for another time. Wes shook his head and waved his hand impatiently. Smiling a half smile, he mimed a drink.

Legs grinned a toothless grin and laughed. It was amazing how different the sound was in a throat missing a great deal of tongue.

Legs and the woman made their way down the hall to Wes's rooms, pausing to gawk at paintings and the gilded finery of an upscale gentlemen's apartment house. The butler and night maid, in contrast, regarded Wes's guests with great wariness. Wes carried on, ignoring the servants and letting Legs and his woman take their time. When they finally arrived, Wes had the door to his rooms unlocked and had gone around the corner to light a lamp.

"S-s-s-sit on the s-s-sofa," he directed his guests as he procured clean glasses from his cabinet. He poured brandy for himself and whiskey for Legs, but he paused and gave the woman an inquiring look.

She held up her hands and shook her head. "No thank you, milord," she replied in a heavy West Indies accent.

Once Wes had given Legs his liquor and taken a seat in the chair opposite him, it was the woman who spoke.

"He say he sorry, but he lost you plant." She scowled and motioned in the general direction of the docks. "That dog Renny called in he debt and sent he to the prison. I get he out, but they take all he things. They sell he hat and he boots, and they throw you plant away."

Wes's heart sank. He'd *nearly* had it, and now it was in the bottom of some garbage bin. Though he knew he should leave well enough alone, he found he had to torture himself. Picking up his notebook from the desk beside him, he passed it over to Legs with a questioning look.

Which one was it?

He knew this would be bittersweet when Legs grimaced before even opening the book, but when Legs pointed to a cattleya gigas orchid and held it up for illustration, Wes had to shut his eyes and lean forward, pressing his hands over his mouth. It was like being told someone had crossed the Alps to bring him a diamond but some idiot had mistaken it for glass and tossed it into the bottom of a lake.

Legs put the book down, shoulders falling forward. "Rah-rah," he said in a rough, thick voice, his tone sorrowful.

Wes sat back up and shook his head as he waved the apology away. "N-n-not y-y-your f-f-fault."

Though Wes reached into his pocket and withdrew his wallet to produce a note, Legs held up his hands. "Rah." He gestured to the woman, who sat up straighter and launched into what had clearly been a prepared speech.

"He want no money for failure, he say. He want to try again. He think he know somebody else who bring black-market flower. Somebody who owe him favor. He get this flower for you for fair price. He say he respect his lordship and want to make things right."

Wes nodded solemnly, biting back a wry smile. Over the past three years, between his own purchases and those for other members of the Royal Botanical Society, Wes had given the sailor at least seven hundred pounds. Yes, he suspected Legs was highly interested in making sure his steady paycheck didn't look elsewhere for specimens. He was curious to know what flower it might be, though, so he tapped the notebook again and gave Legs an inquiring look.

Legs frowned and gave a grunt, leafing through the notebook for some time. Wes was certain he was about to confess he didn't know what flower, but at last Legs flipped all the way to the back and began to slow down.

Wes's heartbeat, however, sped up. Legs was looking at the orchids. When Legs turned the book around again for Wes and pointed at the half-finished illustration of Mrs. Gordon's flower, Wes had to press a hand over the center of his chest in his excitement. Legs gestured animatedly to his translator.

"He say it like this one, but has different leaves and flower."

Wes could scarcely breathe. Wes looked levelly at Legs. "Are y-y-you s-s-s-sure?"

Legs nodded emphatically. He gestured in his crude hand-speaking code to the woman.

"He say he saw the man on the other ship take the flower. He say he know where he likely to be in London."

Wes couldn't take his eyes from the illustration. "L-L-Likely he-he-he already h-h-h-has a b-buyer."

Legs grinned a wicked grin and chuckled before making more sign. When the woman translated, she was grinning too.

"He say this man no know what he have. He say this man idiot."

Legs pounded his chest proudly, then gestured to Wes and to the book. Wes smiled back. That had been his insurance, teaching Legs what were the most valuable plants to search for and where they were likely to hide. No, Legs was no idiot.

Wes nodded and took a few breaths to speak directly to Legs. "I w-w-will w-w-wait to h-h-hear f-from you."

Legs nodded back and rose, pressing his hat to his chest and bowing to Wes. The woman curtseyed again.

"Thank you, milord," she said.

Once they were gone, Wes locked the door. He poured out two more of his pills, made himself another brandy and retired to his bath.

Wes had signed a lease in the building where he lived for several reasons: it had common servants who kept things running but stayed out of his way, it had indoor plumbing, gas lighting, and immense windows facing south. His apartment had three rooms, the sitting room, the bathroom, and his bedroom, and each were glutted with plants.

Plants hung from the ceiling. Plants spilled out of shelves. Plants occupied windowsills and floors and a few claimed chairs. He kept plants which liked an even temperature in the sitting area, for that room was heated by a stove. The plants in his bedroom were ones which could tolerate the dry and soot of a fireplace.

The ones in the bathroom were his prizes.

He had six types of ferns, which was almost standard, but he also had pelargoniums, heliotropes, salvias, lobelias, and cannas, which was something of a trick to pull off in a bathroom. Every inch of the room overflowed with foliage. It was his haven.

Wes whispered to his plants as he stoked the fire to

heat the water for his bath, and as the water boiled, he made his way around the room to stroke petals and leaves, testing soils and sometimes dipping into his own bath water for their drinks. He lingered at the orchids. Currently he had three: a cattleya, and two phalaenopsis. If Legs did indeed produce the leafless orchid, Wes would keep it in here.

As he slipped into the water and sank deep into the warmth to soak, Wes stared at the windowsill and shelves and cabinets overflowing with plants without seeing them. The orchid. He might have the orchid. Oh, but he hoped it was still intact. The odds were grim, if it were brought over by a man who didn't know how to tend to them, but Wes had brought many a plant back from the dead. For as poorly as he did with people, Wes could charm any plant.

He grimaced and reached for the sponge and cake of soap, remembering that on the morrow he was to talk about plants with his father's friend. The very thought of the meeting made him anxious. So anxious, in fact, that he dropped the soap twice into the water, his breath coming out in short pants as he leaned over to fish it out.

He shouldn't be this unsettled, not after two pills. But what should he expect? He took them daily now, and in heavy doses, so that he could spend the day with Michael without dissolving into a trembling idiot. The cost, as the doctor had warned, was that now when he needed it, the drug would fail him.

Still shaking, Wes climbed out of the tub and back to his bedroom. He took two more of the pills, despite the physician's warning never to take more than two at once. Certainly it wouldn't kill him this one time.

To be safe, however, he wrapped himself in a blanket and sat by the stove as he waited for the drug to take hold of him. Waited for the raw panic in his breast to melt away. Waited for the edges of the world to soften. Waited for the sleepy smile of opium to crawl up the sides of his face.

It did. He laughed out loud, tossed the blanket aside and strode boldly naked back to his bathroom where, new brandy in hand, he warmed his bath again. And then he settled back into the tub, letting his thoughts wander. As tendrils of steam wafted over him, so did his thoughts drift inside his mind, rising and mingling and dissipating as quickly as they came into being, colored by the opium swimming through his blood.

Most of his thoughts were of Michael Vallant.

Vallant sitting primly on the coach seat, trying not to let on how much he enjoyed the velvet cushions. Vallant listening with genuine interest as Wes explained in his hesitant speech about the flora and fauna of London. Vallant's blush as he confessed his nearsightedness, his awkwardness as he wore his spectacles.

His naked yearning as he said, "Kiss me."

Wes shut his eyes and let his thoughts drift back further. To Vallant in his silk gown, looking up at Wes with hungry eyes. Vallant's wicked smile as he slid down Wes's chest to take his cock in his mouth.

Vallant's long, lovely throat exposed as he tipped back his head and opened his body for Wes's pleasure.

For a fleeting moment a voice of conscience scolded Wes, telling him he should focus on Vallant's plight, not his carnal allure. He had done so well all week to try to make the other man feel at ease, but two words and the taste of that sweet mouth had undone him entirely.

Legs and the potential new orchid were forgotten, his father's party dismissed to the furthest reaches of his mind. With his cheek pressed hard against the metal rim of the tub and his voice echoing in sharp, breathy cries against the tile, Wes shut his eyes and stroked himself to completion as he imagined himself emptying not into the tepid waters of a bath but into the hot, eager channel of Michael Vallant.

MICHAEL WOKE FROM a nightmare with a scream that went on and on and on until Rodger was found and brought up to the attic. Even then it took him fifteen minutes and several swallows of brandy to calm Michael down, turning the screams into wretched sobs as his dark dreams played over and over again in his mind.

Chapter Eight

DAVENTRY HOUSE WAS aglow the following night when Wes arrived. He was on foot, as he lived only a few blocks away, and he was early, because he did better at highly populated functions if he was able to stake out a place in the drawing room first and watch people arrive. Even so, the house was already afire with light, inside and out. He could hear the gaslights' quiet pops and hisses as he stepped into the main hall. It was an eerie sound, but he rather liked it. It felt modern and oddly safe.

"Good evening, my lord," the butler greeted Wes as he took his hat and coat. "Your father is in the ballroom with your aunt, overseeing the finishing touches of the decorations. Lord Vaughn is not at home but is expected within the hour."

Wes inclined his head in thanks for the information, then geared his mouth up for a question. "L-L-Lord Alten?"

The butler's eyebrows rose briefly, but he replied,

"In the schoolroom, my lord."

Inclining his head again, Wes headed up the stairs.

Wes braced himself for accusing looks and tender pleadings from his nephew over the promised outings to the gardens which had not come to pass. It would be very easy to tell the truth and blame his brother, but that wouldn't help father and son's already greatly strained relationship. He decided best would be to blame the Society, saying they had refused to allow a minor onto the premises, even supervised.

It would of course make Wes appear the weakling, incapable of convincing his peers of a small, simple favor. The thought made his shoulders heavy and sent his hand to his pocket to press against the extra pills he had brought with him. He resisted the urge, reminding himself that at least in this way he could serve his family, however inglorious the deed.

However, when he stepped into the small library-turned-schoolroom, he found his preparations were not necessary.

Edwin sat bent over a table, and he did not look up when Wes entered, not until the tutor rapped the boy on the back of the head to acknowledge his visitor. When Edwin's hollow eyes looked up and saw Wes, some brightness went back into them, and he rose and threw his arms around his uncle.

"Oh, Uncle George!"

"Master Edwin," the tutor chided, "you must not behave in such a wild manner."

Edwin stiffened and tried to pull back, but Wes stayed him with a hand on his shoulder. He leveled his gaze at the tutor.

"Th-Th-Thank you. Th-Th-That will b-be all."

Even full of stammer, it seemed, he held enough gravitas to be obeyed. The tutor stiffened angrily, but he also inclined his head and left the room. Once the door shut, Edwin's posture relaxed somewhat. Wes led the boy to the sofa and sat beside him.

For some time they simply sat in silence. Eventually Edwin's shoulders slumped. "I'm sorry," he said almost in a whisper.

Wes frowned. "Y-You ha-have nothing to be s-s-sorry for." He clenched his hands once before forcing them open again. "Edw-win, I kn-know they t-t-ell you to k-k-keep a st-stiff upper l-l-lip, but I m-m-must know if y-your t-t-t-utor is hur-hur-hurting you."

The boy slumped further and shook his head.

Wes ached. "P-Please. W-What is w-wrong?"

"What's wrong is that he's done nothing but throw temper tantrums and behave like a spoilt child," Lord Vaughn said from the door, his voice booming out over the room. "His behavior is appalling, and I've told him so. He's even more of a disgrace to the family than you are, Wes." Vaughn stopped in front of the fireplace and glared down at his son. "Note well your uncle, boy. If you fancy ending up as pathetic as he is, then by all means continue this behavior. And as for you—" He shifted his glare to Wes. "You can leave my son alone and let the men of the family bring him in hand without your nannying."

Wes had begun to blush at the first insult to his honor, but by the third he was positively fuming. Words filled his heart and spilled into his mouth, and he lifted his chin to spew them at his brother. But though his lips were parted, his whole soul ready, even now they tripped at the gate.

"P-P-P-P-P-P—"

Vaughn sneered. "God's teeth, Wes. *Listen* to yourself. P-P-P-P-P-what? What is it you want? Spit it out, please do. Make something of the thousands of pounds Father sunk into fixing you, all for nothing. But you won't, will you? Because you're damaged and broken. Well, you won't break my son. You've already done more than enough. This isn't going well. He's only getting worse, despite all Father has done. It's because of you, I know it. Because he wants to *be* like you." His face was red, his eyes dark and shiny with his rage. "I won't have him stammer like you. I won't have my heir turn out like you. They coddled you, and that's what did it. It won't happen again. *Not to my son.*" He aimed his finger at the door. "Go. Get out."

Wes went.

He rose to his feet, crossed the room and exited the door, all as if in a dream. In the hall the tutor passed him, looking superior and smug. Wes kept on walking, oddly numb, all the way to the stairs and back into the main salon.

Daventry House felt masculine and somber, full of hush and the whisper of power and money. This sensation only increased as the guests arrived. Dukes and earls and the Prime Minister himself were here, as well as their wives. Oh, there were others, nobodies with power or money but not both, not enough. They hovered as they were meant to along the peripheries of the walls, watching the play of the others respectfully, whispering and admiring from afar. Waiting to be summoned for their moment of utility.

Wes stood with them.

He took up a station near a window in the farthest part of the second drawing room. It had the advantage of being both beside a window and a doorway. The window was for illusion of escape only; the doorway was literal in its promise of freedom, if only into a quieter part of the house. Only half the guests were here, but already he was feeling the panic of the press of bodies, the pressure of the din, the stench of too many exotic perfumes mingling with scorched silk and sweat.

His pouch of pastilles lurked in his pocket, inviting him to swallow the lot of them and escape into calm. He'd already taken several, and even a week ago, he wouldn't have hesitated to take more. But Miss Brannigan's warning still rang in his ears. He would not end up like that from his pastilles, would he?

Yet all he had to do was think of how delicious the feeling was of sliding away, and he decided it didn't matter, just so long as he was able to escape.

His hand slipped into his pocket, feeling the tin case where the pills lay.

"Are you hiding again, George?"

Wes straightened and turned to his father, who was smiling but looked weary, as he always seemed to do with Wes.

"N-no," Wes lied, flushing at the stutter. "Just w-w-watching."

Lord Daventry looked at Wes soberly. "I don't ask much from you. I am content to leave you to your plants most of the time. But tonight I have need of you. Indeed, your country has need of you." He nodded across the room at a sea of men. "Come. I will introduce you now."

The trip across the room was unbearable. Noise, so much noise, and so many bodies. Only the threat of shame should his father see his panic kept him from running or fainting or simply standing there and screaming. That and the memory of his brother holding Wes up as the warning of what would become of his son if he did not come about. Though thirty-seven years of trying had taught him otherwise, he tried to come about himself as well. He could do this. It was as they all told him, all in his head. There was nothing to fear here. He was fine. He was safe and fine, and he would be fine—

But just to be sure, he reached for his pills, took three and popped them quickly into his mouth. He chewed them, gagging on the bitter taste, but the trick worked as it had before. Within seconds he felt the beginning of the drug overtaking his system.

Almost without warning, he stood before a small, sour-faced man with beady black eyes and a well-greased mustache.

"Daventry," the man said coolly. "Such a charming home. Thank you for your invitation."

Wes's father inclined his head. "I am glad you approve, Presley. We discussed, earlier, my second son, the botanist? This is he. Lord George Albert."

Presley's eyes widened, then narrowed. "I see. But I've heard, my lord, that he also has a stammer. Quite a nasty one. I'm not certain I want to trust the acquisition of something so important to me with someone not right in the head."

Daventry's hand on Wes's arm tightened, as did his smile. Wes stared into Presley's beady, suspicious eyes and tried to keep himself from casting up his accounts. "My son is merely shy. When it comes to his plants, you can do no better than he. Isn't that so, George?"

Wes opened his mouth, but terror kept him from so much as making a squeak. It was so loud, so hot, and Presley glared at him, almost sneering—

"We must greet more guests," Daventry said quickly, his grip on Wes's arm nearly cutting off his circulation. "But when the women retire after dinner, perhaps the two of you may discuss your...options."

"Assuming your son can find his tongue by then, of

course." Presley smiled flatly at Daventry. "I shall look forward to it as I have little else," he said, clearly indicating he looked forward to it not at all.

Daventry laughed nervously. "Nonsense. George Albert, explain to the man there's nothing wrong with you but a scholar's quirky disposition."

He nudged Wes hard in the small of his back. Wes tried to smile, but he didn't dare open his mouth. He'd taken too many pills. He wasn't relaxed; he was ill.

Another laugh, this one almost dangerous. "Come, boy." Daventry nudged him harder and lower in the center of his back.

Wes's mouth came open as he cried out in pain—and then vomited all over Presley's shoes.

Daventry hauled Wes away, weaving him through the crowd, the painful grip on Wes's arm the only thing that kept him from being sick again. Once they were in the hall he didn't let up, only dragged Wes to his study. As soon as the door shut, he shoved Wes away and paced angrily across the floor.

"God's teeth, but I don't know what to do with you." He stopped at the window and stared out at it. "All the years I have supported you and allowed you to slip into the shadows of life. I need your aid for this one small thing, and yet you are so self-centered, George, that you cannot give me even this." He turned enough to look wearily over his shoulder. "Or perhaps it is me who has failed. Failed to believe them when they told me you were broken. Determined in my pride not to let my son be so."

Wes had to work harder than ever to form words. "I-I-I am s-s-s-s-s-sorry."

His father wasn't listening. "Power and control. It is everything. And yet you've never had it. And heaven help your brother, but I think we have another one of you in his son. He started to stammer this week. I've been telling Richard we can aid him, but perhaps I'm only fooling myself. He is as worthless as you, it seems." Daventry pushed off the window, shaking his head. "Rest assured, George Albert. I won't ask favors of you again. I shall call a carriage for you and have it take you back to your apartments, and I will make your excuses at dinner." He sighed, then nodded. "Excuse me."

His father left, and Wes stood for some time in the dark room, shaking, feeling angry, feeling guilty, feeling deep pits of despair expand before him.

Once in the carriage, he rallied. He thought of Michael, of Dove Street. He thought of going there, of dragging him into a bedroom and losing himself inside the beautiful whore. He thought of how good it would feel to hear Michael shout out his name.

Unless, of course, he recoiled from him too.

Wes pulled the pill case from his pocket, emptied the remainder of them into his hand and swallowed them down. He was unconscious before the footman so much as opened his door.

He had no idea how he came to be in his rooms.

All he knew was that one moment he was in the carriage and the next he was lying in his bed, soaked in sweat, the taste of vomit in his mouth and a worried maid whispering to the butler beside him.

Wes grunted at them, rolled over, and went back to opium-soaked dreams.

AS HE HAD the night before, Michael woke in the middle of the night in a puddle of sweat, voice hoarse and still ringing with a scream. He stared into the shadowy darkness, cold, shaking hands clutching at the covers.

Then he threw the covers back, reached for his dressing gown and stumbled toward the stairs.

Three girls were giggling and whispering to one another as they fussed at the mirror in the bathroom, but when they got one look at Michael, their smiles died. Michael tried not to think of what new gossip they would spread and slammed around as he drew his bath and heated water to fill the great porcelain tub. He had just bathed the day before, but he felt gritty and filthy from head to toe, as if he'd slept buried in a heap of dirt crawling with bugs and worms. While he waited for the tub to fill, he paced the room, trying to outrun the feeling of unease and mild nausea that kept creeping up behind him like a shadow. It was with a great sigh of relief that he sank into the water at last, leaning all the way back against the rim and tipping his face up to the ceiling. He shut his eyes.

Fine white linen pressed against his face and bitter male seed coated his tongue. Pressing his forehead to the bed, he reached back with cold, shaking hands and parted his cheeks.

"That's the way," a smooth, darkly sensual voice praised him, as if he were a very good dog. "Yes. Open yourself for me, Michael, and let me see my prize."

Michael's eyes opened and he scrambled desperately to get out of the tub even before he realized what he was doing—he fell twice, choked on a strangled sound, then landed in a heap on the rug beside the bath. Wet, bruised, and shaking, he curled into a ball and stared at the dirt caked against the clawed feet of the tub until the terror faded.

He climbed back into the tub, but he did not relax. He took vicious hold of the cake of soap and scrubbed himself vigorously from head to toe with it, rubbing and scrubbing until his skin throbbed with heat. As the water drained, he toweled himself off with the same angry determination. After storming upstairs to dress, he tucked his hair into a queue, stuffed it under a cap, and reached for his spectacles and his purse.

It was raining and cold, technically morning but still so early the sun hadn't even begun to peek through the clouds, so Michael hunched into his coat and kept himself under eaves as much as he could as he made his way down the back streets and out onto the main roads. For almost an hour he simply wandered aimlessly, shivering and drenched now to the bone. Eventually he saw the call sign of a pub he knew well enough to enter, and after ordering a plate of breakfast, a pot of tea, and a paper, he tucked himself into a corner by the fire, and before his order even arrived, he fell asleep.

The barkeep had been kind enough to serve him again with hot food once he'd woken, and Michael ate gratefully and sipped his freshened tea. He was still slightly damp from his walk in the rain, but he was mostly dried out now, which he supposed was something.

There were still shadows in his head. They were just ghosts now, dull images that made him uneasy: soundless, tasteless, colorless old dreams. But they upset Michael as much now as they had when he'd been dreaming, because he'd thought he was rid of them. He'd been fine. What had happened? What had made them come back?

How could he make them go away again?

When a figure slid into the booth across from him, he startled, then averted his eyes and focused intently on his plate as he saw who it was.

"Why the devil didn't you come and get me?" Rodger asked, sounding weary and frazzled. "Been looking for you for an hour."

Michael pushed a lump of potato into a puddle of runny egg. "You needn't have."

"What, you want me to leave you alone?" When Michael didn't answer, Rodger sighed and reached for Michael's tea. After draining it, he picked up the pot to pour the cup full again. "Do you want to head back or stay out for a while?"

"Out." Michael pushed his plate away and tried to give Rodger a hard look, but he was afraid he appeared mostly dull. "You treat me like your virgin cousin you don't dare let out of your sight. I was only taking a walk and having something to eat."

"You ain't my cousin, and you sure as hell ain't a virgin." Rodger speared the potato and snagged the crust of Michael's toast as he rose. "Come on. I'll take you over to that shop you like in Cheapside."

Friar's Bookshop. Michael's spirits rose in delight before sinking in guilt. "I can't. I haven't earned in a month."

"You brought in eight hundred pounds," Rodger reminded him.

Michael felt the dark that had never fully left him close over his head, and he shrank back into his shadows.

Rodger grabbed his hand. "Come on, love," he urged in a quiet whisper.

"I don't want to keep having the nightmares. I don't know why they've come back." He huddled into himself. "Maybe I shouldn't see him again. Except we've taken his money."

"We'll give it back," Rodger promised.

Michael tried to bite his tongue, but it was no use. "Except I think I *want* to see him again," he whispered.

"Come." Rodger tugged Michael to his feet and led

him through the maze of tables toward the door. "I've a yen to see you smile, ducks, so I'm taking you to go play with your books."

Memory caught up with Michael—he saw Albert stepping forward in the dim light of the bedroom, and he saw Daventry smile his wicked smile in the shadows.

Shaking his head to clear out them both, he pulled free of Rodger and reached for coin to pay his bill and extra for the barkeep's trouble.

"I just want to go home," he said.

Rodger nodded and rested his hand briefly on Michael's shoulder before he turned and headed for the door. Anxious and confused, Michael lifted his heavy feet one after the other and followed Rodger out into the morning London fog.

WES NEARLY SENT a message to Dove Street with his regrets several times. He had been unable to eat breakfast and shook like a leaf until he'd doctored his tea with laudanum, enough to put most men to sleep. Even then the thought of riding a short distance in a carriage made him reach for the chamber pot. Clearly any kind of outing with Vallant would be impossible.

But though he drafted two missives to excuse himself, he tossed both into the fire. After choking down some toast and peppermint-leaf tea, he loaded his pill pouch, ordered his carriage brought around, and headed for Dove Street. At the very least he could deliver his regrets in person.

Upon his arrival, Wes smiled and tipped his hat at the gardener tending to the boxes outside the bawdy house. Often he would stop and inspect the man's work, offering tips and praise, but today he was too fixated on collapsing into a settee in the drawing room. By the time he passed through the doorway and handed his coat and hat to Barrows's man, he was shaking.

When he started down the hall, Barrows himself appeared from a doorway and stopped him with a grim look, jerking his head to indicate the room behind him. "Michael's curled up in my office, asleep at last. He's had nightmares the past few nights, and they're starting to wear on him." Barrows grimaced. "I'd send you on your way, but he'll be furious when he wakes if I do. So your choices are to wait him out here with a copy of the *Times*, or I send a lad over to fetch you when he comes around."

Wes knew there was no way he could make a trip back and again. He nodded toward an open armchair near the fire. "H-H-Here."

"Done and done." Barrows held the door open wide for him. "I'll send a gel 'round with tea and nibbles. Let her know if you need anything else."

With that Barrows headed down the hallway. Wes watched him for a moment before slipping inside, heading for the chair he'd seen from the doorway. As he came fully into the room he caught sight of the figure on the sofa, and he stopped, stricken.

Michael was curled up in the corner, lying on his side with his back to the cushions, all but his eyes covered by a knitted afghan someone had tucked all around his sleeping form. His long blond hair tumbled across the pillow, over the blanket and into his face. He looked like a child sleeping.

All around the sofa were books, at least twenty of them, ranging from the very ragged to pristine, and the shelves behind the sofa were full of them as well, most stacked haphazardly. They were books of all sorts, ranging from novels to serials to nonfiction. To Wes's surprise, one stack contained nothing but books on botany, one of them a volume to which Wes had contributed.

A young man entered, bearing a tray unsteadily. When he saw Wes, he smiled and blushed, trying to bow and not drop his tray, barely succeeding at both.

"Your tea, milord." The boy looked around anxiously. "Where should I put it, sir?"

Wes nodded at the floor before the chair. "Th-Thank you." He opened the volume he had picked up and thumbed through the pages.

The boy lingered. "You a reader like our Michael? He's famous for it, you know. Them's all his books, but he has more in his room. Acres of them." His cheeks went crimson. "He's teaching me to read. Says I'm natural with letters. And Mr. Barrows will get me a good job once I learn them all."

Wes nodded hesitantly, not wanting to encourage

him exactly but not wanting to wound him either. He suspected he needn't have bothered, for the boy clearly had something he wanted to say and would not leave until he'd managed the courage to say it.

The boy shifted on his feet, lifting his chin higher and higher as if courage could be gained by becoming more vertical. "I—I wanted to tell you, sir," he began, his voice shaking a little in his eagerness or fear, or both, "that I'm keen." His entire face became red. "I'm not shamed to be a nancy boy. And—and if you know another gent wh-who wants to pamper a lad like you do our Michael—I *am* keen, sir. Very keen. Or—" He took a deep breath and said the next very quickly. "Or if you and Michael ever want a bit of sport with a lad, I'm keen there as well. Just wanting you to know, sir. How very keen I am."

Wes had no idea what to say to this. He simply nodded and stammered, "Th-Th-Thank you," exhaling a quiet sigh of relief as the lad bowed and hurried from the room.

A soft, sleepy laugh came from the sofa, and when Wes turned toward the sound, Michael was awake.

"Peter's a good lad," he said quietly, his voice still sleep-rough. "A bit too naive, but he's a good lad. Rodger's very careful with who beds him. He has quite a crush on me, but I've never been able to stomach the idea of indulging him of an evening. He's barely older than I was when—" He cut himself off, his smile fading, and his gaze lowered to the floor. "Well. Let's just say I have no taste for young boys in bed."

Wes stared after Peter with new eyes, suddenly envisioning his nephew. He felt slightly ill. Clearing his throat, he shook the image away.

"Sit," Michael urged him, tucking his feet as he sat up. "You look like hell, darling. Did your party keep you up too late? You could have given me your regrets, you know."

Wes smiled blackly and collapsed into the space Michael made for him. The cushions of the sofa creaked and bounced at his abrupt arrival. He tried to summon a dismissive response, but the disjointed shards of memory flashed before his eyes before piercing his heart, and he swallowed hard.

"Albert?" Michael called softly.

Shaking his head, Wes tried for a brittle laugh, but he choked on it. Panic rose on a tide inside him. He saw his nephew's hollow face, heard his brother's disdainful rebuke, his father's flat dismissal.

"Albert?" Michael touched Wes's arm.

Wes swallowed, barely managing to push the lump down this time. He pinched the bridge of his nose and took a deep breath. Only the terror of falling to pieces in front of Michael kept him in check. Weeping like a child was bad enough, but to do it *now*? He bit his tongue, willing the shock of iron taste to jolt him back. He brushed Michael's hand from his arm and fumbled against his waistcoat.

"P-p-p-p—" Self-revulsion flooded his system, and

the fury gave him the push he needed to find the word. "Pills. In my p-p-pocket."

The sweet scent of Michael's hair filled his nose. Long, deft fingers pressed against his abdomen, poked gently at him. He heard the soft *crack* of the pill case as it opened.

"How many?" Michael asked softly.

All of them. Drug me senseless. Wes's nostrils flared, and he took several unsteady breaths. "Three."

The case rattled, then snapped shut. "I'll fetch some water."

"N-N-N-No." Wes opened his eyes and fumbled for Michael's hand. "D-D-Don't n-n-nee-nee-nee—"

He stopped abruptly as first one, then two, then three pastilles pressed past his lips. Suppressing a shudder of anticipation, Wes rolled them on his tongue and shut his eyes as he swallowed. *Should have chewed them*, he thought, too late, but then he felt the gentle brush of lips against his. When he opened his eyes on a long, slow blink, Michael was there before him, his face only inches away, looking at him with tender concern.

I love you.

For the first time in his life he was relieved for his stammer. The words clanged at the back of his throat, not even making it to his tongue. But they echoed in his head, ridiculous and true. *I love you. I love you. I love you, Michael Vallant, my beautiful whore. Run away with me. Marry me. I will buy you every book in the world.*

Laughing at himself, he shut his eyes again.

When Michael brushed sweet, dry kisses against each lid, his heart turned over.

Michael stroked his cheeks. "I take it the party did not go well."

Wes sighed roughly and shook his head.

Michael's hands slid down to stroke his neck. Softly, almost absently. "I've been dreaming again. Remembering." His fingernails curled briefly against Wes's skin. "I hate it. It makes me feel weak. I thought I left these ghosts so long ago, but now they are back, laughing at me." He pressed a kiss to Wes's chin. "What happened to you, my love?"

Wes opened his eyes, staring at the abruptly blurry ceiling. "W-W-Waste." This time he could not swallow the lump. "S-S-Said I was a w-waste." He shut his eyes as the opium reached up and embraced him, easing the pain. "G-G-Good for n-n-nothing. D-D-Disgrace." He remembered Edwin, and this pain even the opium could not contain. Tears slid into his hair, and his voice was thick with more at the ready. "T-T-Told m-m-my n-n-nephew. N-N-Not t-t-to en-en-en-end up l-l-l—" He broke off, letting the rest out on a shuddering sigh.

Not to end up like me.

This time he could not stop a sob and, despite the opium, it carried him away on the wave, this sorrow. He covered his eyes, but the damned tears streamed on. He tried to breathe, but he choked. Michael cooed gently and stroked his shoulders, and Wes hissed in disgust as he sat up and pushed him away.

"T-T-True," he sputtered. "It's t-t-t-true." He shut his eyes tight and hung his head. Idiot. *Idiot.*

The firm hand on his chin caught him by surprise. He went slack enough for it to lift his face, and the sight of Michael staring at him with such a hard expression made him still.

"You mean something to me." One corner of his mouth quirked in a flat smile. "Though perhaps I'm nothing too?"

Wes touched Michael's cheek.

You are everything.

Michael shut his eyes and leaned into Wes's palm. Beautiful. So beautiful. So precious.

"I'm so tired," Michael whispered.

Wes stroked the line of his jaw with his thumb. "Sleep."

Michael laughed, letting his head fall against Wes's shoulder.

Wes kissed the side of his head. Dizzy with opium, he swung his feet up onto the sofa and adjusted Michael carefully against his body. Michael snuggled in, hesitantly at first, but with one encouraging stroke from Wes down his back, he burrowed in like a ground squirrel, positioning himself between Wes's thighs, pillowing his head on Wes's chest, tucking his arm beneath his back. Wes adjusted as well, and then Michael adjusted again, and eventually they were comfortable and still.

Michael turned his head enough to press a kiss

against Wes's chest. "You are good for *me*."

Wes swallowed a different kind of lump, a full, radiant blockage rather than a hollow one. *I love you. I love you like a fool. I would give up all the orchids in the world just to lie for an afternoon like this with you.*

He shut his eyes and stroked Michael's hair.

He floated away on the opium, dreaming of pink clouds and rays of sun he could catch with his fingers. They briefly faded as someone stuck a pillow beneath his head. Michael nuzzled his chest, the afghan was tucked in place around them, and then he fell back into the dream, holding Michael's hand and laughing as they leapt naked through the clouds, swinging around the beams of sunlight and riding them up to the stars.

Chapter Nine

THANKS TO MICHAEL, the week after the dinner party, instead of marking the beginning of a black funk, ushered in a period of almost idyllic bliss. The habit became, after rising, breakfasting, and seeing to any needs at the gardens, Wes would take a day's worth of pills along and head over to Dove Street, where a bleary Michael would welcome him with a kiss before settling down with him on the couch in Barrows's office to nap. If Barrows's office was busy, they went off in Wes's coach and drove around town, or found a quiet space to park the carriage.

And there was kissing. There was always a great deal of kissing.

They hadn't kissed that first afternoon as they slept together on the sofa, not until the evening bustle began when Wes became unnerved by the noise. Michael shooed him away, looking rested and happy, and as he'd sent him out the door, he'd pressed a kiss to Wes's lips. It was meant to be chaste and quick, but it surprised Wes so much that he lingered. And then it was done, but it seemed heavy between them. It lingered all night until he arrived the next morning, at which point Michael met him in the foyer, pulled him into a dark corner, pressed his back to the wall and kissed him full on the mouth. By the time the kiss ended they were both hard and breathless. And smiling.

And so it was every day: Wes would arrive, they would kiss and then they began a long day of nothing. Michael would nap on him, and Wes would review notes from the gardens or read the paper or one of Michael's books, and then they would drive. While they rode about town, Michael climbed into his lap and made love to his mouth.

That was all. Sometimes Michael ran his hands over Wes's chest, but mostly they kissed. Wes could embrace him, could run his hands up and down his back, could, sometimes, thread fingers into his hair, but if he slid his hands over Michael's backside or ran them over his thighs, Michael shuddered and pulled back.

"I'm sorry." He buried his forehead against Wes's neck. "I don't know what's happening to me."

Wes wanted to tell him he didn't mind, but he settled for brushing a kiss against his ear. When Michael eased, Wes resumed stroking his back, but in a gentling, not arousing manner. Michael ended up curled up beside him with his head in his lap, sleeping heavily for an hour.

At each outing they made sweet love like tender

young fools meeting in the meadow in some sort of fairytale. Wes found that he cherished it more than if they had fucked every afternoon. Certainly Michael seemed to be blossoming beneath it. He said he hadn't had a nightmare since their ritual began.

Barrows, however, was less convinced. He frequently worked in his office while Michael slept draped over Wes, and he did a lot of glowering.

"This isn't a workable solution," he grumbled on the third day as Michael slept. "Ignoring the fact that I have to do my business in the drawing room, you'll notice he can't do this in a bed with you. Only in your carriage or in here."

Wes had noticed. He said nothing, though, only stroked Michael's pale hair as he slept. He didn't know what to do about it. When Michael curled up beside him, when he smiled at him, when he pressed his mouth to Wes's own, he could forget everything his brother or father ever said to him, every slight he received at the Society, every whisper at the club. But yes, beneath this veneer it all still lurked, just as Barrows said. This wasn't a solution. Like everything else in his life, it was a panacea, an escape. He couldn't fix anything but a dying plant.

When the heaviness of this realization got the better of him, he reached into his pocket for his pill pouch and took two. He'd have taken three, but it had been barely two hours since his last dose, and it was getting harder and harder to find the line between mental ease and unconsciousness. He popped the pills in his mouth, closed his eyes, and rolled the pastilles on his tongue, working up enough saliva to swallow them, but also anticipating—hoping for—a moment of bliss as well.

Once he opened his eyes, from the corner of his vision he saw Barrows lean back in his chair, watching Wes. Barrows's face was closed and unreadable. "You're chasing the dragon."

Wes blinked at him, genuinely confused.

Barrows rolled his eyes and grimaced. "God above. You don't even *know* you're chasing the dragon. I suppose a kindly doctor sends you to your bliss, does he?"

The pills. Barrows was speaking of his pills. Wes faltered. "F-F-For-For m-m-my n-n-n—"

"Nerves?" Barrows finished for him acidly. He shook his head in disgust.

Wes felt his cheeks burn. "I c-c-c-can't f-f-f-fun-function w-w-w-without them."

Barrows stared at Wes very hard, his piercing gaze making Wes squirm despite the opium. "I take men out of the gutter every day, my lord, and give them new life. Drunks. Washed-out sailors. Street whores. Any man or woman with a spark left, I tell them, come to Dove Street, and you won't go hungry again, and you'll fuck who you like for real money. We bring in girls who were mothers at thirteen and traded their cunts for a crust of bread, teach them manners and self-respect, and they go on to be maids in decent households or run pubs with their men or retire happy and sated after making themselves a tidy sum on their mattress. I train lads how to steal and not get hanged, who to steal from, and what to do with the stash. I turn street thugs into my thugs, and they're loyal as the day is long. I make ten silk purses out of sows' ears before breakfast each day." His voice hardened. "But as soon as I smell the poppy, I leave them be. Dragon claws are sharp, and they quickly steal what little spark a body has left."

Wes flushed at this, not a blush on his cheeks but a hot rush over his whole body, an odd mix of insult and cold fear. He wanted to argue, to explain to Barrows that it wasn't for pleasure that he took the pills, but for medicine. He wanted to insist no dragon had claws in him, that he hadn't had a spark to steal to begin with. But he could not. Because even as the defiance tried to rise, it drowned in guilt. Guilt that he knew he had long ago left the dose recommended to him by his physician—and had yet to confess this to his medical guardian. Guilt that he hardly waited for true anxiety any longer, dosing himself higher and higher to keep the empty feelings at bay, always hoping for that softening of the edges of the world that he could rarely get any longer, which only severely upping the dose would do.

Which sometimes he did at night, just so he could lie back on his bed and ride away on the rainbow tides of soft, careless pleasure.

Barrows said nothing more on the matter, simply returned to his work with grim determination. His words echoed in Wes's head for two days, however, and one afternoon, having left Michael curled in the window seat of Barrows's office with a new book Wes had brought him as a present, Wes went not to his apartment but to the east side of town, to the docks, to the street where he had meant to meet Legs but had met Penelope Brannigan instead.

He rapped hesitantly on her door. A white-capped old woman ushered him inside, but Miss Brannigan herself rose from a chair beside an invalid on a sofa and hurried over to greet him.

"Lord George," she exclaimed, beaming at him. "What a lovely surprise." Her smile nearly split her face. "What brings you here today, sir?"

Having no idea himself, Wes could only sputter helplessly for a moment before giving up and sliding his gaze away. It helped him not at all that he had done his best to refrain from extra pills all day and the result was he felt so raw and exposed he wouldn't be surprised to learn the skin had come free of his spine, letting all the sensations of the world rush at once into his brain.

His silence didn't seem to upset her. She only smiled and held out her hand. "Come, my lord. Come have some tea."

He let her take his hand, let her lead him to a comfortable chair beside the fire, even though he felt very foolish doing so, as if he were a little boy she had found on the street and was tucking in for some comfort. The thought prompted him to glance around looking for the young man he had seen when he'd visited a few weeks ago. He was in the same place he had been then, even wearing the same clothes. He did not cast a single glance at Wes, and he appeared to be taking great care to do so. Other than the boy, the room was empty, save the white-capped old woman who settled in a rocking chair near the front window, taking some sewing from a basket and losing herself in it at once. The room was quiet and warm, the only sounds the click of the young man's chess pieces, the creak of the old woman's rocker and the crackle of the fire.

Wes wanted to speak, to explain to Miss Brannigan why he had come, or at least to invent some reason, but even in the gentleness of her parlor he found himself tongue-tied. After a few sputters, he gave up and sank back in his chair.

She smiled comfortingly at him. "There, my lord. No need to upset yourself. It's a long journey from your part of town to mine. Take some tea and collect yourself a moment." She stationed herself in the chair across from him. For a few minutes she let him steep in quiet, and then she began a comforting but endless prattle. "The donation your man sent over was most kind. I used it to pay our rent for the next several months, with leftover enough to take the children to

Covent Garden for some ices. Some of them. We have six children here, you see. Four boys and two girls. We could have more easily, God knows, for the streets are littered with homeless children, but I've found six is about all I can manage at once, and even then sometimes that is too many. Difficult, sometimes, knowing the ones I let go will come to bad ends. But better to do what can be done with a few than do badly by many. This is what I tell myself."

She smiled a little sadly. "I find ones who are damaged, you see. Stammerers, sometimes, but sometimes they don't speak at all. Everyone deals with tragedy in different ways. And as I tell them, it doesn't matter to me how one gets out of a hole, just so long as they get out of it and go about their business." She reached for her own cup of tea. "Though to be honest, I do better with older children, or adults. You would think they are more difficult, and it's true. But the honest truth is that I've had more practice helping addicts and full-grown lost souls."

She paused, then looked at Wes kindly. "Don't mind me, dear. I'll just keep prattling on until you feel comfortable enough to speak. Didn't see any reason not to fill you in a bit while I did so."

Wes blinked several times. She was a sort of female Rodger Barrows, he supposed, though she smiled more. Somehow he doubted she also ran an illegal smuggling ring on the side.

He cleared his throat and tried to manage his end

of the conversation a little better. "W-W-Why d-do y-you d-do this?"

"Why, because I'm a silly American. Wasn't it obvious?" She laughed. "To be honest, I can't even sort it out myself. I began nursing one addict, but I lost her. In a sort of stupid grief I simply went out and got myself another. She lived, and for a time that was enough. She kept house for me, and I tried to decide what to do with my life next. Somehow that became helping another, and then another. And then we discovered a pack of urchins living behind our bins in the alley, and of course I brought them in and fed them, and of course they stole anything worth taking once I was asleep." She looked pensive. "I suppose it's gone that way with everything. I ruin my first attempts, but I do all right on my second, and it becomes a habit after that." She shrugged. "That's all I have for an explanation. I didn't fit in at the salons of the other do-gooders, and I hated how we only talked of reform, yet actually achieved so little. It all comes together like a puzzle somehow, I suspect, when laid out on the table."

Simply listening to the woman made Wes dizzy. "H-How-How were y-you ever a st-st-sta-stammerer?"

He expected another laugh and saucy dismissal. But she did not laugh. Not even a smile cracked her lips. She turned to the old woman at the window. "Mrs. Howard, would you take Tommy upstairs?"

The woman looked up startled, but she nodded and

rose, moving with a lumbering, arthritic gait. "Of course, Miss Brannigan." With a whisper in the boy's ear, she helped him from his chair and nudged him toward the stairs. Once the door closed, Miss Brannigan turned back to Wes.

"It's a bit of a grim tale, Your Lordship. But if you truly want to hear it, I will tell it to you."

When Wes gave her a nod, she returned the gesture and smoothed her hands over her skirts.

"I was born in Chicago, but my parents had a yearning to head south, away from the snow. And so when I was five, we packed up a wagon and set off as adventurers. We got as far as Missouri." She kept her eyes on the fire. "We were overtaken by bandits. They murdered my father and raped my mother. Several times. My sister and I were hidden beneath the wagon, where Mother had told us to go if there was trouble. Mary had the shotgun, and after the third time they raped our mother, her cries tore at Mary, and she came out brandishing the weapon."

She shut her eyes. When she spoke, her words were little above a whisper. "Th-They r-raped her with it. They s-s-sodomized her with it until she bl-bled. Then they s-sodomized her themselves. And then my mother." She paused to take several more breaths, but she kept her eyes closed. "I stopped watching then. I c-couldn't take any more."

Wes wasn't sure he could either. *I'm sorry*, he wanted to say. Before he could muster the words she was speaking again, this time with her eyes open as she stared at the fire.

"My memory is faint past that point. I know from others' retelling that once the bandits were passed out from whiskey, my mother freed herself from the rope they'd used to tie her to the tree, and she killed them. She routed the wagon back to the road and drove us hard to St. Louis. And there we lived. Mother sold everything in the wagon, plus the wagon, and we rented a room. She did baking and sewing and charity work. We had money enough—we'd lived quite well in Chicago—but outside of sending Mary to school, she spent none of it. And we never spoke of that night on the road when Father was murdered and they were raped. Mary sobbed often at night, but other than smiling less, even she pretended nothing had happened. For myself, I simply didn't speak. For three years, I was mute. I have dim memories of it, of doctors examining me, of whispers that I had been damaged. That's all, however. I don't remember why I didn't speak. Just that I wouldn't.

"And then when I was eight, a carnival came to town. Mother took me. I remember a bright red tent and rainbow ribbons streaming from it. I wanted so desperately to go inside, but Mother was heading the wrong way, and the next thing she knew I was sobbing and crying, 'Tent! R-Red tent!' And she sobbed as well, and hugged me, and bought me a ticket to the tent. They had a lion inside, in a cage. It looked sad."

She sighed and smoothed her skirts. "And so then I spoke again. Stuttering horribly, but I could speak. Mother kept me at home for fear teasing from schoolgirls would make me stop speaking again, but she taught me well, not just to read and write and do sums but to cook and clean and care for things. I was her shadow on her charity work, which often took us to alms houses. She was particularly tender to the women there, and she would sit and listen to their stories. And then when I was thirteen she took fever, and everything went poorly again.

"Our aunt came to fetch us back to Chicago, but she was hard and slightly cruel to Mary—and Mary ran away the second we arrived. Aunt Millicent only cared for the money that came with us, and she happily spent it and left me with her mother. Though this in the end turned out to be a blessing. Nana Fairchild was a lovely old soul. It was she who taught me how to overcome my stutter. She let me sleep in her room and even in her bed when I woke crying. She finished my lessons and convinced her daughter she was responsible for my education, and she saw that I was sent to a good finishing school. She outlived my aunt as well, by six months. And when she died I was of age, and all our family's money was mine. I used it to find my sister—and I spent nearly all of it to do so, landing all the way over here in England." She smoothed her hands over her skirts. "And that, Your Lordship, is how I came to be a stutterer. Stammerer, of course, as you say."

Wes's tea had grown cold, forgotten in his slack hands. "I h-h-have n-nothing s-s-so g-g-grim." Lord help him, but he felt a fool beside her. Who had troubles such as hers?

"I should say," she went on, "that not every stammerer has a tale of woe. I don't want you to assume so. Something in your eyes, however, insists that you do. And I want you to feel comfortable telling me, which is why I tell you mine. Do you know, everyone who tells me their tale begins as you did: 'it isn't so bad.' As if they should be ashamed for letting it affect them, as if everyone in the world has better right to sorrow than they." She shrugged. "Life is pain, Lord George. We all deal with it as we can. Some of us feel safer swallowing our voices. Some of us hide in our anger. I prefer not to judge the method of coping but to do what I can to help others let go of the pain."

She let him digest this, taking his teacup from his hands and reaching for the pot to refill it.

"I think," she said, her tone light once again, "we should touch only on pleasant subjects from here on today, sir, but I do hope you will come visit me tomorrow? Or would another time be better?"

She added milk and a sugar to his tea and passed it over. Wes sipped absently, still reeling. But after a few moments he said, "F-F-Friday. At t-t-ten. W-W-Would it s-s-suit you?"

Her smile split to show pretty, even teeth. "It suits me very well, Your Lordship." She took up her own cup of tea and sat back. "Now you tell *me*, sir, about your plants. Because from what I have learned, you are famous for them."

Wes laughed. After another sip of tea he was still smiling. And as he launched into an explanation of the Royal Society and the gardens at Regent's Park, he realized he was scarcely stammering at all.

BY THE THIRD week of seeing Albert, Michael began to feel impatient. With himself, with Albert—he wasn't sure of the source, but he couldn't seem to shake the sense that more should be happening. His nightmares had stopped. He had, twice, napped in his own bed, alone. He felt ready for something more. For congress, possibly. Their last few carriage rides had left them both breathless and flushed and rock hard. Kisses had become only the opening act. They soon gave way to fondling beneath waistcoats and groping trousers. Their hair knew no mercy. Their necks were banquets. Any second now Michael suspected he would undo Albert's trousers and reacquaint himself with his lover's cock with the same sort of passion. He simply hadn't quite done so yet.

Albert hadn't ever pushed him to do so, nor to let him have the same pleasure, the pleasure he was, in fact, paying for. In fact, he made no moves of a sexual nature without Michael's express permission, and sometimes even then he had to give him a second encouragement. Though once that was settled, he clearly had no reservations of any kind.

It wasn't just sexual encounters Michael was starting to want. He longed to *do* things with Albert and not tour another bloody garden. He'd managed to get Albert into a bookstore, once. That hadn't been so bad, but Albert had merely waited near the door looking uncomfortable, not browsing with Michael as he'd hoped he would. Forget coffeehouses, and never speak of pubs. Albert simply went white and shook his head when Michael mentioned them.

The thought of taking him to Covent Garden was laughable.

Actual gardens, however, or parks, were fine, and any day the weather was good enough, they toured them. And they were lovely, true. It was only that Michael wanted something more. Something… Something…

Something normal.

He let this revelation rattle around in his head as he stared at his own reflection in a mirror, getting ready for yet another day with Albert. Yes, normal. That was what he wanted. A foolish yen, most likely, and yet no amount of chastising himself kept the desire away. Perhaps *that* was what he was in love with, what Rodger saw.

Normal had evaporated so long ago, and the joke was that even then Michael had struggled for it. He hadn't thought about his school days in years, but every time he was with Albert he couldn't help but remember what it had been like to stride about London as a normal boy, wondering how he could swindle his mother out of more sweets or a new book. He'd closed his heart to that boy so long ago, not letting him out, for the world Michael lived in now was too grim for him. But with Albert, the boy, now a man, always wanted to come out to play. With Albert, Michael wanted to explore London. To share books. To delight in things. And yes, sometimes they did. But all too often just as Michael felt that boy inside him rising from his sleepy corner, ready to play again, Albert was coming up against his own terror of public places and shutting down.

Michael stroked his reflection in the glass. He had a pretty face, he knew. A boyish, pretty face. Many, many men had told him so, had traced the outline of his lips, praising the beauty of their line before nibbling on them as if they were a rare delicacy. When he worked, he made sure to rouge them slightly, and he powdered his face, smoothing and whitening it. His hair was always loose and down, as pampered as a girl's.

But not with Albert. When he prepared himself to spend the day with Albert, he applied no rouge and no powder. His hair went back into a queue, leaving bits on top to style with pomade, and each time he prepared himself he wished he could cut it and give himself a modern style.

Normal. A normal style for normal outings.

He finished his toilet, tugged on his jacket and shoes, and headed downstairs to wait for Albert. He had been coming later and later, explaining that a project was keeping him through most of the mornings. More and more lately he seemed to welcome their naps as much as Michael. Except today Michael didn't want to collapse in Rodger's office, nor did he want to doze as they drove around town. Today Michael had a plan.

When Albert finally arrived, Michael drew a deep breath, steeled himself, and asked, "Could we go to the Athenaeum today?"

He had worked out the phrasing of this carefully, but even now he had to bite his tongue almost literally to keep from tacking on softeners. He wanted to brush this off as a casual, almost random request, but it was not. He'd been waiting for Albert to suggest this himself since they'd first discussed it weeks ago, but he had not once so much as brought it up again. This was another case where that boy inside him had come out again, desperate and eager, determined to let no one and nothing take away his pleasure.

The hardened, world-weary Michael who had spent over a decade whoring braced himself for a rejection. He tried not to look it. He tried to project easiness, as if he didn't really care, it was just a whim, but he suspected he failed.

Albert blinked at him. "M-My club? You w-w-want to g-go?"

Michael did his best to steady himself. "Yes. Please?"

He waited for the excuse, for the dismissal, for the awkwardness. Though Albert did look slightly uncomfortable, he only nodded and said, "Sh-Shall we g-g-go now?"

And they went. After all his preparation and fear, Michael found it hard to believe it had been this easy, but it was, and they were in the carriage and headed for Pall Mall.

Michael had only been to this part of town with Albert a few times when traffic routed them so. He had done his gawking then, trying to be casual until he'd realized the heavy traffic made Albert so uncomfortable he wouldn't notice. Michael was able to temper himself somewhat this time, though he still had to press his face to the glass like an eager child as they passed Trafalgar Square, St. Martin-in-the-Fields, and the line of gentlemen's clubs until at last they arrived at the Athenaeum.

It took every ounce of Michael's control to contain his giddiness. When he'd been a boy in school he'd boasted to the boys in his dormitory that he'd be a member of the Athenaeum one day. He'd wanted to be a scholar of books then, until his mother had pointed out a more practical career would be better. He'd decided to be a lawyer, but he would be the most *literary* lawyer London had ever seen. And he would belong to the Athenaeum, he'd bragged, and he'd take all his meals there, spending evenings he wasn't working on cases discussing the arts and sciences with the most brilliant minds in Britain.

He'd become a whore instead. Yet here he was, at the Athenaeum at last.

It was so *white*. So gleaming clean and classical and *white*, not even a pigeon dropping staining its marble stairs. He longed to crane his head and gape like a country bumpkin at the decorative frieze, but he managed to resist, looking as collected as he could as he followed Albert up the steps. When he felt his queue brush the back of his neck, he touched it self-consciously and tucked it into his collar. He would not play Albert's whore today. He would be a literary man, as he had wanted to be long ago. Just for today.

"Good afternoon, Your Lordship." The doorman welcomed them inside—and Michael gave up and gaped as he saw the foyer.

Grand didn't even begin to describe it. It wasn't ostentatious, either. It was simply…perfect. Elegant, aristocratic, clean, and spare. Great classical arches and curved ceilings with geometric relief contrasted marble statuary and grand tropical plants. Gas lamps burned everywhere, their soft hiss contrasting against the hushed sound of men's footsteps on the parquet. It smelled elegant as well: the gas, to start, but also the mixture of tobacco, sandalwood, and the distant whiff of scrubbed floors. Only a few men lingered in the main entrance, but in the distance he heard muted voices in conversation and laughter. Educated voices, trained in elocution.

Michael faltered, falling back.

Albert turned toward him immediately, looking concerned. "Everything all r-r-right?"

No, it wasn't. Michael tried not to glance around like a nervous cow in the slaughterhouse, but he couldn't help it. What had he been thinking? What on earth had possessed him to think he belonged here, even for a visit? And what if, God help him, he met a client? Rodger kept the *ton* well away from him, but not everyone here was upper class, were they? He ran a nervous hand over his hair.

A firm clasp stopped his arm from falling back down. He'd been so lost in his paranoia he was almost surprised to see it was Albert's grip that had caught him.

Albert smiled at him, a patient, kind, Albert sort of smile. The smile widened and reached his eyes as he nodded at the hall before them. He lowered Michael's arm and held on to his elbow a moment, squeezing it. The touch lingered once he let go, as if he were still holding Michael there as he walked them forward, remaining as close at Michael's side so that, indeed, he could have kept holding him.

Which, Michael realized, he likely would have were others not around to witness them. The thought warmed him deeply and propelled him forward, on into the hall.

It was without question the sort of place one went only if one belonged. The halls were a maze of doors, opening and closing to reveal men in various displays of fine dress. Upon peering discreetly inside one of the rooms, Michael saw men in their shirtsleeves—shirtsleeves rolled up—smoking cigars and drinking brandy and guffawing over something one of their peers had said. In others it appeared the men were conducting some sort of meeting, around a table and all. Other salons saw men grouped around fireplaces, chatting with one another in one and sitting silently together in another. Old men leaned back in chairs and napped with their mouths hanging wide open. Younger men read by windows or sat reviewing papers. Men, men everywhere, existing in pods and groups, united in station, divided by individual and unspoken selection.

In short, just like school had been.

Occasionally Albert offered quiet explanation of where they were, or what a portrait on the wall depicted. At one point they ended back up in the main foyer and headed up the stairs, where on the landing Michael saw a strange clock.

"Why does it have two sevens and no eight on the face?" he whispered to Albert as they finished ascending.

Albert's lips twisted into a wry smile. "N-No one knows. Has always b-been that way."

They toured some more, up and down different sets of stairs. Michael was now hopelessly lost and nearly asked if he could lie down in one of the bedrooms Albert had shown him and rest his dizzy head.

As if he had been working hard to avoid it, Albert took him to a set of double doors behind which could be heard a great deal of commotion and noise. It took him several attempts before he could begin to speak, and when he did, his voice was full of disdain.

"H-H-Here is the c-c-common room. M-Most m-m-members c-c-congregate within."

Michael tried not to laugh. "I take it not you, however?"

He snorted in derision. "D-D-Didn't care for the sch-sch-sch-schoolyard when I was there. D-D-Don't now either."

Now Michael could not stop a smile. "I thought it seemed like school as well. I mean—the whole club." His smile faded. "I had hoped it would be a kind of learned society. All the great minds are allegedly members here."

This seemed to make Albert thoughtful. "That m-m-might happen on oc-c-c-ccasion. But m-m-mostly it is p-p-peers p-p-posturing." He nodded at the doors. "W-Would you like a tour?"

"How can I resist, after such a billing?" After a subversive glance around the hall to be sure they were alone, he brushed his fingers against Albert's hand. "Thank you for showing me, Albert."

This earned Michael a smile, and he suspected had they been alone would have netted him a brush of a kiss as well.

The room was bigger than any of the others, and in truth it better fit the image of a gentlemen's club Michael had harbored. Men were gathered in pods at billiard tables, around the fireplace, at tables and in clusters of chairs, but there was an element of display here that had been absent from the private chambers. Only those at the billiard tables had stripped to shirtsleeves, but even they were not truly relaxed. Everyone was aware of everyone else or was boldly ignoring them. With a single sweeping glance Michael was able to spot the bully, the pack of buffoons, and several braggarts—some deserved with no ability to temper ego, some hiding fear of lack of worth in boasting. A second glance revealed the clusters of men who dealt with the noise of the others by leaning close to one another, ignoring them as much as possible. There were several groups of friends, probably grouped by discipline and social standing and sometimes simply by money. Of course there were the poor wallflowers, hovering at the fringes of sympathetic groups but never joining, or out-and-out stationed alone, alternating between trying not to look as if they noticed the others and trying not to let their depression get the best of them.

Yes. Precisely like the schoolyard.

Albert led them to a table by the window, near the door but far enough away from the loudest of the noise to give a weak reprieve. He indicated for Michael to sit, not seating himself until his guest was settled. Even then it was clear he wouldn't be able to fully relax in the room. Michael felt guilty, knowing he was the cause—clearly Albert generally favored one of the smaller salons. Before he could work out an apology, a handsome young servant came up to them, smiling brightly in greeting.

"Welcome, Lord George. Would you like your usual this afternoon?" When Albert nodded, the servant turned to Michael. "And for your guest?"

Michael froze, having no idea what exactly was happening. Was the man taking drinks? Food orders? Bringing the newspaper? He dared a panicked glance at Albert.

Albert's eyebrow quirked before a flash of understanding, but both expressions had barely registered on his face before he wiped it clean and addressed the servant again. "The s-s-same. But with a p-p-p-plate of scones."

"Very good, my lord." The servant gave a bow as befit his station and Albert's before weaving his way through the room toward a door at the back.

A loud shout across the room made Albert wince. He tried to wipe his face clean and sit easily back in his chair, but the extraordinary care his host took in appearing relaxed gave him away.

"We don't need to stay here," Michael said. "I've seen the common room. We can go elsewhere if you'd rather."

This only seemed to embarrass Albert. "N-N-No. I'll be f-f-f-fine." He forced a little more ease, slouched in his seat and threaded his fingers across his chest. "H-H-How did you sleep last n-n-night?"

This was a question Albert asked every day of him, without fail. Michael smiled. "Well. I nodded off in Rodger's office around three, and at nine I went up and finished the last few hours in my own bed." He rubbed his cheek ruefully. "I wish I dared try beginning there."

"P-P-P-Progress takes t-t-time." The way Albert phrased it had Michael thinking he was repeating it from somewhere else, speaking to himself as much as Michael.

A sharp crack from the billiard table startled them both, but the chorus of male shouts of delighted surprise that followed made Albert jerk again, and much harder. He paled and shut his eyes, swearing through his stammer under his breath.

Michael checked his reach for Albert a hairsbreadth from his wrist. He rested his hand on the armchair beside Albert and let his thumb brush briefly, lovingly over the back of his lover's hand instead. "Albert," he whispered. "Albert, there is no need to stay here and torture yourself."

For a moment Michael thought he would argue, but then Albert nodded. Grimly. Rising shakily, he gestured for Michael to precede him to the door.

"What of your order?" Michael said, glancing back to where the servant had disappeared. "Should we let someone know where we are going?"

Albert stopped and blinked. He looked completely surprised at the thought. Recovering, he shrugged. "They'll f-f-find us," he said with confidence.

And here, Michael realized, was a true gentleman. A man born of a marquess and not a whore. A man who left a room with every confidence that his order would follow him wherever he went within his club. Michael couldn't decide if he was amused, irritated, or envious.

Likely it was a bit of all three.

They weaved through the maze again. More men were in the hall this time, and several nodded to Albert, though most of them did so stiffly. Michael began to study the odd reaction, unable to place it. They were aloof but attempting not to look so. This wasn't any playground maneuver. This was a complicated mix of respect, revulsion, and…fear? It didn't make any sense.

At the end of a hall, Albert stopped at another set of double doors, though this one promised to open into silence, or something at least distinctly more hushed than the common room. He paused before opening them, his hand on the knob. He turned his head back to glance at Michael, looking grim.

"M-My ap-p-pologies," he said.

Now it was Michael's turn to be baffled. "What for?"

A parade of emotions crossed his face in the seconds he struggled with speech. After four false starts, he gritted his teeth, shut his eyes, and exhaled an angry breath. "F-F-For n-n-n-not being n-n-n-normal."

Even butchered, the words went straight to Michael's soul. God in heaven, he wished he could grip Albert's face and push him against the door in a ferocious kiss. He smiled instead. "But, darling. Normal is so very *tedious.*"

His pulse fluttered like a trapped butterfly at Albert's answering smile. Oh, but for a shadowed alcove and a downstairs distraction.

"You l-l-like b-b-books," Albert said, clearly hoping for confirmation.

The butterfly flapped its wings with more sensual languor now. "No, Albert. I *adore* books."

Albert nodded as if this pleased him very much. "Th-Then you should l-l-like this." He opened the doors with quiet flourish. Stepping aside, he revealed the step-down entrance to a large, long room whose walls were filled floor to ceiling with books. "Th-This is the Athen-n-n-naeum's library."

Michael could not move. Not until that butterfly inside him flapped hard enough to propel him forward, taking him inside, down the stairs, onto the thick carpet that hushed his steps. His steps into the library. The Athenaeum's library.

"Oh my," he whispered, his voice shaking. And then he did not speak at all, only walked in a daze along the shelves, hand shaking, blood pounding, soul soaring.

Chapter Ten

WATCHING MICHAEL LOSE himself in the Athenaeum's library, Wes decided, was a pleasure second only to making love to him.

It amused him, in a delighted way, to see how completely his guest forgot him as he wandered about the room, remembering him only when he found a particularly amazing volume and had to share his amazement. Michael didn't register the servant's entrance into the room with their refreshments either, and several attempts to point out his tea was going cold went unheard as well. Wes gave up and enjoyed his lover's enjoyment.

The only mar on the moment was the fact he was still shaking, which meant that more than the raucousness of the common room was upsetting him, that as Miss Brannigan had warned him, he was beginning to feel the effect of withdrawal from the opiates. He had not cut them out entirely, but he had reduced his dosage significantly, and it was beginning to affect him. In an attempt to deflect temptation, he had only brought the usual dose for late afternoon, which he wasn't due to take for another two hours.

"When yearning for the drug seizes you, remind yourself why you are trying to turn away from it." This had been Miss Brannigan's advice, and it was, he would admit, sound. In fact, the very reason he wanted to break opium's hold on him had shed his jacket and was enthusiastically mounting a ladder to investigate a higher shelf. Wes had already been wary of his increasing dependence on the drug, of how his options seemed to be paranoid bouts of the shakes or complete stupefaction. Having Rodger, Michael's self-declared guardian, see this fine line and doubt his ability to walk it, had been what propelled him to try and manage himself better. But it was Michael, the joy of him, the desire to be with him not just here but everywhere—that was what drove him.

To his shame, he found that when the drug gripped him like this, not even Michael was enough deterrent, for the opium had found its own voice, and it whispered to him now.

Where do you think this is going, this affair? Your sponsored month is nearly up. What do you propose to do, set him up in a house and visit him as a normal man would his mistress? You would both be hanged.

Wes's hands tightened on the arms of his chair. He'd sponsor another month.

The opium kept whispering to him. *You think he will*

still want you? What could he possibly see in you? You saw his eyes in the common room. He loved it as much as you detest it. He loves opera too—you think you can stomach such a crush without me? What of Covent Garden? He mentioned it once as a joke, but there was longing in his eyes. He is already restless of the type of entertainment you can stand. Now you want to make yourself more vulnerable? Fool!

Within a half an hour of their entrance to the library, Wes broke and took the dose early. It wasn't nearly enough, but it did take the barest of edges off his nerves and allowed him to force a smile when Michael eventually returned to sit beside him, breathless.

"Albert, it's simply the most amazing library I've ever seen." His cheeks were flushed with color, and his eyes danced with light. "They have everything. Everything in the world, and more, somehow, I swear. And some of them signed. *Dickens.* Three signed volumes by *Dickens.*"

"H-H-He is a m-m-member," Wes said, then added, "P-P-Perhaps w-w-we shall b-b-bump into him."

Michael's hands flew to his mouth, and his eyes widened. "Oh—*oh.* I—Albert, I wouldn't know what to say. I'm sure I'd look like a complete simpleton." But he looked absolutely giddy at the prospect of meeting the author. It made Wes want to pen a note to the man at once and invite him to dinner.

Why would a celebrated author accept the invitation of the Marquess of Daventry's damaged son? New waves of anxiety passed over Wes, and he began to shake again. Michael noticed.

"Darl—Albert," he amended hastily, biting off the endearment as he glanced at the library's few other occupants. "Are you unwell?" He dared a discreet stroke of Wes's knee. "Perhaps you should take some of your medicine."

Yes, Albert. Why don't you? Why didn't you bring more?

Wes shut his eyes as he drew a breath to steady himself. It took him three tries to break into his voice. "I'm f-f-fine. Th-Th-Thank you."

Michael didn't appear convinced. "Perhaps we should get you home. You should rest."

Wes wanted to argue with him, but the truth was he was now so rattled by withdrawal he could barely speak. Eventually he gave in, and within a mere three hours of having collected Michael, he was now returning him to Dove Street.

Back in his own rooms, he paced in agitation for another hour before he gave in and took enough opiate to render him unconscious.

He confessed his failure the next morning with Miss Brannigan. Though he'd expected chastising from her, she surprised him by projecting only empathy.

"Setbacks are expected," she told him as she poured what had become their ritual tea. It was something herbal, not proper British black, and the grassy scent of it had yet to seem palpable to him. "In my experience, it's best to work hard to avoid setbacks, but when they occur, it's wise to forgive one's self and move on."

Wes tried not to make a face. His irritation, however, he could not stow. "It's qu-quite one thing to th-th-th-theorize over addiction and an-n-n-nother to experience it."

She raised an amused eyebrow at him. "I agree. Nevertheless, if your goal is to be free, focusing on the difficulty of the task will not aid you. Only working toward freeing yourself will." She took a sip of her tea. "For the record, it isn't just the drug, I think, whispering to you, telling you that you need it. It's your own fears and sense of desperation trying to keep you from stumbling out into danger, which to your mind is anything that exposes you. Destructive as the opiate is, it feels safer than the alternative."

Wes stared at her, unnerved. How had she known about the voices?

She smiled at him in her kind, patient way. "Before we do exercises today, I believe it's time we delve into some of your history, since these fears seem to be holding great sway with you now. Have you given any further thought to what might have caused the onset of your stutter?"

No, he hadn't, and he had no intention of doing so. "I d-d-don't wish to discuss my p-p-past."

The eyebrow again. He longed to pluck it out. "You have state secrets, my lord, you must preserve?"

He glared at her. "I w-w-was shy. R-R-Reserved. I h-h-had no f-f-friends. They th-th-threatened to send me to a m-m-mental ward. Th-This isn't r-r-reason enough?"

She tilted her head slightly and regarded him with new thoughtfulness. "Except they didn't threaten to commit you until *after* you began stuttering. Yes?"

Wes paused, first confused, and then angry. He had a vague sense that it was irrational, but the thought was easily displaced with the tide. How dare she. Stupid American upstart. If this was not enough, before he could gather himself to give her a piece of his mind, she spoke again, carrying on in the same mild tone as if she had no idea how offensive she was being, prying into his life like this.

"You say you had no friends. Was there a period where that changed? Did you have friends at a previous point, and then things shifted?" She finally seemed to realize he was offended and gentled further. "It isn't my intention to pry into your life. I merely wish to find that moment where things changed for you. And failing a defining moment, I hope to find a pattern. I've been accused of peddling female nonsense and much more colorful things, but I do believe there is some merit in examining our pasts. For myself, it wasn't as if I decided to stop speaking. Certainly I don't remember any such thing. All I remember is being afraid—afraid, and guilty. Afraid somehow I would do or say something that would make horrible, bad things happen again. Afraid that this time they would happen to me. Afraid that I would be spared again, and this time someone would think to be angry with me for not suffering along with them. And none of this of course was even conscious. Just a demon following me wherever I went."

She reached out, tentatively, and placed her hand on the side of Wes's chair, almost touching his knee, but there was nothing remotely sexual in the advance. If it was anything, it was motherly. "Do you have such a demon, my lord?"

Wes stared at her. He didn't know where his rage had gone. He suspected it had evaporated as he'd huddled again with her beneath a wagon in the dark, in the terrified space inside his mind. No, she wasn't poking. She'd suffered beyond anything he'd ever heard, except perhaps Michael, though it was a bit like asking which was worse, cutting off both legs or both arms. Yes, she knew demons. She knew that cold fear, worrying what might come, worrying that one should have done differently, worrying that one might be found out, that they might know—

The room, already still and quiet, seemed to darken at the edges of his vision, and an odd ringing began in his ears as the old, sludgy memory surfaced.

"One," he managed at last, stumbling w-w-w-w-wuh over the word for almost twenty seconds. She sat through the whole of it, patiently, undisturbed by his struggle. Which perhaps was why the rest came much easier. "One d-d-demon."

She didn't look eager. She didn't look apprehensive.

She only looked like Penelope Brannigan, ridiculously patient, kind and eager to listen. To his surprise, Wes found himself willing to speak to her.

"When I was a small b-boy," he began, "just seven years old, a b-burglar broke into our house while I was at home. My n-nurse had fallen asleep, and I had crept off to the library to r-read. A corner by the window boasted a strange little n-nook made by remodeling some thirty years p-prior. The carpenter had simply used a f-false board to cover the gap, and he did not nail it into p-p-place. If I removed it and h-hid it behind the curtain, I could settle inside with an old b-blanket and a few pillows." He smiled, lost in the memory, seeing the space so vividly in his mind's eye. "It was m-my favorite place."

His smile faded. "The burglar, h-h-however, came in through the w-w-window beside me—there was no h-hiding from h-him. I suppose he had expected easy p-p-pickings. The library isn't far from the b-b-butler's p-pantry, and with my p-parents away, they had let most of the st-st-staff take h-h-holiday. My b-b-brother was at school, so it was just my n-nurse left with me at h-home. Who would suspect a thief in m-m-midday with servants still about? But there I was, upsetting his p-p-plans."

Wes stared off into the darkness of a corner of the room. "I r-r-remember that he had a knife. I r-r-remember it glinting in front of my face. I r-r-remember him threatening to c-c-cut m-me—" He shut his eyes, cheeks burning crimson. "I r-r-remember soiling my b-b-breeches. He l-laughed at me." Wes kept his eyes closed and went cold as he recalled the rest. This part took some doing to spit out. "Th-Then h-h-he-he t-t-told m-me he kn-kn-knew where m-my m-m-mama's r-r-room was, and if I w-w-wasn't a g-g-good b-b-boy and h-h-helped, he'd c-c-come b-back and c-c-cut her th-th-throat."

"Oh," Miss Brannigan cried. This time she didn't just place her hand on his knee—she reached for his hands and clasped them tenderly. "You poor boy. And you did, didn't you? You helped him to save your mother. Helped him rob your own house."

Wes had his eyes open again, but he was staring down at the carpet, eyes blurry. "T-T-Took him to all of it. H-Helped him f-f-find m-m-more than he ever c-c-could have alone." She had withdrawn from him as he began to speak, and he reached up to pinch the bridge of his nose. "He m-made me hide b-back in my c-c-corner. S-Said he would be w-w-watching. S-S-Said if they c-c-caught him h-he'd expose me and I'd h-h-hang with him."

She didn't give an outburst this time, but he could hear her fury in her exhale. It soothed him, in an odd way. He pressed on.

"Wh-When my father came home, he was in a r-rage. H-He was v-v-vicious to the staff, c-c-certain it had been an inside j-j-job. I l-l-lurked in the h-h-h-hallway, guilt t-t-t-tearing me ap-p-part." Memory caught him for a moment. He recalled that sick, terrible feeling, knowing that rage should be directed at him. Then came the rest, like lifting a dirty rock and finding worms. He shook a little. "Th-They d-d-decided it w-w-was the sc-sc-scullery boy. B-Beat him b-b-b-bloody. Kn-Knocked out t-t-teeth. N-N-Never kn-knew wh-what happened to him after. Just that he was g-g-gone."

Her hand touched his arm this time, just briefly, like a grounding wire. "And it was after this that it started?" she asked, after a lengthy period of silence. "Your stammer?"

He nodded. He wasn't sure, but he thought so. "N-Not right away. C-Came on s-s-slowly. F-F-Father scolded me for it. M-Made it w-w-worse. At school they t-t-teased m-m-me, m-m-more than b-b-before. T-Teachers s-s-said I w-w-w-was w-w-wrong in the h-h-head. M-M-Mother stood up for me." He let out a ragged, heavy sigh. "B-But th-then she was d-d-d-dead."

It sounded so pathetic, out loud. Like he was a silly child complaining about his lot. His mother had died in childbed: nothing extraordinary. Yet lost as he was in the past, it indeed felt, as it had then, like the most crushing blow the world could deal him. He'd been able to bear it then, but to have his one advocate, his one solace gone—the only person who had ever seemed to understand him, extinguished—it had been too much.

He had stammered after the burglary. After his mother's death was when he'd begun to withdraw.

"I h-had n-no friends," he whispered. He shook his head, staring unseeing at the carpet still. "N-Not before. N-Not after." He swallowed. "Not n-now." He let the words hang in the air for some time, a terrible confession. Part of him hoped she would say something. Offer pity. A cry of dismay. Laugh, even. But she remained quiet, and he couldn't look at her, and somehow he began speaking again. "M-My brother, for a w-w-while. When we were y-young. But I was too sh-shy for other b-boys. I d-didn't d-d-d—"

He stopped abruptly, going cold as he realized what he'd been about to say.

I didn't dare let them find out what it was I truly wanted of them.

Now he had to glance at her, and of course she was looking eager, encouraging. "You didn't what? Go on. It's all right. You can tell me."

"No." He almost barked the word. "No." Sliding back into his chair, regaining his posture, he shook his head. "N-No."

He braced himself, ready for her to goad it out of him—or to try, for he would *not* confess this, not to her, not to anyone—but she did not make the attempt. She only smiled that smile of hers and leaned back in her chair as well, though her posture was much more relaxed.

"That's enough for today, I imagine. Perhaps we

should end with more vocal exercises."

It must have been all the thinking of his youth, for Wes in honesty almost groaned aloud, like a boy at his lessons. He did not, however, and he did her exercises as instructed. "Maw-maw-maw-maw-maw. Moo-moo-moo-moo-moo." Covering his ears and reciting the alphabet at the top of his lungs as she banged on the piano in the corner in discordant clangs and slammed a cymbal against the top of it to add clatter off the beat. Repeating childish rhyming phrases with every word repeated. "The the the the rain rain rain rain fell fell fell fell on on on on the the the the plain plain plain plain." *Trying* to stammer. "T-T-T-T-T-Tickle. P-P-P-Pickle." He didn't know why they did any of it. It wasn't as if it had helped. Just as dragging up his past had not aided him in any way.

It made him angry. Helplessly, maddeningly angry.

When she called their session complete fifteen minutes early, he was relieved, and after stammering the barest of thanks and essential pleasantries, he reached for his coat. When he started for the front door, she stopped him and nodded toward the back of the house.

"There's one more exercise I'd like you to try, my lord. And to do it, we'll need to go to the alley."

He frowned at her, but more out of confusion than anything else. When she reached for a thick woolen shawl and headed into a hallway, he followed her.

She led him through the house, past closed doors

and cupboards, all the way to a set of stairs leading to a door which opened into a sort of crude garden. No plants of any sort grew here, and there was barely any rock to stop the mud. The small space was bordered all around by high walls of brick, wood, and wire—keeping it safe, he realized, from the more usual occupants of east London alleys. Even in its crudeness, there was an elegance about it. A table and chair sat to one side beneath a tarpaulin, a rough-framed child's painting hanging as decoration from the wall beside it. A much-patched ball sat beside bricks clearly used as building blocks for play. All this was separated from the back half of the garden by a wall made of rough planks behind which, Wes assumed, refuse was stowed. As Miss Brannigan led him around it, he realized this was not the case. It seemed another game was set up here, though this one was much stranger. A box of random bits of glass, whole, cracked, and broken, stood to the side. Beneath the opposite wall lay a pile of entirely broken glass.

"We stirred up a great deal today," Miss Brannigan began, her tone breezy, but it belied the grimness he heard beneath. "If I send you away now, you'll be unsettled all day, and very likely you'll fall back onto more opiates again. That may not be something I can halt. But I would like to try." She gestured to the box of glass. "Use as much as you like. Throw as hard as you'd like. Shout. Curse. Weep. Swallow it—whatever suits you, do so, but spend as much of that rage and uncertainty I see on your face against that wall in whatever means seems best to you." She nodded back toward the house. "I will sit at the table and wait for you. Take as long as you'd like."

She disappeared then, and Wes watched her go, more than a little stunned. She wanted him to break glass? As if it would help? Was she mad?

With Penelope Brannigan it was difficult to say for certain. What he did know was that it would be easier to toss a few pieces of glass than it would be to argue that he had no need to do so. Sighing, he turned to the box and tried to decide which piece to pick.

He chose a drinking glass with a large chip on the top. Hefting it in his hand, he measured its weight, feeling slightly ridiculous. Then he lifted it up to his head, tensed his arm and threw.

The glass shattered with a sharp, almost melodic crash and fell to join the heap on the ground.

Wes stared at the point of impact on the brick, feeling a strange sense of…relief? He couldn't quite tell. Generally he detested strong noise, but the glass breaking had an almost quiet shatter. Even so, it drowned out, in that moment, the din from the tavern behind, children's voices from the mouth of the alley, and the sound of wheels and hooves on the streets. It had felt oddly good. Noise. Destruction. His noise. His destruction. And there was a remarkable mischief about it all. Breaking glass was the stuff of accidents and punishments. Messes to be scolded for. There was no scolding now. In fact, he'd been *told* to break it. And encouraged to break more.

He decided that, in fact, he'd be happy to.

The second piece of glass hit much harder, delivered with greater intent, and as such it wasn't just relief but release that coursed through Wes. Good God, *yes*. He'd like to buy out a shop full of the stuff and spend an hour at this. *Crash. Shatter.* One after another, glasses, decanters, bowls, and shards of heaven knew what went sailing against the brick and came down onto the heap.

And he did shout. He swore as well. As he released each bit of glass, Wes insulted its honor, called it names, told it where to fuck itself, and ultimately simply roared at it. All the rage and frustration and confusion he'd felt in the parlor came out of him now, and he suspected some of it came from the boy who'd been tricked by a whoreson thief into giving away not just his family's treasures but his own dignity. His happiness too—that boy had possessed so little true happiness, for all his advantages of birth. The thief had stolen that from Wes as well. He realized that now. It infuriated him. It made him want to scream. And sob. And break every piece of glass in London.

He didn't, though. He didn't even break every piece in the box. After several minutes of destruction and shouting and a bit of frustrated weeping, he surprised himself yet again by reaching the end of that well. The rage was done. He felt tired. He felt lonely and empty.

But he felt…better. Less angry. Less anxious. Now he was simply sad, sad for what he had lost, for what he could not get back.

A glimmer of hope flared deep inside him, a tiny flame in the darkness. *Is that the magic? Is my stammer gone now too, shattered within that pile of glass?*

He took a deep breath, let it out and tried to speak.

"H-H-H—"

He pressed his lips back together quickly, embarrassed and disgusted.

A gentle hand rested on his shoulder. "No, I don't think it works like that. Not for you. Not for me either. I spent years practicing those exercises, and even then I still don't know what really allowed me to relax." Miss Brannigan sighed and let her hand fall away from his arm. "Hopefully, though, this has let go some of what remembering stirred up. I'll see you to your carriage—but if you please, wait a moment. I must see to something of my own first."

To Wes's great surprise, she walked over to the box of glass and selected a piece of her own.

She threw with viciousness and speed, and it didn't take but two throws to wipe away her careful, kind mask. Her eyes were hard with anger, her nose wrinkled and her lips flat as she swore and spat and then, abruptly, sobbed. Her throws slowed a bit as she paused on occasion to wipe her eyes with the back of her glove, then screamed an obscenity and threw again. It was unsettling and yet engaging to watch her.

Then she was done. She drew a few breaths, wiped her eyes again and turned to Wes. Her mask was still down, and as she smiled tentatively at him, the wise mentor Miss Brannigan was gone, replaced by a weary, damp-eyed young woman.

"Penny," she said to him. "It would please me if you would call me Penny from now on."

Wes frowned at her, uncertain as to how to respond.

She turned her gaze back to the wall. "I've been doing this for a while. Rescuing, some have called it, and usually with a bit of a sneer. And yes, I'm aware it's all because I couldn't save my own family. It seems a fair trade, though. Without them I had nothing else to live for, but instead of ending myself messily, I've chosen to help others. It makes their deaths—and my loss—mean something. It gives me a sort of peace." She sighed. "The only trouble, of course, is that it isn't that I have any sort of training for such things. I'm not even sure it exists. I simply do my best and hope it's enough. When I meet people who need help, I try to give them what it seems they need."

She glanced at him with a crooked smile. "I've been trying to give you a strong anchor. It seemed to be what you needed, so proper and formal and with your high rank. I thought I could give you a space you could be at ease. Even if that is what would help you, though, I don't think I can play that any longer." She had to wipe away another tear. "Perhaps you don't see it, but your story felt so much like mine. You were a bit older, but not much. It felt the same, hearing about you sitting in that library, the same as me lying under that wagon. Except you had to walk about with your monster. Odd, how I'd always thought it would have been better to have been hurt. But when I listened to you, I thought of myself and all my what-ifs, and I realized no, it would just be different pain."

She shook her head. "I'm sorry. I can't see you as just another soul I'm helping. And I know most British people find it offensive to be overly familiar, but I can't be your mentor or guide in this any longer. But I would like very much to be your friend. Your friend who listens and helps—and, I'm afraid, bleeds with you." She paused, then flattened her lips briefly before adding, "And I'm not laying bait for you or any such nonsense. I'm not marrying anyone, but if I were, I certainly wouldn't marry the son of a marquess. God in heaven, I don't need that kind of headache."

Wes laughed. The sound simply burst out of him, surprising him as much as it did her. When it faded his smile lingered. "W-Wes." It was her turn to frown at that, so he explained. "W-What my f-friends call me is W-Wes."

He saw the delight and happiness reach her eyes, but she lifted her eyebrow and gave him a mock-stern look. "I thought you had no friends."

He shrugged, but he was still smiling. "P-Perhaps I was f-f-feeling a bit s-s-sorry for myself and exag-ggerated. I have s-some. Not g-g-good ones, but s-some. And they c-c-call me W-Wes."

She nodded, giving in to her own smile at last. "I shall endeavor to fill that void, then, and be a good one." She enveloped him in a gentle, sisterly hug and bussed a dry kiss against his cheek. "Until tomorrow, Wes."

"G-G-Good day, P-Penny," he replied.

He left her in a much better mood than he had anticipated—a much better mood than he'd felt in some time, in fact. He felt light and easy as he lingered in her doorway, waiting for his carriage, for once not even slightly upset by the noise from the tavern beside him.

He wasn't due to meet Michael for another hour, and so he went home and freshened up, catching himself humming every now and again, which made him laugh. Heavens, but it felt good to feel good. His buoyant mood continued as he left the house to meet Michael. Michael, his *very* good friend. His blood quickened, and he let his mind wander over all the things they might do together today. Perhaps he would be brave and try something daring. Perhaps one of the coffeehouses Michael kept mentioning.

Wes was so lost in his own reverie that he didn't notice the urchin until he'd tugged twice on Wes's arm. The boy made a clumsy bow, handed Wes a note, and once Wes had given him a guinea, hurried off. The note was from Legs, written in rough scrawl.

Hav flowr. Bring Tusdy at dark. L.

First all that with Penny, and now a promising day with Michael, and then his flower at last. The day, it seemed, would only get better and better.

He felt full. Full and happy and almost…wild. It was as if he'd ingested too much opium, but instead of putting him to sleep as it buzzed his nerves, it made him want to climb buildings. He wanted to do something rash. Something…something with Michael. Perhaps a longer outing. Perhaps…oh, did he dare consider the opera? Would this euphoria keep his fears at bay?

An idea hit him, and the perfection of it made him stop still in his tracks. *Yes.* It wasn't perfect, no, and not as flashy as the opera, but if he could call in a few favors…well, most men wouldn't find it exciting, but if Michael had been impressed by the Athenaeum, surely…

The plan solidified in his mind, and Wes quickened his steps, not even caring when the pub broke into its usual noontime brawl.

When he got back to his apartments, the butler came out to greet him, holding a letter on a tray.

"From your father, my lord. He said it is most urgent."

Wes took the letter, for all its single sheet feeling like lead. He nodded thanks to the butler and carried it down the hall to his room. He stood staring at it for several moments before going inside.

He didn't open it right away, setting it on the side

table as he gathered what he would need. He started toward it twice, only to walk away and water a few of his plants and pen instructions for the maids.

In the end he left it lying there, unread. Urgent or not, he wouldn't let his father ruin his good mood. Not this day. Not this time.

Feeling reckless and wicked and quite good, he left his rooms, straightened his hat and went to find the butler to hand him the notes and order his carriage.

MICHAEL SAT AT the window in the front parlor, waiting for Albert to arrive, when Rodger sent a message asking him to his office. The summons irritated him, but since Albert's carriage wasn't in sight, he went.

Rodger stood at the window, staring into the courtyard where Cook raised her vegetables and herbs, his right foot resting on the wide ledge where Michael frequently made a nest to read, though Michael always drew the screen taut before it to cloak himself. Rodger kept it folded back now, and when he saw Michael enter, he pushed off the window and nodded to the space, indicating Michael sit.

It was an odd move, and it stayed Michael's chiding remarks about Albert's imminent arrival. He sat where Rodger indicated he should. "Is something wrong?"

In response, Rodger huffed and flattened his lips in a grimace. He didn't pace exactly, but he fidgeted back and forth for some time before he spoke, and when he did, he didn't look Michael in the eye. "You seem to be happy with Lord George."

"Yes, I am," Michael said carefully. Good Lord, was Rodger jealous? "Is *that* the problem?"

Rodger sighed and rubbed his mouth. "I don't know. It might be." He turned to Michael at last. "I don't like where this is going, Michael. I think you should be more careful."

Michael almost laughed. "Careful of what? Rodger, be serious. You think he is a threat? He's nothing like his father. He's nothing like anyone. He'd never hurt me."

"Are you in love with him?" Rodger demanded.

Michael only hesitated a beat. "Yes."

A tic appeared in Rodger's cheek. "And this, ducks, is exactly why I'm worried. If you're in love with him, he can wound you beyond anyone."

Now Michael was irritated. "For heaven's sake. Obviously, yes, he can hurt me. But I meant that he won't hurt me like his father."

"No. He'd hurt you far worse." When Michael started to protest, Rodger stood over him, boring those angry eyes into his. "Have you told him?"

"Told him what?" Michael asked, but his stomach flipped over, for he knew what Rodger meant.

"About what his father did to you."

"Yes," Michael said, willing his cheeks not to color. It wasn't a lie.

But Rodger was no man's fool. He smiled mirthlessly. "And did you mention that it was his *father* who did it?"

Michael longed to lie. He might have, too, except Rodger was certain to test out the truth. Michael averted his eyes and said nothing, which was of course the same as an admission.

Rodger swore under his breath. And then he did pace, wearing a trench in the floorboards as he went on. "Your month is up next week. I have half a mind to tell him thank you for his donation and move on."

"You wouldn't." When Rodger just gave a dark laugh in reply, Michael stood, shaking with fury. "I'm not your property, Rodger Barrows."

"Aren't you?" Rodger shot back. "He's a danger to you, and you won't even hear it, because you're in love with him. You want his protection over mine? Fine. If there's anything left of you once he breaks you, I'll find you somewhere quiet to live, but it won't be here. I can't stomach the thought of cleaning up after that fucking family again."

Michael didn't know if he should be furious or terrified. He ended up both. "Rodger, where is this coming from? Why are you suddenly so adamant against Albert?"

"I've been against him since the moment I met him." He stopped pacing and shut his eyes, looking pained. "I've been talking myself out of my apprehension, trying to give the bugger a chance. But it's no good. Not after the report I got this morning." He turned to Michael. "Your Albert's an addict, love. You can give him your heart, but his soul belongs to the poppy."

Michael blinked a few times, not even sure what Rodger was saying. "You think Albert is addicted to...opium?" He laughed, feeling relieved. "Rodger, your report is wrong. Albert can't even go into a bookstore. You think he could go to an opium den?"

"He doesn't take it in a den, ducks." He held out his hand, cupped like an offering, and smiled grimly. "His little pills. And his tea. Laudanum, they call it, but it comes from the poppy all the same. Been increasing regularly for months. He downplayed it to me, which was why I had the boys look into him. He's even seeing that bluestocking chit down in Southwark—that's why he moved your outings to the afternoon. Spends every morning with her. Won't do a bit of good, though. All her wiles are shite."

Michael's ears had pricked at *chit*, but *wiles* gave him pause. "He—he's seeing a woman?"

Rodger paused, frowning at him, then shook his head. "Not like that, love. God knows I'd love to use that to turn you off him, but no, she's not a doxy. Fuck, she's practically a nun, that bleeding idiot—she thinks she's an angel, Miss Brannigan does, saving lost souls. She has Lord George singing songs and breaking dishes, as if such nonsense will break him away." He rolled his eyes.

Michael calmed somewhat. "But he's trying to quit,

yes? Isn't that a good thing?"

Rodger barked a laugh. "It's a nice sentiment, but it won't work. Not like that. I've seen only a handful of men break free of the dragon, and it marked each one as surely as a scar. It takes a strength of iron to walk through that fire."

"And you're saying Albert doesn't have that strength?"

Rodger snorted.

Michael's cheeks colored again. "He's strong enough," he said, but with less heat than he wanted. "Albert is strong enough to defeat opium. And strong enough to protect me from his father."

"Glad to hear it." Rodger smiled darkly. "You won't mind if I let him know about your history with Daventry, then."

"You wouldn't," Michael cried.

"I will if you don't tell him yourself," Rodger promised.

Michael felt panicked. And sick. "Why?" he demanded. "Why are you being so unreasonable? All because he uses opium, suddenly he's too weak to be with me? And why do you get to make that decision?"

"Because I've made every decision for you for the past fifteen years," Rodger replied, without pity. "Because *you* aren't strong enough to even sleep in your own bed."

That jab cut deep, and Michael all but hissed at the pain. And lashed out to distract from it. "Are you sure it isn't because I'm not warming *yours*?"

Rodger's anger, to Michael's surprise, abruptly gave way, leaving him looking only pained. "No, love. It isn't. But that doesn't mean I don't care enough about you to bleed with you when the house of Daventry guts you all over again."

Michael tried to hold on to his anger. He couldn't. His voice broke as he asked, "Are you telling me I can't see him?"

"I don't know." Rodger ran his hand through his hair. "I don't know, ducks. I don't. I wanted you to have a good fuck with him. Wanted you to play and feel free. But you aren't. You aren't fucking him, and you aren't playing." He turned back to Michael. "Tell me I'm wrong. Tell me you won't be broken if he isn't what you want him to be. Tell me you aren't looking for a fairytale prince who will buy you a cottage in the country and fill it with books and pace the front walk to keep your demons at bay in between making sweet love to you."

Just hearing the words spoken out loud made Michael fill with longing. Yes, he wanted all that, and he wanted it with Albert.

And yes. If Albert betrayed him, it would break him to his core.

He shut his eyes, and Rodger swore. Michael wanted to cry.

"When—" Michael's voice broke, and he swallowed hard before continuing, keeping his eyes shut.

"When will you tell him? Today?"

He braced himself, ready to hear Rodger say yes, that it was already over. When Rodger didn't answer, Michael had to open his eyes. Rodger was looking at him strangely.

"You'd give him up that easily?" He frowned. "Am I wrong and you don't care that deeply—or is it too late, and it's me who's broken you?"

Michael faltered. "I don't know what you mean. Broken me?"

Rodger looked pained. "God's teeth, but I did, didn't I? Fuck me." His laugh was bitter. "That's why I pushed you out of my bed those years ago. I thought if I kept fucking you that you'd never take any control over your life. I didn't want you to become my pet, unable to do anything without my say-so. But it didn't matter, did it. You were my pet anyway."

"But you just said—" Michael shook his head. "You just told me I'm too weak to make a decision, just ordered me to end it with Albert and told me he was too weak to—"

"And you didn't fight for him," Rodger cut in. He watched very carefully. "Because you don't love him, or because..."

He left the rest unfinished.

Michael tried not to understand him. Tried to be angry, but all he felt was fear. Why was Rodger doing this? The ground kept shifting beneath him, and he hated it, hated this feeling. He felt exposed, confused, and afraid. All at once it was just as it had been when he'd been with the men in the rooms, before Rodger had brought in Albert, and he panicked.

"Rodger," he said, trying to not let the panic show, but he couldn't keep the pleading from his voice. "Rodger, why—" His palms began to sweat, and the room felt too close, the air too heavy. "Why are you doing this to me? Why are you trying to turn me mad?"

Even before Rodger's face crumpled in despair, a deep part of Michael realized the answer. *Rodger is right. You are his slave. Rodger's slave, Albert's—both. You aren't just weak. You don't even know how to think for yourself.*

Like a snake, the old memory crept from the back of his mind, Daventry smiling down at him, running his hand over Michael's hair as he suckled his master's cock. *"Such a sweet pet. One day I'll put a collar on you, boy, and keep you beside me forever."*

Michael had gagged on the cock, swearing he would never let him do it, that he'd run away first. And yet after all this time, the joke was on him. He'd collared himself.

The knock at the door startled them both.

"Sir," a servant said, sticking his head inside the room, "Lord George has arrived."

Rodger waved the man away without looking at him, his eyes staying on Michael.

Michael wanted to sob. "What do I do?" he whispered.

Rodger rubbed at his cheek. "Good God, I've no

idea."

"Don't tell him," Michael pleaded. "Don't tell him about Daventry."

"Will you tell him, then?" Rodger asked.

No. Never. But Michael swallowed hard and nodded. "Just—not today."

"I'll give you three days," Rodger replied.

"Three! *Days?*" Michael cried. "It isn't anywhere near enough time."

"It's more than I should give you." Rodger sighed and reached out to brush his fingers across Michael's cheek. "If it goes badly, ducks, you're done whoring for me. I won't send you away," he amended quickly, when Michael stiffened, "but this can't go on. I should have seen it long ago. I'm sorry I didn't." He grimaced, exhaled hard, then smiled placatingly at Michael. "Shall I send him away and have him come back tomorrow? I can do so without letting him know anything is amiss."

Michael wanted to scream. He wanted to shout, scream, cry out, kick—at Rodger, at Albert, at the whole world. How had this happened? How had everything run so abruptly mad?

I only have three days left with him.

"No," he said hotly. A tear ran down his cheek, which he hated but could not stop. He wiped angrily at it. "I will see him today." He drew a breath. "And I will tell him within three days' time. Myself. I will tell him about Daventry myself." Pride made him add, "I'll prove to you that I don't need either of you. That I'm strong enough to take care of myself."

He was ready for condescension, but Rodger only looked at him with weary sadness. "I hope you do, ducks. I hope you do."

Rodger leaned forward and brushed a kiss against his forehead before heading back to his desk.

Michael stood there stupidly a moment. Then he squared his shoulders and left the room, slamming the door behind him.

Before he could go to the parlor he had to step into the dark alcove by the water closet and press his face into the wall. When he stopped shaking, he wiped the wet from his cheeks, drew a deep breath, and pinched his cheeks to give them color as he went out into the parlor to meet his lover.

"LET'S GO SOMEWHERE different today."

To Michael's credit, he managed to keep his voice largely in line. Even better, Albert wasn't just receptive to the idea—rather, he almost seemed pleased. In fact, he was in a mood Michael hadn't ever quite seen in him before.

"Wh-Where would you like?" He leaned back against the carriage cushions and smiled. "An-n-nother bookstore? Club?" His smile curled up at one corner, and his eyes twinkled. "Or p-perhaps something…out of town?"

Michael stilled. "Are you jesting?" He realized what

Albert must mean and relaxed a little. "You want to take me to some suburban garden, don't you."

He must not have marshaled his tone very well, for Albert's smile turned from devilish to wry. "I've t-t-taken you to t-t-too m-many gardens." He sighed and turned his palm up in a conciliatory gesture. "No g-g-garden. Something j-just for y-y-you." He paused. "Though w-w-we w-w-will need to st-st-stay the n-night. Is that a p-p-problem?"

Michael didn't know. Was it? "How far out of town are we going?"

Albert's lips quirked as he shook his head. Ah. So it was a secret.

Well.

Michael tried to think quickly, though he wasn't sure if that meant reason or heart were leading. He hadn't been out of town in years. In fact, he'd left town exactly twice in his entire life, and both had been…before. It shouldn't make any difference, but…well, it did. Overnight with Albert. There would be no running away if things went badly. No bursting into the streets, finding an urchin and summoning Rodger.

Rodger, who'd accused him of being unable to think for himself, take care of himself.

"H-How long?" Michael asked. Despite his best efforts, it came out a whisper. His blood wasn't just pounding in his ears now. It was banging at the back of his throat.

Albert looked somewhat chagrined. “I m-must be back by tom-m-morrow evening.”

Michael let out a relieved breath. “That’s fine.” One night. One night with Albert.

Three days.

He swallowed his fear and nodded. “Yes. Yes—I can go.”

“Do y-you need anything?”

Michael shook his head. “I’ll need to send a messenger to Rodger, but other than that, no.” His cheeks colored as he added, “Though I don’t have any coin with me.”

Albert waved this idea away with his hand. “W-We will s-send word from the st-station.”

Michael blinked. “Station?”

Albert nodded. “I th-thought you m-might enjoy the t-t-train. Is th-that all r-r-right?”

Michael didn’t know. He’d seen the trains, of course—he’d gone down to watch them for a lark. He’d read several papers about them. But ride one? Of course he’d love to. But it just seemed so…so…

Well.

He cleared his throat. “Of course. I only—you surprise me, Albert. I would think trains would be a bit…busy for you.”

Albert grimaced. “I w-w-wear c-cotton in my ears.”

“So you’ve been on the train before?”

He nodded. He was still watching Michael closely. “W-We could take a c-c-carriage, if you’d r-r-rather.”

On a bumpy country road. Michael remembered that part very well. He shook his head. "No, a train would be lovely. I'm simply...surprised."

"In a g-g-good way?" Albert pressed.

Michael smiled. "In a good way."

The carriage stopped shortly after that, taking them to Euston Station, which Michael had ridden past a thousand times but never entered. They didn't enter it now, either. First Albert scribbled a few notes and gave them plus a small satchel to a porter who promised, "I'll deliver them right away, m'lord, and see to it that your bag makes it safe onto the train." Then they headed toward a coffee shop across the way. It was noisy and crowded, and Michael glanced at Albert, worried.

Albert, who had gone white, tried to smile back.

Relieved when he saw a small park and a bench beneath a tree, Michael pointed at it. "We'll be stuck on the train all afternoon. Perhaps we should sit outside for a while?"

Albert gave him a long, strange look. "It's r-r-raining and c-c-cold," he pointed out.

Michael squinted up at the gray sky. "Well—yes, but—" He searched for a polite way to duck around Albert's fear of crowds, but it wasn't easy. "It's...so busy in there, and I don't feel like—I had coffee at Dove Street, really, and—"

Albert's bemusement gave way to comprehension, and his mouth flattened into a thin line. Before Michael could decide how to react, his escort took hold of his forearm and walked with grim purpose toward the shop.

It was loud outside, but the din was deafening within. Michael stepped in to guard Albert's wallet as he recognized a few of the *gentlemen* at the bar working unsuspecting travelers. There wasn't a free table anywhere.

"We don't have to do this," Michael said, leaning in close to Albert.

Albert ignored him, pressing on white-lipped to wave down a host. Retrieving his handy notebook and paper, he scribbled a note and showed it to the host, who nodded and motioned to a waiter. Just like that, they were led down a hall to a parlor, not empty, but with better chairs and a lot more quiet. The waiter seated them, Albert scribbled another note, and then he collapsed carefully into his seat, shutting his eyes with a shuddering breath. He stayed that way for several seconds, at which point he withdrew his pill case from his vest pocket with a shaking hand.

The opium.

Michael watched the white pill tumble into Albert's hand. He thought of everything Rodger had said about it, of how it ruined lives. Of how it was the reason Rodger wanted Michael to end their affair.

As Albert lifted the pill to his lips, Michael reached out without thinking and knocked it out of his hand.

Albert stilled. Michael drew his hand back quickly

as the pill sailed over the edge of their table and onto the floor. It felt like he'd walked into a dream. Had he seriously done that? Knocked the pill out of Albert's hand? He had. Oh God in heaven, but he had.

"I—I'm sorry," he whispered to the tablecloth, unable to meet Albert's eyes. "I shouldn't have done that. I just—" He swallowed hard, and then it all came out in a hushed torrent. "Rodger told me you take opium, told me what it does to people, and I saw it in your hand and thought of it destroying you like he said it did so many people, and I didn't think." He shut his eyes. Good God, he should just get a shovel and make burying himself so much simpler. "I'm sorry. Truly, I'm very sorry. It won't happen again."

He kept his gaze down as a waiter appeared with their coffees. Neither of them spoke. Michael made a few tentative sips, then sank back in his chair, wishing he could crawl under the table.

A hand pressed gently against his knee.

Darting a glance at Albert, at first he thought he must have imagined it, for Albert was engrossed in his coffee, not looking at him at all—but no, that was his arm disappearing beneath the table. And that had to be his hand, his large, strong hand on Michael's knee, drifting to the edge of his thigh.

Stroking.

Gently—not hard, not angrily. And not sensually, either. His hand shook a little, and his face was pale. But the touch was…odd. Michael didn't know what to do with it. He reached down to close his hand over Albert's, worried that he might not be well.

Albert's hand captured his—and squeezed.

Lord George Albert Westin, he supposed, had made a lifetime's practice of expressing himself without words. Looks, glances, mannerisms—and now this, a touch. It was odd, because Michael had been touched so much, but never like this. Never beneath a table in a fine salon. And never with such…passion. Intensity.

Abruptly Albert's hand went away, withdrawn almost guiltily. "V-Vaughn."

Michael turned to where Albert was looking, and he felt himself go pale too.

Standing before them was Daventry's eldest son.

Chapter Eleven

VAUGHN'S SMILE WAS strained as he regarded his brother. It vanished almost completely as he took in Michael. "George Albert. Good to see you. And your…friend."

A movement beside the earl caught Michael's attention. A small, pale boy stood beside Vaughn.

Albert saw this too and frowned. "Wh-What is w-wrong with Edwin?"

Vaughn's lips flattened into a line. "I think Father is running him a bit too hard. Or perhaps the tutor. I don't know. He simply—" He cut himself off, but Michael thought the man seemed worried before he erased the emotion from his countenance. "At any rate, Edwin's mother wants to see him, so it works out. He gets a reprieve from the old man's schooling on how to be a marquess, and his mother gets to coddle him for a time."

Michael made eye contact with the boy and shivered at the vacantness he saw there.

"We should get going to our train," Vaughn said. "Alice is already waiting in Bristol for us." His thin smile returned, and he made a slight bow with his head. "Good to see you, George Albert. Sir," he added, making an even tighter bow to Michael. He tugged on his son's hand. "Come along, Edwin."

For several minutes Albert and Michael sat silent at their table, the earl's interruption resonating between them. Eventually Albert cleared his throat and stood. "We sh-should get to our t-train."

Michael rose too, but he did not miss Albert slipping one of his pastilles into his mouth.

Albert kept a hand on Michael as they pushed through the crush to the door, trying not to lose him.

Inside the station it was madness, hundreds of voices and harpers echoing against the high ceiling, but Albert pressed on, huddling close to the wall, eschewing ticket stations and leading them straight to the platform.

Their coach was sleek and black, boasting glass windows, the only car to do so. Glancing forward, Michael saw the second class had a roof and open walls, and third had no roof at all and not even seats, everyone clustered in like cattle. In their car, Michael and Albert had fine leather seats, cushioned, and with lap rugs, which Michael didn't hesitate to put on. He sat beside Albert, who after tucking his own rug into place, withdrew his notepad and began to write.

Michael settled in to wait. After several seconds of

dutiful scribbling, Albert handed it over. His writing looked rushed and slightly frantic.

I am not an addict. The laudanum is for my nerves. It's true I've used too much lately, but I am working on using less.

Michael glanced around the car, which wasn't crowded but seemed too full of ears. He took the pencil from Albert and wrote back.

But if you hadn't gone into the coffeehouse, you wouldn't have needed it. I wouldn't have minded waiting outside.

This only made Albert frown and scribble faster.

I will not have you thinking I am some pathetic weakling. It's true that I don't do well in crowds. But I am not incapable. Only out of practice.

Michael barely had time to read this before Albert, looking pained, snatched the notebook back and wrote again.

I wanted to do something special with you today. I wanted to see you smile again the way you did when you saw the Athenaeum. I didn't want you to think of me as an addict. Michael had read over his shoulder, but at this point Albert paused. Then he went on. *I would tell you I would stop entirely, but I don't think that's wise. But I promise you I will use it as little as I can.*

Michael claimed the pencil again, but he fingered it nervously. *I don't think you're weak*, he wrote at last. *You don't need to prove yourself to me. Especially at such cost. I am content—*

He stopped, the lie catching him up. Content to tour gardens and ride in his coach? No. He wanted more. But he couldn't say that to Albert.

Albert took the pencil and paper back.

You aren't content. I can tell. Please, don't worry. You were right, I didn't need the drug just then. It's a habit as well, taking a pill when I need to calm myself. The pills, yes, are a weakness. I apologize. But I want to do this with you. To spend time with you. To prove to you—he paused, smiled sadly, and went on—*and perhaps to myself, that I can do this.*

Michael replied.

That's well and good, but please don't ever hurt yourself for me. I don't care how bored I get of gardens. I don't wish harm for you, Albert. I care—

He stopped abruptly, realizing what he'd been about to write. He tried to scribble it out, but Albert stayed his hand. He was looking intently at the paper.

"F-Finish," he demanded.

With a shaking hand, Michael dislodged Albert's enough to write the rest.

I care about you. He swallowed a lump of fear and pressed on. *I care very much about you.*

They stared at the words. Around them the porters arranged the other passengers, wealthy men and women chattering and complaining and speaking in excitement to one another.

Albert gently took the pencil from Michael's hand and wrote, in careful letters with the notebook still on Michael's lap, *I care for you as well. Very, very much.*

He left the notebook in Michael's lap, their twin confessions laid bare. When the porter came by, Michael shut the book, but he held it close, remembering the look of those sentences together, in his handwriting and in Albert's own. Those words, so simple, so dear.

They were seated at the back of the train, with no one behind them and only a single seat across. The seats were all arranged like benches facing front, as if they were in a church without a pulpit. The other passengers seated themselves and looked around, but never back.

Beneath their lap rugs, their legs were pressed together, knees touching intimately. Michael could feel the heat of Albert, could smell his toilet water, the lavender his maid used on his clothes.

Albert, who cared for him.

When the train pulled out of the station, rain pattered down upon the windows. Wearing his glasses as he always did with Albert now, Michael could see outside, but everything was runny and vague, blurred by the rain. He watched the London he knew go by, while before him the rich prattled on, settling into their seats, and beside him Albert remained still, except for his foot, which tentatively reached over to brush his toes.

Michael smiled.

An old woman was seated across from them, and she was asleep before they left the city limits. Soon there was only the rhythmic clack of the train along the rails, the creaking of the car and the leather seats, and the hushed conversation of the passengers.

Albert leaned down to Michael's ear. "There is a t-tunnel ahead," he whispered.

He kept his face nearby, and Michael turned toward him slightly as well, keeping one eye on the window. He could see it, a mound of earth with a dark mouth to swallow the train. He remembered what the girls who had ridden the train down from the northern cities had told him about the tunnels. If you didn't like the look of the man beside you, put your hatpins in your mouth to keep him from stealing a kiss in the dark.

But Michael very much liked the look of the man beside him, and he was more concerned with making sure he *did* steal a kiss.

When the darkness enfolded them, he turned to his lover. Their mouths met like magic in the darkness, finding each other without a fumble. It was a soft, sweet kiss—innocent and desperate as a kiss stolen in the first-class train car should be. He tasted Albert's breath, felt his sigh, felt him shake, just a little, echoing the trembling Michael felt inside himself.

The light grew—they pulled away quickly, but not too quickly. Their eyes locked.

Albert smiled.

There were no more tunnels, but there was the lap rug. Beneath it, all the way to their destination, Michael and Albert discreetly held hands. No groping. No fondling. Just hands touching, lightly teasing, silently celebrating what they had confessed in Albert's notebook.

I care for you.

Just when Michael began to nod off, the train pulled over for another stop, and this time Albert rose, urging Michael up as well.

"Where are we?" Michael asked.

Albert smiled at him, looking delighted again. "Oxford."

AS MUCH AS the coffeehouse had been a mistake, Oxford was all Wes had wanted for Michael and more.

After securing umbrellas from a porter, they began their tour of the town. The rain was coming down in buckets now, but Wes suspected it could have been sheets and a degree above freezing, and even without an umbrella Michael would have delighted in it all.

"It's so charming," he said, over and over. "Like a toy village. So busy, and yet, after London, it's—" He laughed. "Charming. Completely, utterly charming. I could stay here forever."

"You haven't even b-been inside a shop," Wes pointed out, aiming them toward a bakery. "And you m-m-must be hungry."

Michael, Wes had come to learn, was always hungry, or rather, he could always eat. Meat pies, sweet rolls, hot cross buns—Wes thought even with half the bakery at his disposal Michael would find somewhere to put the food away. They ate as they walked, Wes only nibbling at a bun and Michael wolfishly consuming not one but two pies, and when Wes tempted him with a gooey sweet roll, he hesitated only a moment before taking that up as well.

"You shall make me fat," Michael accused, falling to the sweet with relish.

Wes sincerely doubted that, but in any case, he wouldn't mind. He would feed Michael all day long, were he allowed. But he only said, "Eat quickly. There is a b-b-bookstore ahead."

This, as he knew it would, made Michael's eyes go wide. "A bookstore—in Oxford?" he said around a mouthful. "Oh, I imagine it's heavenly. I wonder what I should find there. If only I had made you go back to fetch my purse."

"I sh-shall buy whatever you l-like," Wes promised, but nudged his elbow and looked meaningfully at the roll. "Eat."

"I can't eat it all that quickly." Michael tore half the roll away and held it up to Wes's mouth. "Here. Take this. You must try it, Albert. It's heaven."

Wes longed to take the sweet directly from Michael's fingers. He wondered, glancing up and down the street, if he could. Hedging caution, he accepted with his fingers instead, tucking his umbrella into the crook of his arm as he popped the roll into his mouth. It was heaven, yes. But better was to watch Michael lick the sweet from his fingers after.

The bookstore proved to fulfill all Michael desired. He found three volumes immediately that looked as if they might make him weep on the spot, and another half hour's perusal provided four more. He then tried to spread the pile out on a table and choose his favorite, but Wes only motioned to the shopkeeper to wrap them all. He gave the man a slip of paper with an address to deliver them to and ushered a protesting Michael back onto the street.

"Albert, that will cost a fortune," he hissed. He glanced back over his shoulder. "And where are you sending them?"

"To our l-lodgings," Wes replied. "We cross h-here."

Michael went, but he seemed oddly subdued. "Is it true that you have your own money? Apart from your father's allowance?"

Wes nodded. "From my m-m-mother's uncle."

"I wonder that you don't purchase a house with it." Michael gestured to the town at large. "Somewhere quaint and quiet like this. Somewhere you could have your own garden."

This was something Wes had considered many times, often to the point of sending his solicitor to examine houses. But to Michael he only shook his head. "Too l-l-lonely."

Did Michael blush there? And why? Wes wished he could ask.

"Where do you live in town?" Michael went on. "In some bachelor apartments, I suppose? Or a boardinghouse?"

"Ap-p-partments. In M-Mayfair." Wes smiled. "First fl-floor. Gas l-lighting and r-r-running w-w-water."

Michael laughed. "Goodness, Albert, you're a prince. But then I already know you like the finer things in life."

Wes directed them around a puddle, still smiling. He felt so very good with Michael. "I d-do."

"I don't mind them," Michael said, sighing, "but there must be quiet, good light, and many books. That is luxury to me. That and a hot stove. I do detest the damp."

"D-Do you have your own r-r-room at Dove Street?"

"Yes. In the attic," Michael supplied. "Well away from the sighing and banging of headboards. And with plenty of space for my books."

"And l-l-light?" Wes ventured.

"Excellent light," Michael agreed.

"You sh-should have pl-plants," Wes suggested.

Michael turned to look at him severely. "You would wish the plants *dead*, my lord? I scarcely remember to take care of myself, and no maids are allowed in my room."

Wes grinned. "I w-w-will give you a c-c-cactus."

Michael blinked at him. "A what? That sounds like a disease."

As they crossed the streets, Wes described in detail the prickly plant found in American deserts. He began to stammer as he realize he'd gone on and on, but a glance at Michael found him only listening intently, careless of the rain that drenched their boots and poured off the tarpaulin above their heads. He continued on, hesitating less as he warmed to his topic, explaining the beauty and even religious importance of the cactus. At one point Michael mentioned he would like to read a book about the Americas and the native cultures there, and Wes vowed privately to find him one as soon as he returned to London.

And then they arrived at the university.

Wes led Michael through the colleges, letting him linger and delight at porticos and arches, taking his own pleasure in watching Michael light up over so many simple things, like narrow passages and lanes and doors that looked "absolutely medieval!" But he kept him going, herding him onward to his ultimate destination. In truth he should have left it for the morrow, for the day was growing long, but he couldn't wait. When he'd envisioned this trip, he had one place in mind in which to take his lover, and they were now nearly there. A turn down New College Lane onto Cattle Street, and there, across from Hertford College, it stood waiting.

Bodleian.

Best of all was that Michael had no notion of what it was. He only marveled at the architecture and the door, imagining dragons and princesses, then amending it to "nefarious professors, waiting to pile books atop unsuspecting boys' heads." Wes only smiled and ushered him inside. And watched. And enjoyed as it dawned on Michael that he was in a library. An old, monstrously large, musty old library.

When on occasion librarians and caretakers came forward to question who they were, Wes took care of dispatching them, making certain nothing came between Michael and his discoveries. It was, Wes decided, rather as if someone could take him into a museum of plants, where all the species of the world were contained, greater than any botanical garden Wes had ever dreamed existed. Michael walked slowly, hushing his footsteps and behaving as if he had entered the holiest of churches. For almost an hour he simply wandered, touching nothing, only taking in the great halls, the alcoves, the stacks that reached all the way to the top of the vaulted ceiling. And then, as if it had finally become too much, he collapsed against a pillar and pressed his hands together over his mouth, his eyes full and dark and shining.

"Oh, Albert," he whispered, staring off at another hall, another avenue of books. "Oh, *Albert.*"

"G-Go on," Wes urged him. "Explore."

Michael did. He ran his fingers over spines. He asked librarians where he might find such-and-such, or the volume written by so-and-so. Several times he ended up in happily spirited debates with other browsing scholars, students, and sometimes the librarians themselves.

The man, Wes realized, was at home. As much as

Wes was at home in a garden, this library was where Michael Vallant bloomed.

In total they were there for three hours, leaving only when the building itself shut down. Michael was disappointed, but he refused to believe they'd been there that long, and once he was proved that they had been, he chastised Wes for not removing him earlier.

"We've missed dinner." He shook his head as they exited the building. "You should have told me."

"I w-w-will find you something to eat," Wes promised, smiling. He swore he had done nothing but smile since the moment he picked Michael up that day.

Michael stopped their walking, and after a glance around, he pulled Wes into a dark corner of an arched door, blocked the view from the street with his umbrella and pressed his lips to Wes's own.

It was a soft, sweet, almost magical kiss. A kiss of thanks. A kiss of wonder and lightness. And for all that, it made Wes's eyes close and stole directly into his soul.

When they finally drew apart, they walked in silence. Wes longed to take Michael's arm—in fact, he had to check the gesture several times. But of course that would not do. They walked as close as possible, back through the maze of colleges and passages, back to the city center, stopping at last at the warm light of an inn. Wes secured them a private dining room, where they sat close together and talked quietly as they drank wine and ate bowls of stew.

"Did you go to Oxford?" Michael asked. "You

seem so familiar with it."

Wes shook his head and refilled Michael's glass. "N-No. I was t-t-tutored at home until I was s-s-sixteen. Then I took up my p-plants in earnest. But I have c-c-come here to do research and to h-help with gardens." He cast Michael a wry glance. "D-Do I d-d-dare offer to show you the B-Botanical G-Garden tomorrow?"

"Albert darling, after that library, you could plant me in a pot and I would be content." He touched Wes's arm, his eyes shining. "I shall never forget it. Never." He squeezed. "Thank you."

The door opened to a maid, and Michael drew back his hand, but Wes felt the burn of it lingering there.

"W-What of y-you?" Wes asked. "Would you h-have liked to g-go to university?"

He worried that the question strayed into delicate territory, and a shadow did cross Michael's face before he shrugged. "It was never a given. I longed to, yes, but I never let myself get attached, even—before. I had dreams of being a scholarship boy, but likely those were phantoms as well. Who would grant money to a whore's son?" He laughed without mirth. "Honestly, it would have come to nothing. I longed to be a barrister, but at best I suspect I would have been a clerk. I would have been one of the lonely souls I service." He paused, a different shadow passing over his face.

There seemed to be a story there, but instinct led Wes to redirect the conversation entirely. He asked what books Michael had found, what had been the most interesting, and this let loose a torrent of words, most of which swirled around Wes's head without landing, but he smiled and nodded and listened, being careful to pick up enough detail to press him with deeper questions.

He kept Michael's glass full as well, letting his companion grow tipsy, but when he began to *tip* as well, Wes called for his bill and laid out his coin before handing a note of instruction to the innkeeper. Michael listed against him, looking confused as Wes led him outside.

"We aren't staying at the inn?" he asked.

"No." Wes helped Michael into the carriage that pulled into the inn's drive.

He sat across from Michael as they drove, enjoying the way the streetlights played across his face, his loosened necktie, his open waistcoat. Michael stared back, looking relaxed and sated.

"You got me drunk," he accused without rancor.

"A b-bit," Wes admitted.

"To have your way with me?" The question was playful, but Wes could hear the sliver of unease behind it.

He shook his head. "To r-relax you."

Michael was quiet a moment. "I want you to have your way with me."

Heat seeped through Wes, but he kept himself neutral. "B-But you are af-fraid."

Michael frowned. "I don't wish to be."

Wes pushed all carnal thoughts aside and leaned forward to make sure Michael could see the earnestness on his face. "I expect n-nothing from you," he assured him. "N-Nothing need h-happen tonight."

This only seemed to upset Michael further. "You don't want me any longer—not as a lover? Only as a friend?"

The heat crept back into Wes. "I w-w-want you m-more than I can s-s-say."

"But you'll do nothing if that's what I wish." Michael considered this. "But—that makes no sense, Albert. You *should* expect something. You *bought* me."

Wes drew back. He sputtered for several seconds before he could speak. "N-N-No! I b-b-b-b—" He drew a breath. "I p-p-paid for your t-time. Your c-company."

"My company," Michael drawled, "implies using me for sex."

"I would n-never," Wes said, unable to keep the anger from his tone, "use you for th-that."

Michael seemed more confused than ever. He tried several times to speak, but in the end he could say nothing, only look at Wes with a stunned expression.

Blessedly, the carriage slowed and stopped, and the coachman came around to let them out at their destination.

The small cottage was completely dark, which was to be expected, but the door, happily, was unlocked and waiting for him, which meant the larder was filled as well, and the coalbin—yes, he saw, peering into the sitting room—filled to the brim. He tried to decide if he should bother lighting a fire downstairs or simply show Michael to bed when Michael spoke behind him from the foyer.

"What is this place?"

Wes gestured around the front rooms. "A c-c-cottage. Belongs to an ac-c-cquaintance at the gardens. I b-b-borrow it when I'm in Oxford." He tried to read Michael's face in the dark, but it was impossible. Too many shadows. "W-Would you rather w-w-we return to t-t-town?" He wondered if he could still catch the coachman.

"Oh—no!" Michael said quickly. He rubbed his hands over his arms as he glanced around the room. "No. It's charming. And there are no servants, I assume? Just the pair of us?"

"Y-Yes," Wes confirmed, watching again.

Michael said nothing, only continued looking around. Abruptly, he turned back to Wes.

"What do you mean, you would never use me for sex?"

He seemed upset, and Wes couldn't figure out why. He also had no idea how to further explain himself, so he simply shook his head.

"You *have*," Michael pressed. "You've used me twice. Once at the party, and once at Dove Street."

Wes frowned. "N-No. At the p-p-party you emb-braced me. I th-th—" The truth was, it had been a delightfully spontaneous moment, a sort of celebration of...life, or something equally, beautifully daft. But he could hardly say that. He swallowed. "And at D-D-Dove Street you as-as-as-asked for me. I n-n-never used you."

"What were you doing then?" Michael demanded. He wasn't angry, but he seemed...oddly agitated. "What do you call that, if it isn't using me for sex? Making love?"

He spat the last two words with such derision that Wes couldn't speak for several seconds, until at last he was able to overcome his stammer and say, "Y-Y-Y-Y-Yes."

Michael stared at him. Outside the rain beat down on the cottage roof, relentless. Inside it was cold and dark, but Wes could see Michael's face, the wine leaving him bare. Confused. Upset. Doubting, almost angry. Wes began to shake. He'd taken a pill, quietly, at dinner. He'd taken one as well in the library, when Michael hadn't been looking. He longed for one now. He felt jagged and raw, no envelope of calm. He needed one. This was too much. He didn't know what to do. He was too weak. He couldn't do this. He couldn't—

"You were making love to me." Michael took a step forward. His eyes bore into Wes. "Even that first time. Not hot release with the confessed whore who wanted to thank you. Making love. *Love.*"

Wes couldn't answer. He wanted to reach for his notebook, to let it give him his words, but it was too dark for Michael to read them. He nodded instead, his breath coming in short, sharp bursts. He pressed his back to the wall, hating himself, hating his weakness. He couldn't do this. He couldn't do this!

Michael closed the distance between them, his eyes drunken and wild. "Do you love me, Albert?"

Wes's breath caught. He stared at Michael. He gripped the wall.

He nodded and closed his eyes, too terrified to look any longer. The words burst from him, driven out by the fear. "Y-Yes," he whispered. "Y-Y-Yes, I l-l-love you."

Michael's hands pressed against Wes's chest, and he startled.

"No you don't," Michael whispered back. He sounded terrified too.

Wes nodded again. "Y-Yes. I d-d-do."

Fingers curled into his chest. "When? When!"

Panic—Michael was panicked. Wes wanted to laugh. He wasn't alone in that.

Michael gripped him tighter. "When? When did you fall in love with me, Albert?"

Wes tried to think. When? He searched back, trying to find the moment. At the gardens, when he asked for a kiss? No. Before that. In the blue room at Dove Street? No. He'd been gone before then. When? When—

He did laugh, then. He opened his eyes, trying to

speak, but he only sputtered. Claiming Michael's hand, he moved it, slowly, down to his groin.

"Th-Then," he whispered.

Michael frowned. Then he frowned harder. "When I thought you were Rodger?" He pursed his lips together and tried to push away. "Be serious, Albert."

Wes held him in place. Wes's cock was soft, but at their combined touch, it started to stir. "Then," he insisted. He fought for his words. "S-So bold. S-So b-beautiful." He steadied himself with a breath and made himself look Michael in the eye. "S-So f-f-fragile. L-Like a f-f-flower." He pressed Michael's hand closer. "And th-then you k-k-kissed me. I was l-lost."

Michael was like a flower now. A beautiful, travel-weary orchid, petals ready to fall. "But I was just a whore."

Now Wes frowned, and he shook his head. "B-Beautiful. You were b-beautiful." He let go of Michael's hand and reached up to touch his face. "Y-You are b-beautiful. Always."

Michael's eyes were shining again, and he was very still. "You love me," he whispered.

"I l-love you," Wes agreed. Michael shivered, and Wes stroked his cheek. "It's c-c-cold," he said. "We should m-make a f-fire."

"Yes." A tear ran down Michael's cheek. "Yes, we should."

Leaning forward, Michael pressed his body hard against Wes's own as he swallowed him in a kiss.

Chapter Twelve

AFTER SEVERAL WONDERFUL, disoriented minutes, Wes decided it would be best if they went upstairs.

Kissing and touching until Wes's hip hit the rail, they stumbled upward, stopping on occasion to fall against the stairs as hands and lips had their way. By the time they reached the top, Michael had Wes's jacket halfway off his body and his own necktie dangled around his neck.

Inside the room, things immediately became more intense, more desperate. Jackets and waistcoats fell away completely, and when the lawn of shirts opened to reveal skin, they both tried to attack each other at once. Michael won that round, pressing Wes back upon the bed and keeping his arms prisoner as he made a feast of his lover's chest, kissing the line of hair, teasing nipples with his tongue. Wes gained some ground when Michael stood to divest himself of his trousers—he leaned forward and caught his lover's waist, holding him in place as he dove straight for the proud, erect root before him and drove it deep into his own throat. Michael cried out and gripped Wes's hair—Wes groaned and urged those slim hips forward to fuck him gently. He tasted the salty, bittersweet tang of Michael, just a tease, but enough to spur him on.

And then Michael pulled back, grabbed Wes's shoulders and straddled him.

They moaned and shouted and grunted as they fought to pleasure one another. Managing to lose all clothing save their socks, they wrestled across the bed. Wes thought he had Michael good to rights, gripping his lover's bottom from beneath, sliding into place to take Michael's cock back into his mouth again, but Michael, after more gasping and breathless thrusts, bent around Wes's hip and applied his tongue directly to Wes's bunghole. Electricity shot through Wes, and he went weak—weak enough for Michael to flip him to his stomach, straddle him, pry his cheeks apart and feast on that dark entrance until Wes was incoherent.

Michael rolled him back over, rested on his knees and presented his own backside for the same.

Wes went to the job eagerly, his cock throbbing at the whimpering sounds Michael made. He slicked his lover well, pushing his tongue into the flexing opening before carefully inserting a finger.

Michael arched back and pressed down to swallow the digit deep.

Soon Michael was bent over the pillows, knees

spread wide as Wes slicked him with spit and speared him over and over, making him sigh and plead and shudder. Wes wanted more. He wanted to go downstairs and find the satchel and the salve he'd tucked inside so he could drive himself home. He wanted it more than he had ever wanted anything in the world. But even lost in passion, even with the wine and his confession—perhaps because of it—he knew Michael's panic could return.

Eventually it did.

At first Michael thrust back against Wes's fingers, but then he slowed, and then he stilled. Wes withdrew, returning to kisses, trailing them over Michael's backside and up his spine, but by the time he got to Michael's collarbone, his lover was rigid, his knuckles white in the moonlight as they gripped the sheets.

Wes shifted his erection away from Michael's leg, put a hand over those clenched fingers and kissed the side of his head. "It's all r-r-ight," he whispered.

Michael's voice broke on a soft sob. "I'm sorry."

"Shh." Wes eased himself down beside Michael on the bed and drew him into his arms. "It's all r-right."

"No." Michael settled onto Wes's shoulder, but his right hand closed angrily over the center of Wes's chest. "No, it's not. I hate that I'm like this. I hate that I'm like this with *you*."

Wes weighed his words before speaking. "Is it y-your past?"

"Yes," Michael admitted wearily. "It is. Which is

why it makes me so furious. Why? Why can't I let it go? Why must I be beaten by something so stupid? It never upset me before. Why now? And most of all, why when it isn't angry revenge or cold-hearted, empty fucking—why with you?" He shuddered as his voice lowered to an angry whisper. "Why am I so *weak*?"

"You aren't weak, Michael," Wes said firmly, and sealed the statement with a kiss against Michael's hairline.

Michael sagged into him. "You said all that without a single stammer."

Wes smiled to himself and stroked Michael's arm. "I am c-comfortable with you."

"You love me," Michael repeated.

"Yes," Wes agreed, drawing him closer for a brief, affirming embrace. "I l-love you."

"Even though I am a complete idiot and fall to pieces when you try to make love to me?"

"You aren't an idiot." Wes stroked his arm again. "You are w-wonderful." He gentled Michael with a few more strokes. "Y-Your fear isn't unlike m-my st-stammer. Be g-gentle with it." He thought of his confession to Penny about the thief, about Penny herself, huddled beneath the wagon, and of Michael, young and vulnerable and finding out his mother had sold him. "Treat that p-part of you like a y-young child you find w-w-weeping. It isn't f-far from the truth, I s-suspect."

Michael seemed to consider this a moment. "I hadn't thought of it that way." He lifted his head to smile at Wes and place a kiss on his chin. "I didn't take you for such a sage."

Wes felt himself flush, and he shook his head with a wry smile. "N-Not my w-wisdom. I've b-borrowed it from a f-f-friend."

Michael leaned back to rest in the corner of Wes's shoulder, staring up at Wes's face. His fingers drifted up to trace delicate trails as he spoke. "Even that frightened part wants to make love back to you, and be made love to." His face clouded. "Rodger told me this morning that I don't make any decisions for myself. Said, essentially, that I'm waiting for someone to rescue me. That I can't care for myself." His fingers circled Wes's lips. "The sad truth is that I think he's right. It makes me feel so ashamed. I've harbored this image of myself as so above what my mother made me, told myself I'm better even than what I would have been had she limited her exchanges to selling her own flesh."

He laughed sadly. "I felt so independent and smug. But I'm not. All I do is hide in my attic, in my books, and I whore for who Rodger picks out for me. He even told me"—another laugh, this one quite black—"that he ended our affair all those years ago because he didn't want me to attach to him nor he to me, that he wanted to be able to keep objective and protect me within reason and that he didn't want me to fixate on him. Then he said it hadn't worked, that even with that I'd turned over my life to him. No, it's true," he said, when Wes grimaced and sputtered angrily over an objection.

"He wasn't polite about how he said it, but I know what he means, and it's true." His expression grew fierce, though still crowded by desperation and futility. "I want to change that, Albert. I want to conquer that fear—both how it manifests between us and how it has, I've come to see, ruled my life ever since that night my mother sold me. I just don't know *how*."

"B-Begin with me," Wes said.

Michael frowned at him, and the truth was Wes wasn't sure himself exactly how this would work, but he didn't try to form the words, just let them flow as easily as he could manage directly from the germ of the idea in the back of his mind.

"Ch-Change it with m-me. Y-You say you w-want me." He stroked Michael's hair. "You may h-have anything of me you d-desire. If y-you wish to m-make love with m-me, you may make love t-to me. I w-will lie quiet, or wh-whatever you wish. I w-will serve y-you, or d-deliver y-you. S-Support you." He drew Michael's hand to his mouth and brushed his lips over his lover's knuckles. "Y-You are s-safe with m-me. Always."

He liked that Michael seemed to consider him, that he didn't just dismiss him out of hand. He liked the way Michael's eyes sharpened and darkened, the way his frustration and weariness seemed to bleed away, replaced by the beginnings of eagerness and desire.

"Make love to you," Michael repeated. He blushed just a little. "I am so used to being the object of sex. I feel ridiculous for not thinking of it myself, to reverse the roles." He stroked Wes's cheek a moment. "The truth is, I think I might *like* being the object. I think, sometimes, the shame of that is where the fear starts."

"It isn't sh-shameful," Wes countered gently. He kissed Michael's fingers again and threaded theirs together. "W-Work up to that, however. D-Don't begin there."

Michael's thumb traced the side of Wes's hand. "Yes. I suppose that makes a sort of sense."

"P-Perhaps I should light a fire and get us some t-tea while you p-plot your course."

"No." Michael sat up, disentangling himself. He turned to straddle Wes, his now-soft sex resting against Wes's thigh. There was a look of determination on his face.

"No?" Wes echoed.

"I think," Michael said, his voice growing stronger with each word, "I think, my lord, I should like you to keep still and quiet, for I'd like to make love to you right now."

Michael loomed over Wes like a conqueror, moonlight making his pale face and hair shine blue-silver in the dark. He was beautiful. Confident.

Powerful.

Wes smiled. "As y-you wish, sir." He pinned his arms to his sides and waited to be told what to do.

Michael didn't do anything at first, but Wes didn't rush him. He had a great deal of patience, an appreciation gleaned from years of people impatient for him to complete a sentence and speaking over him to hurry things along, guessing his intent or disregarding him entirely. Michael could stammer over lovemaking as long as he cared to. Wes certainly wouldn't hurry him along.

He held still and watched as Michael considered Wes's body, looking uncertain and charming as he bit absently at his bottom lip and surveyed. After several minutes, he ran his left hand down the center of Wes's chest, a delightfully soft touch that ended just an inch above his belly button. At this point, Michael looked up at Wes's face and frowned.

"I feel ridiculous," he confessed.

"You d-don't look it," Wes assured him. He shut his eyes, deciding he would keep them closed. "T-Take your t-time."

Michael did. For many, many minutes all he did was touch Wes's chest, exploring tentatively at first and then more boldly. His touches became strokes. When he strayed too close to a ticklish or sensitive area, Wes would spasm, and Michael would stop, but when Wes only continued to remain still, Michael would resume again.

The hands departed, Michael's weight shifted, and Wes felt the soft, damp press of Michael's lips on his skin.

It became harder and harder to remain still, and so Wes gave in to the urge to shiver, to arch, and he suspected most importantly, to moan. It wasn't difficult for him to play the passive role. In his amorous encounters, he'd largely split the difference between giver and receiver. Sometimes the arrangements sorted themselves out, and sometimes he'd negotiated his preference. But never had he been with someone where pleasure was so shared. Where he knew his gasps and tremors would be received not as fuel for further ardor but as an acknowledgment of Michael's power over him, of his trust for Michael. It made him feel vulnerable, but in a very good and safe way. He hoped the reverse was true for his lover.

It seemed to be. Michael used both hands and mouth upon him now, tweaking his nipple as he licked at the pit of his elbow, kneading his shoulder as he trailed his mouth down Wes's abdomen. When Wes's weeping erection nudged Michael's throat, Michael laughed, a soft, playful sound that made Wes's heart tumble over itself. When Michael took Wes's cock in hand and laved his way up to a nipple where he sucked and nipped in concert to his long, tight strokes, Wes clutched at the bedsheets and gasped, thrusting mindlessly as he gave himself up to Michael's pleasure.

Michael's erection poked his thigh, and his mouth teased Wes's throat. "Would you let me fuck you?" he whispered, his voice rough with passion.

"Yes," Wes rasped, no hesitation at all.

Michael nipped at Wes's jaw as his strokes on Wes's cock became more intent. "I don't know that I'm ready to do that," he confessed. "I never have. But I'd like to, someday, with you."

For some strange reason that made Michael falter. Wes longed to quickly affirm his eagerness for such an event. "Wh-Whatever day you wish." He bucked and gasped as Michael's thumb pressed in just the right spot at the base of his cock.

"I want you inside me. I want to feel you pounding hard inside me." His hand that didn't hold Wes's cock gripped desperately at Wes's shoulder. "I want you so much that I ache, Albert."

Wes ached as well. His cock, long past ache and well into blind yearning, took over most of his thinking and gained control of his mouth. "M-Mount me," he rasped. "H-Hold me down and f-fuck me w-with your body. T-Take me. I am h-helpless beneath you."

Michael shivered and thrust against Wes's leg. "I want to. I want to fuck you so desperately."

"Use me," Wes urged him. "Use my b-body. I am y-your slave, M-Michael Vallant."

Michael's grip in both hands became tight. "I have no unguent."

"Use all of m-me." Wes drew his right hand to his mouth. He sucked hard on his fingers, then withdrew them, letting the saliva drip onto his neck. "I am y-your s-slave," he repeated.

Michael shuddered again. Wes's eyes opened, slowly, heavy with lust. He watched as Michael loomed over him, his hair falling like a silver curtain around his face as he bent to take Wes's mouth in a carnal kiss.

"Then prepare me, slave." Michael rose, turned and placed his spread hole before Wes's mouth.

Wes obeyed. Leaning forward, he made sweet love to Michael's hole once more, kissing it, spearing it, easing the muscles and filling him with slick spit. He held back none of his groans and cries at how much he loved his task, and when Michael's hands began to torment him, he twitched and shuddered in happy helplessness. When Michael turned back around and positioned himself over Wes's straining cock, he tried to open his eyes, but he couldn't, he was so lost in passion.

"Fuck me, Michael," he rasped, thrusting his hips into the air. "Fuck me, p-please."

He felt Michael positioning over him, teasing the tip of his penis, rubbing it ruthlessly against his opening. "Tell me you love me, Albert," he demanded.

"I love you," Wes said obediently.

"I love you too."

Michael drove them both home.

Wes forgot everything. He forgot to worry for Michael, to soothe his fear—he only cried out and fucked, chasing as Michael rode him. He shuddered and gripped at Michael's legs, begging and pleading, so helpless, so wild with need as he sought that tight heat over and over again. But when he came toward the edge, he stopped, not letting himself cross over, determined to wait for Michael to find his release first. And he did—bucking hard and crying out, jerking hard on his own cock and calling out to Wes, "Albert, Albert, *Albert!*" He spent hard against Wes's chest, shooting cream all the way up to his neck, a few droplets landing on his chin. He wanted to let go then, but he still held back, not wanting to take even this from Michael, not without his permission.

Michael slid off, collapsed beside Wes on the bed and drunkenly pushed one of Wes's own hands to his cock. "Come, Albert," he whispered wearily. With three sharp strokes, Wes did, sending his own seed up to mingle with Michael's against his chest.

They lay there a long time, heaving for breath.

I love you too.

Wes shut his eyes and turned his head to place a kiss on Michael's hair. Michael drew himself closer and snuggled against Wes's side.

Wes reached down without displacing him, drew up the covers and nestled in close to his lover as they both settled into sleep. They lay together without moving until morning was high and a chirping bird outside the cottage window woke him.

Opening his eyes, Wes felt Michael hot and close beside him, their sticky spendings dried and cold against his chest.

He smiled.

MICHAEL HAD NO nightmares, and when he woke, it was to find himself in Albert's arms.

Several times that day he wondered if he'd stumbled into a dream. After making lingering, sweet love in bed until they could stand it no longer, they made breakfast together out of the supplies they'd foraged from the cottage larder and enjoyed quiet conversation peppered by comfortable silence over this and their morning tea. After that Albert took Michael on a walk through the neighboring countryside. It was as picturesque as a painting—indeed, everything about Oxford seemed carefully crafted to be exquisitely charming and beautiful.

They meandered all the way back into town, where they shopped once more, this time not just in bookshops but anywhere that caught their fancy. They revisited the bakery and the inn. They wandered down the narrow streets and passages around the campus—Michael couldn't get over how close everything felt, like dangerous alleys in London that weren't dangerous any longer.

The only part that brought him any pain were the boys. The bright, happy boys laughing and joking with one another between classes. It didn't matter that he knew many of them weren't happy at all. That the smaller ones were probably fagging, both literally and metaphorically, for the bigger ones. That they had overbearing or disinterested fathers, that they had nightmares of their own. He couldn't stop yearning after them, wishing he had been one of them. Because much as their lives weren't perfect, he also knew none of them would end up whoring for a living. He'd told Albert he'd rather his life than that of a boring clerk, but as he watched the boys, he admitted that boast was a lie.

He hated his life. Rodger was right—he wanted out of it. But where on earth would he go?

Albert. I can go to Albert. Yes, he could, because Albert loved him. Albert would do anything for him. In fact, he thought Albert often looked as if he were working up to asking him serious questions, possibly ones that revolved around spending much, much more time together on outings like this. In cottages like the one they'd slept in the night before. Yes. Albert would take him in.

Until he learned about Michael's connection to his father.

As Albert's satchel and Michael's purchases were loaded onto the train, Michael tried to reassure himself that his confession might not go entirely awry. Certainly Albert would be shocked, yes. But he'd hardly refuse to see Michael any longer because of it. It wasn't as if it was Michael's fault. Nor was it Albert's. It was just a gruesome, unfortunate fact that it was Albert's father who had bought and raped him.

Of course, it was possible that Albert wouldn't believe him.

Also possible that he would be so disgusted he couldn't stand to see him.

Truth be told, there were many unpleasant outcomes possible.

He barely noticed anything on the train ride home, he was so preoccupied with how, even when, to tell Albert. *Two days.* He could put it off until tomorrow. Or he could get it over with tonight. Instinct told him now was good. Now when Albert was so soft and affectionate. Now when Albert kept holding his hand beneath the lap blanket. Obviously not that very second, he shouldn't tell him, not on the train. But he knew men, and he knew Albert. He had the feeling Albert would try to stay the evening with him. Perhaps that would be best. Perhaps they could go back to Dove Street, and he would take Albert up to his room. Show him his books. Ply him with wine. Light candles and open the windows so the music from the ballroom drifted up. Tell his tale slowly, carefully. Explain.

But when Albert looked at him all soft and in love, he said, "W-Would you c-come to m-my ap-partment?"

Albert's apartment. Ah.

Michael gave him as seductive a smile as he dared in public as they exited the train. "I could make you quite comfortable at Dove Street. In my room." He squeezed Albert's hand surreptitiously. "I would love to show you where the lovely books you bought me go."

If anything, Albert seemed more upset. He stammered incoherently for several seconds, then managed to get out his words. "Ap-p-pologies. I h-h-h-have r-un out of m-m-medicine." He paused for breath, glancing around at the crowd.

Michael's spirits sank. Yes, this had been quite the public airing for his recluse. Which meant he shouldn't even go home with him at all, let alone tell him horror stories about his father.

Before he could say anything, Albert took his arm, maneuvering him against a wall behind a crowd of people lining up for a food stall. He leaned in close so his lips brushed Michael's ear as he spoke.

"St-stay with me." His hand squeezed on Michael's shoulder. "Please."

Michael dared a brush of his lips against his collar. "Of course."

Wes loaded them into a fine black carriage, Michael's books and parcels carefully packed inside too, and the coachman drove them into the heart of Mayfair. As they made their way up the stately walk to Albert's front door, a smart-looking butler came out to greet them.

"Good evening, Lord George." The servant bowed. "You have had several visitors, and much correspondence has been left for you."

Albert waved him off impatiently. "In a m-moment, in a m-m-moment." He hurried Michael down the hall to a room on the left, wrestled with the door, then let them inside.

A fire waited in the sitting room, lighting his way as he fumbled to a side table. It was burned down to embers, but they were hot coals and would rise back to life with just a little fuel. As Albert fumbled with a wooden box and Michael hovered off to the side, a mob-capped maid ducked into the room, built up the fire and exited again without a word.

Now the room was brightly lit, allowing Michael to watch as Albert withdrew a small glass bottle. His hands shook as he held a dropper over an empty glass tumbler, measuring out seven drops with care. After replacing the glass vial in the box, he produced a bottle of wine from the cupboard below, pulled the cork and splashed a bit of red on top of his drops. His hand shook mightily as he brought the glass to his lips and tossed the liquid into his mouth, but when the tumbler came down again, he sighed in ragged relief.

"M-my ap-pologies." His voice was ragged and tinged with shame. "I l-let it go t-too long." His back still to Michael, he ran a hand through his own hair. "I am t-t-trying, but I am st-still d-dependent on the st-stuff."

Michael wanted to reach out and reassure him, but he wasn't entirely sure how. "It's all right," he said, feeling pat, but it seemed to work regardless, for Albert came over and brushed a kiss against his cheek. Michael could smell the sweetness of the wine and the laudanum when Albert spoke.

"I m-must go s-see to our b-belongings and h-hear my c-c-correspondence from Rawlins. I w-won't be long. P-please, make yourself at h-home."

He left, and for a few moments Michael simply stood at the side of the room, looking about idly, trying to decide what to do. He took in a simple set of chairs, a desk, a cabinet.

The wooden box with the opiate inside.

Michael walked toward the box without meaning to. He didn't open it, but he ran his hand over the top. Then he meandered around the room, hushing his footfalls.

He wandered down the hall and into Albert's lavatory.

It was the most impressive bath he'd ever seen: grand copper tub, elegant black tile. More beautiful was the display of plants that filled the place. They stood on shelves, in corners, hung from the ceiling. Some were right in the window and some were pulled back. Apparatus dangled from the ceiling, pipes and tubes and valves that seemed to have nothing to do with the usual features of a bath. Small spouts hung from the ends of some of the tubes. Whole pots of nothing but soil stood on one side of the room.

A series of glass jars lined a long wooden shelf, with green twiglike plants buried within rock inside clear, condensation-riddled containers. Michael was inspecting one as Albert came into the room. When he saw what Michael was looking at, he brightened.

"Th-these are my orchids."

"Oh?" Michael turned back to the plants, more than a little disappointed. These were Albert's prizes? They didn't look terribly interesting. Nothing like the ones at the Regent's Park garden.

Albert stroked the side of one of the jars in the same way most men would stroke their lover. "None of these are b-blooming yet, but they all w-will before I'm through with them." He nodded at the jar he was touching. "Th-This is c-cattleya. They f-form in clumps—you can s-see this sp-specimen starting to do so here, if you p-peer around the side."

He lifted his hand to gesture to another on a higher shelf. "Here is a ph-phalaenopsis. I h-have a blooming plant of this species, though not here. Th-These two are the most p-prevalent species in England just now, though there is also the d-dendrobium."

Michael nodded in what he hoped was a sage gesture, though largely he saw odd little green stems stuck in moss and rock. Albert smiled at him knowingly and pulled a binder down from the shelf above.

"L-Let me show you what these orchids will become."

He opened the binder and laid it on the counter, and Michael couldn't stop an intake of breath.

The colors of the illustrations themselves were half the beauty. Bright pinks fading into white, deep purples, all outlined in charcoal and perched atop bright green stems. The illustrations were works of art, done in expert hand. Beneath each was a carefully inked title: DENDROBRIUM and CATTLEYA.

Michael looked up at him. "Did you paint these?"

Albert nodded. "I h-have trouble still with scale, but otherwise I b-believe I'm quite p-passable as a b-botanical illustrator." He turned one of the heavy vellum pages, giving Michael more minutiae of orchids than he could ever possibly retain. Still, he loved hearing the passion in Albert's voice. The more he spoke of flowers the less and less of his stammer was present.

Turning one last page, Albert sighed. "This is the p-plant I want most of all. It is l-leafless, you see. The f-flower hangs in the m-middle of the air. I've s-seen a few in London—one at L-Lady G-Gordon's p-party the night we met. N-None of them are blooming, however. This illustration is a c-copy of a c-copy." He stroked the page sadly.

Michael leaned against the side of the shelf behind him, feeling a tickle of a bud against the back of his head. "Is that why you love orchids so? Because they're rare?"

"N-N-Not at all." Albert stroked the page of the folio. "Orchids have no p-purpose other than b-beauty. They provide n-no medicine, n-no food. They are d-delicate flowers, difficult to g-g-grow. And y-yet they grow everywhere in the world." He traced a gloved fingertip over the curve of a drawn petal, his soft brown eyes trailing the motion. "B-Beauty for b-b-beauty's sake. G-G-God asks n-n-nothing of them b-beyond that they b-be themselves. Th-That's why they are m-my f-f-favorite."

Was it the yearning in Albert's voice? Was it the way he stroked the image with such love and longing? Was it the gentleness with which his lover spoke? Was it Michael's own pent-up fear simply choosing this moment to burst free? Michael didn't know. All he knew was that his mouth was opening and he was whispering, "Albert—Albert, I have something to tell you."

Albert's expression changed to concern. "W-We should g-go sit d-down."

"No." Michael grabbed at Albert's hands and held them fast before him. His chest hurt. He tried to make himself breathe. "No, if I don't do it right now, I'll frighten myself out of it again." His exhale was a shudder, but he looked Albert in the eye. "I have to tell you. I have to tell you who it was who first bought me when I was a boy."

Tenderness turned to surprise and then to a hard sort of pleasure that vanished quickly beneath steadiness. "Of c-course," Albert said, his voice soothing and strong even with the small hiccough. "I am listening."

"You won't—" Michael had to stop. His throat was so thick he couldn't go on. When he swallowed, his vision swam. "You won't like it," he whispered, a tear sliding down his cheek.

Albert caught the tear and cupped the side of Michael's face tenderly. "Shh. It's all r-right. T-Tell me, and I will help you."

Michael shut his eyes tight. He could barely breathe. "I don't w-want to tell you."

"Then don't." Albert's touches were so strong, so sure. Michael wanted to crawl into that strong, sure hand. He nearly died when it pulled away, only to die all over again when the hand came back bare to press warm skin against his damp cheek. "Don't tell me if it b-brings you pain."

"I have to." Michael turned into his palm, nuzzling it. "Or Rodger will." Anger rippled through Albert's body, making him taut. Michael sighed, the sound half-sob, and kissed the palm that cradled him. "No. He's right. I need to tell you. You'll see why, when I do. I just—" This time the sob caught him at the throat and in his gut at the same time. "I don't want you to hate me," he whispered.

Now he was enfolded in strong arms, pressed against Albert's chest. He smelled of starch and sweat and wind and earth. Albert kissed the top of Michael's head, the gesture hard and desperate. "I would n-never hate you." When this made another sob escape Michael, Albert only drew him closer, rocking him back and forth like a babe. "T-Tell me, love, so I m-may put your m-mind at ease." He stroked Michael's back, his halting words and sure touches a soothing litany. "Just t-tell me. G-Give me his n-name. I w-will still l-love you. N-No m-matter the name."

Over and over he caressed and crooned, lulling Michael. It made him feel soft. Though he knew it could not be so, not truly, it made him feel safe. Eventually it made him feel safe enough to speak.

"You kn-know him," he whispered at last.

"It's all r-r-ight," Albert promised. "Whoever he is,

he is n-nothing to me compared to you."

I hope so. Oh, I hope so, darling Albert. He swallowed another sob and plunged on. "He is very close to you."

"It's all r-right." Albert kept stroking.

It was as if Michael were back at the train station, the steam whistles all blowing at once inside his head. He let the sound and Albert's touch drown out the world. "He—His name—" He choked on bile and had to start again. "He—He—He—" He shut his eyes tight. Oh, he couldn't do it.

"Just tell me," Albert whispered.

The truth sat on his tongue, and Michael willed it out. "He is—"

The firm rapping on the door to Albert's apartments stopped Michael's words and breath. Around him, Albert startled as well. The sound came once more, loud and hard and angry.

"George Albert, this is your father. I demand you open this door at once, or I shall break it down."

"—your father."

The words tumbled out, both an echo and a damnation. As soon as they were out, the full reality of it hit Michael squarely in the center of his chest. He went very, very still.

Albert sighed heavily. "It's all r-right. It's just my father." He let go of Michael reluctantly, kissing the side of his face. "I'll be back."

As Albert left, the room went cold. Colder than it could be with all the heaters, and yet cold it was to him.

Michael felt as if he had been thrown headfirst into the Thames in January.

He was here.

Daventry was here.

With a soft, terrified cry, Michael fell back against the shelves and inched away until he met the wall—the outside wall, damp and cold. He slid down it until he hit the floor, where he curled tight against himself as the terror took him over.

He's here. He's found you at last. He told you he'd have you again, didn't he? He's haunted your dreams, and now he's here. He'll tell Albert about you, and then he'll take you away, and he'll have you. He told you, he told you, he told you—

"No!" he cried, burying his face into the wall. He was shaking so hard his teeth were chattering. "No—no, no, no, no, no!"

But it didn't matter. Even through the terror Michael could hear the voice. *His* voice, low and smooth and elegant and terrible, triggering all the memories Michael had put so carefully away, making him forget himself and remember things he had never wanted to know again, of how those hands had held him down, of how they had invaded him, of how they had coaxed and teased him as that voice droned on, until his own body betrayed him, and the voice laughed, echoing on and on and on—

"No, no, no!" he cried in a broken whisper, but he knew it was pointless, that it was already over, and he only waited, shivering and sobbing quietly, for the hell to begin.

Chapter Thirteen

SOMETHING DARK AND terrible stalked the back of Wes's mind.

His father stood in the middle of his sitting room, lip curled in disgust as he berated Wes for not reading his note, saying he'd convinced his merchant friend to meet Wes again and wanted to set up a new meeting, but Wes hardly heard a word he said. Something was wrong. He felt sick and strange inside, and the worst part of it was that he knew part of him knew why. But whatever it was, it was so nasty that this part of him had gone to hide inside the deepest garden of his soul.

As his father droned on, the darkness hunted, unearthing every corner, determined that the truth would come out. Darkness always slithered inside him when he took opium, especially the drops straight like that, especially so many, but this was different. Normally opium was like a great blanket. It didn't separate him from the fear, not exactly, but he felt…more aware, as it were, of his parts. He could sense the frightened part of him—and most importantly of all, he could calm it. This was key. When he was lucid, he couldn't help this part of himself, for it was far, far too loud, far too strong. The opium let it gentle, and he could talk to it, tell it that nothing bad would happen, and it would listen.

He could see other parts too. He could see the intelligent part of himself, always working in the background, like a clerk sorting papers. He could hear it so much more clearly with the opium, but he'd learned long ago that the amount it took to calm the nervous one turned the intelligent one's language into mush. So he could see his clever self, but it churned out reams of nonsense and nothing more.

Tonight was different. Everything about this moment was wrong. It wasn't a comforting dark inside him, clawing at him as he listened to his father, as Michael hid in his lavatory. It was a yawing, hollow darkness that no opiate could touch, not without killing him first. It was a terrible truth. Instead of comforting him, all the opiate did was make him more aware that just as one part of him was determined to lift the veil, another part was desperate to keep its eyes firmly closed.

I don't want to tell you, Michael's voice whispered, remembered in Wes's mind.

"I needed you there," his father all but snarled. "One simple thing. You had hardly to speak. You only needed to be there. Your only use, and you could not give me even this."

You won't like it.

"I heard you were on the train. With a man. Good God, but I hope he was only a fellow plant idiot and not what I fear him to be."

I don't want you to hate me.

"Is that what you have sunk to now? Flaunting your perversity in public? It's bad enough you won't marry, not even the desperate souls who would have someone as damaged as you. But to carry on an affair? Are you this stupid, boy, that you don't even know to conduct such things in private? Must I arrange even this for you—your perverted pleasure?"

You know him. You are very close to him.

A thought closed its circle in Wes's mind. Horrible. Terrible. Impossible.

"No," he whispered, but the darkness kept coming.

"Thank God for that." Daventry regarded him with open disgust. "I have rued the day you might fancy yourself in love with one of your perverted bedmates. That would be your way. I promise you, there will be pain if it comes to that. You may be a bugger, but you are a Daventry. Use who you must, but no love. They'll only blackmail you, and by extension me. And then things will get messy, which you won't care for either."

I need to tell you. You'll see why, when I do.

I don't want you to hate me.

Sick. Wes was going to be sick. No, this was just his fancy—no, *no*, he was wrong. But God in heaven help him, as he stared at his father, as he thought of Michael's fear, he could think of nothing else to inspire it.

He is—

He is—

He is—

"No," Wes burst out, stopping his own inner whispers. "No. You w-w-would never d-d-do that. You would n-n-n-never h-hurt someone l-l-like that."

His father laughed in his face. "You fool. You simpering nancy boy. I w-w-w-would, and I have, and I will again."

Wes nearly vomited. *He doesn't know what you're thinking. He thinks you're speaking of his disposing of your paramours.* The reminder did nothing to push back the terror. "But n-n-not a ch-child. You w-would n-n-never h-h-hurt a child."

Too late he realized this was even worse—now his father would think he favored boys. He tried to correct himself, but his stammer swallowed him whole, and he stood paralyzed.

Which was why as his father's face went blank—oh-so-carefully blank—and he stilled, Wes saw it all. And he saw, too, the hint of surprise and—just a shade, but it was there—approval.

"Well," Daventry said at last. "If that's the way of it, you must take great, *great* care."

No! Wes wanted to shout. *No, no, no, no, no!* But he had never been more mute than he was now. Mute and frozen, and this time when the whispers began, he could not stop them, could not turn away.

He is your father.

Daventry was watching him with new eyes. Not admiration, not exactly, but it was sickeningly close. "You surprise me, son. You have more depth than I thought."

Wes wished he could vomit on him. He couldn't even manage a single sound, but inside he was screaming. *Not like that. I don't have depth like that.*

His father retrieved his hat from a side table. "On that note, I shall leave you. But come by the house soon, and we will…discuss things. Including how you will make it up to me for missing this party."

The Marquess of Daventry placed his hat upon his head and smiled at Wes. He let himself out the door, leaving his son to stand there swimming in horror as his footsteps disappeared down the hall.

He wasn't sure when, exactly, he began to move. All he knew was that he found himself in the doorway of the lavatory, clutching tight to something in his hand. On the other side of the room, Michael was curled into a ball between two pots of empty soil, a small, trembling splash of blue and pale yellow. When Wes went to him, Michael cried out and shrank into the shadows.

Wes's heart cleaved in two. "M-M-Michael," he whispered.

Michael tucked tighter into himself, but as he shifted, Wes could see his face. It was pale and streaked with tears. "I can't. I can't. I can't."

He murmured the words like a litany. He was lost in panic, in fear—a place Wes knew too well. And it was then Wes realized what he had in his hand, recognizing it by feel but confirming it with a glance: the bottle of laudanum drops.

Swallowing the sea inside himself, he uncapped the bottle and smeared a drop on his finger. Gently, carefully, he rubbed the droplet onto Michael's trembling lips. Michael drew back, startled, but it didn't matter. As he tucked his lip into his mouth, the opiate went too. He stilled somewhat almost immediately, though most of that was from surprise.

"Sweet," he murmured. "And…tart." But he was still shaking.

"Let me g-give you a bit m-more in w-water."

Michael did not respond, but neither did he cringe as Wes rose to fetch a glass from the top of a cabinet. He startled slightly when Wes turned on a tap, but when Wes returned to his side, bringing the glass to his lips, Michael only stared down at it in a daze.

"Opium." He looked uneasy.

"It w-w-will help you," Wes promised.

Michael blinked at the glass. His eyes shifted to Wes, then filled with tears.

"You know." There was no question.

Wes affirmed the statement with a curt nod.

Michael reached for the glass and tossed the liquid down. He did not look at Wes again, and Wes waited patiently for the drug to take effect—both the drug he had given Michael and the extra nip he had taken himself before returning to Michael's side.

Eventually Michael lifted a hand in front of himself, watching it oddly. "Feel so strange. Everything…floats."

"L-Let it calm you," Wes urged. "L-Let it take your fear."

Michael looked up at him blearily. "Daventry."

My father. Wes swallowed and replied, with some effort, "Y-Yes."

Tears leaked from the corners of Michael's eyes. "I'm sorry."

Wes made a strange, strangled sound. He'd apologized? *He?* The opium tried to carry him away, but this was too terrible. Michael. *Michael.*

My father raped Michael.

While I was hiding at home, too terrified to go to school.

Gentle hands touched his face. "Albert—Albert, please don't cry."

Wes opened his mouth to deny this, but stopped as he found with no small amount of surprise that he was indeed weeping. Tears were streaming down his face, and he couldn't stop them. But still he couldn't speak.

Michael kissed him softly on the cheek. "Albert, don't cry. It's all right."

"S-S-S-S-S-S-S-S—" Wes choked, coughed and tried again, but everything caught at his teeth. "S-S-S-S-S-S—"

Both Michael's hands gripped his face now—clumsily, and when he spoke, Michael's words were slurred too. "No. *No*, Albert—I won't let him hurt you too."

That statement of protection only made Wes weep harder. His chest hurt, and his body ached as if it were splitting in half. When Michael kissed the bridge of his nose, he choked on a sob and reached up to grip his shoulders.

You must be very, very careful.

"S-S-S-S-S-S-S-Sorry," he choked out. "S-S-S-S-So s-s-s-s-s-orry, s-s-s-s-s-s-s-s—"

"Shh." Michael kissed one of Wes's eyes, then the other, then his lips. "Hush, love."

The pain tore Wes to pieces inside. Not pain—sorrow, shame, and guilt like he had never known. His father—*his father*! After all the names he had called Wes, all the accusations—and he had done this? *This?*

And to *Michael*?

The sob that had been choking the back of his throat broke free.

Michael caught it with his mouth. "Don't hate me," Michael whispered against Wes's lips. He was crying too. "I could bear him using me again, anything in the world but that you would hate me."

Wes held him fast. "N-N-No."

Michael clutched at him. "I'll do whatever you want. Just don't go, Albert—please, please don't leave me because it was him." He kissed Wes's cheek, his ear.

"Just don't leave me, Albert, please."

Wes could not answer. He could barely think. He needed more opium. He needed an entire bottle of brandy.

He needed a knife to carve this horrible truth from his head.

This time when the knock came on the door, they both yelped, but when Wes heard Rawlins's familiar voice, he calmed at once. "B-B-Butler. It's m-m-my b-butler." He dragged a kiss across his cheek. "I'll be r-right back."

He rose carefully, listing back and forth as he made his way to the door. When he opened it, the butler was standing there holding a lumpy burlap bag.

"This was just delivered for you, my lord." Rawlins's nose curled slightly. "The…gentleman gave it to me, and his companion said they would 'settle up' with you later." He handed over the bag, made a proper bow and left.

Wes shut the door, opened the bag and looked down at a slightly ragged but otherwise perfect orchid, an exact copy of the one he'd seen at Mrs. Gordon's house.

He didn't know how long he stared at it. He only knew that eventually he heard a soft voice down the hall, and he turned to see Michael standing there, swaying on his feet, looking as if he had just climbed through and were poised at the portal to hell.

"Albert?" he whispered, his entire world in the

word.

Wes put down the orchid and its bag on the table, not even bothering to rewrap it. He stumbled down the hall toward Michael.

On the way he picked up the bottle of wine he'd opened earlier. After a brief, reassuring kiss to Michael, he picked up the laudanum and put a liberal amount in the bottle.

He took a deep, deep drink directly from the mouth.

As the now-dangerous amount of opium swirled inside him, he stumbled back into the hall. Wrapping his arm around Michael, he led him back into his bedroom.

Michael sagged against him. "I'm sorry."

Wes kissed him, gently, then took another swig from the bottle, deeply. "F-Forget." He kissed him again.

Forget.

Forget everything.

Everything.

He laid Michael down on the bed. He kissed him. He made slow, sweet, opiate-laced love to him. He let Michael cry, and he cried too. He held Michael close as he quieted and drifted fitfully to sleep.

Then Wes rose. He penned several notes at his desk. He paused at the orchid, closed his eyes and turned away.

He slipped out of his apartments and out of his

house, out of Mayfair and into the night, not knowing where he was going, not caring. He wandered on and on, trying to outrun the feeling of despair no opium could hide, the despair that as the drug wore off would only get worse.

How long he wandered, he didn't know. He had vague, distant memories of strange rooms full of smoke and naked women who tried to entice him, but all Wes wanted of them was the pipes they held in their hands. He remembered a great deal of vomiting. That was the way of life, with opium, but there was so much more vomiting now, it seemed. And then there was the other problem. His gut twisted in knots so tight he wanted to drive a knife into them to loosen his stool. Another curse of opium. Wes wanted oblivion, but opium now only gave him hell. All he knew now was despair, the yawning portal of deep terror that chased him, growing ever closer.

In the bowels of the darkest alley in London it found him, and he knew he could run no more. He let go, ready now for the end.

It did not come.

He had tried. He had found a knife, or a piece of glass—he couldn't tell which in his delirium—but whatever it was, it was sharp, and it would work. Even here he failed. A vision stopped him, a sad, beautiful vision of a man who reached out and stayed his hand. When Wes shut his eyes, the man began to weep, and Wes ran, stumbling, nearly fainting, but running on and on, trying to get away from that terrible sound.

MICHAEL'S HEAD AND mouth felt as if they were full of cotton. Only the top of his head, though, because his ears felt far, far too open, and every sound was magnified, and the barest scrape of a fingernail seemed likely to make him cast up his accounts.

"The bastard drugged him. *Drugged Michael.*"

The words sounded funny, echoing as if they were being spoken through a speaking tube, but Michael knew the voice even so. He lifted his head.

"Rodger?"

He opened his eyes, but everything was blurry. His stomach threatened to heave.

"Rodger?" he called with more panic. "Rodger, I don't feel w—"

A hand thrust him forward as a disgusting torrent came out of his mouth. Michael had just enough time to whimper and smack his lips against the foul acid of his stomach when it happened again. One time more, and then strong hands were lowering him back down as a cool cloth rested upon his sweaty brow.

"Good God in heaven," Michael slurred, letting his suddenly very heavy eyelids close.

"Hush." This was Rodger again. The cool cloth slid gently down his cheek. "You hush, love. I've got you."

"What happened?" Michael couldn't remember. He couldn't remember anything at all.

"Lord George drugged you is what happened," Rodger said tightly. "And I'll kill the bastard when I find him."

Lord George.

Albert.

Michael's eyes flew open, and he tried to sit up. Then moaned and sank back down.

"I have to—" His stomach heaved in protest of his attempts to move, and he held his breath a moment, trying to recover. "Albert. I must—"

"He's gone, love." The anger in Rodger's voice was acute. "He fucking up and left. Left you here. Sent a runner for me, so he gets some credit for that, but he left you here in the meantime and run off like the snake he is."

Michael's eyes opened again. "Ran off?"

Rodger's bleary face suggested a grimace. Michael needed to see him. "Where are my—?"

Rodger handed him his spectacles without a word.

Michael slipped the glasses onto his face. Rodger was scowling.

And sad.

"Where is Albert?" Michael repeated. "Where has he gone?"

The tic in Rodger's cheek grew deeper. "I don't know."

Michael's blood ran cold. "No." He looked up in despair and desperation at Rodger. "Why—?"

But then he began to remember.

I have something to tell you.

Michael's hands trembled. "Daventry. Daventry was here."

All sorrow evaporated into anger as Rodger's hand seized his shoulder. "If that bastard harmed you—"

Michael shook his head. "No. No, he was…" He shut his eyes, remembering. "He was at the door. He came to the door—I don't know if he came in. I think…." He ran a hand over his face. "I think I went into some kind of hysterics. I don't remember. I only know that I was terrified and that Albert tried to comfort me." The last piece of the puzzle clicked into place. "And that was why he gave me the opiates, I would imagine."

"He could bloody well have sent for me then."

Michael ignored Rodger. He could remember all of it now. The cold fear, the old terror rising inside him, choking him.

"I hope he is rotting in some alley, damn him," Rodger swore.

"*No.*" Michael didn't know if he was speaking to Rodger or the terrible swirl of memory. He'd told him. Told Albert. Albert knew. Albert knew, and he'd given Michael opium.

And gone. Left in the middle of the night and disappeared.

To kill himself, a dark part of Michael's mind whispered.

When he cried out this time, Rodger drew him into

a gruff embrace. "It's all right, love."

Michael's throat was almost too thick to speak. "He means to be dead. He will drug himself until he is dead."

"He isn't worthy of you," Rodger shot back, but Michael shook his head. "He might as well be dead."

"I love him. I am in love with him. If you wish him ill, you wish me ill as well."

"He's a coward who descends into drugs and runs when confronted with the truth."

"*No!*" Michael cried.

Rodger didn't yield. "He ran, love. You need him right now more than ever, and he ran."

Tears had been brimming in Michael's eyes for some time, but at this, he gave in and let them flow. Yes. That cut. It cut like a saber across his chest, that Albert had run. It was worse than a rejection, somehow. But it still didn't matter. "I love him. I don't want him to die."

Rodger sighed and kissed Michael's cheek. "I already have the boys out looking for him. I want to kill him myself for leaving you, but if you want him, Michael, you shall have him."

Michael leaned forward and kissed Rodger softly on the cheek.

Rodger grunted and rose from the bed, calling for the men who were with him. They tried to carry Michael, but he refused them, insisting on standing on his own feet. He made it all the way to the sitting room.

There he saw what could only be an orchid, exotic and frail, roots exposed and drying as it lay helpless and half-broken on the floor.

That was when it hit him, not fear, not panic, just sorrow, and he fell to the floor, took the orchid carefully in his hands and cried.

Chapter Fourteen

THEY COULD NOT find Albert anywhere.

Rodger pointed out, almost hourly, that they had found no sign of his body, either, and that a man of his birth would not be lost for too long even in death. But with each passing day, Michael grew more and more frantic. Because he could, he took it out on Rodger.

"You always brag that you can find anyone in London." Michael stood over Rodger's desk in his dressing gown, doing his best to loom. "You say no one can slip away from you, that this is your city." He folded his arms over his chest. "Where is he, then?"

"I don't know." Rodger tightened his lips into a thin line. "He went out the back door and down the alley. He got into a cab somewhere around Grosvenor." He ran his hand through his hair. "And that's where I lose him. I interviewed the man who picked him up myself. He says he let him out on a street, but there was no one on that street who saw him get into another cab. I know where every cab that ran down that street went. I've investigated every route, every destination. Everything runs cold."

Michael sat down and wrapped his gown closer to his body. He stared at Rodger's desk for a long, terrible moment.

Rodger shook his head, reading his mind. "He's not dead, lad. I've been watching the corpses too. The only thing I can think of is that he isn't in town. All his usual places I have eyes on. Even some of his unusual. But I don't get anywhere checking non-London options either. The only thing that confounds me is that his family isn't looking. Even a bastard like the marquess would want this handled delicately. Either they're accustomed to this, or someone has warned them off, that he's invisible but fine. Something is odd here. He can't go missing this long, not this easily. Not by accident."

This pinched at Michael. "You're saying he's hiding from me deliberately?"

Rodger snorted. "That's exactly what I'm saying, ducks."

"But why? I understand his being upset, but—hiding?"

Rodger leveled a look at him.

"I don't believe you," Michael said. "I don't think he's hiding from me. I think something's wrong."

"And now you're being a ninny." He waved in irritation at Michael. "Go on with you. I have other things to do in addition to hunting down your idiot of a lover, and your nagging helps none of it."

Michael left Rodger, reluctantly, and returned to his room.

He tried to read, but he couldn't keep his attention on anything. He tried a bath and some lunch in the kitchen.

As the days turned into a week, he even tried working.

Not sex. Not even hand jobs—they didn't frighten him, but it felt like a betrayal, so he didn't allow them. He flirted and danced and teased, working the customers into such a state they could barely make it to a booth to relieve themselves. Every night he took a shift at the ballroom, trying to distract himself from the fact that he was dying inside.

But it didn't work. He still pined for Albert, and on top of it all he didn't feel the thrill in working anymore. He didn't hate it, didn't feel sick doing it, and didn't panic. It only felt…strange to smile and tease men who were not Albert. It didn't feel wrong, either. It just didn't feel…satisfying.

Which was a revelation in and of itself. Was that why he had been a whore? Because it was satisfying? He would have laughed at the idea before, but now the question loomed in his mind. Why *was* he a whore?

He found Rodger late one evening and asked him.

Rodger gave him a very strange look, one that seemed to question Michael's sanity in earnest. "Are you ill, love? Or simply tired?"

"Neither." Michael rested his elbows on Rodger's desk. "Honestly, why am I doing this? Because it seems something I should be able to answer, and I can't. I don't even remember precisely how it started. It just seemed to happen."

Rodger leaned back and threaded his fingers over his chest. "You asked me to let you try. A man had been eyeing you, and I commented on it, and you went still and quiet. I thought you would be upset, but you just said, 'Is he still looking?' and he was, so I said so. You told me you were going to go up to him and offer to jerk him off, and how much should you ask for? Could have knocked me over with a feather. I told you to go on ahead, and I'd keep an eye out for you. After that night, you never looked back."

Michael remembered now. He smiled absently as he stared unseeing at the wall, letting the old scene pass through his vision. "Yes. I remember now as well. There was something about him I liked. He was hungry, but not domineering like Daventry. And handsome. I liked the idea of watching his face while he came—and getting paid for it."

Rodger nodded. "It's always been about power for you. About pleasure too, but mostly power. Which I thought was a proper attitude for a prostitute, so I encouraged you. And here we are."

Power. Michael frowned, still staring off at nothing. "Then why don't I care about it anymore?"

"We been over this, ducks. Lord George reminded you of Daventry—"

"No, that's not what I mean." Michael gestured vaguely toward the front room. "I've been flirting with the men all week. I even went into the booths a few times—I didn't let them touch me, but even if they had, I could tell it wouldn't have mattered. It was almost boring. I felt nothing at all. Not disgust, not aversion. Just…disinterest."

Now he had Rodger's attention. He sat forward, looking hard at Michael. "No panic?"

Michael shook his head. "None."

"Hmm," Rodger said, and returned to his ledgers.

Three days after that Michael was called into Rodger's office to find his friend looking angry and grim.

"I have had word," he spat out, "of Lord George."

Michael's stomach became abruptly hollow. "You have?"

Rodger nodded tersely. "He is on the east side, down by the docks." His fist tightened on the desk. "With that damned woman."

The pit in Michael's abdomen widened. "Pardon?"

"He's with Brannigan. It took me a week to confirm it, and that's all I can get. Not without creating a royal fracas, and I won't do such for the likes of that bastard."

With a woman. Michael tried to shove his doubts aside. "But—did you explain? Did you tell him—her—I was looking for Albert? Me, Michael?"

There was a horrible pause. Eventually Rodger nodded again. “Aye.”

Michael stood there a long time, until the silence pressed on him and he turned away without speaking.

“Michael, love,” Rodger called out, but Michael spoke over him.

“I need to go for a walk,” he said, heading for the door. Blessedly, Rodger let him go.

He didn’t go outside, however, but to his room. For several minutes he sat on his bed, staring at the floor, thinking. Then he rose and rifled through his closet.

As he dressed, his eyes fell on the space beneath his window, and out of habit, he crossed to the shelf and stroked the glass jar.

With the help of some books, Albert’s notes, and advice Rodger had hunted down for him, the orchid was still alive. In a very narrow sort of way Michael fancied he was one of London’s top orchid experts now. Whenever possible, he took the jar—carefully, so carefully—to the bath with him, steaming up the room as much as he dared. He kept a pot of boiling water atop his stove, making the attic as humid as possible. Likely he had ruined scores of books. He cared for none of them now. Only Albert’s orchid mattered.

Only Albert mattered.

If only I mattered to him.

He knew without question Albert would never hurt him deliberately, that he ignored him not to wound, not to mock. Yet Michael found that didn't change the fact that he did hurt. In a strange way the idea that Albert simply didn't think of him now, too wrapped up in his pain to notice, hurt worse than any deliberate slight.

Turning away from the orchid, he caught a look at himself in the mirror, at his long hair. He thought of all the men who had stroked it. He thought of how Rodger called them his golden locks, rubbing his fingers together to indicate coin.

He thought of how he had lain in bed with Albert at Oxford, safe and loved as Albert held him and methodically stroked the long, silken strands, calling him beautiful.

He thought of Albert with the unknown woman even Rodger couldn't reach.

Michael touched his hair sadly.

Gathering the rest of his things, he headed down the stairs. He found Clary in the ready room, drew a breath, and said, "Darling, do you have time to cut my hair?"

EVERY NIGHTMARE WES had ever had in his life was haunting him at once, and as days turned into weeks and the weeks into a month, he very, very sincerely wanted to die.

He didn't even remember coming to Penny. As the opium left his system, his memory began to scramble, and he could recall both her finding him in an alley and falling through her door in a faint. He also thought sometimes he was with his father, or underwater. But his faulty memories came and went. Penny herself was always there when they receded.

She took the opium from him slowly. To do otherwise might kill him, she said, though as the withdrawal set its teeth into Wes he wished he were dead. The road back was full of nightmares, literal and metaphorical both. Shakes, fevers, retching, tortured visions—his body and mind were melting away, and there was nowhere for him to hide.

Penny stayed by him through it all. No matter how he wept, no matter how he shouted, no matter that he vomited or soiled himself, she remained. She listened to him plead. She heard his bargains with God and with the devil. She witnessed his hallucinations, most of them about his father.

His father and Michael.

Over and over again he watched his father rape his lover. Over and over again Michael called to him, but Albert could never move. He could barely speak.

"You're worthless," his father told him. "You're pathetic and worthless. How could you ever save him? You cannot even save yourself."

His father became the burglar. The burglar became the nasty boys at school. The nasty boys at school became the superior members of the Botanical Society, all of them sneering at him as they raped Michael over and over and over. Night and day, waking or sleeping, the visions never stopped, and they were worse than the chills, or the fevers, or the sick or the spiders and lizards and monsters that erupted from the walls. None of them held a candle to his failure, his worthlessness, played like a bad, endless opera before the backs of his eyes.

He would have run mad, he was sure of it, had it not been for Penny.

"You are not worthless," she told him every time he repeated the nightmare's accusations aloud. "You are not pathetic. You are not weak. You are strong, George Albert Westin. You are strong and capable, and you are alive."

"No," he would weep. "No, I'm not," he would insist, but she held fast to his hands and whispered in his ear.

"Yes you are. And your Michael thinks so too."

On and on this went, torture that seemed like years, that seemed it would never end. Yet end it did. Not at once. But the nightmares began to get weaker, and wonder of wonders, Wes grew stronger. One day he found himself shouting back at his father, at the burglar, at all the boys and men who mocked him, parroting Penny's words.

"I am n-not worthless. I am n-n-not w-w-weak."

Whenever he defended himself, Michael would look up at Wes, his beautiful eyes cutting right to Albert's soul, and he would whisper, "I love you."

He was still very sick. He threw up on Penny as often as not, but now there was no blood. It took him over a month to stand. Walking seemed years away. But he was getting better.

"Rest," Penny urged him when the panic tried to drown him. "Think only of getting better. Don't dwell on troubling things."

"M-M-Michael," he rasped. "M-M-M-M—"

Penny rubbed his back, the same soothing strokes his mother had once given him. "Michael can wait. You're no good to him until you're better. Rest, Wes. Rest."

In the end Wes had no choice. He was so weak he could barely sit, let alone compose sentences enough to explain. But he could still think. And though the monsters were slain, this duty was far worse, far more terrible an outcome left untended, and unlike the hallucinations, this one was real.

He saved his strength. He used every trick Penny had taught him. He practiced over and over inside his mind. When he knew he was able, he spoke.

"Michael," he whispered one day as Penny held his head over a bowl. "You m-m-must tell M-M-M-Michael."

"I sent word to your butler," Penny soothed him. "I told him to tell anyone concerned that you had gone unexpectedly out of town. Someone is even looking after your plants."

He didn't give a damn about his plants. She didn't understand. He shoved the bowl away, wiped his mouth with his sleeve and sat up, forcing himself not to wobble. "Michael," he repeated, looking her as squarely in the eye as he could. "M-M-Must tell M-M-ichael."

She paused, regarding him carefully before putting down the bowl. She spoke slowly. "Is…this the Michael that you spoke of as you dreamed?" Another pause. "The Michael that you…love?"

He froze. Would she abandon him over this? Would she love an addict but despise a sodomite? He thought of Michael and decided it didn't matter. If she tossed him out, he would find a way to stumble to Dove Street himself.

"Y-Yes."

The awkward moment expanded painfully. And then she nodded, reached into her pocket, and withdrew a notebook and pencil. "What is his address?"

Half-laughing, half-sobbing in relief, Wes gave it to her.

A MONTH AND three weeks after Albert had gone, Michael took himself to Oxford.

Rodger went with him. They took the mail coach, not the train, and they did not speak for the whole of the journey. This was nothing new. It had become Michael's habit to go for long walks all across London, and Rodger always went with him, his silent companion. It was only partly, Michael knew, to keep from intruding on his thoughts. A great deal of it was because for once Rodger did not know what to say.

Once in Oxford, as he had hoped, Michael felt lighter. He knew a bit of pain at walking the paths he had walked so happily with Albert, but they still gave him pleasure, and so he cherished them. He went to the shops. He went to the inn.

He went to Bodleian.

Here a bit in him began to stir. Perhaps it was the smell of the books, the hush that swallowed his footsteps across the marble floors. Perhaps—oh, he didn't know what it was, but the library made him feel strange, to the point he almost wanted to leave. It was for this reason he kept himself moving, kept himself wandering the shelves of books, selecting some, ignoring most. He stationed Rodger in a reading room and went off on his own, searching from floor to floor, from room to room, on and on as if somewhere, somehow, within these endless lines of pages, he could find himself.

He came down one dark hallway, ducking around a group of quietly laughing young men, trying to stay out of their way. But they were a veritable herd, a new clutch of them appearing as soon as the last were gone. Eventually Michael gave up and slipped past them through the doorway, sliding up to an empty glass display cabinet someone had propped into the corner, apparently to take up more space in the narrow passage. He pressed up against it and stared at the black backdrop behind it—and there. There it was.

There he was.

It was his reflection—Michael Vallant, in the glass. Distorted by the warp, shadowed by the dim light of the hall and the ripple made by the endless pass of bodies. He didn't even recognize himself. His short hair curled around his head, around his ears, falling over his forehead. His face was thin from lack of appetite, his cheeks sunken. There were shadows under his eyes—eyes outlined by his thick spectacles. His lips were parted in surprise. He wore his traveling clothes, garments chosen not with care but because they were simple, serviceable.

In the glass was not a whore. Not a witty, clever scholar eclipsing the discovery of his sodomy. Not a lawyer, not a thief. Not anything at all. Simply Michael Vallant, the man.

The man, and the boy within.

There he was, staring back at Michael in the empty curio case, in the shadowy glass. The boy who had been lost. The boy who had been so rudely used. The boy who had run into the night, his home having burned down around him.

The boy Michael had thought had died.

He was not aware of when exactly he began to weep. The tears were silent, and few, sliding down his face into his collar like drops of rain that did not know if it meant to begin in earnest or simply go back to bed inside the clouds. Little dewdrops of sorrow. Not keening, not release. Simply those few tears, leaving salt trails across his cheeks as Michael stared at himself, afraid to move, afraid the self might go away.

"Sir?"

Michael jumped, turning away guiltily. A man stood there, about his age. He looked concerned. "Sir, are you well?"

Michael nodded hastily and wiped at his eyes. "Yes. Sorry—only—sorry." He longed to cast one last glance at the case, but he feared to see the reflection gone or changed. He gave a thin smile to the man. "Apologies," he said, and pushed the rest of the way down the hall.

He went outside, into the courtyard, into what seemed a disgustingly bright sun. It should be gray and soft, but no, the world beamed intensity at him he did not want. He wandered, feeling empty, confused, until he could take it no more and sat down before a fountain, collapsing onto a bench, afraid he would weep again, afraid he might not.

The image from the glass remained in his brain. Did he look like that? That quiet, sad man? No brass, no whore, no flirt.

Only Michael.

He laughed, the sound turning into a sob, and he covered his mouth, his eyes blurring as he stared at the water.

When the bell tolled two, he rose and began to wander again. He collected Rodger and went back to the inn where he ordered a plate of food that he largely pushed around, a glass of ale he did not drink. He sat in the corner, looking out the window at the town, the university—and he knew.

"I'm going to live here," he said.

Rodger looked up at him, possibly as surprised to hear him speak as to hear what he said. "What—here? Now?"

Michael considered this, then shook his head. "No. Not now. Not just yet. But soon."

The idea warmed him. He would find himself a set of rooms. He would like a house, but he wouldn't have the money for such things. He would need an income of some sort—Rodger would find him something, or set him up with an income, because that was what he did. But Michael would be here. He would move about the town, about the library, about the countryside on long walks alone. They would not know him as the whore, the sodomite. He would be the scholar. The kind man who lived upstairs and frequented that corner of the pub.

A quiet gentleman.

When the call came for the coach, Michael rose with Rodger and boarded. As they rode out of town, Michael played the day over in his head.

"I will miss you," Rodger said gruffly.

Michael didn't even look to see if the other passengers were awake or asleep. He simply laid his head on Rodger's shoulder and took his hand. "I will miss you too."

And then, because they were still English, they broke apart and resumed their silence. Michael felt both light and heavy as they took their cab to Dove Street, feeling as if he had traveled much farther than the distance to Oxford and back. He was ready to tuck himself into bed with a novel and a cup of tea and lose himself in fiction for the evening.

When Michael got out of the cab, Rodger had gone still and stiff on the walk. Peering around him to see what had upset his friend, Michael saw a tall, titian-haired and eccentrically dressed woman standing there smiling at him.

"Hello," she said, ignoring Rodger and looking straight at Michael as she spoke in a bright American accent. "You must be Michael Vallant."

Chapter Fifteen

THE WOMAN WAS, Michael decided as he watched her standing in the middle of Rodger's office, quite possibly the tallest female he'd ever seen. She dwarfed Rodger by several inches, and she would even if she weren't wearing boots with heavy heels. She looked as if she should be bearing a shield and leading dead Vikings to Valhalla—except that she was red-haired, not blonde. Her face was not precisely pretty, but she was striking all the same—something about her declared that there would be no more nonsense, and that was the end of the discussion. She looked to be in her thirties. No ring glinted on her finger, either.

Rodger was standing between the woman and the window, chest out, hands resting defiantly on his hips.

"Who the devil do you think you are," he began, using his clipped and proper high-Brit voice, "to come barging into my establishment and bark out orders like some sort of manic seal?"

"I am Penelope Brannigan," she replied in her flat

tones, not cowered in the slightest. "Not that it's any of your business. Because you aren't Michael Vallant, and therefore I have no business with you." She gave him a quelling glance. "And I'm not barking out orders. I'm simply asking to speak with him in private. I understand that I terrify *you*, Barrows, but I promise I shall not bite your friend. Not even a little."

Rodger began to sputter, his accent falling into cant in his rage. "You rabid bit of baggage. I'll have you know—"

Penelope Brannigan stepped around Rodger, ignoring him completely, and smiled at Michael. "I'm sorry, it appears I shall have to give you my message in public. I am here on behalf of Lord George Albert Westin, and—"

Michael tried to step in front of Miss Brannigan. "You know Albert?" Hope and wariness battled within him. *A woman. Rodger said he was with a woman.* "You know where he is?"

Rodger shoved him—gently—back out of the way and aimed a finger in Miss Brannigan's face. "Listen here, Madam Harpy, woman or no, I don't mind giving you a taste of my fist."

Brannigan wrinkled her nose at him as if he were a piece of garbage stuck to her heel in the street. "Oh, I loathe your kind of man more than any other. You're nothing but a bully, aren't you?"

"Bloody hell, woman, but you have a lot of nerve, barging into my establishment *and* my office and insulting me. I'm not above having you thrown out."

"By all means, try," she said sweetly.

Michael stepped between them again. "Please—please, madam, you said you have word of Albert?"

Rodger swore and stalked out of the room, slamming the door behind him.

Brannigan relaxed significantly with Rodger gone, and now for Michael she was all smiles and softness, leading him to a settee. "He is staying with me, at a house I run down by the docks." Her smile died. "I will not lie to you. He has been very, very sick, and he is still not even close to recovered. I thought he was dead several times. He is stable now, but very weak, and it was only today that he was able to explain to me what I think he has been trying to tell me for some time. He asked me to come here to tell you that he is sorry." She squeezed his hand and added, "And that he loves you."

It amazed Michael he had any tears left to shed over that man, but it appeared he did, for they were rolling down his cheeks. He wiped them away with the back of his hand.

"Your pardon," he murmured. He realized what the woman had just confessed to him and with what acceptance, and he looked at her with new eyes. "You are not offended to be charged to tell one man that another loves him?"

Her smile was enigmatic. "I have learned in my life, Mr. Vallant, that love does not share the prejudices we humans have—and that it is rare and precious." She sighed. "I am sorry I did not come to you sooner. When Barrows's men came to the door, I believe they mentioned your name, but I didn't understand. I thought they meant to collect on a debt—I didn't know."

"It's all right," Michael said.

"You must understand. He was soaked in opium when he came to me. It is a wonder he did not die from what he took." She shook her head. "He was doing so well. He had been coming to me with help in elocution, and I thought he was even cutting back on his doses of laudanum—I don't know what threw him so badly, but something did."

"I know." Michael stared down at the floor. "But it is a long story to tell, and unpleasant."

"I would love to hear it." She glanced around Rodger's office in distaste. "Perhaps not in a brothel, however."

Michael had to laugh at that. But then he thought of Albert, wrecked as she said he was, and his smile died. "I want to see him. Please—I need to see him."

He did not like the way she hesitated. "You will, but not yet. Let him be ready. Let him become a little stronger."

"But I want to help him," Michael protested.

A strange shadow passed over her face. When she spoke, it startled him at how soft she had become, how she could not look him in the eye. "As one who has witnessed a loved one in this state, I advise you to wait.

It is a s-special kind of hell to see them too s-s-soon." She shut her eyes. "And if they d-d-on't make it all the way through, it is unb-b-bearable."

Now it was Michael who squeezed her hand. "Very well," he said quietly. "I will trust your judgment. For now."

She rose, dabbing at her eyes with a handkerchief. "I must get back to him now. But I will come by soon to hear your tale."

She gave him a smile and a nod goodbye, but as she headed for the door, an idea struck Michael, and he called out, "Wait! Wait—I have something I wish you to give him." He rushed past her, pausing to touch her arm. "You will wait? It's up in my room."

"I will wait," she promised.

He hurried as best he could, afraid she would disappear, afraid that Rodger would shout her out before he returned. They were only glaring at one another in the front hallway as he entered it, and so he pressed the glass jar into her arms.

"What is this?" she asked, looking confused.

"He will know. Tell him I did my best, but that I expect him to take over from here. And tell him—" A lump in his throat caught, but he pushed past it. "Tell him I expect him to show me how it blooms."

"Michael," Rodger warned, "don't let him drag you back in. He already hurt you once. If you go back to that no-good—"

Michael stepped forward hastily and clapped a hand

over Rodger's mouth as Brannigan's body went taut. "Don't, Rodger. I believe she truly will hit you. And you're ugly enough as it is without a broken tooth to boot."

Rodger glared at Brannigan, then looked pleadingly at Michael. "Don't let him hurt you again."

Michael smiled and kissed Rodger on the cheek. "Thank you, mother hen. But I'll be fine." He turned back to Miss Brannigan. "Besides, I won't be seeing him anytime soon, it seems."

"I will endeavor to make it as soon as I possibly can," she promised. "And I will give him this and tell him what you said." She gave one last warning look to Rodger, then turned to several large men Michael did not recognize, men who he'd thought were new bodyguards of Rodger's but indeed they appeared to be hers. "We should go. Traffic will be ghastly at this time of day."

They left, and Michael felt as if it was his heart in that jar being carried away.

Rodger sighed heavily and put his arm around Michael. "I hope to God he's worth it, ducks."

"He is." Michael leaned on Rodger's shoulder and watched Penelope Brannigan's coach drive off into the evening fog. "He is."

THREE WEEKS LATER, Wes sat in the sitting room of Penny's house, waiting for Michael to come.

"There's no reason to be nervous." Penny rested her hand on Wes's shoulder as she sat beside him. "It's Michael, not the devil." Her hand squeezed lightly. "And he's lovely. Handsome, charming, and unless I am completely fooled, utterly in love with you."

Wes smiled wryly despite his nerves but kept his eyes on the door to the hall. Eventually footsteps sounded, and Penny urged him to his feet.

"Look sharp, Wes. He's coming."

Rising unsteadily, Wes faced the opening door. The fears roared inside Wes, nearly weighing him down. He could not help his nerves, nor could he his fears. What if he had waited too long? What if Michael found him weak? What if he couldn't forgive Wes because of his father?

What if someone else had come along, and Michael loved him instead?

Michael appeared in the door, and Wes forgot to breathe.

Beautiful—he was so beautiful, as beautiful as ever. He was dressed more soberly than he ever had been before, even on outings, but he still looked so smart and handsome that Wes wanted to take him up in his arms and spin him around, he was so lovely. His beautiful face, his thin, sensual lips, his glowing cheeks, his bright, large eyes—Wes could not stop his smile. Michael wore his spectacles. They only added to his charm.

Wes's eyes widened, and before he could stop himself, the words tumbled out of his mouth. "You c-cut your hair."

Michael had been hovering in the doorway, looking quietly uncertain, but now he seemed very self-conscious, and his hand lifted up to his shorn hair. "I'm sorry. I was angry."

Wes smiled, no artifice, and shook his head. "I l-like it. It s-suits you."

Michael's hand ran along his hairline again, then lowered. He smiled, but hesitantly. "It's easier, I confess." Clasping his hands together in front of himself, he rocked slightly on his heels. "Are you well, my lord?"

My lord. Wes's smile melted away, and he tried to mask his hurt, but he wasn't sure he succeeded. *My lord. We will be formal now? Have you only come to say goodbye?* He replaced his smile as best he could, and offered a nod. "Y-Yes. Th-Th-Th—"

Yes, thank you, my beloved. Come here so I may embrace you properly.

Wes stopped, shut his eyes and started to turn away.

When he opened his eyes, he saw the orchid thriving in the sun beside his bed. He gathered his courage and turned to face his lover again.

"Please come in," Penny said to Michael, "and have a seat."

She directed Michael to the chair beside Wes's sofa, and Michael placed himself primly on the front part of the chair. He looked ready to bolt. Wes sat as well, though he mirrored Michael's position. He foresaw half an hour of stilted, painful conversation ahead of him. His only consolation was that Penny would be there to keep things from being too stilted and awkward.

Except she was heading toward the door.

"I'll leave the two of you alone," she said, a sparkle in her eyes. "Ring if you need anything, but other than that, I'll be sure to see you're not disturbed."

Horrified, Wes stared at the door, watching her leave. When the door shut, he turned, palms sweating, to Michael.

Michael smiled—a little thinly. Was he nervous, or was he uncomfortable because he didn't want to be here?

Michael cleared his throat. "You look—" He stopped, hesitated, biting his lip. "You look too thin."

Was that worry in his tone, or horror? Wes smoothed his hands over his thighs nervously. "Th-The op-p-p—" His hands shook, and he shut his eyes. God help him, he wasn't ready, he should never have done this—

A warm hand closed over his knee. "Where is your pad and pencil?"

Wes laughed darkly and shook his head. "N-N-No. Sh-Sh-Sh—" He stopped, drew a breath and let it out. *Calm. Calm. You can do this.* "I'm m-m-meant to t-t-t-try and r-relax." He sighed, a ragged exhale. "I'm-m s-s-s-sorry. I th-th-ought I w-w-was b-b-better."

The hand on his knee stroked gently. "But why—?" The hand hesitated, then made as if to withdraw. "Is it I making you nervous, Albert?"

Wes's eyes snapped open. Squeezing Michael's hand, he searched for his words and a sense of calm. *I'm sorry, Michael. Sorry for leaving you. Sorry for being gone so long. Sorry for my father. For my clumsiness. For my failures.*

"I l-love you," Wes said.

For a moment Michael stared at him, his expression fixed, his eyes wide. Then they filled with water, and Michael leaned forward, took gentle hold of Wes's chin and kissed him. Wes opened his mouth to Michael and reached up to touch the back of his lover's neck.

Michael made a soft mew, shivered, and slid onto Wes's lap.

"I was so frightened for you," he whispered. "I thought you were lost. I thought you were dead." His arms tightened around Wes. "I thought you didn't want me."

"I'm s-s-sorry. I w-w-was w-w-w-weak. I'm s-s-s-sorry." Wes clung to his lover. "I'm s-s-s-sorry f-f-f-for my f-f-father."

"I don't give a damn about your father," Michael cried. "I only want you, Albert. Only you." He nuzzled deeper into the collar of Wes's dressing gown. "I love you too."

Wes shut his eyes and held him close. As Penny had warned him, he was tired, completely exhausted in fact. But Michael was here now. Michael was here, and he loved him.

It was medicine more heady than any opiate could ever be.

Chapter Sixteen

"I M-MISSED YOU."

The words, Albert's words, the ones he had so longed to hear, rumbled from his lover's chest, and Michael smiled, his head upon Albert's shoulder as he reached out to trace his nipple. "I missed you too."

"Th-Thank you for taking care of my o-orchid."

Michael glanced at the glass jar on the shelf near the window, where the orchid was indeed thriving once more. "It was my pleasure."

"I worried you w-w-would not come." Albert's fingers teased in Michael's hair. "I f-feared I had w-waited too l-long."

"No." Michael turned and kissed Albert's salty skin.

Albert looked sad. "I'm s-sorry for my f-father," he said again. He didn't know that he could ever say it enough.

Michael pressed a finger against Albert's lips. "You have no cause to apologize for what he did. You aren't Daventry. Not even close."

Albert's smile turned black. "For so many years, that w-was my p-prison. W-Wanting to be D-Daventry." His fingers teased Michael's hair. "To be good enough for him."

Michael shut his eyes against the pleasant sensation of Albert's touch. "Your stammer is so much improved."

"Penny has t-taught me tricks." He kissed Michael's hair. "I ap-pologize I couldn't use them earlier. I was too nervous that you w-would not want me."

Michael laughed and slid his naked leg up along Albert's thigh. "I hope I've put that fear to rest?"

"Mmm." Albert's hand slid down Michael's back to the top of his bottom. "I m-may require a reminder."

"Anytime, darling." Michael rolled over slightly to press his body closer, but he looked up at his lover in earnest. "Will you go home now?"

Albert looked away. "I c-can't."

Michael tensed. "But why not? Are you—do you fear you will go back to the opium again?"

Albert's hand stroked idly against Michael's naked hip for several seconds before he responded. "Sometimes. But I kn-know now the true issue is wh-what drives me to it." He stilled, then sagged helplessly. "I c-cannot face my f-father. N-Not kn-knowing what he has done to you."

It upset Michael to hear this.

Dejected him, even—it wasn't that he'd wanted a

champion, but that Albert feared his father? Hid from him? Hid more now than before?

Leave it alone, a voice cautioned quickly in Michael's mind, but he could not. He would admit he had hoped...for anger, perhaps, or for Albert to decry his father.

"You still fear him?"

The space between this question and Albert's answer was vast and heavy. Albert's fingers strayed occasionally across Michael's skin, but it was as if they were thinking and considering too. Finally Albert spoke, his voice soft and slow and careful, marked more than anything by not just what he said, but how calmly he said it.

"Once I heard m-my father b-boast to another lord that his p-p-power and will was s-subject only to the Queen herself, and even there h-he thought he had more leeway than m-m-most. 'I c-can have anything I w-want in this world,' he told his f-f-friend. 'Whatever I d-d-desire from it is m-m-mine.'" His hand on Michael's body stilled again. "N-N-Never, not once, did I d-d-dream he would use it to harm someone h-h-helpless." His hand fell away from Michael. "F-Fear *him*? No. I h-hate him. I l-l-loathe him. I want to sp-spit in his face. But do I have f-fear of something else? Yes. I f-fear that I have been t-timid so long that now, now w-w-when it truly matters, I will try to f-face him and be cowardly out of h-h-habit."

Michael moved out of Albert's embrace but did not

leave his side. He pushed himself up on both hands, sliding his body against Albert's, needing to keep him close. His soul felt so full, so warm—for once, it was he who could not make the words leave his mouth. "I would n—" He stroked Albert's cheeks. "I would not ask you to face him. You need not—I do not need defending, my love."

Albert drew Michael against him, capturing a hand and kissing it softly. "It is n-not for you that I must f-face him." He placed Michael's hand over his own heart. "For m-me. For m-my own injured little boy." His fingers tangled with Michael's, and he looked up at him hesitantly, almost questioningly. "D-Does th-that d-d-disap-point you?"

Michael could only shake his head as he bent forward to kiss him softly on the lips. "No."

This made Albert smile and turn his head to kiss Michael's hand. "I should have l-liked to have known you when I was a b-boy. We could have h-hidden and r-read together. You could h-have fit in my h-hideaways with me."

"And I would have gone with you to school," Michael vowed. "I would have kicked the bullies and given them a scathing put-down. Then I would have put mud in their shoes and snails in their beds. Were Rodger there as well, he would have organized a gang to steal all their pocket money, and we could have picnicked together on a hillside, dining on fine things and drinking wine as Rodger plotted to take over the headmaster's quarters and we read books of faraway places."

Albert smiled up at him. "I love you."

It caught at Michael's heart every time—*I love you.* Clear and bold, no hesitation.

Let there never be hesitation between us again.

He threaded his fingers in Albert's. "I want to help you with your father." When Albert looked uneasy and opened his mouth to object, Michael overrode him. "I will admit, I'm still nervous to face him. But I could do it for you, if it came to it. Which it may not. More than anything else, I want to help you. I want you to be as free as I feel." He tightened his grip on Albert's hand. "And then I want to be with you. Wherever you go, for the rest of our lives."

Albert hesitated a moment, then said, very carefully, "W-Will y-you still w-work for R-Rodger?"

Michael went still. "Does it matter?"

More quiet. "Yes. B-But I will l-learn to l-live with it."

Oh, the pleasure, the deep, rich pleasure Michael took in smiling down at Albert. "In point of fact, I am done with whoring." He slid his body against Albert's sensuously. "Though I would not mind reprising the role on occasion for you."

Albert drew him down for a hard kiss, and they did not speak again for some time.

WES APPROACHED PENNY in hopes she could help think of a way for him to face his father. He told her the entire story, with Michael's help. She was not encouraging. Even more depressing was the fact that Rodger wasn't either.

"Going up against gentry is never simple, but going against Daventry is suicide," Rodger said bluntly. His jaw set briefly before he added, "If it weren't, I'd have done so years ago."

Penny had tried to soften the blow. "What is it, Wes, that you chiefly want? Revenge? Justice? It isn't that I don't think you're entitled to either, but the truth, and even the practicality is, both will be difficult to come by against a man like your father. Even if he had been caught at the time, a nobleman dallying for sport with a whore's son, willing or not, wouldn't cost him much in society's eye." She glanced apologetically at Michael. "Casting no aspersions on you or your mother—I mean only to state facts."

Michael waved this aside. "Cast aspersions on my mother all you like, but I agree with you." He returned his focus to Wes. "I consider their concern warranted, love. What is it, precisely, you wish to achieve? That would likely make a better start in finding how to face him."

Wes considered carefully, framing his thoughts before voicing them. "Self-respect," he said at last, feeling a deep satisfaction in not hesitating. "I w-wish to stand before my father, call him out for his actions and n-not back down. I d-do not wish to publicly shame him—" He paused. "I do, but I understand that I cannot likely have this." He ran a hand through his hair. "What I desire is to be f-free. F-Free of my shame I c-cast on myself."

Michael took his hand, stroking the back of his knuckles with his thumb.

"You do understand," Penny said gently, "that your father will not likely cower before you? That he will brush you off?" She sighed. "I don't wish to discourage you, but I cannot be convinced this goal, however noble, is not best achieved simply within yourself."

Wes took his time with his reply, wanting very much to be clear and understood. "I n-n-need to know I have this strength."

Penny held up her hands. "Men. Men and their tests of bravery. Do you not understand that bravery is not inherent—it is made? Not by circumstance, but by believing you possess it? Do you not understand how brave you are even to consider this? How brave Michael is for enduring what he did—and carrying on?" She shook her head. "You do not require your father's pound of flesh for courage—in fact, it may taint it. Let him answer to God for what he has done."

"God damns men like Albert and me," Michael pointed out.

Penny snorted. "Does He? I have often wondered that. Everyone seems so quick to insist God damns ones they dislike but carves out exceptions for those who they like and for themselves. If God is, as Jesus said, nothing but love, and if our only task is to love—how is the love between the two of you wrong?" She gestured vaguely at the air. "Men like your father, Wes, will one day reap their own reward. Perhaps we will see it, and perhaps we will not. And perhaps they won't. Perhaps there truly is no justice of any kind. But how much of your life are you willing to give him? What does this gain you, when you could simply walk away and enjoy the happiness you have found with Michael?"

Wes didn't like this conversation, largely because Penny seemed to make such a valid point. He didn't know why he had to do this, only that he knew he did.

But did he really? He was beginning not to even know that any longer.

Penny held his hand. "Don't act just yet. Not until you have calmed down. I don't want to see them put you away, which is what they will do to you. Declare you mad, and then where will you be? Your father will have won again. Have patience. A moment will come, or something else will arise, and you'll know what to do. Just don't act rashly."

Wes didn't like this, and he was so upset that later when he tried to discuss it with Michael in bed, it tangled his tongue all over again.

"Slowly, love," Michael urged him. "Slowly." He kissed him, teasing his tongue. "Shut your eyes if need be."

Wes did. "I c-can't let him get away with w-w-what he did. I c-c-can't face him. I c-can't just let him go free. Not after this. Not n-now."

Michael kissed his face. "I don't want him to hurt you too."

"You don't think I'm strong enough?"

"That's not what I mean at all. I think that Daventry is powerful, though, and I don't think your being his son will save you. Be strong with me, love. Stay with me. We can forget him. I have lived all this time without retribution. I can live the rest of my life as well."

"But he haunts you."

"Yes—and he will continue to do so even if he is dead and the whole world knows what he did. It can't help me. Only I can help me." He kissed Wes's nose. "You help me, beloved."

Wes settled in beside him with a frustrated sigh. "I want to f-fix it."

"You already have," Michael whispered. "You already have." He ran his hand along Wes's leg. "Make love to me, darling. Now. Here. Let me show you how fixed I am."

Wes met his kiss, and stroked him, and pushed him into the bed and loved him, all the night long.

Out of deference to Michael, to Penny, even to Rodger, Wes tried. He truly tried to let it go, to do what Penny said and give himself his own worth. He thought he'd at least gotten a handle on a corner of the concept too, when one morning when Michael was visiting,

Rodger came storming through the front door and into Penny's salon.

"Thank God," Rodger burst out at the sight of Wes, not bothering with a greeting. He collapsed against a wall, catching his breath. "I was afraid you'd hear before I got here and be gone already."

Wes sat up in alarm, and Michael rose. "What's going on, Rodger?" Michael asked. Penny had appeared in the doorway, and she listened too.

Rodger held up a hand. "I wasn't looking for anything. I swear. I'd only sent Jane over when we first couldn't find you to see if Daventry House would give us any leads, and when we located you, I called her back. But she took it upon herself to keep tabs on the boy Edwin, not wanting to come to me until she had solid information." His mouth flattened into a grim line before he continued. "And now she has it. Goddamn the bastard."

"What do you know?" Penny said, her voice a hard warning.

Somehow Wes knew before Rodger said the words. He couldn't have, of course—it was just that once he saw the expression on Rodger's face he began to try and imagine the worst, and once the thought was lodged there, it stuck. He could only imagine one thing at Daventry House that would involve Edwin and invoke such a look on Rodger's face. He could only hope and pray that he was wrong.

He wasn't.

"Daventry," Rodger said at last, looking sick and almost choking on the words. "Daventry has been using him."

MICHAEL SAT BACK down next to Albert, feeling cold.

He was dimly aware of the others. Penny had come fully into the room and was ushering Rodger into a chair. Beside him on the sofa, Albert went very still. Despite their presence, Rodger's declaration made him feel as if he were sitting alone in a long, echoing hall, listening to the others discuss the situation at the other end.

"He w-w-would not," Albert said to Rodger. "Edwin is h-his heir."

Rodger sagged into his chair and rubbed wearily at the side of his face. "That's what I told Jane. Said she had to be wrong. No way on earth would Daventry harm his own heir like that. A second son, yes. A servant boy. A *stranger*'s heir. But his own? No. It would be like fucking himself." His expression turned grim. "But perhaps that was the thrill of it. Or perhaps he's gone mad. Or—bloody hell. I don't know." He shut his eyes and pinched the bridge of his nose. "What I do know is that Jane hid herself beneath the boy's bed for a full night. Hid herself there, and waited, and then sure enough, the marquess came to the lad. She said she heard the lad whimper, heard him say, 'No, I don't want to do it again' but the marquess just laughed and told him he wanted it, he knew he did. Told him—" Rodger looked like he might choke. "Told him this was part of making him a man, since he was failing every other way."

Michael had no trouble imagining such a speech from Daventry. In point of fact he could hear the marquess's voice echoing around the words inside his head, and he could smell the spice of his tobacco as he leaned in close to move his hand around Michael's waist, sliding the other down to his groin.

Michael pressed his hands against his stomach.

Rodger went on, his voice strained. "Jane says the marquess had the boy get on his knees. Said he didn't fuck him right off, that at first she thought it would just be a spanking. But then the marquess asked if the boy wanted more spankings or wanted something else. This went on until the boy, sobbing, said he wanted 'something else'. Which was when the marquess told him to—"

Rodger stopped for several seconds before continuing.

"Jane said she cut her palms with her own fingernails wanting to go out from under the bed and help the boy. If she'd thought for a moment she could get away, she would have, but she figured, and rightly so, that Daventry would have her killed. So she waited. And while she was there, she saw the box, up in the springs. A box with a knife inside, razor sharp. And a journal. Written in some sort of odd code."

Michael had turned away, only half listening, but at this he returned his full attention to Rodger. He had the journal with him, a small, beaten and bound leather diary. Penelope looked at it, but she shook her head and passed it to Albert. Michael glanced over his lover's shoulder at the tremulously penned passages and knew instantly what code the boy had used.

"Latin," he whispered. "Inverted Latin. With some French tossed in, I suspect to make it difficult to read. But it isn't, not truly."

"What does it say?" Rodger asked.

Michael took the journal from Albert and held it carefully in his hands. He examined it for several minutes before speaking. When he did, his voice was quiet.

"He says his grandfather does terrible things to him, things to make him a man, but things he thinks cannot be so. He says they hurt worse than a beating and make him feel ashamed and confused." Michael's hand trembled a bit on the edge of the journal. "He hates himself for letting them happen. He—he wants to kill himself, but he is afraid it will hurt. He hates himself for this as well, fearing his grandfather is right, that he is weak and not a true man." Michael flipped through, hoping for a better entry, but they were all the same. A few detailed the acts Daventry made him perform.

Michael pressed the book back to Albert and rose. "Excuse me," he whispered. Or rather, he tried to, but his throat was thick, and he hurried from the room.

He went through the kitchens out back to the small garden, where at last he felt he could breathe. It should have been the stale, stinking air of a London slum, but Albert had been staying here, and so it was now a paradise of foliage. He sat on a crudely constructed bench and let himself crumple forward, not weeping, but not feeling well, either.

He wasn't surprised to hear the door open to admit another to the garden—and he was relieved it was Rodger, not Albert, because he didn't think he could stand to comfort his lover just now. He needed too much of that himself. To his surprise, Rodger didn't come to him, only sank against the wall.

"I'm so sorry, Michael," he whispered.

Michael frowned. "Why? What are you sorry for?"

Rodger looked wrecked. "I should have just killed him," he whispered. "I should have gone then like I wanted all those years ago, killed him, then let them hang me. Because God only knows how many others there have been since you."

Michael stood and went to Rodger, stunned, moved, and upset. "You think I would want you dead?"

"Better me dead and all those other lives saved."

Michael took Rodger's face in his hands, displacing his palms. "You saved mine," he said quietly.

"To make you a whore," Rodger shot back.

"To make me myself," Michael corrected. He

kissed Rodger. "Hush. It's all right."

He found, somehow, that in saying the words, they were true. Yes, Daventry made him sick. The thought of him using another boy, right now possibly, one as sweet as Edwin, made him physically ill.

But it was all right—*he* was all right.

"You got me out," he said to Rodger, speaking the revelation aloud as it came to him. "You rescued me and took me in. And you taught me, Rodger. You taught me to respect myself. To be strong. You taught me to forget the past and to look ahead."

"I tried," Rodger said, sounding a little stronger. "I should have done more."

"We will do more—now. We'll help that boy somehow. We'll go back inside, and the four of us will think of a way." He squeezed Rodger's hand. "We'll save him too. And we'll take our time and do it right."

The door burst open, and Penny came through, looking harried and upset.

"He's gone," she cried. "Lord George is gone—I tried to stop him, but he was so angry, and he wouldn't listen."

Rodger straightened. "Where did he go?"

Penny shook her head. "He didn't say."

But they all could guess. Just like that, Michael felt cold again. "We have to stop him."

Rodger took hold of his arm. "You don't have to go, ducks. I can do this for you."

Michael withdrew. "No. I'm going with you. I

won't let Daventry take him too."

"We have to hurry, I'm afraid," Penny said.

Michael nodded and followed her, back into the house, back through the parlor, out onto the street where Rodger's man shouted for a carriage that would take them across town to Mayfair and into the lion's den.

Chapter Seventeen

WES'S FATHER WAS having a party.

It was a small gathering of political players and their wives: some lords, some ministers, some businessmen. They were in the drawing room, talking and laughing. In the center of it all was the Marquess of Daventry. Wes's father.

Michael's demon.

Edwin's tormentor.

When Wes had stood in Penny's salon listening to Michael read from Edwin's journal, Wes had nearly been sick. Sick with disgust, rage, and despair. But he had felt no fear whatsoever, which was why, once his emotions reached a fever pitch, he had ignored Penny's pleas and headed out the door. He hadn't even taken his carriage. He had walked, moving so fast each step jarred his jaw, until he came to Bond Street, where he had hired a cab to the edge of Mayfair. There he had walked again, on and on, through traffic, across the park, through a crowd which had gathered to watch a boat launch in a pond. None of the noise or crush bothered him, because he could see nothing, hear nothing but Edwin crying as his grandfather, Wes's father—*his father*—

Now he was here, at his father's party. He was not wearing the appropriate clothes. He was dirty and full of sweat. Now that he had slowed down, now that the moment was upon him, fear blocked his throat. Now that he could hear his father, now—now—

Wes shut his eyes, pushed the fear aside, letting it rest like metal in his mouth, and he bit down on it, pushed open the doors and entered the drawing room.

The conversation did not still, but it hushed, going from a burble to a murmur. They were talking of him, Wes knew. Laughing. Fear tried to grip him.

He shoved it away and aimed a finger at his father. His angry accusations rose like fire inside him.

And lodged at the back of his throat, unable to move.

Wes stood frozen and mute—and the worst was that he didn't know why. No more fear, not half so much as rage, and yet still he could not speak.

His father came over, concerned. His brother loomed behind him, looking uneasy and uncomfortable. Wes fixed his focus on his brother instead.

Your son, Wes tried to say, but remained mute.

"George? Where on earth have you been all this time?" Daventry tilted his head to the side, still regarding Wes carefully. "George Albert, are you unwell?"

Mad, son? Are you mad?

Wes hated him. He longed to decry him here, in front of them all, in front of Vaughn, but still, *still* the words would not come. He drew a deep breath, but all he could let out was a strangled cry.

And then he drew his fist back, stepped forward and punched his father hard across the jaw.

The room erupted into shouts and screams as the marquess stumbled backward—it was a clumsy blow as Wes's punches always were, and his hand was injured more than his father's face, but it had done the work after all, for now, finally now, Wes was able to speak.

He spoke loudly and in a constant stream, fueled by rage, fueled by pain, fueled by decades of misery, of cowering before a man he had thought was a god but was only a monster—he bared it all, all in one nonsensical, incomprehensible stream. Not a word of his furious ravings could be understood. He didn't even care. It felt so good. It felt like heaven to speak like this: incoherent, yes, but without hesitation. His speech was unending, blissfully connected to itself, never halting, simply pouring out of him, words and words and words, one after another until they fell at a heap at his feet. He felt drunk, higher than any opium could ever take him.

"Hurt him!" he shouted. "You hurt him, hurt M-Michael, hurt Edwin, hurt me. Hurt everyone. Wretched m-monster. Vile devil. M-Make us all worship you, but you are *the d-d-devil, you bastard.* Your soul is full of m-m-maggots. You bastard. You vile, seething, b-b-bastard."

They were coming for him now—men brave enough to tame the madman, to stop his tirade. Not Daventry—he seemed, somehow, to understand, and just stood there coldly, staring through Wes as if he did not exist. As if he did not matter—because of course, he didn't. Not to Daventry. No one did. The world was full of his playthings. And now that Wes was no longer interesting, he would be removed.

One of the men removing him was Vaughn. As the hands closed over Wes, he turned to his brother, looked him in the eye and said, clear as a bell, no slurring, no stops, no hesitations, "Our father is raping your son."

His brother blinked and recoiled.

And then he turned to their father.

They were dragging Wes off. They were carrying him away, and Wes knew it was over—he would never escape now. Nothing could undo this. No one could shout at a marquess in public like this, not with his history. He would lose Michael, which he could feel the pain of distantly now, but much as he loved him, it did not matter, not next to this. And it was worth it. Because he could see his brother's face, could see the shock and the pain, and maybe he was mad—maybe he had broken finally after all. As they dragged him off, out the door—he thought he saw his brother break. His brother believed him, or at least he doubted.

Wes hoped it would be enough. It was too late for him, but for Edwin he hoped with all his soul it would be all right.

They bundled him into a carriage, and Wes went quietly, almost eager for a bit of respite, wherever it came from.

The shouts began, and panic rose like an old friend—and then a fist caught up alongside his head, and he had his rest after all.

MICHAEL CRIED OUT as he watched Wes crumple inside the carriage, but Rodger held him fast and angled him toward the door to Daventry House.

"The boys have him, love," Rodger rumbled in his ear. "They'll keep him safe. I hope to Christ we're meeting up back at Dove Street, but if not, they'll head straight on out of town, and we'll meet up with him after. We'll sail to bloody France if we have to." He nudged Michael toward the door. "Come on, love. Let's finish this, one way or another."

He had dressed well, but still, Michael had never felt more naked. Daventry's house. They were walking into Daventry's *house*, with Daventry himself there.

He shut his eyes, reached into his jacket to close his hand on the journal, trying to focus on the child upstairs.

There was so much commotion in the foyer that it was easy enough to slip inside. It was easy to find

Daventry, for he was speaking loudly and calmly. Vaughn was shouting.

"What did he mean? Why would he say you would do that to my son?" Albert's brother demanded.

"You are overwrought," Daventry said. "You have let your brother's madness delude you as well. Someone please pour my son a drink."

"He said—he said that you—that you—"

Rodger stepped forward into the room, held out his hands and smiled. "Ah. A party. Wonderful. And everyone here. Good evening, Daventry. And Vaughn too. How excellent."

"Who is this?" Daventry leveled a stare at him. Michael looked quickly away, but he could feel those eyes pass over him, and they made him cold. "Who are these fools? Remove them at once."

"Not quite," Rodger said. "Not yet. Not until I tell Vaughn what you've been doing with his son."

"*Remove them*," Daventry shouted, but Vaughn stepped forward, staying the few who tried to follow Daventry's demand.

"No." The earl's voice was raw and hoarse. "No. I want to hear them speak."

"You don't even know who they are," Daventry shot back.

Rodger inclined his head in a bow and reached into his vest pocket. "Allow me to introduce myself. I am Herbert Williams, and I am an investigator. You may check with my references at the Yard." He handed the card to Vaughn. "I was contracted by Lord George as he was concerned for the welfare of his nephew. It turns out his concerns were justified. I hope you shall all forgive him his unruly outburst. Were you to know what he knew, what I have discovered, you would likely be inclined to do the same."

"Get them out of here," Daventry snarled. Vaughn stayed him with a hard look and motioned for Rodger to continue.

And Rodger did. He spun a fancy story about Jane being his agent—which she was, though she was also a first-class whore. He told the truth, the grisly whole of it. Through it all, Daventry stared daggers at him, while Vaughn gaped at him, looking ill.

"This is all a mad stunt," Daventry said, calm and cool. "I am sorry you have all been exposed to such chicanery, but I promise you, this man and *all* his associates will hang."

"We have proof, of course," Rodger replied calmly. "Beyond the witness." He motioned to Michael. "A journal."

The room went quiet. Michael withdrew the book from inside his jacket.

Daventry, for the first time, seemed afraid.

His eyes met Michael's, and though the book was in his hands, though he was but a moment from exposing the monster, Michael was caught.

He was a boy again. He was in his mother's house, and Daventry stood there smiling, as he was now, and he was holding out his hand—

"Give that to me," Daventry demanded.

Michael faltered. *No*, he tried to reply, but his throat would not work.

Vaughn stepped between them and took it from Michael's hand. He closed it in disgust. "It's nonsense."

"As I assured you," Daventry drawled. "These men are frauds." His gaze sharpened on Michael. "I promise you, they will be dealt with."

You're such a good whore, young man. Such a very, very good whore.

"Code."

The word burst out like a shot through the room, and it took Michael almost a full minute to realize it was his own voice he heard.

"The journal is written in a code." He looked at Daventry, so terrifying, still, in the face of this, so confident, and he said, "I can read it to you."

And he did. He read with Vaughn holding the book open for him when Michael's hands began to shake, as the earl comprehended the code and read along with him—then Michael held the book alone, reading as if from far away, the voice not for himself, not for the boy within him, but the boy who was still in this house, the boy—

"My lord! My lord!" The housekeeper burst into the room, her face white, her cap askew. "My lord—Lord Vaughn, he has taken a knife! He has cut himself—"

It all turned to madness then—people ran everywhere, Vaughn chief among them, bolting up the stairs, shouting, "Edwin! Edwin!" The servants wept, the women fainted or screamed. Some of the men slipped quietly out the front door. Rodger stood still beside Michael, not touching him, but holding him up all the same.

Daventry stared at him, his eyes burning with hatred. Did he recognize him, Michael wondered? Did he know he was looking at another boy he had ruined, or had he pushed him cleanly out of his mind? Would it matter?

Would he, as he appeared to suggest, find a way to destroy them, to use his power he wielded so confidently, and simply continue on?

Daventry was moving. He walked toward Rodger and Michael, and Michael tried to withdraw, but now Rodger grabbed his arm and held him. Inside, the boy flinched; outside, Michael was wooden, trying desperately not to let him see how frightened he was.

Daventry smiled a cold, terrible smile.

"I will ruin you," he whispered. "I will throw you to the wolves, all of you, and I will teach you what happens to those who dare oppose me."

"No," a voice said behind Michael—a voice quiet but strong and sure. "No. You won't."

Albert was there. He was rattled, battered, and half held up by one of Rodger's men, but he was there.

He looked into his father's face, his own full of fury.

He spat at his father.

Gasps from the far sides of the room made Michael turn away from the scene, and he remembered they weren't alone. He didn't recognize the other guests by name, but he knew they were all important. They were leaders of the community. Peers of the realm.

And they were all looking at Daventry, uncertain.

Daventry saw them too. He had turned away from his son and back to his crowd, ready to reassure them, but it was too late. They were already doubting.

"What is this?" he sneered. "You would believe my damaged son and his whore over me?"

"Your undamaged son charges you too," Roger pointed out. "And several maids and scullery boys will attest to it." He rocked back on his heels and smiled at Daventry with savage glee. "I have kept tabs on you a long time, my lord. You've dallied with a number of young men over the years, some of them from very well-to-do families. How will you explain it away should *they* come forward?"

"This is all lies," the marquess hissed.

Rodger had to be making some bald guesses, for surely he hadn't tracked the marquess all this time. Though perhaps he had. Michael supposed it didn't matter, for once again, Rodger proved himself the master of manipulation—his proof was immaterial. The marquess's peers were watching him carefully, watching him with new eyes.

Eyes full of concern—and doubt.

The marquess saw it too. For a few minutes he seemed to be trying to think of something to say. Finally, Daventry calmly wiped the spittle from his face, turned and headed down the hall toward the kitchen.

The remaining guests, murmuring to each other, quietly filed out.

Michael moved. As the door shut behind the last of the marquess's guests, Michael ran to his love and, swallowing the sound of his cry, threw himself into Albert's arms.

Chapter Eighteen

VAUGHN AND WES sat together by Edwin's bedside, not speaking. The boy's arm was bandaged, tucked beneath the blanket. On the mantle a clock ticked, and hushed voices could be heard in the hall.

Outside, the wind rustled in the trees.

Inside, the brothers kept silent.

Eventually Vaughn said, in a hoarse voice, "Wes, what do I do?"

Wes didn't answer, only reached out and stroked his nephew's sweat-damp forehead.

Vaughn stared at his son, looking hollow and beaten. "What do I do? How do I help him? What—what do I tell him? How do I explain that I—that I—" He broke off and buried his face in his hands, bent double over his knees.

Wes put a weary hand on his brother's shoulder. "It's n-not y-your fault," he whispered. "N-no more th-than it is Edwin's."

"It *is* my fault," Vaughn insisted, despair tearing at his voice. "I am his father. I should have protected him. I should have known—I should have believed you when you—" He broke down again.

Wes sat with his brother for several minutes. Then he sent for Penny.

Wes didn't know what she told Vaughn, but whatever it was seemed to ease him, and he tried to hire her as a nurse on the spot. She politely refused, but she gave him several names and promised to work with him.

Lord Daventry. For that was his brother, now. His father had gone up to his study and put a bullet through the back of his head. There would be that to deal with too, but their father could do no more damage now. Edwin needed them.

And Vaughn needed Wes, and his friends.

For Michael met with Vaughn—now Lord Daventry—too. Uncertain at first and with Wes at his side, Michael told the new marquess what their father had done to him. Calmly, succinctly, but he gave Wes's brother the truth. Wes sat beside him as he did so.

"Is that why—?" His brother turned to Wes. "Is that why you are the way you are? Did he—to you—?" He paled.

Wes shook his head. "N-no." He held out his hand. "I d-do not ask th-that y-you accept us. Only that y-you do not p-p-persecute us. W-we will stay f-f-f-far away—"

Daventry looked crestfallen. "Good God, man—you want me to tell his mother on my own? Not about the two of you—she could never understand that, and no, I won't persecute you, for heaven's sake. But—" He gestured upstairs to the room where Edwin rested. "He adores you. Why would you leave him now?"

Wes paused. "I th-th-thought—" He turned to Michael.

Michael took over for him. "You don't think we would be a poor influence on him?"

"What—for being sodomites?" Wes's brother made a face, though at himself. "God's teeth, isn't there a better word? For being lovers, then. Oh, yes, it's deuced odd, but—" His expression turned hollow. "I don't know. I should say I never thought Father could do such things, so I suppose…" He sank back in his chair.

Wes swallowed the bile in his throat. "I would n-never," he whispered, "n-never h-h-hurt Edwin."

"Nor would I," Michael said.

Daventry was a ship lost at sea. "The Brannigan woman said she thought you could be a help, having gone through the same." This was directed at Michael. "And I would welcome it. Even with this—" He gestured at the two of them. His eyes were damp. "I don't know how he shall ever be normal again. How he can ever be the heir I need him to be."

"We will help," Michael promised.

"Would you come with us to the country?" Daventry asked, glancing between the two of them. "Both of you? Perhaps you could stay at Ballyglen. You could have the run of the dower house, and I don't care what people say. It's humble, but it's not far from London. You could turn the gardens into whatever you like, Wes."

Wes smiled, wanting to laugh, his spirit felt so full. "Ballyglen—yes. I would l-love to." His smile went so wide it nearly broke his face as he turned to Michael. "Would you st-stay with me there? In a ch-charming cottage just outs-side of Oxford?"

Michael's eyes danced, his face shining as bright as the sun. "Yes."

WITHIN A WEEK they had retired to the family estate, Daventry and his wife and Edwin at the main house, Michael and Wes in the dowager cottage. Rodger had found them a small cache of servants who wouldn't blink at two men sharing a bed together, and that had been that.

Edwin, once the doctors Penny had sent him declared him well, was almost always in their house. If he wasn't reading with Michael, he was out in the garden with Wes. The boy was still skittish, and he wasn't exactly the same as he had been before, but his nightmares had stopped. And, as Penny had pointed out, he was living his life.

"He isn't hiding, and he isn't dwelling on it." They watched from a distance as Edwin played with a paper boat in a pond.

Wes shook his head. "I h-hate that it had to happen at all."

Penny shrugged. "We all have pain, Wes. It isn't life without it. What matters in life isn't that we escape pain. What matters is that we overcome it." She smiled and took his hand. "Come. Let's go help him with his boat."

Wes rose to do so, but as Penny set out across the grass, he heard his name echoing from back at the main house, and when he turned toward the sound he saw Michael beckoning to him. He made his apologies to Penny and hurried his strides across the lawn to his lover, who was beaming.

When he asked Michael what he wanted, all he did was smile, hold out his hand, and say, "Come with me."

Michael led him back toward their cottage, to the greenhouse in the back.

The stovehouse smelled of new wood, and a month past its introduction, it was still a delight to Wes. It had more apparatus for heating and watering than what he had at Regent's Park, for as Penny no longer wanted for money for her house by the docks, neither did the marquess ever let Wes want for a botanist's luxury. He hadn't yet asked for exotic plants to be delivered, but he suspected his brother wouldn't hesitate to procure them.

It was August, and there were as many blooms

around the house as there were inside it, but the most exotic and precious plants still remained within.

"I just noticed it this morning," Michael said, sounding very excited. "It must have happened overnight."

Michael led Wes around the corner past a great potted palm, behind four exotic ferns, and there in the back where his orchids were, he saw it.

The leafless orchid was blooming.

It was just a small bloom. The petals were thin and white and open against the long green stem—it was the most amazing bloom Wes had ever seen. The top part was like a star, each petal a thin and delicate arm, but the bottom produced a lip that extended out like a slipper—and then from *that*, as if it had not done enough, two slender arms snaked from each side.

Pale, delicate and lovely—and healthy.

He didn't know how long he sat there. Michael brought him his notebook and pencil, and later a spot of tea, but eventually he took away both and led Wes back out into the sunshine, declaring he'd been a botanist long enough.

"To celebrate the blooming," Michael declared, linking their arms, "we will take the train back to London and spend the night at Dove Street." He ran his hand seductively down Wes's arm. "And you shall take me to the ballroom, and we will go dancing."

Wes had been smiling, his blood humming at the thought of all that they would and could do in a room at Dove Street, but when he heard *dancing*, his face fell. "I c-can't dance," he reminded Michael.

Michael gave him an impatient look. "It isn't terribly difficult to dance, dear Albert. I can teach you in a trifle."

"M-Many have t-tried," Wes said, sensing disaster and wishing to avoid it. "All have f-f-failed."

"Half an hour," Michael declared. "Give me half an hour to teach you, and if I can't, then I shall believe you that you are in fact unteachable, and I will never bring up the subject again."

Wes rubbed at his forehead, hating this with a fiery passion, but not seeing any way out, either. He sighed. "Very w-well."

They ended up in their parlor, all the couches and chairs pushed back and rugs rolled up. Michael stood in the center of the room, held his arms up, and gestured with his wrist. "Come here, please. I can't dance with you from fifteen feet away."

Wes came forward, lifting his hands into dancing position. Michael nodded in approval and slipped into his embrace. This made Wes's body hum. He'd never danced with a man before. He found he was more relaxed already. This was so much better. Though he knew it would still end in disaster.

"All dances are patterns," Michael explained. "The trick is to find the basic pattern and teach it to your feet. As the leader, you'll also need to guide the dance steps of your partner, who in this case is me. Even then, however, you stick to the same pattern. When you're ready, you move a bit about the room. You must look out for furniture and, if there are others dancing with you, other couples. But essentially, Albert darling, that is all there is to dancing."

Wes's eyebrows lifted briefly. Put like that, it didn't sound difficult at all.

He had to give Michael credit—Wes did better with him than he'd ever done. While they were dancing side by side, Wes mimicking Michael, he did quite, quite well indeed. When Michael stood before him, mirroring his steps, he also did fairly well.

And then Michael stepped into his embrace, Wes tried to lead, and it fell to pieces. Every single time.

"Sorry," Wes murmured, blushing furiously. "I t-told you—"

Michael lifted a hand and waved him into silence. He stared thoughtfully at Wes for several seconds. "Hmm. Do you know, it never occurred to me before, but—yes. Why not?" His smile became wicked. "Again, my lord."

Wes raised his arms, swallowing a weary sigh. Michael kept grinning, and he shook his head.

"No, darling." He shifted Wes's hands, placing one on Michael's right shoulder and clasped his other hand with his left. "This time, it's you who will follow me." When Wes blinked, Michael continued grinning. "The same steps, but this time beginning with the other foot. I'll lead the way. You only have to let your body move in the direction I tell it to go."

Wes felt a bit strange, he had to admit, as if he had been unmanned somehow. And yet—well, hadn't that been Michael, only moments before? Had he thought him unmanly?

A bit, he admitted to himself.

No longer. For Michael moved Wes with strength and grace about the floor, and when Wes tripped, he recovered them so smoothly that anyone watching them wouldn't even have known. For what felt like hours, they simply turned about the room, Michael humming a tune softly under his breath to give them time and rhythm. They danced, and they danced, and they danced.

Lord George Albert Westin was dancing.

All these years. All these *years*, an entire lifetime of years of parties, of home dances, dances at school—his sainted mother even had been frustrated with him for not being able to dance. The tutors. The daughters of mothers who hoped to win favor with the marquess by helping him with his socially awkward son. "Teach him to dance," that was the excuse. What everyone meant, of course, was *Teach him how to be in the world. How to get out of the house. How to be able to bear a party without passing out. How to not disgrace the family. How to dance, not just in the arms of a woman, but in life.*

Michael's mouth brushed Wes's ear, and Wes could hear the smile in Michael's voice as he said, "It didn't even take me fifteen minutes."

Wes wanted to laugh—laugh, cry, shout, leap through the air. For the first time in his life, even, he wanted to run out into the street and run up to strangers and shout in their faces and spin them around. *I can dance. I can dance, and I can speak. I can love, I can laugh—I can live. There's nothing wrong with me. There never was. I just needed to find the right way to do it. The right place to do it.*

He looked down at Michael.

The right man to do it with.

Wes stopped dancing—not tripping, just stopping, and he held Michael fast about the waist, clutching him, drawing him close. Shivering, he shut his eyes and buried his face in Michael's neck, drawing in deep draughts of him.

"Albert?" Michael called softly. "Are you all right?"

Wes pulled back, swallowing hard. He looked Michael in the eye, but he still couldn't say anything. He touched Michael's face in wonder.

"Albert?" Michael stroked Wes's cheek.

"Yes," Wes said, spirit soaring, his throat full of words, and his tongue—at least for this moment—content to get completely out of the way. "Yes. I am perfectly fine."

Wes bent and kissed his lover, at which point, though his words were still ready to slide out on command, he had no need of them at all.

ABOUT THE AUTHOR

Heidi Cullinan has always enjoyed a good love story, provided it has a happy ending. Proud to be from the first Midwestern state with full marriage equality, Heidi writes positive-outcome romances for LGBT characters struggling against insurmountable odds because she believes there's no such thing as too much happy ever after. Heidi is a two-time RITA® finalist and her books have been recommended by *Library Journal*, *USA Today*, *RT Magazine*, and *Publisher's Weekly*. When Heidi isn't writing, she enjoys cooking, reading romance and manga, playing with her cats, and watching too much anime. Find out more about Heidi at heidicullinan.com.

Did you enjoy this book?

If you did, please consider leaving a review online or recommending it to a friend. There's absolutely nothing that helps an author more than a reader's enthusiasm. Your word of mouth is greatly appreciated and helps me sell more books, which helps me write more books.

OTHER BOOKS BY HEIDI CULLINAN

There's a lot happening with my books right now! Sign up for my **release-announcement-only newsletter** on my website to be sure you don't miss a single release or re-release.

www.heidicullinan.com/newssignup

Want the inside scoop on upcoming releases, automatic delivery of all my titles in your preferred format, with option for signed paperbacks shipped worldwide? Consider joining my Patreon. You can learn more about it on my website.

www.patreon.com/heidicullinan

THE COPPER POINT MEDICAL SERIES

Where love is just a heartbeat away

The Doctor's Secret

The Doctor's Date

The Doctor's Orders

Coming in 2019 from Dreamspinner Press

THE ROOSEVELT SERIES

Carry the Ocean

Shelter the Sea

More titles in this series coming soon

LOVE LESSONS SERIES

Love Lessons (also available in German)

Frozen Heart

Fever Pitch (also available in German)

Lonely Hearts (also available in German)

Short Stay

Rebel Heart (coming summer 2018)

THE DANCING SERIES

Dance With Me (also available in French, Italian)

Enjoy the Dance

Burn the Floor (coming in 2019)

MINNESOTA CHRISTMAS SERIES

Let It Snow

Sleigh Ride

Winter Wonderland

Santa Baby

THE CHRISTMAS TOWN SERIES

The Christmas Fling

More adventures in Logan, Minnesota coming soon

CLOCKWORK LOVE SERIES

Clockwork Heart

Clockwork Pirate (coming 2019)

Clockwork Princess (coming soon)

SPECIAL DELIVERY SERIES

Special Delivery (also available in German)
Hooch and Cake
Double Blind (also available in German)
The Twelve Days of Randy
Tough Love

TUCKER SPRINGS SERIES

Second Hand (written with Marie Sexton) (available in French)
Dirty Laundry (available in French)
More titles in this series by other authors
More titles in this series from Dreamspinner Press coming soon

SINGLE TITLES

Antisocial
Nowhere Ranch (available in Italian)
Family Man (written with Marie Sexton)
The Devil Will Do
Hero
Miles and the Magic Flute

NONFICTION

Your A Game: Winning Promo for Genre Fiction (written with Damon Suede)

Many titles are also available in audio and more are in production. Check the listings wherever you purchase audiobooks to see which titles are available.

Printed in the USA
CPSIA information can be obtained
at www.ICGtesting.com
CBHW020233050924
13971CB00023B/123